The Kingmaker's Banshee

By T.S. Petersen

Works by T.S. Petersen

The Evanee Sheperd Series:

Moribund

Exitus

The Immortals of Death:

The Kingmaker's Banshee

Brad and Paige, your love is a shinning beacon through thick and thin. I hope my love for you shines as bright as yours and guides you through the tough times.

Druid's Prayer

Grant, my God and Goddess, Thy Protection;

And in protection, strength;

And in strength, understanding;

And in understanding, knowledge;

And in knowledge, the knowledge of justice;

And in the knowledge of justice, the love of it;

And in that love, the love of all existence;

And in the love of all existence the love of Earth, the

love you my God and Goddess. – Originally written by

Iolo Morganwg

Prologue

Tristan

The stallion beneath my thighs snorted with agitation, and I reached forward to stroke his neck. The air reeked of death, and decay sat heavily in the air, heightened by the blistering rays of the day's sun. It had long since set. Stars twinkled above my head, and I resisted the urge to study the constellations scattered through the heavens.

"Sire, what would you have us do?" I encouraged the young prince sitting astride his horse beside me.

The young prince gazed upon the fire and blood-drenched earth, his teeth grinding in frustration.

He lifted his weary gaze to the stars I'd fought hard not to lose myself in. "I tire of all this bloodshed,

Tristan. I wish to call a truce but fear father does not see the future I see.”

Shoulders heavy with a burden born too young slumped before the young prince remembered his audience and sat rigid once more. With Alexandru's forced exile after he'd declared his love for a human witch, Erick now bore responsibility and weariness beyond his youthful two-hundred and forty years. Young Erick had the makings of a great king, despite his earlier temper and the mischievousness that had seen him in more trouble than was wise.

“Sire, you will be king of this land someday. You must be decisive and firm in your decisions if your father is to believe in your vision.”

“And when have you known father to believe in my visions for the future of this kingdom. The man would see me take up a wife and land of my own. He refuses to acknowledge this era is over. We stand on a cliff's edge overlooking a future where men such as this Sir Isaac Newton gentleman will rule. We as a species need to evolve, or humans will leave us behind. And have no need for a wife."

Erick stared at me, his raised eyebrow eliciting a chuckle from me.

Our stallions snorted impatiently beneath us. I leaned forward to pat the sweat-slicked coat of my Lipizzan stead. The horse was a creature of beauty and had served me well these past three years.

"True, Sire. I would advise against saying such things in front of your family, especially Sophia." I smiled ruefully at him.

"How is my dear sister? Does she still write you?"

Erick studied my expression, and I fought a cringe.

"Your sister is like most newlyweds, Sire. She struggles to find her place within a new family. But I am keeping an eye on her as best I can, and she has asked that you not worry yourself on her account."

Erick rolled his eyes heavenwards in exasperation. "I'll always worry about her. I don't like Nikolai, and I have little trust in the family. That was not a match I would have made for her."

I said nothing, sharing his sentiments. I was still formulating a plan to remove Sophia safely from Nikolai's grasp. Jordan and my spies had returned with word of the beatings she'd suffered at his and his brother's hands, and I'd sent a command to intervene as much as possible. But there were only so many places spies could go within the castle without being discovered.

"So what decision have you come to, Sire?" I avoided the topic of Sophia and her scoundrel of a husband.

Erick contemplated his next move in silence.

"Withdraw the troops and send word to their King that we wish to meet." he advised, determination creasing his brow.

"As you wish. And what of the banshees and ghouls?"

Our gaze drifted to the white-clothed women drifting along the landscape, their crimson hair floating behind them. Their cries and screams surpassed the loudest of death howls from the lycanthrope bounding between surviving vampires. Ghouls feasted on the innards of both humans loyal to the Tenebris family and wounded werewolves.

"They are the Dark God's servants. I have little doubt his children roam between us, plucking what's left of us off. They are not under my or my father's rule. I have no desire to command their obedience or attract their attention any more than need be."

A ripple on the charred and blood-drenched landscape drew our attention. A blonde, leather-clad female warrior roamed between the fallen bodies. Here and there she would dip, placing a hand to the chest of a fallen human or werewolf.

Erick shuddered at the sight of the reaper, then murmured, "Any word about Jordan?"

"He survives. He is lucky to be alive, and I look forward to the tale of how he came to survive the attack of so many werewolves."

"As do I. No doubt it will be lengthy and embellished." Erick chuckled, and I shook my head.

"No doubt," I replied drily, then summoned the nearest soldier.

"Sire," the young vampire greeted formerly.

"Send a message to King Leonard. Have him request a meeting within the hour, to be held at the centre of that field if it should suit the king," I commanded.

"At once." With that, the male nudged his horse, spurring the animal forward.

"I find being surrounded by the dead of one's people to encourage negotiation for the better. Don't you?" I nudged my horse toward the main tent.

"It does indeed. Should my negotiations succeed, we may see the end of this war. You realise though, it may end with us being sent off to some forsaken continent in some little-explored corner of the globe. We'd never hear the end of Jordan's complaining if he were to part from his mistresses and ale." Erick smirked, his blood-streaked face crinkling with the first genuine smile I'd seen in weeks, if not months.

"Aye, the man will never let us live it down. We'd best find his mate amongst the females of whatever forsaken continent we land on." I groaned.

Erick's deep laughter echoed through the camp, stirring our weary brethren. They smiled along with him, no doubt remembering their happy memories shared alongside him or with others. I chuckled, following the vampire already respected more than his father. He'd fought hard and long beside his men, with me at his back, as it would always be. Greatness awaited him and whichever woman destined to walk beside him. My only hope was for a mate of my own to share the moment he became king. The hope I'd held close for so long was growing thin, and I grew weary of the search to find her. Once, I had thought Sophia might be the one. In the end, our friendship wasn't enough to ignite the spark that would sustain us until the All-Father and Great Queen came to see us to our resting place.

Please let her exist, Dagda. Please let me find the one to soothe the beast within.

Chapter One

Tristan

Fear permeated the air, at odds with the soothing sounds of the Brisbane River lapping against the stone wall at the front of the townhouse. The twinkling lights and random shouts of laughter from locals and tourists sailing and admiring Brisbane's nightlife reached my heightened hearing. I'd never been a fan of big cities, and Australia's cities were no different. Two weeping women knelt at the centre of the white, cream and beige lounge room. The cream Persian rug beneath them grew darker as the urine puddle beneath them expanded outwards, absorbed by the silky soft fibres beneath them.

I leaned forward on the couch, watching the pathetic blonde creatures cry useless tears. I'd never enjoyed torture. In a past life, I'd been a healer to my people —

a Druid. That life was long gone now, faded into the mist

along with my people. The images of atrocities

committed by the women pierced my mind, but I ignored

them. They were of no use to me. There was nothing that

to gain from that knowledge, nothing I needed to know.

"I've been tasked with your deaths. It surprised me

at first, but having read your thoughts and seen your sins,

I now understand why my Queen requested I do it. She

needed someone impartial, someone methodical and

logical. And that's me," I whispered, drumming the ends

of my fingers against my thigh. The blue of the Nitril

gloves encasing my hands a stark contrast against the

creams and beige décor.

"Plea… please. If it's money you need, we can get

it. Just tell us what you want, and it's yours. I have a

husband and a son who will miss me," the tallest of the two women begged.

"You're Brian's mother?" I clarified.

Hope sparkled in the depths of her hazel eyes. Her hoarse voice at odds with that hope. "Yes, I am. But how do you know my son's name? Do you know him?"

I grimaced, sitting back in the chair to put more distance between the two whimpering women and me. "Oh, I know Brian. Just as I know he's dead. Dead at the hands of my Queen."

Silence fell, and I sat patiently waiting for my words to sink in. It didn't take as long as I thought it would.

"Whaa… what. That can't be right. My darling boy's bed-bound in his apartment as we speak. I saw him this morning."

"I highly doubt that considering Evanee Sheperd killed him four nights ago. Then again, a reaper's magic is powerful, and your human mind would be no match for it." At the mention of Evanee's name, Mrs Turner stilled, her face reddening. "The name rings a bell, I see."

"That bitch ruined my son's life. How could I forget her name?"

"Now, a few months ago I'd have agreed with you. On the life-ruining-bitch part, that is. But I've gotten to know Evanee, and I find her delightful. Oh, don't get me wrong, she can be a right pain, but she truly cares about those around her. It's rare to find someone as selfless as she is. She's surprised me at every turn, to be honest."

I unfurled my legs, allowing them to stretch before me. The movement didn't go unnoticed by the two women who, despite their dire situation, watched with a spark of lust twinkling in the depths of their eyes. It was a side-effect of vampirism, designed to attract our prey.

"But I digress. Your dear, sweet boy hasn't been in that bedroom for some time, Mrs Turner. In fact, he's been downright unpleasant these last few months, what with murdering all those women in Acrasin City, and attempting and failing to kill Evanee. My King is rather displeased about all these attempts on his mate's life, and when Erick is angry, I become someone's worst nightmare," I purred, the vibration eliciting a shiver of apprehension from the women before me.

"I don't know any Erick, and I barely know Evanee. I only know about her because of Brian," Mrs Reilly sniffled.

"No, you haven't, but your son, Desmond, was the one responsible for her death."

A deep frown creased Mrs Turner's forehead. "But you just said that Evanee was alive? So how could Desmond have killed her if she's still alive?"

"Desmond's plan to avenge his ailing cousin ended Evanee's human life," I explained.

"Human life? What are you talking about? She's either dead, or she isn't," Mrs Reilly snapped before she sniffed indelicately.

"Humans aren't the only creatures to walk this earth, and they won't be the last."

I surged upward, my body nothing but a blur. In an instant, I knelt before them, dismissing their astonished gasps.

Twin looks of horror slithered across the women's faces before Brian's mother plucked up the nerve to ask. "Who are you?"

A wicked smile twisted my lips, my fangs descending to peek beneath my upper lip. "It's not who I am that you should concern you, Turner. It's what I am, you should worry about."

"A… and what are you?" Mrs Reilly stuttered.

The soft lavender of my glowing eyes reflected in the wide stares of my victims. The stench of their fear stirred the barely leashed beast within me, and I embraced it.

"I'm the living dead. A vampire, to be specific. I am Tristan Cathbad, son of the druid Cathbad, who sat at the side of the cursed King Conor MacNess of Ulster. I am claíomh to his Royal Highness Erick Tenebris and chosen soothsayer by the Dagda himself." My brogue increased the longer I continued my declaration.

It'd been decades since I'd been able to use my full title. It felt strange announcing my connection to the Great Father, Dagda himself. Most beings I came into contact with already knew my name and title, but I'd not killed a human since Erick's sister, Sophia's fiancé brutally betrayed her, resulting in an ambush by human hunters. I reserved my skills for those beings who broke the vampiric laws set by Erick in Australia.

At the women's vacant stares, I leaned closer. "Ladies, I'm what's known as the king's sword or bringer of death."

Both women shook violently. The foul stench of faeces permeated the air. I cringed at the reek and leaned back. There were no more words for these two, only the fear of what knelt before them, rendering them speechless.

I could have mesmerised them, but the fear was part of their punishment.

"As I said, Evanee tasked me with your deaths, and I intend on seeing that come to pass." I made to stand but hesitated a second. "Oh, there was one other thing she asked for. She's well aware of your extra-curricular activities but feels they should be publicised. I concur with her thoughts, and I'm happy to fulfil her request."

"Wh… what are you talking about?" Mrs Turner chattered through her shaking jaw.

"Your abuse of young children, including both your sons. You daft cow," I hissed. "Evanee wants a full confession on video along with the names of each of your victims. It'll be left with your cooling corpses as I leave. Now, we need to hurry this along. Your husbands are due to return in a couple of hours and I still need to feed."

When neither woman moved, I stepped behind them, snagging their bound hands to pull them up. Forced to decide between broken arms or rising, they chose the latter.

The blubbering began again, but I tuned it out. I had no sympathy for these perverted creatures. They were the lowest of low in human society, yet sat on a hill filled with material riches.

My beast swirled beneath the surface, and I rotated my neck in anticipation of what was to come. From healer to executioner, it was both my curse and blessing for the immortality I'd gained. Yet, it was a role I'd do over and over for my king and best friend, Erick Tenebris.

A gentle pulse at the back of my mind stopped me short, and I held on to the squirming women, waiting to see if it would come again.

When it didn't, I shook my head to clear it. Releasing the women, my claws extended. With an upward slash, the stockings binding their wrists dropped to the ground. Stockings worked remarkably well as restraints because they rarely ever left marks on the deceased. Sensing their freedom, both women tensed before they made to dart separate ways.

Predictable.

Hands snapping outward, I caught hold of the back of their silk shirts, tugging forcefully so they fell hard against the couch behind me.

"Sit and don't move. I'm not interested in playing a game of chase with either of you," I ordered.

When neither woman moved a muscle, I stepped in front of Mrs Turner. I leaned forward, and the petrified woman all but tried to sink into the leather couch.

My hand snapped out to secure Mrs Turner's square jaw. I stared into the depths of her muddy brown irises, willing her mind to bend to my demands. When her eyes glazed over in submission, I released her jaw. "You will sit on this couch until I instruct you otherwise. At my nod, you will stare at the camera and hit record with this remote." I withdrew a remote from my pocket, placing it in her limp hand. "You will confess your sins. Every single one of them. I want the names of every child you've hurt and abused, including your son's name. You will give details of what you did, where you did it, and when you did it. You will also give the names of anyone who took part."

Mrs Turner's eyes cleared, and I moved on to Desmond's mother. My command delivered, I positioned the tripod in the centre of the carpet just beyond the urine stain. Satisfied with the adjustment, I nodded for the women to begin.

I reclaimed my position in the armchair, my ears and mind burning with each confession uttered by the vial creatures before me. With each name given and what was done, my stomach tightened, and I fought my beast and its need to seek vengeance. I understood now why Evanee couldn't complete this task.

She'd have ripped these two women limb from limb after the second name. It's such a pity that isn't an option.

The swirl I'd felt moments before resurfaced, and I stilled yet again. I waited patiently for it to come again, and when it did, I smiled despite the words passing from the foul lips of the women before me.

'Ellie.' I mentally sighed.

'I'm here. I can feel your anger.' She hesitated before a menacing growl shivered through my mind. *'I can also taste fear. It's feminine. Tristan. Why am I tasting a woman's fear?'*

'Are you jealous, mo ghrá?' I was baiting her, but I couldn't help myself.

'Don't call me that, Tristan.' Ellie's snap whipped through our bond, and I grimaced, barely hearing her whisper. *'I'm nobody's love. I can't be.'*

'You still haven't told me why. Are you afraid your mother would disapprove of me?' I kept the uncertainty from my tone, but I suspected she'd feel it through the link we now shared.

'I couldn't give a crap what my mother thinks, and you know that. I told you when we began our friendship that we couldn't be anything but friends with benefits. You agreed, remember?' she seethed.

'I remember. But things have changed, and you know it. We have exchanged blood twice since that night you emerged from the bushland.'

My jaw clenched as the image of Ellie cradling a dying Evanee's head in her lap rose to the surface. The sight of infected humans and vampires emerging from the long grass in the background still chilled me to the core. Ellie was beautiful at that moment, her blonde hair floating around her head as though it were her halo. Her black, unseeing pupils and deafening screams only stopping when I'd scooped her up and rushed her from the scene.

Until that night, it never occurred to me the petite and feisty female housed a banshee beneath her flesh. Despite my best effort to stay away from her, Ellie stirred things within me I'd long since dismissed. After walking this earth for over two thousand years, I'd given up hope of ever finding a mate; resigning myself to a long and lonely life serving Erick and any offspring he might produce. My father had served a noble king, and I too would serve one of the greatest kings I'd ever known or seen. Until the night I met Ellie.

I resisted the urge to grind my teeth. *'There's no going back. You knew that the night we first exchanged blood.'*

I grew tired of her pushing me away and then pulling me back in. She refused to tell me what was eating her from within. Was it her heritage fuelling her indecision about how she felt about me, or was it something else?

'Tristan. I'm… Look, I know exchanging blood was a big deal, but I don't do commitment. I can't, and I wish I could explain why, but I'm forbidden.'

Her sad sigh constricted my heart as she confirmed my suspicions.

'I see. Well, I'm in the middle of something. Come back when you've decided what it is you want from me,' I murmured, my mood plummeting even further.

My skin crawled at the atrocities these two women had committed. I longed to rip their throats out and leave them a bloody mess resembling the emotional and physical trauma they'd caused to so many innocents.

Ellie's presence swirled once again at the back of my mind, and my lips quirked at her tenacity and determination.

'*Mo ghrá, what are you searching for?*' My whisper curled around her presence, surrounding it.

She shivered before responding distractedly, '*The source of your rage. I can only assume it has something to do with the two women you're with.*'

Surprised she'd discovered there were two women in the room with me, I snapped, '*This is not something I want to share with you, Ellie. There are parts of who I am and what I do that I don't want you to see.*'

The two women sat staring at the camera, their confessions complete. With a flick of my wrist to Brian's mother, she raised the remote and hit stop.

'*I've seen ugly my entire life, Tristan. Whatever you're experiencing or are about to do won't be new to me. You forget, my mother is the head Banshee of our clan. I've lived around death all my life.*'

I chuckled at the sudden image of her rolling her eyes at me.

'I don't doubt that, Ellie. However, I'm too old to want to do anything but shield you from the ugly in this world.' Rising from my seat, I palmed the kitchen knife I'd placed on the arm of the sofa when I'd first arrived and approached the two abusers, my fangs extending.

'You need to leave now, Ellie.' I focused on my prey and the chaotic beat of their pulse trapped beneath the skin at their necks.

The stench of fear grew more potent in the room. Ellie sighed with pleasure, as though she could smell and taste the fear through our link.

'I'm not going anywhere, Tristan,' she whispered.

This wasn't a battle I'd win tonight. With a mental sigh, I bent and placed the vegetable knife in Mrs Turner's hand.

"I want you to slit your wrists. Be sure to do it vertically. I don't want there to be any chance of saving you." When she raised the blade to the wrist, I cooed, "Not too deep now, or you won't have enough function to slit the other wrist."

I stepped toward the wet bar and lifted a crystal tumbler sitting beside the scotch decanter. I returned to Mrs Turner's side, tracking the blood escaping the cut.

"Your turn, Mrs Reilly. Pick up the knife and slit your throat," I ordered, standing at the ready.

Without hesitation, Mrs Reilly grasped the bloodied knife and placed the tip at her throat. With a steady hand, she drew the tip across the soft flesh. It puckered at first, but gave way beneath the sharpness of the blade. The scorching heat of the fresh blood hit the tumbler and splattered over my hand. Angling the glass, I caught the hot, red liquid.

I sipped the ruby liquid, watching the light bleed from both women's eyes. Satisfied justice was served, I made my way toward the kitchen. Washing the blood from my gloved hand and the tumbler, I dried and replaced it on the wet bar.

I snagged my coat from the armchair and shrugged into it. My palm found the disposable phone in my coat pocket, and I dialled triple zero. The soothing voice of a female operator greeted me. I grumbled about a disturbance with little effort and gave them the address, a fake name and number before hanging up. The open patio door and a fresh breeze coming off of the water beckoned me.

'Why didn't you drain them?'

Ellie's essence still lingered in my mind, despite my actions.

'It needed to appear as though it was suicide. The authorities would have become suspicious if I'd drained their blood,' I explained.

'Oh, I see. Doesn't their blood taste rotten from their many sins?' Ellie whispered.

'Blood is blood. It's nourishment. When do you get back?' I asked, tiredness creeping into my voice.

The separation in the last few weeks had been harder than I'd thought it would be. Loneliness had settled in during Ellie's visit to her family to secure an alliance with the Arnam clan. I'd expected her to travel to New South Wales and return, but her family had other ideas.

'Tomorrow evening. When will you be back in Murder Point Bay?' she asked.

'I'm booked on a flight home in an hour. So yes, I'll be home.'

'*Okay. Well, that's a good thing then. I guess I'll see you around?*' She was putting on a good front of acting indifferent, but she'd been unable to hide the brief spurt of hurt.

'*I dare say so. Safe travels, mo ghrá.*' I farewelled her before slamming a barrier in place, effectively shutting her out before she could feel my hurt at her distance.

Hand on my neck, I rubbed at it to ease the tension, turning back to the scene of death. The two women lay slumped on the leather couch. I pitied the police officers who would find them and those who would bear witness to the confessions of these two monsters. But justice had been served, and the victims would receive the recognition they deserved. An investigation would no doubt lead to those who'd taken part, and if the law didn't find them guilty, they too would receive a visit from me. I'd burnt their names into my mind. It would be easy enough to locate them once criminal proceedings began.

A turn toward the river, a blur of movement, and I was at the black sedan I'd parked five blocks away, and folding myself in. My head met the cold leather of the headrest, and I shut my eyes, trying my best to wash the images and thoughts of the women from my mind.

My fatigued eyelids lifted, and I hit the ignition, turning the car toward Brisbane's airport.

My job was complete.

Chapter Two

Ellie

You'll arrive back with one arm as long as the other.

The front door lock released, and I depressed the silver handle, shoving at the door with my foot. I lugged my bags through the silent house to my room and threw them in. My exhausted body collapsed onto my mattress, and I allowed my eyelids to drift shut, inhaling the familiar lavender scent drifting up from my bedding.

Home at last. Thank goodness for minor miracles.

There was a chill to the air that only autumn could deliver to Murder Point Bay. The country town in Australia's Far North Queensland had the perfect weather. Not too hot in summer and perfectly chilled in winter.

The winters in Murder Point Bay were pleasant compared to the bone-numbing chill of Ireland's winter. The toe of my shoe caught on the heel of the other and I flicked it off, moving onto the other one. I stood and shrugged out of my maxi dress and bra. I dug through my drawers, finding a pair of stretch pants I'd dubbed my 'fat pants'. I stepped into them and tugged on a loose-fitting t-shirt. I sidestepped my bags, knowing they would still be there later this evening, and kept walking toward the kitchen at the back of the house. The last rays of the afternoon sun filtered through the row of orange and emerald windowpanes, glimmering against the tulip oak floorboards.

My gaze moved around the room, and my shoulders drooped when my brain registered I was home and safe.

Relief washed through my body, tears making their way down my cheeks. My purposely over-due return to the family farm in Bray had been a test of my wits and strengths in every way. There'd been more than one occasion I'd been grateful to Brad for training me at the local Mixed Martial Arts gym.

The attacks were constant and draining from the day I set foot on the Arnam Farm in New South Wales until I'd landed in Ireland. In between clan meetings and the rebirths of four of my female cousins as banshees, I'd sat with my back to the wall and a knife in my grip at all times. I'd put four of my male cousins in hospital this time, two more than last time.

The clan was beside themselves. I was still a living and breathing female with a pulse who'd made it to my twenty-eighth birthday. I was supposed to have died and transitioned at twenty-five, but I'd been away from the homestead in Orchard Hills in New South Wales, completing my studies on that birthday. I'd found every reason under the sun that would prevent me from returning to Orchard Hills or Bray. But there'd been no avoiding it this time. I'd needed to approach the high council and inform them of my allegiance to Evanee. That information had gone down about as well as a bottle of cod liver oil. There'd been yells and curses hurled at me, as well as cries for my banishment.

The wooden countertop bit into my hip, the pain of their words slicing at my heart all over again. Máthair had sat in silence, never once calling for order. I'd known then she'd never stand behind me. I was the failure of the family, the runt of the litter. My five sisters had all converted on their twenty-fifth birthdays without the blink of an eye; my three oldest brothers being tasked with their deaths, as was the tradition in our clan.

Destined to be murdered by the men of our clan as they came of age, the women in our family completed the transition to a full-blooded banshee. The clan expected the men to join the army or my father's private security company. Mercenaries for hire, but to the locals and the government they were bodyguards. Of course, any female offspring they produced would be cursed just as their predecessors were. The apple didn't fall far from my mother's DNA.

Ronan's warning rattled around my mind. My twin brother's blunt statement that I never return to the homestead in Orchard Hills or the farm in Bray as I was, or I'd face permanent death, shivered up my spine. A bounty hung over my head. It was a free for all, and the cousins and second cousins would come out of the woodwork.

I drew in a deep breath, scooped an errant strand of hair behind my ear, and approached the fridge. With a sharp jerk, the door opened, and I lifted the hem of my shirt and wiped my tears away. I smiled at the pile of food my housemate and best friend, Brad, had stocked in anticipation of my homecoming. I bypassed the food and reached for the bottle of vodka cradled in the door. I withdrew the chilled glass from the fridge and poured three fingers' worth, then downed it. I cringed at the instant burn, but topped the glass up again, grateful Brad knew me well enough to have a glass waiting for me.

With a shuffle that would make any zombie proud, I headed toward the lounge room, only to stall when my reflection in the hall mirror caught my attention. I stiffened at the sight that greeted me, dread swirling within. The vividness of my green eyes now sat dull and drained against the almost black skin beneath my eye sockets, a stark contrast against my ivory skin. My petite frame was now tiny, the weight I'd gained since living with Brad having melted away in my attempt to avoid being drugged. But it was my hair that scared me the most. There in amongst the blonde strands were light strawberry-blonde highlights. Each strand was a reminder I was running out of time. When I died and transitioned to a full-blooded banshee, my hair would bleed red, and my tears would be forever black as I wept and wailed, heralding Death's coming. There was so much to do before my death came. Vaccines I needed to work on, a bucket list I needed to complete. There would be no completing the bucket list after my death. The clan expected me to return to the compound and take my place as the chief's daughter.

A series of knocks echoed through the house from the front door, and I spun toward it. The cold glass of the vodka bottle bit into my hand reassuringly as I tiptoed toward the front door, placing the tumbler on a side table as I passed the lounge. A bottle wouldn't make an ideal weapon, but it would give me enough time to run if I needed to.

My breath stalled in my chest when a deep, soothing voice slid through the cracks of the door. "Mo ghrá, are you going to stand there all night, or are you going to open the door for me?"

Instantaneous relief flooded my body, so the vodka bottle shook violently in my hand. The door was barely open before my arms were around Tristan's supple neck. He'd secured his shoulder-length, feathery, platinum blonde hair as he'd anticipated my reaction. His large, bare arms circled my waist, and I held on tighter, my legs rising to circle his taut, narrow waist despite the groan of protest from my almost healed rib and bruised organs. Without missing a beat, Tristan's arms moved to support my weight as he pressed his nose to my neck, inhaling my scent. For the first time in what felt like ages, I allowed my body to relax, knowing I was safe.

Tristan stepped forward before he kicked the door shut, making his way toward my bedroom.

"How did you know I'd be home?" I mumbled against his neck, the sweet, delicate scent of holly calming me.

His chest vibrated as he replied, "I'm psychic."

"No, you're not," my scoff muffled against his neck.

"You're right, I'm not, but you mentioned you were returning today, and I felt your relief through our connection."

He felt my relief? What else did he feel?

"I felt your fear and sadness. You're hurting and have lost weight since I last saw you. What happened with your family, Ellie?"

Tristan lowered us to the edge of the bed, his arms circling my back once more as he hugged me to him.

"You smell like holly. I don't think I've ever asked why?" I sat back, still clutching the bottle of vodka.

My eyes searched his pale oval face, marking the lines of worry and the gentle lavender glow of his intelligent eyes. Ruby flecks peeked beneath his lavender irises, the only hint at his vampirism.

"I've always smelled of holly. The scent was unique to my mother's family. She was a sacrificer amongst the Druids. It was the scent of her power. And you're avoiding my question."

I brought the bottle to my lips, gulping more of its content down. I gasped against the burn, forced to answer Tristan in a breathless whisper. "Ireland was Ireland. It went about as well as I expected. My mother refused to align with Evanee, and the clan was enraged that I swore allegiance to her."

"That was to be expected, but that doesn't explain why you're so frail. Your body's shrunk, and the dark circles under your eyes look like bruises."

Tristan's nimble fingers pried the bottle from my hand. He set it on the floor before his fingers resumed their delicate journey across my nose, cheeks and finally, my lips.

"I can't talk about what happened, Tristan. It's clan business. It's forbidden to outsiders."

When his hand stalled, my eyelids fluttered open. I stroked at his clenched jaw, hoping he'd relax.

"I'm okay, Tristan. This happens when I return to my family, more so when a trip to Ireland is involved.

It's why I don't visit often and why I moved halfway across Australia. Brad knows the drill and filled the fridge with all manner of deliciousness, including the bottle of vodka." I tried hard to smile, but it refused to reach my eyes.

"That's not good enough, Ellie. I want to check you over and make sure malnutrition is the only thing you are suffering from. I can smell the increased blood circulation to the various spots in your body, so save it."

Tristan twisted to lower me onto the middle of my queen bed. Tiredness crept upon me, but I fought it as I had since Orchard Hill.

"Relax, Ellie. I mean you no harm. You know I'd never hurt you."

Tristan's melodic voice drifted over my body, and I sighed.

"I know you wouldn't, Tristan. It's the residual adrenaline from my fight response. It'll dissipate after a week," I murmured tiredly, accidentally giving away a small piece of the puzzle about my family life.

Tristan wisely ignored my slip-up. Instead, he focused on stripping my baggy shirt from my body. I closed my eyes, not wanting to see his eyes when he saw the bruises. At least one of my ribs was fractured, but it was well on its way to healing.

"Fucking hell, Ellie. Who the hell did this to you? And don't give me some bullshit about it being clan business. These wounds are far too close to major organs to be anything but kill shots."

"Tristan, it's fine. The injuries were meant to incapacitate me until… Look, the ones who did this won't be coming for me anytime soon. I put every one of them in the hospital. Some are even in ICU." I opened my eyes to smile at him in reassurance.

A growl more beast than man rumbled from his thinned lips. "It's been a long time since I visited New South Wales or Ireland, but perhaps a visit is in order."

I shivered at the emergence of his beast simmering beneath the surface. The fear that beast could elicit would feed the banshee within me well.

"Leave it alone, Tristan. The farms are both warded by magic and technology. You wouldn't make it too far. Now, are you planning on staring at my delightful bruises all day, or did you have something else planned?"

"Fine, but that was the last time you are returning to the farms without me, Ellie. I mean it. If this happens each time you return home, it'll only be a matter of time before they achieve what they want. I won't allow your death, Ellie."

My heart constricted at his declaration.

You don't have a choice. My death is inevitable; it's who delivers it that will be the true surprise.

My hand scrubbed at my face to hide the small tear that escaped.

"I can smell your tears, mo ghrá. You don't have to hide them from me."

His shadow fell over my face, and I regarded his gorgeous slender face hovering inches from mine.

"I wasn't crying. I have dust in my eyes, that's all." I smiled weakly.

"Oh, do you now? Should I carry you to the bathroom so we can wash your eyes out?"

His cheeky grin filled my heart with happiness that had no right being there.

"It's all gone now. See no dust. The tears did their job and washed it out. The wonders of the human body." I grinned.

"Ah-huh." Large hands framed my face, brushing at the strands along my temples.

I fought the heaviness in my relaxed arms to lift them around his neck. With a tug, his lips found my seeking ones. I took my time devouring their softness, the taste of fresh rain on a hot summer's evening calming my racing heart. I'd missed this; I'd missed him. He drove me to the point of insanity with his macho crap, but his heart was the size of Australia. He cared about me and what happened to me. I wasn't some descendent of Aibell the Ua Briain banshee. I was Ellie Arnam, a virologist in the Scientific Research Department of Aeternum Limited. He centred me, despite the shit storm circling me.

I have to let him go, if not to save my heart, then to save his. But not tonight.

With care, I raised my legs around his waist, holding onto him tighter, trying to press every inch of my body to his. His kisses were delicious yet restrained, and I hissed with impatience. I didn't want controlled.

My growl of displeasure rumbled in my chest when Tristan pulled away from me, eliciting a soft chuckle from him.

"Not tonight, Ellie. You're injured and tired." The warmth and affection in his tone drew a groan from me.

"I'm fine, Tristan. Really."

He stilled for a split second, then rose to his knees in between my parted legs, his tongue clicking at me in reprimand. "Liar. Now lie still. I'd like to inspect you."

"Fine, but wake me if I fall asleep, please. I have a bag to unpack."

When he didn't answer me, I lifted my head to see his hand hovering over my abdomen, seeking out my injuries.

I guess having a vampire whose power revolves around inflicting pain within the body has its advantages.

"Your rib is almost healed. Your kidney's bruised but on the mend. The ligaments in your shoulder are torn, and you have muscles in your abdomen that aren't far off snapping. Overall, you're healing, but I'd like you to heal quicker. I want to give you a small amount of blood to speed up the healing process."

I forgot the polite refusal on the tip of my lips when Tristan leaned forward. "Don't refuse this, Ellie," his voice little more than a murmur falling from his tender lips. "I can do this for you, shorten your healing time and have you back to normal. It wouldn't be a significant exchange, just a prick of my finger. Enough vampiric blood to aid your banshee blood. Your human DNA is slowing the healing down, but you're still healing quicker than the average human would."

Crap, he's right. I can't afford to be weak, not when the attacks will keep coming. Damn it all to hell!

"Fine. You're right. There are you happy?" I snarled, angrier at my vulnerability than I was at his logic.

"It's a start. I'd prefer complete transparency and honesty between us. But I guess I'll settle with you admitting I'm right, for now." He shrugged at me.

"Don't be a wanker, Tristan. I have enough of them in my family."

His deep bellied laughter startled me.

Perplexed, I frowned. "Why are you laughing? You realise calling you a wanker isn't a good thing, right?"

He laughed harder, wiping at a soft pink tear that escaped at the corner of his long-lashed eye.

When he'd calmed down, at last, he answered with shaking shoulders, "Yes, I realise that wanker isn't a *good thing.* Since meeting you and Evanee, I've been called many names. I've not had this since my childhood. It's quite refreshing and somewhat grounding. I've been feared and respected for most of my life, but not by you or Evanee, it seems."

I stilled at the last part. Rising onto my elbow, I breathed through the pain of my rib and torn muscles, reaching for the collar of his cotton shirt. "I respect you, Tristan. Never think I don't. I don't fear you, but I respect you. I'm sorry I called you a wanker. You're not one. I'm angrier at my vulnerability and the implications it might have on not just me, but you and the others."

His laughter drained from him at my apology.

"You're not vulnerable, Ellie. I'm right here. If anyone is stupid enough to take you on with me beside you, then they deserve the death they'll inevitably suffer at my hands."

My mind went blank at his statement, and I had no response.

With a grin, he rolled his eyes toward the ceiling and then back to me as he exclaimed, "At last, she's speechless. Now lie down and let me heal you, please. You still need to eat and sleep."

Tristan pulled my upper arm gently, displacing my elbow, so I dropped back to the bed.

"No food. I can't eat right now. I'll eat tomorrow morning, I promise." He hesitated, but the resolve in my eyes must have been warning enough because he simply nodded.

I watched, fixated as his fangs lengthened. The tip of his index finger rose to his sharp canine, and he drew it sharply across the tip. Crimson liquid pooled at the tip. His finger reached out to my lips, and I parted them. I gripped his wrist, holding it in place as I opened wider so my tongue darted out to lap at the liquid. The taste of fresh rain I'd smelled earlier danced across my tongue. My eyes drifted shut at the sensation, and I drew his finger deeper into my mouth. I suckled at the wound, gently drawing more of his blood to the surface.

A long, low growl from above me snapped my eyes open. Tristan hovered over me, and I watched as something I'd sensed on more than one occasion rippled beneath the surface, tightening his features ever so slightly. I stilled, waiting for Tristan to decide what happened next.

He shut his eyes, a hard shudder shaking his body. When the rippling ceased, his features were once again serene.

"I said not tonight, and I meant it, Ellie. Another night though," he ground out through clenched teeth.

He withdrew his wrist from my loosened grip.

He dipped his head, and his luscious lips met mine. Our kiss was light and tender. A promise of nights to come that would have us tangled in sheets or falling from the bed like we'd done the night before I'd left for Ireland.

"Another night," I promised.

I allowed my weighted eyelids to shut and finally passed out, knowing I'd be safe tonight.

Chapter Three

Ellie

Blood isn't always thicker than water.

The spray of the scalding water beat at my aching shoulders, and I leaned my heavy head between my braced forearms against the tiled wall of my shower. I inhaled the moist, warm air, trying desperately to shake off the nightmare still lingering at the forefront of my memory. My ears still rung with the high-pitched whistle of the wind that sneaked through the cracks in the old stone barn on my family's farm in Bray.

I shut my eyes tight, the sound and sting of my repeated wet slaps of my hand on the dove grey tile useless against the surfacing memory. The smell of the fire and straw roof filled my nostrils, despite the fifteen thousand plus kilometres distance. One by one, the faces of the thirty banshees and half-human women in my family flickered behind my closed eyelids. Their anger and outrage had echoed off the stone walls, but I'd stood tall knowing what I was fighting for was more important than the anger of my family.

"You cannot be serious. You would have us side with some reaper halfbreed bitch because she's your friend?" Aibell junior spat from beside Máthair.

I willed my spine straighter, if it was even possible, unafraid to meet the icy white stare of my oldest half-sister.

You're such a hateful bitch. You always have been.

I clenched my fists against the anger coursing through my veins and forced myself to meet her mocking eyes. "No, Aibell. I would have you pick a side in the upcoming war. Evanee will be queen, and we swore allegiance to Death millennia ago. Are you willing to piss Death off to stick it to my friend and me?"

Máthair sat unblinking at the head of the room. The flicker of flames from behind me from the fire at the centre of the room cast eerie shadows around the room. The old barn hadn't changed since its build during my grandmother's reign.

Aibell glared at me. "Death's not made an appearance since he lost his bride. Why would now be any different? This is no doubt some rich brat and her prince's bid to put themselves at the forefront. There have been others before them, and they won't be the last."

Oh, Death's made an appearance alright.

I ignored my sister to focus on my still silent mother. "What say you, Máthair? Will you enter an alliance with Evanee and Erick?"

The room stilled, and I was sure every occupant in the room held her breath—dead or not.

Máthair continued to stare at me, never blinking.

I hate when she does that. I fought the urge to shudder beneath the tingles of my skin crawling.

"No."

Frustration speared through my gut, and I clenched my jaw tighter in an effort not to tell her to go fuck herself.

Breathe, Ellie. You know she's never given a shit about anything you wanted. You've only ever been a number to add to the clan.

"Very well, Máthair. What should I tell them is your excuse for not wanting to enter an alliance with them?" I returned Máthair's stare.

"Ellie, I care little what you tell them. I will not enter an alliance when your friend will be dead soon."

Fear seized my heart. "What do you mean dead soon? She's already the undead."

Máthair rose from her high-backed wooden chair, and the tips of my nails bit into my damp palms as I willed myself to remain still.

"The penalty for mixing the species must be paid, as Erick and your Tristan would know."

At the mention of Tristan, I bit down on my bottom lip. The sweet metallic taste of blood filling my mouth.

Shit! She knows about Tristan.

My panic must have shown because Máthair stepped in front of me, her smirk chilling me to my soul. "Did you think I wouldn't find out about your vampire lover? I'm impressed you'd have the stomach to date Erick Tenebris' claíomh. Tell me, does he whisper about his latest slaughter when you lie in bed? Does he reminisce about the lands he's laid waste to in the name of the Tenebris family?"

I ignored Máthair's taunt, knowing it would get me nowhere to retaliate. It never had in the past. "I'll pass on your answer to Evanee when I return to Australia."

I spun on my heel, holding my head high as I made my way past the fire pit. From behind me, Máthair called out, "You will stop fucking Tristan, Ellie, or you will receive the same death sentence hanging over the young prince's head. Then again, you may yet transition during this trip, in which case, that warning was pointless."

Something inside me snapped, and my banshee screeched happily within me at the fiery white anger bubbling up. I spun in a tight circle to face the woman I'd hated for most of my short life.

"Hear me, Máthair, because I won't be repeating myself. My relationship with Tristan has nothing to do with you or anyone else in this godsforsaken clan. You send anyone after him, and I'll rip out every one of their organs one by one, feasting on their fear as I do. I'm done with you and your bullshit rules. Send your best after me, Máthair, because as far as I'm concerned, you can all go fuck yourselves. I'll never be a part of this clan. I stand with Evanee and Erick."

Shocked gasps rose from the congregation, but I ignored them. Middle finger held up clear and proud, I made my way out into the raging storm.

The heavens were truly weeping, their tears hitting the hood of my jacket. I'd have said they were sobbing the tears I refused to let fall.

Holy shit, holy shit! You've just walked away from your family. What the hell were you thinking, Ellie?

Trapped in my misery and the beginning of a panic attack, I failed to see the four hulking figures surrounding me until it was too late.

"You've done it now, haven't you, Ellie?" John taunted, his American accent at odds with the brogue I'd heard seconds before. The pretentious twit had married one of my cousins, no doubt hoping to marry in the infamous Arnam family. Our fingers were in so many private and public military organisations, I doubted he even knew the true extent.

"Yeah, you know what they say? In for a penny, in for a pound." Panic setting in, I took in the four figures surrounding me.

My half-brother, Oisin, shifted from foot to foot, the mud beneath his boot squelching. "You're the only woman to make it past her twenty-fifth birthday. It's time, Ellie."

"Oh, I know that Oisin. So, how's this going to go? You all going to rush me and see who gets the best shot in, or you lining up for turns?" I said, shrugging out of my jacket and slinging it over my arm.

I soaked through instantly, the deluge adding to the ice encasing my bitter and broken heart.

"The aim is to kill you without too much damage, not slaughter you. Don't make this hard, Ellie. We can make it painless, and we've sharpened the ceremonial knife. The incision will only be a faint, thin white line once we're done cutting your heart out." Oisin promised, as though the idea of cutting my heart out of my dead body was an everyday occurrence.

For them, it is.

I swayed between embracing my banshee, but I didn't trust her not to hinder me during the fight to free herself entirely from my mortal body.

"As appealing as that sounds, I'm going to tell you what I told dear old Máthair in there." I widened my stance and wiped my eyes to clear the rain from them. It didn't work. "You can all go fuck yourselves," I spat, then launched my sopping wet jacket at John's face.

My missile hit its target, and I launched my soaked body to the right. I stopped short in front of my second-oldest sister's husband, Finn. With my left leg braced, my right booted foot found its target above his right knee. The rumble of thunder from above drowned the snap of his knee cap shattering. His hoarse screech of pain wasn't. Finn dropped to the ground, cradling his knee. But I was already moving with a speed I was sure I'd never had before meeting Tristan.

Note to self, ask Tristan if his blood has given me super powers.

I grinned and circled John. His training with my sisters wouldn't save him from what was coming next. I'd always disliked John and his know-it-all attitude. His 'God's gift to humanity' attitude never sat well with me. Arm raised, I drove my fist into where his ribs connected with the left side of his spine.

His breath left his lungs with a whoosh, but I was far from done. With a twirl, I appeared in front of him. Rigid with pain, John's only defence was to raise his right arm. I shackled his wrist with one hand, twisting side on as he leaned into his defence. I drove my left arm up into the crease of his arm and hooked my left hand around his wrist as his arm bowed upward. My right hand now free, I slammed my fist into his sternum, driving him to the ground. Fear flashed across his hazel eyes, and I smiled down at him.

"Smile pretty, you pompous prick," I yelled over the next crash of thunder.

I fisted his shirt and lifted his upper body. He stared dazedly up at me as I smashed my fist into the side of his head. His body went limp, and I released him.

Strong arms linked around mine from behind, and I stiffened. My body lifted from the ground, the world blurring when my captor spun me to face the other direction. Orion met me, and by the stench of home-grown tobacco wafting off of my captor, my cousin Nevin held me captive.

"Come on, Ellie. Just give up. You can't win with the two of us against you."

He grunted with the effort it took to keep my struggling body in his grasp.

A flash of lightning light the sky above, illuminating Orion and the blade he held away from his body.

My mind froze at the glint of that cold steel. I wanted to reach out to Tristan, ask for his help, but then he'd know just how much danger I was in.

If you die tonight, you know he'll bathe these hills and the farm in rivers of the family's blood. Then there's the risk Evanee and Brad will follow him. You know they'll be right behind him, sharpening whatever weapon they can get their hands on. You risk losing them and possibly Ronan and Pa during their three-person war.

The world sped up as though someone hit fast forward, and I scrambled to remember Brad's many drills and training sessions. With each memory I pulled up and disregarded, Orion stepped closer.

The banshee within me screeched in happiness at my fear and her imminent release from the prison that was my body.

At last, a memory flashed through my mind. With as little movement as possible, I slid my right foot back. At the last second, I pushed my upper body forward, sliding my left arm from Nevin's grip when his hands failed to hold me. The skin on my left arm burned from the friction of the material of his jacket against my bare arms.

Ahead of me, Orion cursed, and I caught the flash of his blade when the next fork of lightning spread across the sky. A sharp sting followed by a fiery burn radiated from my exposed side, but I dared not stop, knowing what was at stake. I dove forward, jerking my right arm, still trapped in Nevin's grip, up. I twisted to grip behind his knees, lifting his right leg to throw him off balance.

When he caught at the loose strands of my hair, dragging me down with him, I cursed.

And this, ladies and gentlemen, is why you don't wear your hair down when your family is hell-bent on murdering you.

I tucked into a roll, crying out when I came out of the somersault, and my head snapped back. I reached back to grab hold of the strands still in Nevin's grasp and pulled hard. Some strands ripped from my skull, and I screeched in pain. With another hard pull, the rest came free, but I'd lost precious seconds I didn't have.

Orion towered over me. Both hands gripping his military knife, he reared back before he plunged the blade down toward my gut. The rain had stopped at some stage during the fight, but the land was still a field of sludge. I twisted hard, my momentum catching Orion by surprise. He slid out thanks to the mud-clogged tread of his boots. Once again, searing pain exploded from the side of my body, and I twisted to find he'd lodged his blade.

"Mother fucker," I screamed, anger fuelling the adrenaline pumping through my veins.

With a simultaneous grunt and whimper, I ripped the blade from my side, then rolled onto my back, reaching over to plunge the knife into Orion's gut.

He bellowed, and I grunted as I got to my feet, ready to take on Nevin, who knelt panting behind Nevin's head.

"My sentiments exactly," I spat.

A rock caught my attention while I hunched over in pain.

"You'll do," I grumbled, reaching to pick it up.

With a long groan, I straightened, slipping and sliding to where Nevin was trying and failing to climb to his feet.

His head lifted, anger reddening his pale face. "You know it'll never stop. It's only the beginning."

"Keep it coming, jackass. I'll put every one of you in the hospital like I have tonight."

He gaped at me, and I gave him my best shit-eating grin as I brought the rock down, connecting with the side of his head.

His body went limp before it slumped over.

I stepped toward Orion. "You still alive, Orion?"

"Yes," he hissed.

"You want me to knock you out too, or do you want to lie there and wait for one of the others to rescue you?"

I was pissed and tired, but I wasn't completely heartless. He was my half-brother, after all.

"I'll probably pass out soon, so don't bother."

The rock rolled from my fingers, and I slipped and slid my way to the beam of light shining from the open back door. A tall, imposing figure stood at the door, and I stiffened.

"You going to have a go too, Pa?"

I dared not breathe, praying my father loved me enough to not condemn me to a life like the other women in my family.

"Your technique's improved, darlin'. You made your old pa proud tonight." Pa stepped to the side, making way for me to enter. "Ronan's waiting for you in the bathroom. I've booked you a flight back to Australia the day after tomorrow. Ronan will drive you to Dublin tonight once you're patched up."

"Thanks, Pa. You know she'll be pissed you helped me, right?" I squinted at my dad through the pain.

"I'll handle your mother. Now go get patched up and be on your way." Pa leaned forward to press a tender kiss to my temple. "Your old pa loves you, darlin'. Always remember that."

"I love you too, Pa. No matter what." I choked out through the pain of my wounds and breaking heart.

With a last kiss, he stepped out into the night. His broad shoulders pulled back, and his head held high.

Steam enveloped me as I dragged myself back into the present. With a gut-wrenching sob, I dropped to my knees, giving way to the knowledge I'd never see my twin brother or father again.

Sacred Trees

BLACKTHORN (Prunus spinosa)

Purification and protection.

Combats fear, depression and anger.

Use for inner work and assessment, protection,

and grounding.

Fate's presence is strong, and outside influences

should be obeyed. – Tristan Cathbad.

Chapter Four

Tristan

"How often has this happened since you've known her, Brad?" My mind was still reeling at the sight of Ellie's tiny figure and terrified eyes when she'd opened the front door yesterday afternoon.

"Two or three times. She's never visited for as long as she did this visit." Brad gingerly stirred the scrambled eggs cooking on the stovetop before he reached for the tongs to flip the bacon. "The first time she returned from a visit, I drove her up to the hospital, petrified she had some kind of aggressive cancer we didn't know about or some other disease. Of course, she tried telling me I was overreacting, but I refused to listen," Brad said, then sighed.

"I'd have acted no differently. And the second and third time?" I pressed.

"Each visit got worse. There were healing cuts, bruises and breaks. Of course, I had no idea she was part banshee, so her healing was quicker than the average human. What was the damage this time?" Brad ground out.

"A fractured rib, bruised kidneys, torn ligaments in various spots. I noticed a healing laceration and what looks to have been a deep stab wound."

"Good, good. Less than the last time." Brad huffed, his broad shoulders sagging.

"Good? What the hell do you mean 'good'? Her body looks as though it was used as a crash-test dummy." The floor shuddered beneath our feet, my rage seeping through my barriers. Sharp fangs erupted, and I zeroed in on Brad's erratic heartbeat as he spun wide-eyed to face me.

Brad's eyes darted to something behind me, and I tensed, ready to react.

"Calm down, Tristan," came a soothing feminine voice.

Slim arms snaked around my waist before Ellie's head came to rest at my spine. My eyes drifted shut when her sweet rose scent encased me, and I forced my canines to retract. My claws followed next, reluctantly receding.

"What he means is that the mixed martial arts training he made me take up after he witnessed the aftermath of my visit home when we first started living together is working. My injuries are lessening with each trip home. It's why I survived as long as I did this trip.

But things have changed." Her voice caught on the last part.

The tears in her voice were too much for me. I turned in her arms and embraced her, stroking at her silky blonde strands. Gazing down at the crown of her head, I marvelled at the woman Fate had bestowed upon me. She was the fun to my sombreness, the petite to my tallness and the light to my darkness. We were a juxtaposition, yet her intelligence and loyalty were as fierce as my own.

"Did you get highlights in your hair?" I mumbled into the soft threads of her hair.

"Kind of. Why? Don't you like them?" Ellie leant back.

"Dude, before you answer that question. From one bro to another, you want to answer yes to that question every time. Trust me."

Brad chuckled, dishing eggs and bacon onto two plates as though my intention to rip his throat out seconds ago hadn't even happened.

"Shut up, Brad. You're such an arse, you know that." Ellie's middle finger flew into the air, and I laughed at her crassness.

"I'll remember that, Brad. Thank you. And, yes, despite Brad's warning, I do, in fact, like it. But you could dye your hair black, and I'd still love it."

Relief passed over her features, and I frowned at it. With a quick nod, she cleared her throat.

"Good, because I'll probably end up with a head of flaming red hair at this point."

"Well, if that were to be the case, I'd still love the way you look. Come to think of it, I think you might suit red hair." I grinned, tugging gently at a strawberry blonde strand.

Brad snorted at the display of affection. With papers between his teeth, he snagged his plate and a glass of orange juice before taking his place at the small round table shoved into the corner of the kitchen. Brad took a second to inspect the garden below through the open window before adjusting the papers clenched between his teeth.

With reluctance, I released Ellie, giving her a gentle push in Brad's direction. She shuffled forward and sat tiredly on the seat opposite Brad. Satisfied, I retrieved her meal and orange juice, placing them in front of her.

Ellie smiled up at me, and I worried at the dullness in her bottle-green eyes.

When she made no move to eat the food before her, I cooed to her softly, "Eat, Ellie. You need to regain your weight and strength."

"I'm not hungry. I'll just drink my orange juice for now," Ellie whispered distractedly, as though she were far away.

"Eat the damned food, Ellie. Or I'll blend that shit up and shovel it down your throat. You know I'll do it, so don't tempt me," Brad snapped.

I inched forward, only to stop at the sharp shake of Ellie's head.

She stared at her food for a few seconds, then she picked up her fork, tentatively taking a bite of the fluffy scrambled eggs. Her eyelids drifted shut, and her shoulders drooped as though she were no longer shouldering the weight of the world.

The clatter of Ellie's fork hitting the corner of her plate echoed in the quiet kitchen as she snatched up the dessert spoon I hadn't noticed beside her plate. She shovelled spoonful after spoonful of egg into her mouth. She'd barely swallowed one mouthful before she shoved another one in. The bacon suffered the same fate.

Jaw clenched, my heart contracted painfully at the sight before me. Brad's gaze sought mine, his eyes reflecting my heartache. Without a word, he dropped his toast onto her plate, then went back to reading the journal in his hand.

Despite what I was witnessing, the beginnings of jealousy and envy crept beneath my shields. Brad acted as though he were her mate, yet I knew their relationship was more that of a brother and sister.

Her plate empty at last, Ellie's head dropped to the side, resting on the window frame.

I can't just stand here like some useless idiot. I'm her damned mate; I should know what to do next.

Guilt tightened my throat, and my shoulders grew rigid with my frustration and anger. The scraping of Brad's chair proved a welcome distraction. He glided past me to stow his dish in the dishwasher, and came to stand beside me.

"She's stubborn and broken. When she's like this, her thoughts aren't here. Don't worry, mate, she'll return, but it'll take a couple of days. I ended up having to threaten her to eat, or she'd have kept living the way she did in Ireland. Her trips to the farm in Orchard Hills aren't normally as bad as this. With you on the scene, I'm hoping this will be the last time I have to see her like this. I'd normally take time off after her return to care for her, but Erick's asked me to visit," Brad admitted reluctantly.

"It's fine. I've already relayed Ellie's condition to Erick last night. He's agreed to me spending time with her while she heals." I turned from the sight of my broken mate and walked with Brad toward the front door.

"Erick said he wished to speak to the both of you, but with Ellie's current condition, it'll have to wait," I informed Brad.

Scooping up the leather satchel resting against the cream wall, Brad asked, "Do you know what it's about?"

"I believe it's a matter regarding a new employment opportunity." Brad made to argue, but I raised my hand, silencing his protests. "I understand your reluctance to leave Aeternum, but I believe the offer Erick has for you will suit you and Ellie well."

"Fine, but it better be a bloody magnanimous offer. My work's important to me, Tristan. It's the only thing I have left, apart from Ellie and Evanee. I'm hoping to eventually create something that will be strong enough to attack any cancerous cells no matter where they are in the body."

I buried my smile at Brad's determination and tenacity; instead, I offered what little reassurance I could. "I'm sure Erick will make it worth your while."

"Righto. Well, look after our girl, and I guess I'll see you tonight."

With a backward wave, Brad was out the door before I could snap Ellie was my girl, not his.

The scrape of a chair against wooden floorboards drew my attention toward the back of the house. With preternatural speed, I came to a sudden stop before Ellie, who'd stepped into the hallway leading to her bedroom.

"Shit!" she screeched, her fist driving toward my gut. I sidestepped, my large hands trapping her tiny fist.

"Ellie, stop! It's me, Tristan." When her chest didn't move for a few seconds, I cooed, "Breathe, mo ghrá. Breathe."

Ellie gasped once before her knees buckled. I lunged forward and caught her shaking body. Knees dipping, I lowered myself to the wooden floor, taking Ellie with me until I sat back against the wall, cradling the woman who meant so much to me.

"Breathe, my darling. That's it. Slow breaths, in and out. I'm here, no one else, just me." I rocked her slightly as though she were a frightened child. The wetness seeping through my shirt drew my arms tighter around her petite body.

Ellie sniffed, trying her hardest to hide her wet face in the softness of my cotton shirt.

"What did I say yesterday? Don't hide your tears from me. I can't help you if you hide from me," I chided her, my voice husky with tenderness.

"There's no one. No one's in my corner. They'll come, and I'll have no choice but to give in. I'm running out of time, and I still have so much to do." She panicked her body stiffening.

"What do you mean no one's in your corner? Who's coming, Ellie?" Terror like I hadn't felt since my youth filled my heart. My fingers bit into her flesh as though it would be enough to shield her from those that sought to harm her.

What does she mean she's running out of time? Damn it! Who the hell's after her? Surely, she can't mean her family?

"Ellie, tell me what's going on, please? I've respected your need for privacy, and I've refrained from reading your mind. Your silence is not helping my resolve to stay out of your head," I beseeched. "Please, don't make me break my promise to you."

"Until now, I've always had Ronan in my corner. He's sworn to help me escape my fate. He swore an oath to me," Ellie cried. "But there's nothing more he or Pa can do for me. They've brought me all the time they can. There were so many vaccines I hoped to complete, but there's no more time." She hiccupped, her tears falling all the harder.

Red tinged my vision at the mention of another man protecting her. I ignored the mention of her father.

"Who's Ronan?" My growl vibrated through my body.

Startled by my question, Ellie pulled her head from my chest, her tear-stained eyes frowning back at me. "My twin brother, Ronan. I'm sure I've mentioned him before."

"No, you haven't," I seethed. "You haven't told me a thing about your family, other than they live in Orchard Hills in New South Wales and visit Ireland a few times a year. It was pure coincidence I discovered you were part banshee the night you were chased from the hospital. You hid your power well."

"Oh. Thank you. I actually have four half-sisters, two half-brothers and my twin brother. There are eight of us kids all up. My brothers carry the banshee curse within them, passing it to their daughters. Aside from being able to detect danger, they only have above human strength and no other abilities. It's nothing like the females of my family have, even as half mortals."

I held my tongue, hoping she'd continue. This was the most she'd shared with me since we first met all those months ago.

Ellie's trembling voice reached my ears, rewarding my patience and silence. "I'm the only one left in Australia now. Máthair, sorry Mother, has returned to Bray and has demanded all members of the clan return. It's as though she suspects something's coming. She's been rallying the family to her side." Ellie sighed with frustration. "I've ignored her orders to return to Orchard Hill since I began my internship with Aeternum in Sydney. When I joined the virology team in Acrasin City two years ago, it was a strategic move to put even more distance between my family and me. But, Aibell is not a patient woman; she's a woman of action and death. From the way my siblings have talked in the past, my father and brother's calming influence over her is the only reason she hasn't come here personally and hauled me home."

I resisted the urge to smooth the small frown lines at her brow. I worried any slight movement might stop her sweet confessions.

"Us exchanging blood did something to me, didn't it?" she whispered, changing the topic.

"Yes," I murmured. "It would have likely heightened your hearing, smell, taste and sight. Not a drastic amount, but enough that you'd have noticed a difference. It probably increased your strength. Why do you ask?" I pressed a kiss to her head.

"At night, I'd sit in the corner of my room beside the window. I'd listen to the whispers throughout the house whenever my mother and father were out. My sisters talked about how my mother had grown soft in the last four decades. They blamed my father and to some extent Ronan and me. There were whispers of a rebellion. They see my disobedience and my mother's lack of reaction as a sign she's fading or losing her grip on the clan. They believe Aibell Junior should take up my mother's position." She lifted her face to stare into my eyes again, and the horror stamped on her features churned my stomach. "Tristan, I love my family, but Aibell Junior would be disastrous as the head of the family. She's conniving and impetuous at best. Her idea of a good time is to instigate fights or wars. While we're there at the head of any battles, our jobs aren't to start them. We are or were meant to predict or warn of impending death."

A memory tugged at me, and I closed my eyes. Ascending the branches of my mind, I spotted the glowing leaf calling to me. I reached for it and brushed my fingers along it, embracing the images that assaulted my mind.

"As a little boy, I spent most of my youth travelling with my mother. She was a Druidess and highly respected." I smiled at the memory of my mother's kind yet shrewd eyes and her golden hair that changed colour in the sun's embrace. "She was called to a king's castle to provide guidance and wisdom. I was six at the time. On the last night, we were there, I had a terrible nightmare of burning bodies, a black hooded man carrying some kind of weapon and horrible monsters roaming between the dead in the hills surrounding us. When I woke, I was drenched in sweat and petrified of the things I'd seen. That's when I heard it; the cries and keening of a woman." My mind shuddered at the memory of the woman's soulless white eyes with black tears streaming down her face. "I snuck to the window and peeked out to find the woman crying below the king's window. Her cries grew louder the longer I watched her until she let out a screech so loud it left my ears ringing. It was then that I bolted from my bed and ran to my mother. I remember the sheer terror on my mother's face as I recited my dream and the description of the crying woman at the king's window. We left at morning's first light. It wasn't until I was much older that I learned of the battle that took place after we'd left. The king died in that battle."

"How long ago was that?" Ellie murmured, smoothing the crinkles from my shirt.

I released the memory before blinking the room back into focus, scratching my head in thought. "Mmm, roughly two thousand and twenty-two years ago."

Ellie's body twitched hard, and in a flash, she rolled off my lap.

"What the hell? You're two thousand years old?" She gaped at me.

"Two thousand and twenty-eight to be precise." I grinned.

"Tristan, this isn't funny! You're freaking ancient."

That my age might bother her hadn't occurred to me, but judging by her shock, I should have foreseen it being an issue.

"Ellie, my age isn't all that important," I soothed, weariness drawing my back forward, away from the wall.

"Don't be ridiculous, Tristan. Of course, it's important. If you're over two thousand years old, then how old is Erick?" She dropped onto her bum, and her back thumped against the cream wooden wall behind her so the picture hanging above her head wobbled precariously.

"Um, Erick's over the five-hundred-year mark. He's still a bit of a baby. Don't tell him I said that. He'd probably send me back to Romania as punishment," I joked, knowing full well Erick would never do such a thing.

Ellie's tinkling laughter eased the unseen weight from my shoulders.

"Wow, so you've seen a lot in your time, haven't you?" At my nod, she rushed on, "I have so many questions, but I can't decide where to start?" Ellie's bottle-green eyes twinkled with excitement, drawing a chuckle from me.

"How about we go into the kitchen, and I'll get started on tonight's dinner for you and Brad? You can ask me as many questions as you want over a bowl of fruit."

Ellie's head bobbed in agreement. "Deal. Hang on, you cook?"

"I do indeed. As a young Druid roaming the countryside, I had to learn the basics. Now, shall we get started on all those questions you have?"

"You're so freaking perfect," Ellie squealed, jumping to her feet. Her excitement was infectious.

If my heart had been beating, I was sure it would have stopped at her words.

You're the perfect one.

I smirked at her retreating figure.

Ellie halted her retreat and whipped around, staring pointedly at me.

"Stop smirking. Don't think I don't know this is all a plan to get me to eat."

My laughter at being caught was met with a soft huff from her. Ellie turned back around and began talking animatedly about the plague, smallpox, and the potential my blood held for the future of medicine.

Should I be concerned she's going to lock me in a laboratory somewhere?

Ellie stopped short, then turned and bolted down the hallway and into her bedroom. I waited in the hallway, listening as she rustled around her room. She rushed out of the room with a handful of pens, a Dictaphone, and a journal clutched tightly in her nimble fingers.

"Well? What are you waiting for, old man? There's so much to learn and so little time to do it in. Oh, and I don't have a personal laboratory, but I'm considering using my handcuffs to cuff you to my bed."

With an air kiss, she passed me, practically bouncing from foot to foot.

Surprised she'd heard my thought, I shrugged my shoulders and rolled my eyes skyward, following her into the kitchen. Ellie found a seat at the round table, prepping her journal and pens, laying them out in front of her in some kind of order, only she understood.

"Before the inquisition begins, what meat do you want in your stew tonight? And what fruit would you like in your salad?"

"Um, let's do beef for the stew, and I don't care what fruit you put into the salad," she answered distractedly, fiddling with her Dictaphone.

"Ellie, you'd better eat, or I won't be answering a single question," I bit out.

"Tristan, you answer my questions, and I'll not only eat whatever you put in front of me; I'll also screw your brains out. I mean that in a sexual way and not a reach for the cranial drill way." She stared pointedly at me, then giggled at her joke.

With a shake of my head, I opened the fridge, staring into its depths.

What the hell have I gotten myself into?

Chapter Five

Ellie

Life is like a cup of tea; it's all in how you make it.

I rested my heavy head against the leather headrest. Tristan sat silently at the wheel of his Hilux. His hands appeared to be barely touching the steering wheel, yet he manoeuvred the ute with ease and confidence. The soulful strains of a violin drifted around the car, and I frowned. It wasn't that I didn't like classical, because I did, it was that I felt old whenever I listened to it. That and I expected some shrink to pop up in the back seat and start asking how I really felt. I so wasn't prepared to go there.

"What has you so riled up, Ellie?"

I jumped at Tristan's deep voice.

"Nothing." I lied, focusing on the stars scattered across the sky before me.

"Liar," he baited.

"Reading my mind, are you?" At the shake of his head, I huffed, manoeuvring my body to face him. "Fine. I don't like to listen to classical music while I'm driving."

With a raised eyebrow, Tristan reached forward and hit a button. The car came alive with the strains of Lady Gaga's latest release. My body relaxed, my foot finding the beat to bounce along with.

"Thank you." I sighed with relief.

"That's it. I change the music and you're automatically relaxed?" He chuckled at my nod before muttering, "Remind me to put music on whenever you're in a foul mood or we have an argument. I might win."

"Haha. Hilarious. I like music. I listen to it whenever I'm in the lab on an all-night bender. Brad and I have similar tastes in music, so he usually goes along with what I put on and vice versa. The work determines the music genre we listen to." I smiled as memories of me shimmying around my lab when I'd hit a dead-end popped into my mind.

"I see," Tristan said, his long nimble fingers tightening against the steering wheel.

"Stop pouting, Tristan. Jealousy's a nasty emotion. I have no room in my life for it. Brad and I are best friends. He's my brother from another mother, and I'll always have a special bond with him."

We sat in tense silence for a minute.

Tristan's grip loosened on the steering wheel. "Sorry. This is new to me. You're new to me. I know there's nothing for me to be jealous of. You never answered my question though, and until you do, I won't know where I stand."

"What question was that, Tristan?" I knew I should have kept my mouth shut the moment the words slipped out.

With a heavy sigh, Tristan swung right onto the dirt road that led up into the hills and toward Erick's property. "What do you want from me, Ellie?"

I want everything. But I have no right wanting it.

It hurt that I couldn't tell him. To tell him would give him hope we could be an Evanee and Erick, though with fewer trust issues. He was too good for that. He was too good for a soon-to-be-dead woman.

I readjusted my body, my thoughts drifting to one of the best days I'd enjoyed in a long time. The man's mind was a treasure trove of knowledge on ancient viruses and bacteria, and I was the pirate discovering those buried gems of information. My stomach fluttered with excitement at the two notepads with notes on his thoughts and observations of the viruses of his time. The man had met Edward Jenner, the man who'd popularized the practice of vaccination, in 1795. I was in awe. His attention to the illnesses that plagued ancient civilisations was fascinating.

Despite being forced to undergo the conversion to the living dead at twenty-five, Tristan continued to maintain The Druid Way. His thirst for knowledge and healing meant he'd travelled the world, providing what little relief he could to those ill. His talent as a healer hadn't left him after he'd woken as a vampire; instead, his ability to heal was also a means to inflict pain.

~

"I hid from the world for a long time after my master abandoned me," Tristan explained, his loneliness during that period, and I suspected after it, tugging at the corners of his almond-shaped eyes. "The night he abandoned me was the night I accidentally killed my first human. He was nothing more than a drunken sailor. I stood in the shadows watching a group of them laughing and cursing. I was after nothing more than their stories from their time at sea and a quick feed. One of the more inebriated men left the group to relieve himself and he spotted me in the shadows."

He laughed at the memory, then shook his head.

"I hadn't yet learned the art of blending in. The poor guy decided I was hiding in the shadows with the intention of either mugging or killing one of them."

I leaned forward, my chin resting on my fists. My eyes widened, my lips creeping up in amusement. His broad smile and shinning lavender eyes captivated me, and I wished the rest of the world could see him this way—happy and carefree.

"He was right on one account. I had every intention of stealing someone's blood that night, but I never went there to kill. My belief in love and respect for all beings forbade me to kill unless necessary. Even after I first rose, I showed remarkable restraint over my hunger."

He tried to reassure me unnecessarily.

"The next thing I know, the drunk fool's waving a knife at me, yelling at the top of his lungs for his mates. I reacted without thought. I only wanted him to shut the hell up. I sliced his damned throat with a flick of my wrist. He was a good two metres from me and I was still rooted to my spot. I remember surveying the area, thinking my master had returned. It took a good few seconds and the sounds of the petrified screams of his mates running off into the night, to realise it was me who'd killed the poor man."

I winced, imagining how frightening it would've been for Tristan to have little to no support or training. I'd always had the support of the clan and the knowledge of the women passed on through each generation. When I converted to a banshee, I knew what to expect. Tristan didn't have that advantage.

I sat up straight and reached for his hand, squeezing it lightly to comfort him. "Tristan, that's called survival of the fittest, or self-defence if you like."

"Thank you, mo ghrá, but I've fully accepted what I am. I'm at peace with who I've become. Even if some believe I have a stick shoved up my arse."

His eyebrow lifted, and I laughed.

"Okay, yes, I thought you had a stick up your arse. In my defence, you're always so serious."

I scrunched my face at him, stopping short at the bright glow of his gorgeous lavender irises.

"You and I both know that I'm not always serious. I know at least two couches at Murder Point Bay Library that would disagree with you. I'm also positive the lock I manipulated to get us in there after-hours would disagree with you."

Tristan's seductive whisper skittered down my spine, tightening my nipples so they raised the cotton of my shirt ever so slightly.

"If I recall correctly, I was the one who begged you to tick that little gem off my bucket list." I breathed.

"That's true. But it was me who was on his knees for a good portion of that date."

My fingers bit into the palm of my hand as I fought the urge to jump over the small table and straddle him.

~

"We're here." Tristan's taut announcement snapped my head to the windshield in surprise.

"What? That was quick," I mumbled.

Tristan remained silent. His window slid down, and he keyed his password into the security panel.

The huge, black wrought-iron gates that marked the entrance to Erick's driveway swung inward, their heaviness clear by the creaks and groans with each slow centimetre they moved. We crept forward at a sedate pace, the light of the ute illuminating the first of two trees lining the driveway. I smiled at the thick trunk with its branches exploding every which way. In the daylight, the trunk would vary between a light grey-brown to a muddier brown, while its small clusters of evergreen leaves changed colour whenever the breeze rustled through them, exposing the newly interspersed lime-green shoots. I would never grow sick of seeing their majestic beauty and knowing they'd likely still be here well after I'd transitioned into a full-blooded banshee. They would be a constant in a changing world.

"Do you know what the names of these trees are?" I asked, unable to hide the awe in my tone.

"They're Toona Ciliata, better knowns as Red Cedar. I had the saplings transplanted and protected after settlers arrived here in 1881 in search of them for logging. They're beautiful, aren't they? You're no longer allowed to cut them down unless they prove hazardous to your property." The harsh lighting of the dashboard illuminated his warm smile.

"And for good reason. They're so majestic. I'm glad you saved these."

We passed beneath the grove of trees, the ute's high beams flashing across the front entrance to Erick's manor in all its splendour. The two stories on display were a perfect blend of raw local stone and warm redwood. The two wrap-around verandas shielded the rooms hidden within from more than just the heat of the day. It was a shining testament to the age it was built in.

The heavy wooden front door swung open and two familiar figures emerged to stand side by side. Tristan killed the high beams before he swung wide, coming to a stop in front of the stone-grey garage doors. I was out and moving to open the back door before I noticed Tristan's hand snagging my bag from the back.

I side-stepped the tray and whispered, "Thank you."

Tristan nodded sharply from the other side of the tray-back.

Together we approached Evanee and Erick. I snatched up his hand, selfishly using it as a distraction from the bad news I was about to share with my best friend and her mate. I hated failure at the best of times, but knowing I'd failed to secure something as important as the support of the Arnam clan for Evanee left a decidedly bitter taste across my tongue. She'd put her life on the line for me the night Jared's creatures pursued us through the forest, and I had yet to repay her for her sacrifice.

"Ell, you're home at last," Evanee called out excitedly. Lifting her foot, she made to step forward, only to appear in front of me a millisecond later.

My nervousness forgotten, I dropped Tristan's hand and threw my arms around her neck with a delighted laugh. I didn't care that I was hugging a fledgling vampire. The last few weeks of separation had been torture. I'd missed my best friend.

I breathed in the warm scent of cinnamon and sweet delicate rose, comforted by the scent that was uniquely Evanee. Her snow-white hair was pulled back into a loose bun this evening, and I grinned, knowing she only ever tied it up if she was working, cooking or training.

I pressed my mouth near her ear and breathed, "It's so good to see you. I'm sorry I couldn't do more."

"You did the best you could, and that's all that matters to me."

Evanee held me back from her, and her electric blue eyes assessed me, the flecks of red dotted through her iris similar to Tristan and Erick's. "You feeling okay? You're paler and slimmer than before you left."

"I'm fine. Tristan's been a tremendous help with my healing," I hedged, not wanting to discuss it any further.

"Your damned family at it again?" she asked through gritted teeth.

Not long after Evanee and I had first met, I'd been forced to return to Ireland for a funeral. I'd secluded myself for two days before Evanee had come knocking and demanding to see me. My excuse I was contagious hadn't meant a thing to her. Brad, likewise, hadn't been able to stop her once she got in the front door. I still remember her angry retort to Brad all these years later.

"I may be Doctor Death, but I'm still a bloody doctor, Brad. Now move your backside or I'll move it for you."

One look at my emaciated frame and blood-red eyes, and she'd yelled for Brad to order a pizza and to get down to the shops for some ice-cream stat. She'd stayed with me for two days, just holding me and loading comedy after comedy into the DVD player until I'd laughed again. Her friendship would always mean the world to me.

There's no doubt she'll fight for me when my family comes to collect me.

'*Why is your family coming for you, Ellie? Do you think Evanee would be the only one to fight for you?*' Tristan's voice tumbled through my mind.

'*I know you'd fight for me, Tristan. I don't want you to suffer unnecessarily. Few could stand up to my mother and the full brunt of the entire Arnam clan. You mean too much to me to let anything happen to you.*'

With a nod to Evanee, I sighed, "You know how they are."

I reached back for Tristan's hand in reassurance. There was no hesitation. He gripped my hand tightly.

Studying us for a second, Evanee shrugged. "Fair enough. Thank goodness for Elf Boy here and his magic touch." Evanee waggled her rounded eyebrows at the last bit, and I giggled.

Behind Evanee, Erick did his best to smother his snort of laughter at Evanee's nickname for Tristan. I looked back at Tristan, my gaze fixed on his shoulder-length, thick, silvery hair. He'd opted to leave it loose tonight, the strands lifting in the cool night air. Tristan rolled his eyes upward with exasperation, the light from within the house catching on the red specks in amongst the lavender of his irises.

"Well, let's get inside then. There's a bit to discuss. I believe my mate is itching to get her friend to herself, and you and I have business to attend to, Tristan." Erick smiled politely before he stretched his hand out to Evanee.

With a shy smile, Evanee appeared at Erick's side. Erick's 6'1" height dwarfed Evanee's 5'6" hourglass figure. His arm circled her waist, the muscles flexing ever so slightly as he secured her to his side lovingly. This was the happiest I'd seen her since I'd known her, and it suited her.

'Erick's been working hard to reassure her he isn't going anywhere, and what they have is genuine.' My gaze flicked up to Tristan. His face could have been carved out of stone. There was no emotion. He was in work mode.

'That's good. I'm glad she found someone as good as Erick. What she's been through and what Desmond and Brian did to her, no one should have to experience or suffer that.'

The night I'd met Tristan at Desmond and Jared's house party fluttered through my mind. The moment I'd felt his tender touch against my mind, I'd known he was different. His unique lavender eyes snared me in their web the second my eyelids fluttered open. There'd been no denying the quivering in my stomach or the alarming sensation of coming home. I'd ignored the attraction for as long as I could, but those eyes haunted my dreams.

My reflection was interrupted when I stepped into the library. I stood contemplating the room, then smiled when I noted nothing in it had changed since my last visit. The leather sofas still sat at the centre with a solid wooden desk at the helm. Books embraced the walls, and I breathed in deeply, appreciating the scent of their paper pages.

We sat with Evanee and Erick facing Tristan and me.

"I think it'd be best to jump right on into things." Erick smiled warmly.

"Sounds good to me. Will Jordan be joining us?" I searched the room, fully expecting Evanee's left hand and a giant of a man to waltz in.

Jordan's beautiful russet skin tone, bright smile and sense of humour hid how dangerous he was well. I'd watched him rip appendages from infected vampires the night Evanee freed herself from the creature within her. His hand had left a hole the size of a rock melon. The man's thighs alone were the size of at least three of mine. His biceps were no different.

"No, he's been a bit busy over the last week." My curiosity piqued at Evanee's evil grin

I watched her for a split second before my gaze darted to Erick's grinning face and back to Evanee. "What did you do, Evie?"

"Let's just say he's met his match, and Karma truly is a bitch," Tristan chortled beside me.

"Huh?"

"He's found his mate, and it would seem she's giving him a run for his money," Erick replied lightheartedly, his lips tugging at the corners.

"Oh, he did? That's wonderful. Who is it? Do I know her, or is it him?" At my question, Erick and Tristan roared with laughter, their heads dropping back.

Perplexed, my gaze met Evanee's, and my eyebrows rose in question. Her eyes sparkled with humour, and she said two words.

"My mother."

My gasp was loud in the room, despite the men's soft chuckles. "Oh." Then it hit me. Reagan was mated to Jordan. Strong-willed, bad-tempered, could-reap-you-if-you-pissed-her-off-enough Reagan. "Ooh. Well, who'd have thought?"

I sat stunned for a minute, processing just how weird it was that Jordan would likely become Evanee's stepfather.

"Not us, but it sure as hell is fun to watch." Erick squeezed Evanee's shoulder, then kissed her temple.

"I bet it is. It sounds like we have a lot to catch up on then, Evie."

"We sure do, Ell. But first, what's the word from your bat-shit-crazy family?" she queried softly, knowing it would be a sore topic for me.

"Same old shit, different day. Come home or face the consequences. I told them to shove it where the sun doesn't shine." I shrugged. Beside me, Tristan stiffened, and my hand found his in reassurance. "My mother and her council have refused to align themselves with you or Erick. They feel you overstepped and should face the consequences of the vampire council as your mate is a vampire. It turns out my mother knew about Tristan and has forbidden me to have any further contact with him or face the same consequences as you, Erick."

Tristan's body grew stiff before he bellowed, "What! Why didn't you tell me?"

Shocked at his outburst, I sat back, watching his calm demeanour vanish in the blink of an eye.

"Calm down, Tristan. It's okay; I don't care." I shrugged, regretting my confession.

"What exactly are the consequences, Ellie?"

Evanee's voice dropped an octave, and my gaze dropped to the coffee table between us.

My eyes met Erick's. Sadness tugged at the corners of his lips, tugging them down infinitesimally. We both understood what the price was. Judging by the slight tremor in Evanee's hand, I suspected she knew too but wanted confirmation.

"Death," I wheezed.

Silence rung like Notre Dame's bells.

Beside Erick, Evanee shrank further into the couch, her eyes widening with fear and horror. Despite her lower lip parting, she remained silent.

Tristan jumped from the couch, his eyes burning brightly, and his canines distended. "That's bullshit! Why the hell didn't you tell me this when I first saw you.

We've been lying around your damned place like there's no threat hanging over your head. You're not going back to your house, Ellie." His brow furrowing, Tristan shoved his hands into his hair. "You'll have to stay on the property until I can figure out how best to protect you."

Tristan's eyes were wild. Gone was the calm and patient man I knew before me stood a man with fear in his heart.

This is precisely why I didn't want us to get involved. That fear and sadness will only worsen after I'm murdered.

My heart clenched at the knowledge I would be the one to hurt him in the end. I knew I needed to distance myself from him, but I didn't have the courage to give up something or someone as unique and special as him.

Erick rose from the couch, his calm exterior pierced by the shine of his emerald eyes and raised eyebrows. He reached forward to calm his second in command and best friend, addressing him tentatively. "Tristan, you need to calm yourself."

"Don't tell me what to do, Erick." The floor shuddered, Tristan's anger leaching from his body and into the floorboards beneath booted feet. Books trembled on their shelves, some thumping to the ground. "Have you acted calm or rationally since meeting Evanee?" he accused.

Red flecks shimmered in the depths of his glowing lavender eyes. The air around his figure wavered and pulsed with something I'd only ever glimpsed but never seen in full.

"No, you're right. But you're not helping anyone right now. You need to walk this off," Erick reasoned.

With clenched fists, Tristan reigned in that pulsing power. When at last his eyes lost their glow, Tristan blurred his body, escaping through the French doors and into the gardens beyond.

I stood and made to follow him, but Erick's large hand on my upper arm stopped me short.

"Leave him be. He needs to gather himself with no one to witness it. Losing control of his emotions is not something he has regularly experienced, if ever." When I made to argue, Erick raised his hand. "I'll find him in a minute. First, though, I'd like to talk to you about your employment with Aeternum."

My gaze darted between Erick and the French doors, but I stood my ground. I'd hurt Tristan, and every fibre in my body demanded I ease the hurt he was feeling.

"Ellie, you can't help him right now. Listen to what Erick has to offer, and then he'll check on Tristan. Okay?" Evanee sat forward, drawing my attention to her grimace.

"Okay. But hurry, Erick. I don't want him out there on his own. I can feel his anger and pain," I urged, anxiety churning my stomach.

"Very well. I've spoken with Tristan, Evanee, Jordan and Brad. We're all in agreement that it's getting too dangerous for you or Brad to continue to work for Aeternum. We feel it'd be best for you to remove yourself from the company altogether."

Chapter Six

Ellie

A windy day is not a day for thatching.

My body stilled, and I narrowed my eyes dangerously at Erick. The prince and future king towered over me, his broad shoulders reminding me of a swimmer's shoulders. Clad in black jeans, a hunter green polo shirt stretched across his chest, hiding the toned physique I knew lay beneath. I'd been to enough of Evanee's training sessions with Erick, Jordan, and Tristan to know they could use their stomachs as a washing board if the washing machine broke down.

"What do you mean, you feel I should remove myself? Do you understand what that would mean for me?" I hissed, my anger thrumming through my rigid body.

"Ellie, we know how important your work is to you and Brad. And I'm so sorry knowing me has put you in this position. If I could change things, I would, but I can't," Evanee whispered, her hands shifting to her lap where they clenched into fists.

"It took a lot of convincing for these two. You and Brad mean too much to Evanee to risk leaving you in harm's way. And with a rogue reaper as the head of Aeternum, we feel it's too risky," Erick reasoned.

"So, what the hell am I supposed to do for income? Do you expect me to return to Orchard Hill or Bray?" Panic set in.

Evanee sat forward. "No one expects you to return to your fam…."

"You understand that if I leave Aeternum, I'd have no choice but to go crawling back to Bray. It's been my buffer against my family. No child of Aibell would dare shirk their work duties for fear of my mother's wrath." Anger took panic's hand, and together they danced in me. The banshee shifted uncomfortably beneath my skin, and I stretched my neck from side to side to release the tension.

"Ellie, Evanee and I wouldn't allow that; neither would Tristan. You mean too much to all of us," Erick reassured.

The banshee shifted once again, and I clenched my fists against its need to take over. "Give it a rest, Erick. You don't understand what you're asking. None of you do."

"Ellie, please listen to Erick's offer. You wouldn't have to leave Murder Point Bay, let alone Australia. Your family wouldn't have to know you had resigned from Aeternum." Evanee pleaded.

My scoff at Evanee wasn't one of my finer moments. I knew she was trying her best to keep me safe, but my anger wouldn't be reasoned with. "Don't be so damned naïve, Evanee. You and I both know my mother would find out. It would only be a matter of time. She has spies everywhere, and I work on hospital grounds. It's a damned buffet for my kind."

A gentle breeze lifted my hair from my waist, heralding my imminent loss of control.

White bled across Evanee's irises, and I watched, captivated by the forks of obsidian and electric blue peeking through the white.

"Mic Luptător, breathe." Erick's shifted to stand side-on, his emerald gaze shifting between the two of us.

A high-pitched wail ripped from my throat, and black tears streamed down my face, staining my cheeks and pale pink shirt. "You ask me to do this, and you're condemning me to death."

Evanee's head dropped forward, her chin touching her chest while her hands clenched atop of her knees. I continued to wail, the banshee within sliding into place. In front of me, a fog poured from beneath Evanee's bare feet, rolling over the top of the carpeted floor of the library. Fear tainted the mist, tickling my taste buds, and the Banshee grinned. I'd denied it food for too long. It was hungry, and Evanee was offering a free meal.

"Ellie, you need to calm down. I have a solution that will help. It'll offer the full protection of the

Tenebris Family and three members of the Messorem Family. Not even your mother would dare risk offending or challenging Death and two of his descendants." Erick lowered himself to his knees beside Evanee's thigh, rubbing at it gently to bring her back from wherever she was within her mind.

"You don't understand, Erick. None of you...." My moan cut short when Evanee's head snapped up, and her mesmerising gaze shackled mine.

Evanee rose from her seat, the fog beneath her feet remaining undisturbed by her movement. Erick rose with her, weary of what she might do. The dead moaned from deep within the fog, their bodies wreathing and surfacing in amongst the dense mist. My banshee smiled in delight, eager to drink the fear drifting up from those trapped within.

The rip of material shredding echoed loudly within the library. From behind Evanee, a giant pair of opaque wings unfurled. A calmness brushed at my mind, and my banshee hissed at it in frustration. I stood transfixed by the beauty of those shredded, moth-like wings with their gold and pale blue veins.

Evanee's head cocked to the side, her smile haunting. "Did you think you could escape Fate forever, Ellie Arnam? Did you think she wouldn't hunt you down as she hunted me down?"

My muscles at my spine tightened and strained at her questions, and Erick froze at the mention of Fate.

"How did you find out?"

"I tasted it the second you leapt out of the ute. Your aura's changed; it's shrinking with each passing second."

"Please tell me that doesn't mean what I think it does," Erick groaned, his emerald green gaze flicking up to meet mine.

"You can't outrun Fate, Ellie. I tried and failed, and so too will you. Don't worry though, sweet Ellie, for death is but a state, not the end." Evanee's disembodied voice drifted up from the fog.

Her smile widened, chilling me to my core. My banshee cowered at that smile, hiding deeper within me.

Salty tears replaced the banshee's black tears staining my face.

I met Erick's shocked gaze and pleaded, "Don't tell Tristan, please. I'm begging you."

Erick's shock gave way to sadness, his grim nod doing nothing to dull the pain that my time with Tristan was ending.

"I won't tell him, but Ellie, he needs to know. It'll break him to find out any other way." Erick warned.

Grief consuming me, and I sniffed indelicately.

I stood to leave the library when Erick sighed. "The offer of employment I made to Brad still stands, Ellie. You and Brad would take up positions as head virologists at our new laboratory. I'll exceed your current pay package. Talk to Brad; he'll confirm the details."

"Thank you, Erick. Under the circumstances, I think I'll take your offer," I whispered before making my way out of the library.

Working for Erick will have one advantage. I'll at least have more time with those I love before I'm forced to return to Ireland and the death waiting for me. It looks like Máthair might get her way after all.

My shoulder dug into the doorframe. I knew lingering at the door to the gym would achieve nothing, but it gave me the chance to laugh at Brad, who was currently getting his arse handed to him by an amused Jordan. Brad cursed Jordan, then moved in for his next punch to the gut, which Jordan blocked.

"Holding up the door frame?" My body jumped a foot in the air at the soft voice behind me, and I cursed myself for not being more observant.

"Holy crap, Evie. You need a damn collar with a bell on it." I laughed.

"Where would the fun be in that? Can't very well do sneak attacks with a bell giving away my position, now can I?"

Evanee stopped beside me and leaned against the other side of the door frame in time to see Brad get nailed to the mat hard.

"Ouch," we both hissed in sympathy.

After a few seconds of silence, Evanee scrutinised me. "You want to talk about what happened in the library?"

"Not really. There's nothing I can do to change it. I've known for a long time this day was coming." I hesitated for a split second. "Do me a favour?"

"Anything."

"Don't tell Brad." Evanee's eyes narrowed in question, and I straightened up. "I don't want him to know. He's lost so much in his life. He watched cancer ravage his mother in his late teens and then buried her in his first year of Uni. It'd be like history repeating itself;

only this time it wouldn't be cancer, it would be a when and where will she die."

"Ellie, I won't tell anyone; it's not my secret to tell. But for the record, I think you should tell Tristan and Brad. I can and will always support you, but the support of the two men who love you would be even better."

Pain sliced at my heart at her words. I couldn't bear to see the looks of grief and anger that I knew I'd see on Tristan and Brad's faces when I told them.

"Thank you. You seem to be handling this well."

"For now. I'm fully expecting a freak-out to happen at some point. I think Erick knows because he seems to float through my mind an awful lot at the moment." Evanee's bright blue eyes twinkled. "He's currently chastising me for not resting."

We giggled. Evanee wrapped her arm around my shoulder and spoke loudly, "Now, let's do some training. Nothing like a good workout to alleviate stress. I hear sex works, but it's not something I'd consider as bonding time for friends." I giggled at her wince. "Erick seems to agree that sex would not be a great bonding method for you, Brad and I. I think he's considering getting savage dogs again."

I frowned at the last part. "Why savage dogs?"

"So he can set them on anyone looking at me the wrong way."

I laughed at her indelicate snort, then shook my head. "I'd say that's on the medieval side of things, but considering Erick's age, I think it's quite restrained for him."

We grinned at each other and approached the mat at the centre of the room. Jordan and Brad stood facing each other. They shook hands. Brad released first and grabbed his towel and water bottle from the corner of the mat.

Jordan waved cheerfully, loose tendrils of raven hair tickling the sides of his face and neck. He turned, then sped from the room, his body a blur.

"Where's he off to in a hurry?" I twisted to follow his movement, only to give up.

"My mother just teleported in from a reap. I believe they're about to have another yelling match. She left without telling him." Evanee giggled.

"Man, I'm glad my hearing isn't as sharp as you guys," I responded with a giggle of my own. "Hey, Brad. Good work out?"

"Great. I've been struggling to find partners who move like the supernatural do at the gym. At least here I can train for whatever's headed our way." That was Brad, practical and always preparing himself for the worst.

"True. You up for instructor duties?" Evanee grinned devilishly.

"For you two? Always." His goofy grin wrapped around my heart, and refused to let go.

I clapped with delight and pulled out my phone. "We'll need music, and I have the perfect music to get us in the mood. Where's the small speaker you keep in here, Evie?"

"Oh, that's in my room. I asked Erick to install a music system in here. It's Bluetooth, so play away."

"Ooh, brilliant," I squealed, connecting to the Bluetooth.

I scrolled through to one of my mixed albums. The first words of Inner Circle's 'Sweat' blared through the speakers hidden within the roof.

Brad groaned. "Come on, Ellie, you can't be serious."

My laughter took flight through the room as my hips swayed in time to the beat. Evanee's deep bellied chuckle joined mine, and together we twirled and swayed to the beat. The world melted away as the music took over. Brad gave up when 'Dancing in the Moonlight' blared through the speakers. The three of us laughed, dancing around the mat.

We were a bunch of uncoordinated fools dancing as though this was the last time we would ever dance together. Brad threw a sprinkler move in, leaving Evanee and me in stitches.

"I thought you said you wanted to train?" Brad yelled over the music.

"We are training. It's a warm-up." Evanee reassured him, and I gave her a thumbs up in agreement.

"This warm-up is way better than the ones I've done all week. I've had enough arse-kicking this week from my grandfather, Erick and Jordan to last me a lifetime." Evanee agreed.

"Fine, we'll keep the music from nineties hell going," Brad agreed reluctantly. "But you get the moves wrong, and you do ten push-ups and ten burpees. Evanee, that's a hundred each for you. We're switching between four different martial arts, so keep your wits about you."

The three of us manoeuvred into the middle of the mat.

The strains of the piano introduction of Robert Miles' 'Children' pumped through the speakers, and Brad yelled his first set of instructions. Evanee and I flowed. Our punches delivered in quick and precise movements. Brad switched between Tai Chi and boxing depending on the beat. The two of us messed up twice midway to Brad's delight. The cheeky bugger danced around us as we got down and began our push-ups, my shoulders and abdominals protesting with each downward movement.

We moved into a second, more upbeat tune, Brad switching to Capoeira and karate. Sweat dripped from my brow as I breathed through the stitch in my side, trying my hardest to draw in more oxygen than my lungs could hold.

The fear and panic I'd felt at the start of the workout melted from my body. My mind freed itself from the shackles of my impending doom, and the urge to cry drifted through my body. I threw every emotion hammering through my body into my workout, determined to make every second count.

At last, Brad ended the workout, and I collapsed with Evanee onto the sweat dotted mat.

"How am I this unfit?" I groaned.

"That'd be because you're still recovering from the damage done to you in Ireland. You're struggling too, Evie." We squirmed under Brad's assessing gaze.

"Hey, I was moving at a human pace," Evanee retorted. "And my power may have gotten the better of me today," Evanee confessed.

"Okay then. Well, let's move onto stick work then." Brad grinned evilly.

"Since when do you teach stick work?" I panted, grimacing at the burn deep within my chest.

"Oh, I don't. But they do." Brad chuckled.

With a nod of his head toward the gym door, I lifted my head as Evanee exclaimed, "Turn around and walk back out, Elf Boy. I can smell your shit-eating grin from over here."

The back of my skull met the mat before I rotated my neck to study Evanee. "How d'you know Tristan was here?"

"Because I'm the only one in this house aside from Erick, who trains with staffs." Tristan peered down at me, and I poked my tongue out at him. The hairs on the back of my neck rose at Tristan's dark chuckle as he knelt beside me. "And even then, it was me who trained Erick. That's why Evanee is in a foul mood. She hasn't beaten me yet, and from our last session, that isn't likely to happen within this century."

"Considering you were once a druid, I can't say I'm surprised," I muttered.

"Hang on, were you really a druid, Tristan?" Evanee's head shot up from the mat.

Tristan's lavender gaze never left mine as he responded, "Yes, I was, and in some ways still am."

"Well, hell! I guess Elf Boy was the right name for you. You must tell me all about Merlin," Evanee baited.

Tristan rolled his eyes heavenward at Evanee's taunt and sighed. "Merlin did one noble thing and lived off the story for the rest of his life. He was no better than my father and just as vengeful. Their curses were as notorious as their one significant achievement.”

“Fair enough. So, hang on, if you were a druid before you were converted, how old would that make you?” Evanee frowned, rolling to her knees.

“Including my mortal life, I am roughly two thousand and twenty-eight years old.” Tristan shrugged.

Brad, who’d been quietly observing the exchange, spluttered and coughed loudly, forcing me to look back at him to be sure he wasn’t choking.

Evanee observed Erick and Tristan before her neck relaxed enough, so her head drooped heavily between her braced arms. If she’d been human, I’d have said she looked as though she might be sick. She knelt, silent and unmoving, the seconds ticking by.

"I believe you've successfully stunned Evie into silence, Tristan. I'd claim that as a win, bro and run with it," Brad gasped between racking cough, his fist beating at his chest to help clear his windpipe.

"Does my age bother you, Evanee?" Tristan frowned lightly.

"Um… I'd like to say no, but the truth is I'm not sure what I'm feeling right at this moment. It's strange knowing I'm supposed to be a queen to members older than me and with more experience. I'd always assumed Erick converted you." Evanee rose from the mat, not meeting anyone's eyes.

Tristan's lavender eyes shone with suppressed laughter. "I was there the day Erick was born. He was a fangy little bugger and notoriously bad-tempered."

"Hey, my fangs were just fine. Don't listen to him, mic luptător," Erick growled jokingly at Tristan.

"Oh, he was. I believe your sister asked whether your mother had mated with a werewolf. She'd never seen fangs as long as yours. That didn't go down well." Tristan's bark of laughter surprised me. He rarely showed any emotion around others, but I was glad he felt relaxed enough to do it now.

"You knew Sophia?" Evanee's curiosity peeked through.

Tristan shifted subtly, and my curiosity surged. "Yes, Tristan. Tell us, how did you know *Sophia?*"

My mind brushed against his, and I hissed aloud, rolling to my feet when he blocked me out.

"He didn't tell you, Ellie?" Erick clicked his tongue at Tristan.

"Don't, Erick," Tristan pleaded with a pained expression.

"Come now, Tristan. You felt the need to share childhood stories with Evanee; I think it's only fair I share some with Ellie," Erick chortled. "Tristan here was nearly my brother-in-law."

"What!" Evanee and I screeched at the same time.

"Erick!" Tristan snapped. "Ellie, mo ghrá, Sophia and I merely dated; we were never engaged to be married. We separated when we realised what we had wasn't what either of us wanted," he explained. Worry crept across his lavender eyes, widening them a little more than usual.

"Don't placate me, Tristan. How long were you together?" I seethed with frustration, a hint of jealousy creeping into my heart.

I hated myself for that jealousy. It had no right being there when I was lying to him daily.

Erick drifted over to Evanee, who attempted to deliver a swift, hard punch to his shoulder. Erick snatched her fist mid-air, placing a gentle kiss against her knuckles.

"Three hundred years," Tristan confessed grudgingly, a pained expression creasing his face.

Three hundred fucking years! How the hell am I supposed to beat that?

At the slightest brush of Tristan's mind against mine, I slammed my walls in place.

I can't beat three hundred years. Maybe as a banshee, but that won't happen when my mother hauls my butt to Ireland and commands my oath to the clan.

It took all of my willpower to force my rising heartache down deep.

A change of topic was needed. "I think I'm done for the night, guys. Erick, perhaps we could discuss the paperwork for the position you want me to take up."

"Ellie, please let me explain." Tristan approached me cautiously.

"Tristan, it's fine; I'm not angry at you. I'm tired, that's all. When's your next night off, Evie?"

Evanee thought for a second before she answered. "Friday."

With a curt nod, I asked, "Brilliant. You up for a session?"

"Of course. I'm sure my shit-stirring boyfriend here could spare me for a night." She stared hard at Erick, who was rubbing the back of his neck.

"Of course," he muttered. "Ellie, I'm sorry, I never meant to…." I stopped his apology short.

"Erick, it's okay. I'm tired, that's all. Let's look at the paperwork now and discuss logistics before I head to bed." I padded towards Tristan and stood on my tippy toes to press a tender kiss on his cheek. Stepping back, I touched his forearm. "I know you have work to do."

Shoulders stiff, Tristan eyed me warily. "Nothing that can't wait."

"Tristan, I need a long hot bath to soak out the aches and sleep. We'll talk tomorrow."

With a curt nod, Tristan stepped to one side. "Very well. I'll walk you to Erick's office."

Together the five of us left the gym, the silence deafening.

My mind buzzed annoyingly in the awkward silence. "Is my bag in your room?"

"Yes, it is," he nodded.

His gaze sought mine, and the love and uncertainty I saw within it wrapped tight around my weary heart.

"Thank you," I muttered, coming to a halt outside a solid pine door.

Tristan depressed the handle before he stepped back. We waited for Brad, Evanee and Erick to walk past.

My gaze caught on the simple rectangular desk sitting in front of a large window overlooking the forest. I'd figured Erick for an antique desk kind of guy. I'd fully expected to find a desk similar to the one in the library, with deep rich colours gracing the walls similar to what I'd seen throughout the house. A couple of rugs and a stone fireplace offered the only source of warmth in the otherwise sterile and modern room.

My gaze landed on Tristan, and I offered him a small smile. "I'll see you in the morning," I offered, stepping into the room.

"I'll see you later," he murmured and shut the door behind me.

I turned toward the others. "Well, let's get this sorted then."

Sacred Trees

The Rowan Tree (Sorbus Aucuparia)

Symbolises death.

Bury with loved ones to ensure protection from

evil.

Berries are flavourful when added to alcohol and

treated with heat.

May also accompany game in the form of jams

and preserves.

Chapter Seven

Tristan

With the upper half of my back pressed firmly against the wall, I watched Erick and Evanee's dual from afar, allowing my mind to drift to thoughts of Ellie. It'd been two days since we'd spoken, two days since she'd clammed up and gone into her version of hiding. Power trickled sluggishly through my veins. I clenched my hands against the tingling in my fingers and observed the two figures at the heart of the mat. The clang of their swords reverberated through the room.

"Not good enough, Evanee," Erick bellowed. "Your feet are out." He pointed to Evanee's misaligned back foot with the tip of his sword.

When she looked down, Erick stepped into her space, forcing Evanee to step back and lose her footing. She landed on her arse with a dulled thud, thanks to the mat.

A chuckle caught in my chest. A memory of another time and another place hovered in my mind's eye, and I gave into it.

~

"Tsk, tsk, Tristan. Where has your concentration gone, young druid?" The tall raven-haired goddess teased.

I swallowed, not brave enough to tell her my attention centred on the cleavage of her ample breasts. Their gentle curves glimmered beneath the moonlight, as though she'd sprinkled the dust of crushed diamonds on her skin.

"My apologies, my queen." I bowed, my hand and the staff within it extending outward.

A harsh cry escaped my lips when the sharp sting blossomed at the crease of my elbow.

"Let that be a lesson for getting distracted by a woman's body, Tristan." The All-Father hissed into my ear.

I flinched at the harshness of his words and the sting working its way up my arm.

"My love, that was unnecessary," the Great Queen, Morrigan chastised.

"The boy will learn nothing if you continue to treat him as such. He is well into his manhood and has already had his first fuck. If he is man enough to be distracted by your breasts, then he is man enough to face the consequences. Men will not be your only opponents on the battlefield, lad. Allowing yourself to be distracted by a woman's body is a sure way to have your head removed from your body. Would you like me to demonstrate how that feels?" The All-Father taunted.

The blood drained from my head so that I grew faint.

I shook my head and gulped. "No, All-Father. My apologies for the disrespect."

"I should remove your head right this second for your footing." A large hand pressed to my back and gave a gentle push.

I stumbled forward, falling face first in front of my goddess.

Dew soaked through my tunic, and I grimaced at the sting of abrasion on my palms. My staff lay beside me, where I'd dropped it.

"Now get up and do it again. This time you will face me and not your queen. You drop that staff again and I will flog you as though you were a boy," the All-Father growled.

~

The past merged with the present, and I shook my head to clear the fog from it in time to catch Evanee's rant. "Why the hell am I even learning to fight with a sword, Erick? It's not like I'm going to walk out the front door and suddenly get challenged to a dual by sword."

I approached the mat, answering before Erick could. "We've discussed this Evanee. Not all vampires are as progressive as we are. There are those that prefer to wield a sword in battle. You need to be prepared for any situation. You can't rely on your powers, no matter how deep your reserve is."

"I know, I know," Evanee huffed. "I'm done for today."

"We're not done until you get your feet positions right," Erick commanded in a tone I'd not heard since he'd led his father's army into battle in 1701.

I'd ridden beside him, guiding him where necessary for thirteen years, charging into battle after battle. The bodies of both humans and supernatural creatures we'd left in our wake still lay forgotten beneath the bustling streets that had been constructed over them. The War of the Spanish Succession had secured my position as Erick's claíomh, the humans' war a front for an interspecies war that raged for the better part of thirteen years. Reapers, banshees, ghouls, wraths, and vampires at each other's throats for a kingdom that had been left in shreds after Death had disappeared. Word of the rift between the species reached the werewolves, and they'd pounced on the opportunity to secure a larger slice of land. Their loss felt as keenly today as it was then.

"I'm done, Erick. Don't push it," Evanee growled in warning.

I smirked at my king and his future queen. When it came to her work and helping those in need, Evanee had all the patience in the world. But lie to her or try to force her to do something she had no interest in doing, and she'd likely rip your head off before ripping out your heart and shoving it inside your gaping jaw.

"I'm doing this for your own good," Erick hit back, his temper getting the better of him.

I shook my head at the two of them. Erick usually had the patience of a saint with Evanee, which was astounding considering how ill-tempered he'd been as a young lad. But today was not one of those days.

Evanee visibly shivered. The skin at her back beneath her sports bra straps rippling against the wings hidden beneath. I breezed forward, sending my power ahead of me to wash over her body. From the corner of my eye, Jordan's power reached for Evanee, a frown creasing his forehead. I mentally skimmed over her organs, and frowned when I noted signs of mild strain.

"Erick, you need to back down," Jordan cautioned.

Erick hissed at him, stopping Jordan dead in his tracks. With both his hands raised in surrender, Jordan glanced to me for help. I studied Erick and Evanee, my brow furrowed in concentration, searching.

There!

Deep within Evanee's body, barely leashed, swirled her power. The strain from containing it was putting stress on her vital organs.

It would seem I'm not the only one struggling to contain my power this afternoon.

"I'd have to agree with Jordan, Erick."

I was met with the same hiss of anger and warning.

Comprehension dawned, and I darted forward, my fist connecting with Erick's jaw hard, hoping to provide a distraction.

"Erick," I yelled. "Snap out of it! You're reacting to whatever is affecting your mate. She doesn't need your childish temper; she needs your support." I reprimanded him as a father would a child. It wasn't the first time I'd done it over the centuries, and I was sure it wouldn't be the last.

With a shake of his head, Erick rubbed at his jaw dazedly. His bright emerald green eyes locked with my lavender ones. His gaze darted past me to Jordan and then to Evanee. Searching her body, Erick's eyes widened when what I'd said sunk in. He handed me his sword and approached Evanee with small steps. As though she were a skittish animal and any sudden movement might frighten her.

"Baby, I'm sorry. I didn't mean to snap at you. Tell me what's going on? What's got you so on edge?"

Evanee clenched one fist hard around the sword, hissing long and low, her inner struggle with her magic and emotions manifesting externally. When Erick took another step, she reared back and launched her sword into the wall beside the door. Erick stopped short. Her power pulsed once more, and my own responded, seeking someone to maim.

This is getting us nowhere.

With an inward sigh, I brushed past Erick, shoving his sword back at him. My hand shot out to grip Evanee's jaw, while the other shackled her taloned hand aiming for my face.

"Hold her hands, Jordan," I commanded.

"What are you doing, Tristan?" Erick's snarl warned my next words needed to be well thought out or there would be consequences.

"Her power is barely leashed and her organs are under strain, Erick." Looking deep into Evanee's snowy eyes, I shuddered when I met her safeguards.

She's strong.

"When was the last time you fed?" I murmured in the soothing voice I'd once used on the sick as a young apprenticed druid.

"Before training," she bit out.

"And sleep? When was the last time you allowed your body to succumb to the sleep of the dead?" The sudden appearance of pink tears welling within her eyes was answer enough.

"I can't sleep."

I remained silent, waiting for her to explain why.

Exhausted, Evanee broke down. "The nightmares, they're too much," she sobbed.

I released her jaw with a frown and nodded for Jordan to follow suit. "If you succumbed to the sleep of the dead, you wouldn't have nightmares."

"Don't you think I know that?" she argued, her voice thick with tears. "I'm having nightmares no matter what state of sleep I'm in. I can't bloody sleep, and there's this sensation… it keeps clawing at the back of my damned mind."

"What do you mean?" Erick came to stand beside me.

"The sensation that the other shoe's about to drop."

I tensed at her admission.

"When did the sensation start?" I already suspected the answer, but needed to hear it from her.

"The day Ellie returned."

Beside me, Erick's shoulders slumped. The air soured with the pungent odour of defeat and sadness.

"I wish you'd shared your struggles with me, mic luptător," Erick muttered grimly.

I spoke over him. "What happens in your dreams, Evanee?"

Evanee shook her head at me, looking to Erick, who stepped up to her, his arms circling her waist. Blinking up at the ceiling, she fought the tears sliding down her cheeks.

"You're worried about Ellie, aren't you?" I swallowed hard.

She nodded, and my shoulders slumped in defeat. "You aren't the only one feeling a disturbance. It's affecting me as well," I admitted.

"Why would you both be worried about Ellie? She seemed fine the last time I saw her?" Jordan asked, confused.

My ragged confession clawed its way out of my mouth, leaving a bitter taste. "Because she has a death sentence hanging over her head, and I'm the reason it's there. She's been ordered to return to her family."

"Not this crap again. If Erick can mate with a reaper, then why the hell can't you mate with a banshee?" Jordan huffed in exasperation. "I'm sure the big fella wouldn't care. Death seems to be pretty easy with the whole mixed mating topic."

"It has something to do with her clan. I don't understand it myself, considering her mother would have had to mate with a human to produce offspring."

"You do something to piss her mother off in one of your other lives?" Jordan joked.

I thought about his question for a second, but couldn't recollect ever coming across a banshee or a woman named Aibell.

"Not that I'm aware of. Then again, there have been many years between my human death and now." I shrugged.

"Well, it's simple then. We'll just keep her here. Unless they have a reaper in their back pocket, it's not like they could drag her back home if she has us surrounding her." Jordan reasoned.

"That's true. She could…" Pain exploded through my mind, and my knees wobbled under the agony before I stiffened them.

Erick was on alert in seconds, his body moving to block Evanee's from whatever threat I'd perceived. "Can you sense where the threat is?" His head swung from side to side, seeking the threat he'd felt through our shared connection.

I swivelled to Evanee and groaned one word. "Ellie."

Evanee shoved Erick from her, her fangs exploding and her plump cheeks tightening against her skull. The skin around her eye sockets thinned, her vampiric features replacing her human appearance.

Fear gripped my heart, triggering my beast so it roared to the surface. A long, low growl pushed past my elongated fangs. My body whirled when a fresh breeze drifted over my body from behind. There, sitting beside the sparring mat larger than life, stood Evanee's portal. Tiny waves of power pulsed from the whole in the middle of the room.

Thank the Dagda for Evanee.

I sprinted toward it, Evanee keeping pace beside me. Erick and Jordan raced to beat us through the portal, but our motivation was greater.

We emerged from the portal, and my head swivelled wildly, fear tightening the back of my scalp. A chilled wind rustled through the tall paperbark's leaves, bringing with it the heavy scent of burning wood. Winter's darkness had settled in and with it the mist. Ellie's fresh scent of dew settled on the grass, and blossoming roses at dawn's first light drifted to me from the far-right corner. My gaze snapped to the back of a local mechanic's garage. His workshop bordered Murder Point Bay's scenic walking track and dense bush.

A male grunt drifted along with the cool breeze, and I took off toward where it had originated. The sight of Ellie's tiny figure surrounded by four hulking males would have seized my heart if it'd been beating. The anger and desperation in her eyes fanned my fury, driving me into action.

I reached for the nearest male, my fangs sinking deep. I stared at Ellie's tight shoulders, sending my power deep within the man, liquefying his organs one by one as I drank. His corpse dropped, forgotten when my gaze locked on my next target. I stopped short when a short figure blurred up behind the stunned man, who stared at me in horror. Blood and tissue erupted from where his heart had once sat, tainting the mist and ground. The brunette's eyes widened, his mouth gaping as his head dropped forward to see a small fist clutching his still-beating heart. Evanee withdrew her hand from the man's chest, and he dropped uselessly to the ground. Her rage sought its next target, the inanimate organ already forgotten as it splattered against the stones.

Ellie twisted, delivering a solid kick to the male blocking her path. The sound of air rushing from his lungs wasn't nearly as satisfactory as it should have been. Ellie's movements were quick and precise, leaving the red-haired male no time to think when she delivered a solid punch to the side of his head. I smiled savagely when the crack of bone reached my ears; the redhead dropped where he stood, his body hitting the stone driveway with a dull crunch.

"Enough!" Erick roared, a blast of power sizzling through the air and veins of those present.

The male struggling against Erick's taloned grip screeched in pain, before sagging in his grip.

My blood heated uncomfortably within my veins, and I stiffened, almost sympathetic to the man's pain. Almost.

Ellie stumbled at Erick's power, then spun to face us. Her black eyes widened, then closed in relief.

I studied Erick and then Jordan, who stood behind us, his arms hanging loose at his sides as though he expected more trouble.

Erick released the man within his grasp, so he dropped to his booted feet. Too weak to support his weight, the male fell to his knees in defeat.

Erick circled the slumped figure, then knelt before him. "Why are you attacking one of my people?"

"She's not yours. She's an Arnam and daughter of Aibell, the Ua Briain of Banshees. The general has summoned her home."

Despite being Australian, the man had been affiliated with Ellie's family for some time to have perfected the brogue so well. He lifted his head and stared hard at a panting Ellie.

My hand reached out to Ellie, who grasped. Her hand shook in mine and I clamped down on my beast prowling within me. My eyes narrowed on the stranger's brown ones.

"The woman you're talking about is my mate. I've waited for not one but two millennia for her arrival. Do you think I give a shit whose daughter she is?" I spat.

"It's forbidden to mate with vampires. Aibell decreed it so. I may not be a banshee, but I'm a part of the clan, and I know the rules."

His haughtiness grated on every one of my last nerves but confirmed my theory.

"Yeah, yeah. We've all heard the no mixing of species crap before." Evanee stepped around Ellie and I, coming to a stop beside her mate, her bloodied hand resting on his shoulder. "But here's the thing, buddy, we already well and truly broke that rule."

"I am well aware of who you are, Evanee Sheperd. As I know that he's Prince Erick Tenebris, and you're Tristan Cathbad. The big fella behind me is Jordan, no last name known," the man recited.

"Patrick here is ex-military. He gave it up to go into the private sector after he married one of my cousins," Ellie scowled.

"Well, that explains it then." Evanee snorted. "Your mother loves them compliant, doesn't she?"

I cringed inwardly at Ellie's harsh laugh. "Yup, another reason I'm on the top of her shit and unloved list. The only reason she wants me home is so she can close the gates, force me into some useless relationship to some ex-military twat. I'll then become a broodmare, good for nothing more than pumping out the future generation of banshee females and guardsmen. My original purpose forgotten like so many of my sisters and cousins."

"Like hell, you will," I snarled. "Another man touches you and he won't be waking up the next morning," I exploded, red tinging my sight at the thought of another man laying a hand on her.

"It's okay gorgeous, I'd likely cut off his dick before he got the chance to do anything." Ellie smiled evilly.

I looked back at her, and I grinned. "That's my mate." Her sweet laugh warmed me. My attention returned to Patrick, and my smile dropped. "Now back to you. I have a message for your general. Are you listening?" I spoke slow and careful, each word hanging in the air between us. "Aibell can't have Ellie. I don't care if I have to face all of you bastards to prove my point. I'll wade a bloody path through every one of you, including the women who dare to come for her. If Aibell is as old as I think she is, we'd have crossed paths in at least one war. Remind her, of the destruction I wrought during the war of 1701. Remind her of the slivers of my enemies that I left to the flies in those bloody fields."

I allowed the memory of that day to shine through. The blood that had warmed my hands and drenched my hair that day had taken hours to scrub clean, as had the cries of my victims. No one but me knew the toll it'd taken on whatever piece of my soul remained. The healer in me had cursed and cringed at the destruction I wrought and the life I'd claimed so savagely.

"Tristan won't be standing alone. Ellie is now a member of my coven and is under my protection. Should Aibell pursue her path, she'll risk a war with me and mine," Erick added, his voice quiet, yet commanding.

"Don't forget me, baby." Evanee pouted.

Erick chuckled darkly. "You're a part of my coven, mic luptător."

"That's sweet, but not what I meant. Patrick, was it?" When he said nothing, Evanee shrugged and continued. "Ellie not only has the protection of my mate and his coven, but she's also under the protection of three of the Messorem family members and my clipeum back there. We're quite attached to Ellie, Death in particular. And when you piss off Death, well, let's say it ends nasty." She cringed dramatically.

Evanee's face settled into a look so fierce, I was grateful I wasn't on the receiving end of it.

"You touch either of them, and I'll make it a family reunion to be remembered by all for centuries to come."

Patrick's eyes widened slightly, his fear seeping through his pores at the last bit of Evanee's threat.

"I'd say we've about covered things," I declared, relieved to have the backing of not only my king but Evanee too. Not that I'd doubted Erick's loyalty, but Evanee's meant more to me than she'd know, even if it was purely for Ellie's sake. "Perhaps we should give them a helping hand. I wouldn't want it said I wasn't kind to my mate's family."

"You're right. Give me a second to reap these two idiots. The dark brunette might survive if they get him to a hospital in time; otherwise, whoever's assigned to him can deal with it," Evanee agreed.

The tightness in the set of her mouth denounced her calm exterior. These deaths would become an additional weight within her, no matter how much she reasoned with herself. Each death weighed heavily within our hearts as healers and truthseekers.

"Where's your loyalty? We're family," Patrick accused.

"Don't talk to me about loyalty, Paddy. I've kept my oath to the clan and have no intention of revealing our secrets. But you can all go to hell if you think I'll calmly let Máthair marry me off to one of your friends, brothers, or cousins so I can produce the next generation. I'd rather succumb to eternal death than live that life," Ellie exclaimed with a shudder of disgust.

"Your sisters and cousins have never voiced their displeasure and welcomed the chance to contribute to the family."

"I am not one of them. I am my own woman," Ellie yelled, her heartache and fear vibrating through my mind.

"Enough." My power pulsed once, and a thin cut appeared across Patrick's cheek.

I pulled a visibly shaking Ellie to me. "Are you done yet, Evanee?"

"Yup, that was the last one. Jordan, would you help me with the corpses?"

"Of course. Do your thing." Jordan strode over to the two limp bodies, his giant hands gripping one body in each hand. The men's boots collected dead eucalyptus leaves and fallen gumnuts with them as he dragged them toward Evanee's portal.

Evanee bent, retrieving the unconscious man from where he'd fallen. "You get him to a hospital ASAP. You don't, and Death will greet him on his way to his final destination," she warned Patrick as she drifted past him.

"You're next, mate." Erick reached for Patrick, hauling him up to march him toward the portal.

From beside the portal, Jordan bellowed to the perplexed figures standing on the other side, "Delivery for Aibell." He lifted the first body and launched it through the portal. "We don't accept refunds or exchanges." He chuckled at his joke.

My body shook with repressed laughter, but I held it in, conscious it was Ellie's family members being thrown so carelessly through the portal.

"At least he knows how to lighten the moment." Ellie sniffed.

I pressed a tender kiss to the top of her head. "He sure does. But don't tell him I said that."

We watched as Erick and Evanee stepped through the portal side by side. Evanee gently laid the dying man atop the lush green grass. I inhaled until my lungs reached their capacity, taking in the earthy scents of Ireland. Memories of my mother cooking beside the fire on a rainy night and the soft lilt of her voice as she'd sung to me on stormy nights made me smile. Her natural beauty enhanced by the billowing curls framing her face. The only time she ever wore her hair loose was at night.

She secured it with a leather strap not that dissimilar to the one I was wearing during the day.

It'd been a long time since I'd visited my motherland. I missed her in some ways but was at peace with my decision to make Australia my home.

With all four men delivered, Evanee and Erick clasped hands and returned, shutting the portal behind them.

Evanee reached out to hug Ellie, concern drawing her eyebrows together. "You okay, Ell?"

Ellie hugged Evanee tightly, nodding silently.

"Let's go back to the manor," Evanee whispered, summoning a portal back to the mansion.

Chapter Eight

Tristan

Cradled in my lap, Ellie's warmth seeped into me as we sat on the wrap-around deck that circled the dark green Queenslander style home I'd built. My arms tightened involuntarily around her, the images of her surrounded by the four idiots she called family continuing to assault my mind.

Tonight was too close. I almost lost her.

My beast shivered within me, roaming the branches of the giant oak within my mind, unsettled and on edge. My nightmares of Ellie lying in a bloody puddle stirred my magic, so the timber railing in front of us groaned beneath the long gouge marks running across it, as though a giant cat swiped at it.

'You need to calm down, Tristan. I'm fine. I'm sitting in your lap, solid and real.'

Ellie's sweet voice drifted through my mind, wrapping itself around my beast. He stopped in his tracks to embrace the caress of her voice.

'It was too close. What if Evanee hadn't been nearby when they attacked? I'd have arrived too late.' Tension's hand gripped my neck, and a lightness expanded over my brain. If I peered close enough, I was sure I'd see my hands vibrating; it sure felt as though my entire body was shaking on the inside.

Ellie manoeuvred herself to straddle my hips. Her hot, tiny hands clasped my icy cold jaw, forcing me to peer straight into her shimmering bottle-green eyes.

"Tristan, you need to calm yourself. I'm right here. You're on the verge of a panic attack; I can feel it.

There's no point in both of us being a mess. Who'd cook me dinner?" A small smile crept through at the thought of her trying to cook for herself.

"Vampires don't get panic attacks, mo ghrá," I corrected.

"Don't give me that crap. I can feel it, you goofball. That sensation of vibration throughout your body, that's you responding to stress. You're not shaking on the outside. Your heart may not be galloping, but I'd bet anything that it would be if you were human."

Her reprimand was cute and working by the judge of the receding light-headedness.

I clasped her hands in mine, drawing them to my chest as I moved my neck from side to side to loosen the tight muscles.

"I'd like to argue with you, but I think I'd lose this one." I pressed my lips to the tip of her nose before my forehead touched hers gently, and I whispered, "Thank you, Ellie."

"You're welcome, gorgeous."

I chuckled at her nickname. It was the second time she'd used it.

"Is that my new nickname? Gorgeous? Because I have to say, it's an improvement on Elf Boy."

"It's my nickname for you, and if anyone else uses it, I'll jam a syringe full of flesh-eating bacteria into them," Ellie snarled threateningly.

My head dropped back, and I laughed hard, delighting in her threat. "I'll be sure to remember that," I reassured her.

"Damned straight." Ellie's adorable pout emphasised her plump bottom lip.

Still laughing, I pulled her head toward mine, seeking the softness of her pouting lips. I growled with displeasure when she made to pull back. With a sultry chuckle, Ellie worked her arms around my neck, her fingers spearing into my hairline at the base of my head. I wrapped my arms around her waist, shackling her body to my chest and groin. The tip of her tongue teased my upper lip, and I grinned wickedly at where she was leading us.

I tugged at the neon pink tank top, and Ellie's hands dislodged from around my neck. The mesh material trailed along her taut stomach, her six-pack rippling beneath her fair skin. The useless piece of material dropped onto the cushion beside me, and I groaned at the sight of her sports bra.

Another layer?

I focused on her hair, ignoring the newest obstacle. My fingers reached for the elastic holding her blond tendrils hostage, freeing them with a tug. Fingers spearing through the silken strands, I dragged them through the loose strands, admiring the strawberry-blonde that seemed to be taking over the honey blonde.

"Beautiful," I breathed, entranced.

Ellie grinned, her cheeks flushing at my compliment.

"Your turn, gorgeous," she crooned.

She tugged at the hem of my dark green cotton shirt, and I leaned forward. The material slithered up and over my head, and I smirked at the hitch in Ellie's breath.

My shirt dropped, forgotten, onto the cushion, joining hers. Palms tingling, I slid them along her body, settling on the Lycra covering the gentle curves of her hips. She found my lips once more, and the mouth-watering scent of her strawberry flavoured lip-gloss drifted up, taunting me. Then tips of my fingers dug firmly into her silky hips, yanking her closer still.

Her pulse beckoned me, thudding and pumping with her excitement and lust. The scent of her arousal rose, and I inhaled it as though it were the finest perfume in all the world. I fought not to take what I desperately needed from my mate — a deeper connection. My claws lengthened with need, and I dragged them delicately up and down her spine, sending a trail of goosebumps over her hot flesh. She lifted her head, an ecstasy laden sigh escaping her rose-pink lips. When my hand stopped just beneath her bra, I grinned at the lines of frustration creasing Ellie's brow. Ellie's hands lifted from my shoulders to tug hard at the offending bra, dragging it up and over her head. I grinned with satisfaction, my cock twitching at the sight of her small, perfectly round mounds on display for me and me alone. My lips latched onto her soft pink nipple, begging for my attention. I drew it into my seeking mouth, releasing the nipple with a faint pop. The tips of my extended canines dragged delicately across the jutting peak, eliciting a delighted gasp from Ellie. My attentions swapped to her other breast, and I ran my clawed fingers along the delicate lines of her back.

My cock surged at Ellie's throaty groan, and I shifted uncomfortably against the tightness of my jeans.

With preternatural speed, I stood, gripping Ellie to me. The front door swung inward with a flick of my wrist, and I kicked it shut behind us with my now barefoot. I sped past the entry and toward the magnificent giant Red Cedar sitting in all its majestic glory in the centre of my house.

Ellie's body slid down the front of mine as I lowered her to her feet. Her wide eyes danced with delight as she reached out with both hands to caress the rough bark.

"You have a tree in your house?"

I smiled at the awe in her voice.

My fingers hooked into the waist of her Lycra tights and whispered, "Technically, the Red Cedar has a house built around it."

"Wow."

Ellie's head dropped back, her thoughts no longer focused on me as she stared up through the rustling leaves above, entranced by their beauty.

I lowered myself to my knees, dragging Ellie's Lycra tights and lace panties down her slender legs as I went. I stared up at Ellie, who remained transfixed by the dancing leaves above her. I flung the offending tights to one side, my claws returning to her legs. I wanted her attention back on me. I increased the pressure of my claws as I dragged them up the sides of her calves and thighs. Ellie's head drifted down, her green eyes meeting mine. I watched, captivated by the sight of the midnight swirling amongst the vivid green in her irises. Reaching her stomach, Ellie's hand fisted the loose strands of my hair tightly, tugging so I rose to meet her waiting lips.

She kissed me hard. My cock surged again, and I pinned her to the cedar. Her soft breasts pressed against my naked chest, spurring me on. My palm found her bare thigh, only to stop when she reached for the button on my jeans. The zip released, and my cock sprang free.

Frantic hands pushed at the offending stiff material, and my jeans dropped to my knees. A groan lodged in my throat, transforming into a growl when Ellie bit down on my lower lip.

I pulled back, my chest rumbling. "You're playing with fire, Ellie."

"You love it."

Ellie grinned with devilish delight, reaching down to wrap her warm hand around my cock. She pumped it once, then twice.

"I can feel it."

"You're right, I love it, but I only have so much restraint."

And it's hanging by a mere thread.

I gripped her quivering thighs for emphasis and hoisted them around my waist—the action driving her further into the cedar's embrace.

She tugged on my hair again until our foreheads touched.

"If I wanted restraint, I'd be dating a human."

"Like fuck, you're mine."

The very thought of her with another man, human or not, kindled a fiery rage deep within me.

I'd lay waste to this land if another man even contemplated stealing my sweet, fiery Ellie.

"Then what are you waiting for, gorgeous? Show me I'm all yours; give me all you got," she taunted enticingly against my lips.

Not needing any further encouragement, I adjusted her hips so that the tip of my rock-hard cock nudged against her entrance, finding her slick and ready. She caught at her bottom lip, her fingers dropping to my shoulders, digging into them. I pushed forward, fighting my instinct to shut my eyes, not wanting to miss a single emotion fluttering across Ellie's stunning face. The way her lips parted ever so slightly whenever I entered her, or the way her eyelids fluttered softly drove me crazy.

I buried myself to the hilt, finally succumbing to the blinding pleasure squeezing my body tight and allowing my eyes to drift shut.

"So… fucking… good." My guttural groan travelled from the depths of my stomach.

"Yes… more," Ellie hissed through clenched teeth.

I was drowning in the intense heat and grip of her wet core. The slightest twitch of her hips lit the fuse on my faltering restraint, setting fire to it. But it wasn't enough; I wanted more, wanted to give her more and take more from her at the same time.

Deeper. I need to be deeper.

I withdrew until the tip of my pulsing cock nudged at her entrance. I lowered Ellie to the ground and turned her to face the cedar. Hands covering her wrists, I guided them to one of the giant roots.

I leaned forward, grinding my body against hers from behind and growled harshly, "Don't move your hands."

Her ragged breathing was the only response I received.

Best damn sound in the world.

My hands found her hips once again. I hovered at her dripping entrance for a second, gripping my length to position it at her entrance. My hand tensed against her hip to steady her as I slammed home once more.

My free hand returned to her hip, holding her still as I withdrew my cock out until only the tip of me remained within her. I slammed into her again, watching her grip tighten against the roots and her knuckles turn white. I drove deep into her, each thrust harder than the one before. My hands skimmed from her buttocks, around her upper thigh to her soaked folds and the hard swollen nub of her clit.

"Tristan. Fuck… don't stop… please," Ellie begged with the merest brush.

Her intoxicating cries grew louder with each swirl of my fingers against her clit and deep thrust of my cock.

My balls grew tight, a glorious heavy sensation taking up residence in the pit of my gut.

I released her clit, and reached for her golden hair, latching onto the silken strands as though I were a drowning man on the brink of rescue from the clutches of the turbulent ocean. With a gentle tug of her hair, my hungry gaze narrowed on the graceful line of her neck.

Ellie rose ever so slightly, and my tongue darted out to taste her pulse trapped beneath her delicate flesh. Tiny goosebumps broke out across Ellie's body at the same time her pussy clenched hard around my cock. My tongue trailed across the same spot one more time, giving her time to tell me to stop. When she said nothing, my growl of pleasure breathed across her puckered skin, my canines gently scraping at the pleading pulse again.

When she still said nothing, my canines sunk deep into her delicious, tender flesh. Hot liquid gushed into my seeking mouth, and my throat worked hard to absorb her precious blood.

This was what I'd needed since I'd emerged from the portal and seen her fighting for her life. I needed to feel Ellie's blood coursing within my body. I wanted the reassurance of our joined bodies. The druid power I'd buried deep within me for so many centuries pulsed once, then burst from deep within me. The energy released from me in waves, increasing with each suck of my mouth.

Ellie's breathless scream of orgasm winged its way from her parted lips and up into the swaying emerald and bright green canopy high above us. Releasing her neck, I continued to fuck her with deep strokes. My fingers slid down to dance over her clit with soft circles, enticing her body to release the second softer orgasm trapped within. Her muscles quaked once more, and I let go, my gut clenching hard against the orgasm bursting from deep within.

Stars danced at the corners of my eyes, my loud groan joining with Ellie's softer one, twining together to be caught up by the gentle breeze drifting through the house.

Ellie's gentle pants were loud in the house's quiet, and I withdrew from her, pressing a soft kiss to the crease of her neck. I traced my thumb over the twin punctures at her neck, gently wiping at the small trail of blood. I drew my thumb into my mouth, my eyes closing at the exquisite taste. With gentle hands, I pulled Ellie back toward me. Nicking the tip of my thumb against my lengthened canine, I placed it against her parted lips.

"Take it, mo ghrá. It'll help you recover quicker from tonight's fight. I can smell your adrenaline receding," I whispered encouragingly.

Without hesitating, Ellie's delicate hand cupped mine, guiding my thumb into the heat of her mouth. Her tongue danced along the edge before she suckled it. My cock twitched, and my eyes drifted shut at the pleasure igniting within me once more.

When the wound sealed shut, Ellie released my thumb, her head rolling in toward my chest. I lifted her, kicking at the tangled jeans around my ankles, so they slid across the floor. I made my way towards the sectional in the lounge area with silent footsteps, reaching for the blanket draped across the back of the lounge. I tugged at it, draping it over our exhausted bodies.

"Is this your house?" The pillow beneath her head muffled Ellie's sleepy murmur.

"Yes. I built it the last time Erick and I lived in Murder Point Bay. Do you like it?"

A churning sensation in the pit of my stomach intensified at the thought of her not liking the house I'd built. I'd begun the build in 1993 after I'd received a vision so intense, I'd jolted awake and promptly rolled off the bed and onto the wooden floor in my room at the manor. The ear-splitting cries of the female infant that morphed into the high-pitched wail of a shrouded, petite woman had echoed in my mind for months. I knew then my mate had entered the world. With her in mind, I'd designed and slowly built the house, hopeful our paths would cross one day.

"I love what I've seen so far. The focal point was masterfully designed," Ellie joked, snuggling further into me.

"I'd like to take credit for the Red Cedar, but nature was the artist for that particular masterpiece." I chuckled. "So, you like it?" I checked once more.

"It's probably the most relaxing place I've ever seen. Could I reach it if you weren't here to carry me?"

"Of course, there's a driveway around the side where the garage is." I grinned.

"Oh, good." Ellie breathed. "That means I can come and visit you without having to call and ask for a lift from the main house. Why don't you live here permanently?"

Ellie twisted to regard me, and I brushed my thumb against the slight frown creasing her forehead.

"I don't live here because it's the house I built for my mate. I designed it to be a sanctuary for the tough times that would come, and as a place we would be free to be us. I built it for you, mo ghrá." When her eyes widened with shock, I pushed on, hoping to make my case. "I'm hoping you won't only visit it, but you'll move in and live with me. That way, I could protect you and continue to cook for you."

Her parted lips tugged into an uncertain smile, and nervousness warred with fear she'd reject me and my offer.

"What about Brad? I share a house with him and a mortgage. I can't just desert him." She frowned.

"Ellie, I'll pay your part of the loan out. As for Brad, he, like Evanee, will be welcome here. I'd never make you choose between me and those you love. Hell, if you want to invite your brother over, go for it. He'd be welcome too."

"Let's not get carried away. Brad will be the only brother visiting here. You really built this for me?"

I nodded, and she grew silent for a minute before her tear-filled eyes met mine.

With a soft sniffle, she whispered, "Okay, I'll move in. But only if you promise I don't have to cook."

"Deal." I laughed, giddy at the prospect of having her to myself.

My lips pressed down hard on hers, and I pulled back, grinning like a fool.

"You have no idea how happy you've just made me, Ellie. Thank you."

Chapter Nine

Ellie

A friend's eye is a good mirror.

The fan in the depths of the warmed oven swallowed the soft hiss of the cardboard moving along the metal rack as I slid the pizza boxes in. I nudged the oven door shut with my elbow and reached for the chilled glass of Pinot Grigio. Sipping the chilled white wine, I turned to survey the house that'd been my home for the past three years. My gaze travelled to the hallway leading off the kitchen and winced at the memory of the time Brad and I surfed the hall in our socks. It had ended with Brad in the hospital with a concussion. I stared at the small dent in the floor beside the oven where I'd dropped a metal roasting pan after trying to remove a roast chicken that caught fire. Brad had frantically tried to put it out when the heat burned through the oven-mitts. He'd banned me from cooking after that day. This house held memories of love and warmth for me, more so than the house I grew up in.

The house now shone within an inch of its life after I'd armed myself with disinfectant, wood-polish, and cloths. I'd collected my car this morning, and it relieved me to see the mechanic was now fully healed after one of my cousins knocked him unconscious. I'd forgotten all about Doug during the chaos, but was relieved he'd no recollection of the event. Although grateful they'd done it, I wasn't sure who'd healed him and erased his memory.

Handing my resignation and security passes into Aeternum mid-morning was easier than I'd thought. They'd escorted me from the grounds with instructions

I'd no longer be permitted on the premises, despite giving two weeks' notice. I'd felt no fear or grief during the entire process, reassured with the knowledge my new contract with Erick started on Monday. I filled the rest of the day with research and cleaning, despite Tristan's constant mental check-ins. If the man had his way, I'd be sequestered to his treehouse, as I referred to it.

Keys jangling at the front door pulled me from my thoughts. I pushed off from the bench top and padded into the hall and past my bedroom. Brad stepped through the front door, his auburn locks dishevelled and sticking up at places. I smiled with affection at the chaos that was his hair. The man really couldn't tame it, no matter how hard he tried.

"Good day at the office, weirdo?" I greeted him, my shoulder resting heavily against the door frame.

Brad blinked in surprise at my amused voice.

"Ell, you're home. I thought you'd be with Tristan."

Brad deposited his leather satchel onto the floor and approached me, enveloping me in a giant hug.

My arms circled his ribs, and I hugged him a little longer than I usually did. With misted eyes, I stared hard at the burnt orange stained glass window above the doorway to keep them at bay.

"Did you think I'd forget your mother's birthday? I'm sorry I didn't message and let you know I'd be out; I meant to, but things got hectic," I whispered, my heart clenching at the significance of today.

Maybe today's not the day to tell him he nearly lost me last night, or that I'm moving out. He's already lost one woman he loves.

The confrontation still had my heart galloping at random times during the day, not that I'd tell Tristan or Brad. I'd known this was coming, and if I was any kind of woman, I'd pack my things and leave or at the very least stop fighting while one of my brothers or cousins murdered me. But I couldn't. The life I was born into wasn't the one I wanted, not to mention the people I loved the most lived in this small rural town.

"All good, Ell. I'm not your keeper. I smell food. Please tell me you haven't cooked," he pleaded, dodging past me to rush into the kitchen and save whatever new dish I'd decided to try.

I followed behind him, feigning hurt. "I'll have you know I'm an excellent cook, thank you."

"No, you're not. You're a terrible cook. I'm just glad you're dating a dead guy. That way I won't have to testify in court when you kill him with your cooking."

"Hey, that's just mean and culturally insensitive. Tristan is the living dead, and I cooked nothing. It's pizza. I popped it into the oven to keep it warm until you and Evanee showed up. Not that Evanee will eat it anymore, thank goodness. That woman could put away a cow and still keep going onto the next in the herd," I scoffed playfully.

"That's just mean, but oddly true," Evanee piped in from behind me.

Brad and I jumped, spinning to face the grinning vampire-slash-reaper, or as she liked to call herself, vamper, behind us.

"That's it, you're getting a bell on a collar for Christmas," I complained, my hand against my racing heart.

"I told you, Ell, I can't wear one of those it'd give me away in a fight." She sighed dramatically.

Brad reached for a beer, adding his ten cents worth. "I'm going with Ell on this one. You'll end up giving one of us a heart attack. Plus, Erick would probably like it, what with the leash capabilities and all."

"Dude, the only way that man is putting a leash on her is in the sack. Mind you, she'd probably be the one holding the leash attached to his neck with a crop in the other hand." I laughed.

"You're both arseholes, you know that? And it wouldn't be a crop I'd be holding, it'd a be flogger."

There was a second of stunned silence before the room filled with loud laughter.

Our laughter went on and on, my belly beginning to ache. It occurred to me then that I wasn't the only one stressed and anxious. They say laughter was the best remedy, and it wasn't a lie.

Brad wiped at his watering eyes with a sniff. "What's your poison tonight, Evie?"

"I'll grab a Malibu neat, please."

"Bring the entire bottle of Malibu, Brad. I'll grab the pizza I didn't cook and we can head through to the lounge room." I wiped at my wet face, placing my empty wineglass in the dishwasher, then grabbed the pizzas. Snagging the roll of kitchen paper, I balanced it on top of the boxes.

"Here, I'll take the Malibu bottle through," Evanee volunteered.

"Thanks."

We followed Evanee into the lounge, and I plonked the pizza atop the coffee table. Brad and I reached for the meat-lovers and Hawaiian pizzas, leaving Evanee to her Malibu.

With a slice of pizza in one hand, Brad raised his other, holding a glass of Malibu and Coke. "Well, here's to you, Mum. I hope you're kicking back with a shit ton of Malibu and coke and pizza wherever you may be. Happy birthday, Mum. Love ya."

He choked on the last words, and my throat closed at his pain.

Evanee brushed at an escaping pink tear. We raised our tumblers in unison, murmuring, "To Jeanette."

As one, we gulped down a mouthful of the sweet coconut-flavoured beverage.

It wasn't lost on me Brad and Evanee would one day be doing this for me. Would they mourn the day I was murdered, or would they celebrate my birthday? Technically, I wouldn't be dead and buried. I'd be living as a broodmare in Ireland. Would they try to face-time me on my birthday? I knew they would try their best; I guess the biggest question was, would I care? Most of my human emotions would die with me. I'd barely have enough to love my offspring. My breath caught at the cruelty of it all—Fate's cruelty.

The pizza and booze flowed thick and fast as the three of us talked about everything and anything. The longer we spoke, the more relaxed I became, my body growing heavy and warm from the alcohol, thoughts of Ireland and my family disappearing.

"So, I have something to share with you both," I slurred.

"What?" Brad and Evanee echoed each other.

"Tristan asked me to move in with him." I blurted, swirling the golden wine I'd swapped back to within my glass as I stared into it.

Evanee was the first to speak. "Wow, that's great, Ellie. How do you feel about it?"

I looked up and fought the urge to laugh at Brad's raised eyebrows and Evanee's cautious inspection. "Guys, relax. I'm happy about this. I know I've kept him at arm's length, but you only live once, right?" I stared at Evanee, knowing she'd understand what I meant. "Besides, I can't keep fighting this thing Tristan and I have. At some point, I need to be realistic that what we have was set in motion a long time ago. I should just enjoy it for whatever time I have left on this earth," I finished in a whisper.

"Sheesh, morbid much, Ell." Brad laughed uncomfortably.

"Not morbid, Brad, realistic." I pointed out.

Brad cleared his throat, his heavy-lidded gaze hinting at the sadness that lay within him. "True, true. I can't say I'm happy you'll be moving out, but I get it. You need to be with the people you love while you can."

"I'll still be seeing you a ton, Brad. Hell, we'll be working together every day, pretty much. Plus, Tristan said you're both welcome at the house anytime you want," I reassured them.

"What, at Erick's place? I thought that was a given?" Evanee's head darted between Brad and me.

"No, not Erick's place. Tristan has his own house on Erick's property. Didn't you know?"

"I had no idea. Although, that would make sense. I wonder if Jordan has a place of his own? More importantly, could he move my mother to it?"

Evanee's eyes glazed over, and I knew she was asking Erick.

Her next words confirmed it. "Erick says Jordan never asked for some land of his own. But now you've brought it up, it may be an excellent Christmas gift."

Evanee giggled, and I smirked at her.

"Are they fighting that much?"

"Yes," Brad and Evanee interjected.

"Well, hell. I'm glad Erick agreed to Tristan having his own land then. You guys should see the place. It has a giant tree growing in the middle of it. The house is built around it."

My memory drifted to the square four-bedroom house built of solid timber. The green and blue hues gracing the walls screamed relaxation. If I hadn't already said yes, the master ensuite would have sealed the deal. The giant bathtub set before the wall to wall windows overlooking the creek below was a thing of pure beauty. Not to mention the stone shower with its rainfall showerhead and the wall of ferns. They'd received a good drenching last night.

"That sounds enchanting. Looks like we'll be doing spa nights there," Evanee murmured. "You men can go off and do whatever it is you men like to do, Brad."

"Yeah, I'll do board game and pizza night with you ladies, but I draw the line at spa night. There ain't no way in hell you'll catch me putting crap on my face, or nail polish on my nails," Brad scoffed. "Next you'll want to shave my balls."

"Ew, that's just gross. TMI, Brad," I whined.

Beside me, Evanee sat silently, her small smile at odds considering our conversation.

"Hey, you okay?" I poked her shoulder.

Evanee stretched her neck from side to side, then stared at the coffee table, a frown creasing her face. "I'm exhausted, to be honest."

"The guys working you too hard? You need me to lay the smack-down on them?" Brad joked.

Evanee rubbed at the back of her neck. "No, it's nothing like that. I can't sleep. I keep having these vivid dreams and bloody nightmares, but I'm thinking they're more than that. It's as though I've lived the dreams as a child. And the nightmares; I'm worried they're more than nightmares."

"Hey, you want to talk about them. You know we won't judge you." I encouraged, eyeballing Brad for backup.

"Yeah, if it's bothering you that much, then maybe it's your subconscious telling you that something's off." Brad reasoned.

"I can't talk about it, because I'm scared that if I verbalise them, I'll set something in motion."

Evanee sniffed, then rose with a gracefulness that I'd only ever seen the living dead achieve.

"My power is trying to tell me something, but I'm scared that if I let go, it'll prove more damaging than helpful. Tell me you know what I mean, Ellie." Evanee paced, her body winding tighter and tighter.

"I know what you mean, Evie. I spend half my days making sure the banshee is tucked away tightly, or I'd be walking around screaming my head off every few seconds. There'd be an awful lot of bodies with liquefied brains and shattered eardrums lying around. But I'm lucky I had an entire clan of banshees to teach me how to contain that side of me," I sympathised.

"I can feel something coming." Evanee frowned, her hand patting her flat abdomen. "I can feel it here, and in my mind. It's getting harder and harder to contain it. My magic is getting harder to keep in check."

The power in the room shifted slightly, and I stiffened. Despite being human, Brad's body broke out in goosebumps and his shoulders rolled back to adjust his body to the pressure within the room. The movement had me wondering if he was more psychically in tune than any of us thought.

Crap!

'Ellie, what's wrong?'

Tristan's voice appeared out of nowhere. I hadn't even realised I'd reached for him.

'Something's wrong with Evanee. She's struggling, and I can feel her power rising,' I answered.

'Erick and I are on our way. Try to keep her calm,' Tristan warned.

'*I'll try, but Tristan, hurry,*' I warned.

"Evanee, why don't you come and have another drink. I could get you a whiskey or red wine," I offered.

"I can't drink, Ellie. I can feel something coming, and I don't know how to save any of you." Evanee sobbed.

Horror settled deep within my gut when Evanee flexed her hands, her talons lengthening in place of her fingernails. My gaze darted up to her delicate face, stopping short when I encountered sharp fangs. With her eyes shut tight, Evanee took unnecessary breathes, almost as if she were trying to calm herself. When her chest ceased moving, I naively hoped she'd calmed herself enough to keep that daunting and endless power locked within her.

Her eyes snapped open, and I knew I was wrong.

The banshee within me shivered, and I shuddered with fear at its response. The banshee moaned with delight at the swirling white of Evanee's once electric blue eyes. My eyes never moved from hers, tracking the flecks of red and flashes of blue lightning that appeared in the depths of those white orbs.

The loud rip of Evanee's cotton shirt drew bile into the back of my throat as my mind was transported back in time. To the night I'd helped remove Jared's hideous creature that'd infected Evanee.

"Oh, shit. Evanee, princess, you gotta calm down. Things can't be all that bad. It's just nightmares."

Brad stood, trying his best to soothe his best friend, whose magnificent wings unfurled in the middle of our lounge room.

My new and more improved hearing caught Evanee's soft murmur. Repeatedly she chanted, "I can't lose you guys too."

My blood ran cold, and dread filled me as my gaze found Brad's.

It isn't only me she's been dreaming about. Brad's been in her dreams, too.

I froze, panic setting in.

Is Brad on Death's list? Tell me it's not soon. Someone tell me it's thirty or forty years from now. I prayed.

How did our lives get this fucked up?

A deep, melodic voice filled the room, and I jumped.

Death.

My banshee screeched her excitement within me, shocking me with her delight. Evanee spun, the floorboards beneath my feet vibrating from her angry, deep-throated growl.

"Why are you here?" Evanee snapped, her mouth never moving. Her growl filled the room, as her great-grandfather's voice had.

"Power calls to power, sweet child." Death stepped around the couch, then settled on it, reclining back as though it were a throne, and he was surveying his court.

I had to give it to him. The man was hot for an ancient guy. The 6'2" male who Death appeared as was no older than thirty-three. His snow-white hair had changed since I'd last seen him. It now framed his square jaw, floating softly against his broad shoulders, much like Tristan's. I knew I'd find a set of phenomenal abs beneath the black cotton t-shirt currently clinging for dear life to his chest and back.

"You can't have them," Evanee seethed, her wings flaring out around her.

Gold and topaz blue veins pulsed across the giant, moth-like wings, and I sighed, an odd sense of calm descending over me.

"I wasn't aware I was here to collect any souls tonight." Death's calm response did nothing to calm Evanee.

"Bullshit! My power has called to you in worse situations than tonight, and you've done Jack all to help me then. So, why the hell are you here, Grandfather?"

With a heavy sigh, Death stood. "Like I said, your power…."

Death's response cut short when Evanee blurred across the room, her talons locking around him. She drove him up and over the back of the couch, and a stunned gasp clawed its way past my thinned lips. Death slammed into the wooden wall behind the couch, the wood groaning and splintering under the impact.

Brad reeled back, landing hard in the armchair behind him, then rolling over the arm. He stumbled backward, his eyes wide. I remained standing where I was, my eyes only just catching Evanee's movement.

"Liar! You're here for them. I can feel it!" She screamed with desperation.

Evanee leaned forward, her hiss echoing around the room. "They're mine. Neither you nor that psychotic bitch, Fate, will ever get your hands on them."

Death's eyes darted over Evanee's face, and he frowned at whatever he saw there.

"Evanee, you need to calm down. You're not thinking clearly, and I don't want to have to bring you to heel." Death's warning was smooth as silk, yet the slightest hint of a growl laced his speech the longer he spoke.

A black leathered hilt with a ruby gem cresting it solidified in Evanee's outstretched hand, the blade of her sword solidifying in her grip only to slam through the centre of Death's chest. The old god's eyes widened, and a barely discernible grunt reached my sharp hearing. The acidic taste of fear settled over my tongue.

"Stay," Evanee ordered, a sharp burst of power pulsing through the air. When she stepped back, Death stood unmoving, surprise leaving his mouth slightly parted as he clutched the sword now lodged through the centre of his chest. The only way he was moving was if he ripped the thing out or walked through it. Yet, he never moved.

"Evanee, what's going on?" I squeaked.

Evanee stared fixedly at me, and I gulped, nerves tightening my abdomen.

"I'm doing the only thing I know to save you both. I swore I'd protect you, and I'll not fail you like I failed Bob or my father." Her disembodied voice filled the room, both a whisper yet clear as day.

"But we're okay, princess. Look, we're standing right here—alive." Brad's throat worked hard when Evanee's eyes snapped to his.

"For now," was her response.

"Evanee, don't do this. I can overlook your reaction, but Fate, she's no relation of yours. You have no idea how she'll react," Death cautioned.

The slightest flick of his fingers and the waiver of his body told me whatever Evanee had done to him was wearing off, and I breathed a sigh of relief.

"That bitch owes me. Between the two of you, you've cocked up my life enough. Now it's my turn to take control. I need to be in control again." Evanee's voice hitched before her lips sealed shut, forming a tight line.

Evanee stilled, the air rippling from the power resonating from her. The enticing scent of Brad's fear permeated the air, and I breathed it in deeply. My body shuddered, and my skin undulated as the banshee stretched, screeching her hunger. The softest mewl escaped my tight lips.

Evanee's head cocked to the side, watching me. The grin she gave me should have scared the living daylights out of me. Instead, my banshee raked at my body all the harder, desperate to shed my human skin. I was losing my battle against her. Eyes wide with fear, I blinked at Brad, and I fought the banshee harder, sweat dripping down my forehead. One scream from my lips would render Brad's brain nothing more than a greyish-red goopy slush. His eyeballs might perforate, but that would depend on how unlucky he was. I'd lost control of her once, months ago, but I'd been quick enough to direct my scream skyward, so the only thing that had suffered at my banshee's hands had been the glass pavilion. Pure luck and quick thinking on my part had been the only reason Brad and Evanee walked away unscathed.

Evanee materialised before Brad, and I swallowed hard at her speed.

"Don't worry, Brad. I won't hurt you… too much." Evanee promised. "You have to understand this is the only way I know how to protect you."

"Eva…" Brad's plea cut short when Evanee sprung forward, fangs extended, her power vibrating.

Evanee's fingers speared into Brad's hair, and she pulled it, forcing him to stoop lower to accommodate his neck stretched out before her. In a blur, her fangs latched onto his proffered artery, sinking deep. Brad's cry cut short, his legs wobbling beneath him.

Evanee's throat worked, her eyes drifting shut as she drank deeply. I stood transfixed, unable to move as

Evanee's hand snaked beneath Brad's shirt and up to his heart. His pained yell exploded through the room, raking at my frayed nerves. The room was a mixture of slow and fast motion, and I had no idea how to press pause. A flicker of movement caught my attention, and my petrified gaze found Death. He inclined his head toward the main door, his message clear.

Move now. His deep, pain husked voice drifted through my mind.

Dread gripped my mind. We both knew I'd never make it, but I had to try. I took two steps before Evanee's taloned hand latched around my throat, and my heart all but slammed out of my chest.

"Don't run, please. I don't want to hurt you," Evanee warned. "You need to understand; this is the only way for me to save you."

Evanee breathed into my ear, the metallic tang of fresh blood overwhelming me.

"What do you mean, Evanee?" When she said nothing, I pleaded, "Don't do this, Evanee. Don't complicate your life any more than it already is. You'll always have my loyalty, no matter what my mother does to me."

Evanee shuddered against my back, her voice distant, as though she were talking in her sleep.

"I do this, Ellie Arnam, and you won't be leaving this continent unless you choose to, or I will it. My mark will be your shield and sword. You'll be a part of me, and I part of you. If someone tried to separate you and me, it would insight my wrath. And Ellie, I would devour every soul that stood between you and me. You are my sister in every way other than blood."

I stilled, her words finally sinking in. "So, I'd be able to stay with you, Brad, and Tristan. I wouldn't be forced back to my mother?"

"Yes." Evanee sighed.

"What about Brad? Why didn't you give him this choice?"

"I did. It's why my mark lies heavy against his soul and flesh."

This was Evanee. I'd trusted her with my life once, and I'd do it again, despite the power riding her body.

"Do it."

The sudden burst of power from behind us had Evanee pivoting to meet a furious Death. Evanee's sword still sat where she'd pinned him to the wall. The slightest whisper of Evanee's fangs at the crease of my neck drew a delicious shiver from deep within. This felt different from when Tristan drank from me. It was intimate, yet not in a sexual way. There was a gentle pressure, followed by a brief, sharp sting. The sting washed away instantly, replaced by an overwhelming sense of peace and tranquillity. Eyes drifting shut, I sighed blissfully.

The scent of fresh night air tickled at my face, and my heavy lids lifted in time to see Erick and Tristan drop from a portal in the roof. They landed heavily in a crouch. Their gaze locked with Death's, and they nodded their thanks. They rose, and Tristan's gaze snapped to mine. Those lavender orbs I loved staring into lost all emotion as they focused on my neck, where Evanee drank gracefully from it. The cold, dead stare he focused on Evanee petrified me. I had no way of reassuring him through our link. My mind couldn't concentrate on anything.

My mouth opened once, but no words came out.

Before Erick or Death could utter a warning, Tristan launched himself across the room. Evanee's left hand lifted from my shoulder, reaching for the sword impaled in the wall in front of us. It dissolved, only to appear in her outstretched hand. With a slight flick of her wrist, she re-directed the blade she now held in the general direction of where Tristan had been standing seconds before. The blur of Tristan's body came to an abrupt stop; the blade pointed to where his Adam's apple now bobbed. My mind reeled at the speed at which Evanee reacted. The dread I knew I should feel never rose, my mind refusing to rise above the fog clouding it.

"Fucking hell, Tristan. Are you insane? I said I'd deal with it," Erick bellowed.

"Her fangs are buried in my mate's neck, Erick. How did you think I was going to react?" Tristan roared back, his eyes focusing on me.

I smiled warmly at him before I slurred, "Is okay, gorgeous. I'm okay."

"No offence, Ellie, but you look far from okay. You appear and sound drugged. I'm not exactly sure you know what's going on." Tristan frowned.

"Her bite is different. Feels different." My giddy giggle was at odds with the atmosphere in the room.

Evanee released my neck, her hand gripping my stomach, sliding beneath my singlet. It trailed up toward my left breast, stopping just below it. Goosebumps broke out over my body at the soft caress of her long, icy fingers against the underside of my breast.

'This will hurt, Ellie. I'm sorry.'

Evanee's voice drifted through my mind, and I frowned, not understanding, only to remember too late Brad's yell of pain from before.

A sharp, searing pain spread from beneath Evanee's cool palm. My head dropped back onto her shoulder as pain seared my nerve endings. A scream tore at my throat, erupting when Evanee's hand burned through the muscles and tissue over my ribs and down toward my thumping heart. The banshee wreathed and screeched deep within me, the brand searing not only my human flesh but the supernatural one, too.

At last, it was over. I inhaled deeply, expecting to smell the smoky scent of seared flesh; instead, my lungs filled with cool air. Evanee's palm braced my fragile body against her vibrating one. My head lolled to the side, and I caught sight of Brad leaning heavily against the TV cabinet. The skin over my eyes tightened in a frown at the sweat beading his forehead. His hand

clutched tightly to where Evanee's palm had seared him.

He looked no better than I felt.

Sacred Trees

The Scots pine Tree (Pinus Sylvestris)

Symbolises eternal life, vitality, prosperity and

fertility.

An evergreen conifer native to northern Europe.

Excellent firewood and used by my people to celebrate

the passing of the seasons and to draw back the

loving caress of the sun.—Tristan Cathbad.

Chapter Ten

My body froze, Ellie's pained screams shattering my heart and piercing my soul. Evanee's wings spread out wide, the peace and serenity they imbued at odds with the chaos erupting within the room. I remained still, knowing the slightest nick from the blade hovering over my Adam's apple would send me on my merry way to whatever afterlife awaited a vampire such as myself.

A gentle mist seeped from beneath the tattered ends of Evanee's giant wings, drifting sluggishly over the furniture and floor to where Brad leaned heavily against the TV cabinet. It embraced Brad's body as a mother might embrace her sleeping child and lifted him from the floor. Brad's exhausted eyes widened, yet his body remained still, too fatigued to move. Mist swirled lazily up Ellie's body, and I tensed, ready to reach for her.

"Stay where you are, Tristan." Evanee's swirling white, electric blue, and obsidian eyes snapped to mine. "I won't hurt either of them."

My hands fisted. "You've already hurt them, Evanee."

"The pain I caused will last for only a few minutes. I did what I needed to, Tristan. They'll both be safer this way. They're mine, and no one will take them from me, or you for that matter."

Evanee's dreamy tone sounded unnatural when compared with her usual tenacious one.

"I would have protected her, and Brad," I argued.

"Not like I can. I won't let them have either of them." Evanee's voice broke, and she whimpered, her pink tears a stark contrast to her display of power.

"Who are they, mic luptător?"

Erick's silhouette appeared in my peripheral vision.

"She means me, young prince." Death sighed, tiredly. "Well, me, Fate and Aibell," he corrected.

Terror clenched my gut. "Why would you be after Ellie?"

"I'm not. Well, at least not tonight." Death rounded the couch, dropping gracefully onto it.

"When then?"

"Never," Evanee hissed, her anger palatable. "You can't have them. I've made sure of it. Their souls are bound to me unless I deem otherwise."

Death shook his head in resignation. "Evanee, sweet child, I'm not sure if it's the power, your anxiety or sheer stubbornness, but you're picking a fight with beings a lot older and craftier than you. If you'd asked, I'd have helped you."

"Bullshit," Erick and Evanee spat simultaneously.

Death's gaze snapped to Erick.

"Know your place, young prince." His silky threat skittered down my spine.

I faced Death, ready to protect and serve my king.

"I know my place, Death, it's right here beside my mate. She's suffered enough at your hands. If you'd wanted to help, you'd have done it," Erick fumed, that temper he kept suppressed rising to the surface.

'Not the wisest of moves, Erick,' I sighed.

'I don't care, Tristan. You're not the one who's had to watch your mate overcome more than she thinks her mind can handle. Evanee's exhausted from the nightmares, and the merge with her power is more complicated than any of us could have anticipated.'

Erick's fury barged into my mind. Unphased, I let it seep through me, down my body and into the floor beneath me, the timber groaning under the weight of his fury.

"Enough!" Death thundered.

The room darkened and bulged; the wood groaned and creaked.

"Despite what you think, Erick, Evanee and Reagan are important to me. What she's done tonight won't please Fate, but I'll deal with her when the time comes. Evanee, I understand why you did what you did, but it's a dangerous game you're playing. You can't protect every mortal you come to love." Death sympathised.

Evanee's wings trembled with her agitation. "I have no intention of protecting every mortal. These two are family, and they're mine now," she snapped.

"What do you mean they're yours, Evanee?" Foreboding gripped my body.

"It means, old one, that she'll fight not just Fate and Aibell, but me as well when one of us comes to claim your mate or Brad."

Death's stare was unnerving. It reminded me of a time long passed; a time from my youth.

"Evanee, why would you place yourself in such a position?" Bewildered, I twisted to study Evanee. Her stature was dwarfed beside Erick, Brad, and me, yet she was fast becoming the strongest person I knew.

"I told you, Tristan. It's the only way to protect her." Evanee's power was receding, the mist slowly retreating into her body.

I stepped around Evanee's sword, my shaking hands reaching for Ellie, who'd by now passed out. Love consumed my soul as I tenderly scooped my tiny mate into my arms and gazed down at her peaceful features. Erick reached into the mist and scooped up a passed-out Brad, stepping around Evanee on his way toward the bedrooms.

“Protect her from what exactly, Evanee?” I beseeched.

“From Fate and her destiny, wee lad.”

I froze at that heavy brogue I recognised from my youth. My body turned in slow motion to where Death had been seated. There in his place sat an old man with long greying auburn hair. His light brown and emerald robes lay heavily against his broad chest. My gaze drifted to the staff he clasped, and I shuddered at the memory of that staff breaking bones during our training sessions in the depths of the night.

“Dagda?” I whispered raggedly, tracking the room for Death, only for my gaze to gravitate back to the old man. His body morphed before my eyes, and he once again resumed the figure of Evanee’s great-grandfather.

Confusion warred within me as I struggled to associate Death with the All-Father, Dagda. Morrigan, his wife, had been the one to step through the dark shadows that clung to her shapely figure. Dagda had always followed, his hands caressing her, his eyes filled with laughter and delight. So how was it that Dagda was in fact Death?

"Did you think I'd forget you, Son of Cathbad?"

Death chuckled at my open mouth and wide eyes.

"I feel your confusion, lad. We have much to discuss. It's been an age since we last had a good discussion. Evanee, I'll visit later, but for now, go home and rest. Brad will be safe tonight. And please, for the love of my sanity, stay out of trouble." Death sighed, rising to his feet.

Erick stepped up behind Evanee, his arm sliding around her waist to secure her to his side. With a brisk nod to Death, Erick escorted a stumbling Evanee through the portal Death no doubt had summoned and disappeared. I studied Death, my mind berating me for my stupidity at not having made the connection until tonight.

"Well, Tristan? Shall we retreat to your house?"

My voice stalled in my throat, and I coughed hard to clear it. "Yes, All-Father."

I stepped up beside him hesitantly, unwilling to take my eyes from him. His hand dropped to my shoulder, and I jumped. The surrounding room plummeted into darkness. I clenched Ellie tightly to my body, afraid I'd drop her into the abyss swallowing us whole. Just as quickly as the blackness appeared, the light reappeared. The soft sound of the creek below the house bubbling over rocks and the fallen log that had found its final resting place during the last wet season felt at odds with the god standing beside me.

"Why don't you put your mate to bed, Tristan. I think I'd like to inspect this house you've built," Death instructed.

I knew better than to argue with him. I turned and left Death to his own devices. It was dangerous, but I had little choice in the matter.

In the master bedroom, I lowered a slumbering Ellie onto the king-sized bed. The bed sat against the only solid wall in the room, the unobstructed views of the forest the focal point of the room. A small wood-burning stove sat tucked away in the corner but didn't distract from nature's beauty on full display. My booted feet sunk into the ivory wool shag rug beside the bed. Another three dotted the room to absorb the coolness that sunk into the house during winter.

With a flick of my wrist, the ceiling to floor ivory curtains around the room drew shut. I tugged the moss green blanket at the end of the bed, and laid it across Ellie. Unable to resist, I placed a soft kiss to her cheek.

I can't lose you. I love you too much.

Pain gripped my heart, and I clenched my hands against it.

Ellie rolled to her other side, mumbling, "I love you too, gorgeous."

Those five words hit me like a ton of bricks. My mind went blank for a second before a cacophony of random thoughts filled it again. Hope warred with bewilderment and happiness. She'd never said the words out loud, as though to admit them to me was to commit a serious trespass.

I hesitated, not wanting to leave her side after her sleepy confession. This moment would be forever seared into my heart and mind. With a slight shake of my head, I forced myself to turn and stride from the room in search of Death.

I found him in the centre of the house where I'd left him. His back to me as he stared through the rustling leaves of the great Cedar and to the scattered stars above.

"This is truly a thing of beauty, Tristan," he observed.

"It was my dedication to you and your goddess, All-Father."

"She would have loved it. Life and mischief were what she cherished, aside from me and her children, of course," Death whispered reverently. "Her games led so many to believe she was a goddess of death and war in some cultures. I'd play along because her happiness and safety were everything to me."

Death stared at the tree silently for a few seconds.

"You were always a dedicated worshiper. I felt your prayers even after you were turned. That master of yours was a murderous prick, wasn't he?"

Death turned to me with a smirk tugging at his lips.

"That he was. I've always wondered what happened to him. I searched, but came up empty-handed." I indicated toward the lounge, and we approached it.

"You came up empty-handed because that's what I wanted. I ripped that bastard's heart out the minute he became useless to you."

Shock and astonishment weakened my knees and I dropped to the lounge, speechless for a second.

"But I needed him. It took me years to master my gifts and to control my feeding. Even now I still struggle," I confessed.

"You only ever needed him to teach you the basics, Tristan. You've always been astute, but your parent's notoriety hung over you like a shadow. You, like your father, could have been a king in your own right, but that was not the way of the druids." Death snorted. "Tell me, have you maintained the way of the druids, lad? Did you keep the staff my wife gifted you?"

With a smirk, I clapped my hands together. The sound thundered through the house, rattling the windows. My hands drew apart and violet sparks shot from finger to finger as my staff lengthened between my palms. "Of course, I kept the staff. It is and always will be a part of me."

Death's laughter echoed mine as he clicked his fingers, and a long, thick staff appeared in his hands.

"Let us see if you remember the old ways, lad."

A mischievous grin spread across Death's face, and my smile disappeared.

Death's staff descended upon me, and I had a split second to make a decision.

I thrust my staff up, halting Death's mid-strike. "Shit!" I cursed, pushing hard at his staff.

Rolling over the arm of the couch, I raced past Death. It was a risky move, but retreating was better than being confined to the lounge room.

I skidded to a stop, then spun, extending my staff to meet his incoming one. "You'll wake Ellie," I grunted against the strain.

Death snorted, rolling his eyes, "Relax, lad. I've warded her room. She won't hear a thing tonight. Now, stop stalling and show me you haven't forgotten what we taught you."

I retreated a step, watching Death's shirt disintegrate as it'd done so many times during my youth, whenever the Great Queen Goddess, Morrigan, had been present.

My booted feet slid against the Tulip Oak floorboards and I stood tall, my shoulders setting and my wrists loose. I shucked my boots off and threw them toward the lounge. Claws extending, I shredded my shirt, ignoring the pieces of material that drifted lightly to the floor.

"As you wish, All-Father."

Chapter Eleven

Tristan

I stood side on, facing my staff, knowing the All-Father would strike when he saw fit. He was a crafty bugger, always had been. Right on cue, Death's staff soared through the air, and I twisted hard to avoid it, taking my staff with me as I twirled. The butt of the stick landed hard against the floor. My foot flexed without conscious thought, flicking the end of my staff up to connect with Death's next assault up high. My arms dipped as I bent low to deflect the bottom of Death's staff on its way up.

Within me, my beast roared with joy. I dropped to my back foot so our staffs intersected between our parted bodies. The butt of Death's staff dropped and my abdominals groaned with the effort it took to twist and block the strike.

"Good, lad. Good. You haven't forgotten the basics," Death growled.

"No, I haven't. It's knowledge I've imparted to your great-granddaughter," I huffed.

Death's bark of laughter echoed around the house. "So, I've seen. Can't say I wasn't proud or impressed. Chavas, or Morrigan as you know her, would have been proud. Now enough stalling."

Our staves twirled, their whir loud in the silent house. A breeze raced from them, across the floor and up the trunk of the Red Cedar tree.

We connected once more, Death's staff slamming my own to the ground. If I'd been human, I'd have been sweating in more ways than one. Death only ever trained to teach a lesson, and it usually involved pain. My body dropped to a crouch, narrowly avoiding his staff.

The obsidian stone in the thick end of Death's staff swept beneath my feet, and I jumped to avoid it.

Fuck me, I'm out of shape.

"Yes, you are, lad."

Death's throaty laugh taunted me.

"Stay out of my mind, old man. That's an unfair advantage and you know it."

I slammed my walls into place, as Morrigan had taught me, and blocked Death's next attack, my wrist flexing. The impact resonated up my arm, and I gritted my teeth against the pain.

My feet skimmed the surface of the floorboards, as the smooth wood of my staff slid across the back of my neck, sliding down to connect with my hand once more. The end of the staff closing in on my abdominals missed its target narrowly. My wrist flexed, and my staff zeroed in on Death, only for him to block it with a quick twist and a shoulder to my chest. He dipped and my body sailed over his, my shoulder slamming into the floor. I shot my staff out with pure reflex, and I hissed at the loud clack of his staff connecting with mine.

"My, my Tristan, but you are rusty. Perhaps I should have you in the ring with me and Evanee once a week."

The hairs on my body raised at his taunt.

Hell no!

The bruises and broken bones I'd endured at his hand were enough to make me wary of ever going to war against him, no matter how angry I'd been at him for abandoning me when I'd needed him most.

"I think I'll pass," I scoffed.

Springing to my knee, my staff shot forward in one hand. My stomach taking the strain as I slipped my head and shoulder between Death's parted legs. I flicked the staff around the outside of his leg and up so I caught it mid-roll. The momentum and restraint drove Death to his back. With his foot trapped beneath my arm, Death grinned back at me.

"Now you're getting it, lad," he roared from the floor, excitement swirling within his eyes.

His body disintegrated into a fine mist, and I hissed long and low with frustration. I stilled before I gripped my beast and hauled him to the surface, unafraid of releasing it with Death near. He would never harm Ellie. She meant too much to us.

The beast sniffed at the air, and my power trickled from my body in soft waves as though they were sound waves seeking an object to block them. When they encountered one to the right of me, I purred in anticipation of what was to come.

My body rippled, and my claws thickened, scraping large gouges across the wood. Canines lengthening to below my lower lip, a soft lavender glow emitted from their tips, a distraction from the paralytic acid dripping from their ends. I flexed my hand subtly in the blockage's direction. The scent of fresh blood drifted across the room from the gash across Death's chest. I raced across the room, meeting him head-on. My stick slammed down, and we met once more. Our growls and howls sending the wildlife surrounding the house scurrying in every direction. Obsidian and Byzantium sparks rocketed through the room as our weapons met with a loud clunk. Our bodies became a blur, our battle a relief to more than just me.

It'd been so long since I'd truly let myself fight freely. Aside from Erick, Evanee was the first fighter I'd faced in centuries who'd bested me through cunningness. She would make an excellent fighter once she was trained. Then perhaps I could train as I was now, without the worry of killing or maiming someone I cared about.

The muscles in my back rippled and strained with my next twist and twirl, but Death was there at the end of my twirl, his hand lodging firmly in my gut. My body froze, pink droplets of sweat forming across my temple as stars danced before my eyes.

"Too slow, Elf Boy. Isn't that what my great-granddaughter calls you?"

When I grunted, he leaned forward, his swirling eyes adding to my dizziness.

"Sheath your fangs and claws, lad."

"Fuck you," I spat in defiance.

"Always so defiant in the face of true danger, just like my great-granddaughter." He twisted his hand further into my gut. Blood slid down my stomach and into the waist of my slacks, where it was absorbed. My eyes drifted shut at the agony spreading through every nerve.

"Sheath them, lad, and speak truce," Death ordered.

I chose to fight another day.

Blood dribbled annoyingly from my lips and down my chin as I caved. "Truce."

Death's hand slid from my body and I dropped to my knees, a wet cough raking my body.

Death extended his arm, and blood bubbled to the surface of his slit wrist. "Drink what I offer freely."

Knowing better than to decline the All-Father, I accepted what he offered, taking only what I needed to heal my wounds. Blood coated my tongue, and a power I'd long forgotten slammed into my power. My beast purred, happy to be sated with blood as powerful as Death's.

The beast had sat waiting, hidden behind my human form, for decades. My transformation gave it the outlet it needed to wreak havoc. Its venom and brute strength a rarity amongst the druids and vampires. It was pure magic in its authentic form.

My mouth released Death's arm, and I stood, rejuvenated.

"Thank you."

"You're welcome. Now, let's talk. I felt your heartache and vulnerability this evening. A mate is both a strength and a vulnerability, is it not?" Death smirked before he turned and made his way toward the lounge room once more.

"Truer words if ever I heard them. I've waited centuries for Ellie, and when at last she stumbled across my path I still wasn't prepared for what destiny had install for me." I trailed after him, rubbing at my neck, Ellie's sleepy confession churning within my mind.

"You can never be truly prepared for the other half of your soul. Chavas, or should I say Morrigan, knocked me on my arse the first day we met, and never let me rise past my knees."

Death sat back on the lounge and laughed at whatever image appeared within his mind before he gave me a knowing look.

"Not that I minded all that much. Kneeling before her was my favourite pastime."

I laughed at that as I took up a position opposite him, knowing all too well what he meant. Given the chance, I'd have Ellie's legs wrapped around any part of my body, so long as she was all mine. I reclined into the armchair with a grin, no doubt looking like the love-sick fool I was.

Death sobered first. "Just as they bring joy, they bring sadness too."

"Is that why you never returned to visit me? I noticed the Great Queen has not stood beside you for some time." I trod carefully, unsure of how he would respond to my poking and prodding.

"She was taken from me just after your death. I left my children and creations to their own devices to find her, but it wasn't until many centuries later I realised what Fate had done. The curse she placed on my Chavas was the cruellest she could place upon any mate." Anger bubbled beneath Death's calm exterior, and I pitied him.

"What was the curse, All-Father?"

"I would reap the woman I loved, repeatedly throughout the millennia. I would watch the light bleed from the mortal shell that housed my beloved's soul and power. I'd lost hope, driven to near madness until recently." Death's small smile was one of hope.

I shook my head at his confession. "Evanee."

"Yes, Evanee. She's an extraordinary creature, my great-granddaughter. She would take on the world to protect those she loves, just like her great-grandmother." He grinned.

"She has Morrigan, sorry Chavas', humour too, and her beauty." I returned his grin.

"Yes, she does. She inherited my hair, and temper, but there is so much of her that reminds me of her great-grandmother. Reagan and Evanee were a delight to watch as children. Their stubbornness and defiance filled my days with endless laughter. I'd hoped you would be the one to mate with one of my descendants."

The thought of anyone other than Ellie being my mate churned my stomach. "It would have been an honour. But I believe Erick was a fine choice for Evanee. He balances her and compliments her nature far better than I could. Don't discredit Erick because of his age, All-Father. He's accomplished much in his short time. He'll make a fine king."

"So sayeth the kingmaker. And what he dreams shall come to pass," Death murmured thoughtfully. He paused momentarily before solemnly declaring, "She'll be the one to break Chavas' curse. I can feel it. With yours, Erick's, Ellie's and Jordan's help."

Not knowing how to respond, I remained silent. Faced with a god, it was best to let them lead. Anything else would only end in pain or death. I'd been lucky to get away with defending Erick.

Death studied me carefully as he spoke. "She'll also be the one to redetermine Ellie's fate."

Fear clenched my gut, and my shoulders slumped.

"So, it's true? Ellie will die." My throat clenched tight against the question, and a sinkhole of grief expanded from the centre of my chest, radiating outward.

"It's the fate of all banshees, lad. They must die as mortals to transition to a full banshee. Just as the first banshee was murdered, so too will Ellie be murdered."

I jumped from my seat. Anger rolled from my body in great, crashing waves, and the floorboards groaned beneath my feet.

For the second time in as many days, I lost my struggle to contain my emotions as I yelled, "So how the fuck has Evanee helped then? Ellie will still die, and I'd have spent two fucking millenniums waiting for the woman I love to come into my life. She'll be taken from me before I can even be allowed to show her a life of love."

I hunched forward, spearing my fingers into my hair as I screamed myself hoarse at the floor. "Fuck!"

"You need to calm yourself, Tristan. Let me explain," Death soothed, unfazed by my emotional melt down. "When a banshee dies her mortal death, I reap her soul. True, I leave a sliver behind, but only enough for them to feel some kind of affection for their offspring. They're cold creatures with little love or care for anything other than the fear. They predict death and feed off the fear I bring. Not my finest hour, as Chavas continually reminded me. We should have killed the poor pregnant woman that ingested our blood after drinking from the river. Chavas felt sorry for the baby and the effects the curse had on her after her husband murdered her. Chavas begged me to leave a sliver of her human soul so they might feel something other than hunger, and I obliged," he said with patience honed from his millennia of existence.

A relief so profound it buckled my knees coursed through me, and I dropped to the rug, my head drooping. "So that's why she's resisted our connection for so long. She's known she'll die all this time."

"She's known her entire life. But like my great-granddaughter, she's stubborn. She's forged her path through sheer will and determination. I admire her for it. I believe Ellie felt the need to protect you. By not telling you, she thought she'd protect you from what was coming."

"Her death." I shuddered at the word. "How do I save her from her fate?"

"Tristan, you forget that death is but a state, not the end. True, Ellie will die, but there are other ways one could save her. She has the potential to become the first of her kind. For now, enjoy the time you have. Be together." Death stood, his black cloak materialising. "Now, I am out of time. You were always one of my favourites. I knew you were going to be exceptional the night I found you staring out at Aibell's mother as a child. I sensed your mother's power, and death that clung to her. She was a talented sacrificer. My presence in your room ignited your first vision and with it your power. Ellie is our gift to you, lad. It was Chavas' last act of power before she was taken from me. She saw things I could not. Let things play out as they must,

Tristan. You cannot stop what's coming, and Ellie knows this."

My head lifted in surprise, only to encounter an empty room. I hung my head once more, fighting the despair unfurling within me. Fists clenching, I rose and approached the Red Cedar tree to place my hand against its sturdy trunk, my heart and head full.

I may not be able to stop what's coming, but I'll be by her side when she breathes her last breath. I'll be there to hold my love as she sheds her mortal body.

Chapter Twelve

Ellie

God's help is nearer than the door.

I slid my hands across the smooth, sealed surface of Tristan's giant pine dining room table, marvelling at Tristan's many hidden talents. I had no idea he could build furniture until I'd forced his confession after admiring the craftsmanship in this beautiful piece. My gaze drifted around the room, and I spotted more of his creations. A sharp pain radiated across my sternum, and my hand shot to the ribs below my breast, my teeth clenching against the pain.

A deep masculine chuckle sounded from in front of me. Alarm zapped through me, and my gaze shot to where the chuckle had sounded from.

"I see she layered a warning into her bond. She's too smart, that great-granddaughter of mine." Death materialised from the shadows just beside the red cedar.

"It's one of the many things I love about her. That and her curiosity is as bad as my own." I grinned.

"Oh, I remember it all too well. As a toddler, she tried to crawl through my robes to see if I had legs. You can imagine my reaction." His brow quirked, and I giggled at the thought of Death freaking out over a toddler.

"Evanee never mentioned that." I sat back in my chair, watching Death approach me, his silvery hair catching the beams of light shining in through the kitchen window. He'd dressed in his trademark black jeans and black v-neck t-shirt with leather boots.

Death slid a chair out, seating himself opposite me. "She doesn't remember, but she will soon, I suspect."

"I see. If that was me, and you'd wiped my memories of cherished moments, I'd be pissed. Considering this is Evanee we're talking about, I'd say she'll probably try to nail your balls to the wall when she remembers? She'll be pissed that you took something as precious as that away from her," I warned, and Death winced.

"She will indeed, but eventually I hope her and Reagan will understand it was for their safety. I'm more afraid of when my Chavas returns. When she finds out, I neglected her grandchildren and great-grandchildren, I'll end up feeling the full brunt of her temper."

I chuckled at his cringe.

"I'd like to say I know what you mean, but you and I both know my mother's a heartless bitch," I snorted.

"I'll admit, the banshee's creation was not my finest moment. They were created during a nasty fight between Chavas and me. In all fairness, I was the bastard that flirted with Fate at one of our many gatherings. Our blood and emotions were accidentally ingested by a woman drinking from a river nearby. She was with child. While it didn't affect the mother, the baby girl she was carrying felt the full effects," he admitted.

"My grandmother." I acknowledged.

"Yes. It wasn't until your grandmother's husband murdered her to be with another woman that our blood took full effect. She rose from the half-arsed grave your grandfather dug and drifted into that forsaken cottage you all now use for your gatherings. The man was in bed with his mistress when your grandmother floated into the room. He died of fright, and she carved out the poor young woman's heart, feasting on the fear, the heart, and the brain. Chavas felt so guilty she monitored your grandmother's three daughters and son when a cousin of your grandmother came to raise them. It wasn't until one male died in battle that we realised that only the girls inherited the curse. Your mother, though, she's a smart and conniving creature. She worked out that if she mated with a human, she'd still be able to produce offspring despite already transitioning to a full banshee. She evolved, as it were."

"In some ways."

Death acknowledged my truth with a slow, contemplative nod.

"True. And yet, if Aibell had not been as she is, you'd never have been born or met your mate."

Death stared at me knowingly.

With a heavy sigh, I slumped in my seat, knowing what he said was true. "I was lucky to have my father and twin," I admitted.

I studied the handsome god, and the pain and anger at the cards Fate had dealt me exploded. My open palms slapped at the tabletop. "Why the hell would any of you lump me on Tristan? Hasn't he had enough drama in his life without you idiots gifting him a cursed mate? How the hell am I meant to tell him I'm about to be murdered, that you'll suck my soul from me? I'll be left nothing but an empty shell that feels nothing but hatred, anger and an unquenchable thirst for the fear of the dying." My chair shot backward, and I jumped to my feet.

"Technically, Ellie, a slither of your soul remains. It was the best I could do for your grandmother. But you dear girl, you are not a cursed mate we lumped on Tristan. You were our gift to him, and he was Chavas' gift to you. I knew Tristan would die, and he was one of a few humans I treasured, which is why I did nothing to stop his conversion. But his master was a ruthless, murderous vampire, and I grew tired of the bodies he left in his wake, so I ripped out his heart."

Rendered me speechless, I stared open-mouthed at him.

He ignored my shocked face.

"I would never admit this to Tristan, but Chavas' interference in his destiny on my behalf is part of why Fate cursed her. That and the daft bitch was jealous of our love. Chavas could be crafty when she wanted to be. She somehow wove yours and Tristan's destinies together, but Fate picked up on the weave and extended it to curse Chavas. When I refused her advances, she extended that curse to Reagan and Evanee, only I never realised it until recently. My children are either dead, in hiding or blind to their own ignorance. I did what I could for Evanee and Reagan."

I found my voice, at last, and the courage to ask, "If I was Tristan's gift, does that mean I won't die?"

The sadness in his eyes was answer enough. "Sadly, you'll still meet a banshee's death, but it's my hope you won't become like your female kin."

A portal appeared to his right, and my eyes widened when I glimpsed Evanee sitting at her office desk. She lifted her head and rose on a sigh, rounding the table to step through. When she caught sight of me, she scratched at the back of her neck.

She's nervous about how I'll react after the other night.

'You could say that, Ell.'

"We can talk telepathically now?" I shrieked.

Evanee cringed, then nodded. "Yeah, sorry. It comes with the bite and power exchange."

"Okay. Well, do I get any other gifts other than the scale tattoo on my ribs? Which, by the way, I love. Oh, do I get nifty powers like Jordan, or am I still a useless banshee?"

Relief settled over Evanee's tight features, and she giggled through her nerves. "I couldn't tell you. I'm just trying to keep you and Brad alive."

Death rose and strolled to where Evanee had stopped. "Which is precisely why I brought you here, sweet child."

"So, it didn't work. She'll still die?"

Evanee's broken-hearted tone tightened my throat, and I stepped forward to comfort her, only to stop when Death placed his arm around her.

"Her death is an inevitable, sweet child. But the connection you created between you and Ellie may come in handy." Evanee's silvery brows drew together in a frown, and Death smiled affectionately. "I've always found mental connections intriguing. They have so many fascinating uses."

The soft timbre of his voice washed over me.

Evanee gazed up at her great-grandfather, her slim heart-shaped face filled with hope. The love and adoration in Death's eyes brought a tear to my own. For a second, I allowed myself to think of my father and the love that shone in the depths of his blue eyes whenever he looked at me. I realised then that Evanee honestly didn't remember him being present her whole life. My grief at the thought she could forget something so precious stalled the breath in my lungs.

Will I forget precious moments after I die? Will the love I have for Tristan, Ellie, Brad, and Ronan drift away with my soul?

"You're being cryptic again," Evanee sighed, her eyes rolling skyward. "Can you be more specific on how this connection is supposed to be helpful when her murderous family comes for her?"

Death leaned forward and placed a tender kiss on her forehead; his warm chuckle at his great-granddaughter's curiosity and questions were heart-warming. "Always so sassy. You two will need to figure this out for yourselves. But I'll remind you that you are a descendant of two gods, and with that comes responsibilities and perks."

A tiny crease formed at the bridge of Evanee's nose as she thought on Death's hint.

"I'm not sure about Chavas, but as your descendant, I'm required to reap the souls of humans and supernatural creatures." Evanee eyed Death, a deep frown drawing her blond brows together. "Are you telling me I'm supposed to reap her soul?"

My heart skipped a beat. "Hang on. I thought you said you reaped a banshee's soul but left a sliver there as part of her transformation," I interjected.

"You're both correct. Evanee will be the reaper in charge of your reaping. Consider it my gift to you both. As I said, there are perks to being a descendant rather than one of my creations. I believe Tristan may prove useful in figuring out how to save Ellie."

Death regarded us; his features once again sombre.

"That's as much as I can say on this matter. I've already said too much."

Death paused for a second, his gaze roaming my face. My hands twisted together as I fought the urge to squirm beneath his inspection.

"There's one other matter I wish to discuss with you before I go, Ellie. Once you've risen, you'll become the new Ua Briain. Your mother has turned her back on the true purpose of her role. It's time I reminded her of her place; she'll no longer lead all banshees. She will submit to you, and you will submit to Evanee and me as it was before I neglected my duties."

Every muscle in my body tensed at his speech.

"My mother will never relinquish her place as chief; she'd rather die. It's why no one has taken her spot. No one's beaten her."

A single elegant eyebrow rose, and Death stepped toward me.

"There's already talk of one of your sisters taking her place, and frankly, that girl has more bite than brains. She's a soldier, not a general."

Resignation gripped my shoulders, pulling them down. "You're right there. But I have no experience leading a clan. And they hate me for choosing Tristan over them. They cast me aside long before I met him, though. That I made it so far past my twenty-fifth birthday has never sat well with the clan."

"Ellie, they will submit, or you, Evanee and I will leave a path of blood and bodies until they are ready to submit. It doesn't matter to me whether I wipe them from the face of this insignificant planet."

My stomach churned at his words, and my eyes darted to Evanee and the horror on her face.

"I've often wondered if my greatest mistake with your kind was leaving only a slither of your soul intact. Would a banshee with or without a soul have followed commands and not strayed from her true purpose?"

His enigmatic smile chilled me to my core.

"You're talking as though we're nothing but specimens in a lab. As if you can tinker away with us until you get a positive result," I hissed.

"That's exactly what your kind is, Ellie," he purred dangerously.

Evanee stepped around Death and stood shoulder to shoulder with me.

"What's wrong with you? I don't care that you created each species of death, but you talking about them as though they're nothing but playthings is unacceptable."

A glint of something flickered across Death's eyes, and I blinked, wondering if it was the light playing tricks.

"Watch yourself, Granddaughter. I don't take criticism lightly."

The deep rumble in his voice drew every hair on my body to attention.

'Ah, Tristan, I think we're about to have a family fight in the dining room.' I reached out to Tristan, unsure of how I was supposed to solve this.

'We're on our way.' He sighed wearily.

Evanee scoffed. "What a shocker, a god who can't accept their flaws. It turns out you and Fate have more in common than you thought."

Evanee shoved me aside milliseconds before Death had her by the throat. Her body was into the air before Death slammed her hard into the ground.

The kind and doting grandfather evaporated before my eyes as Death leaned into Evanee's face, his animalistic growl rattling the surrounding windows.

"You're an ungrateful child. I've done more for you and your mother than any of my other children, yet you would compare me to the bitch that took my Chavas from me."

"And who's fault was that, huh?" Evanee retorted.

Death hissed long and low, and I watched, horrified when obsidian wings seeped through the material of his shirt. They unfurled themselves, solidifying before my eyes. Tristan would not arrive in time, and I couldn't tell how far Death would go in his current state. He seemed more animal than human if that were even possible.

I breathed in deep, summoning my banshee and the power that came with it. She offered no resistance this time, as though sensing Evanee were in trouble.

A scream built up within me, the pressure expanding my chest and ribs, so my breastbone ached. I focused on Death, my mouth opening to release the pent up scream trapped within. It blasted from my lips, slamming into Death's upper torso. His plump lips drew back into a cringe, but he never moved.

It's not enough.

Without thinking, I launched my body across the space, spearing Death in a low tackle. Our bodies tumbled, nothing but arms and legs. I'd barely moved when Evanee raced in and grabbed a fist full of Death's shirt. With an almighty tug, Death slid across the floor.

We were one. Best friends against the world as it had been since the day I'd met her. My decision to side with Evanee over my family would not be one I'd ever regret.

I rolled to gaze up at Evanee; she stood tall, her shoulders set. I climbed to my feet, moving to stand beside her as her wings ripped through her lab coat and spread out. She stood steadfast in the face of Death himself.

My goodness, she's magnificent.

Death's wings flared, and a shudder of trepidation slithered down my spine.

"Don't throw a tantrum at me because you don't like hearing the truth, Grandfather. This shit storm we're all in is because of you." Evanee pointed at Death, her face thunderous. She spoke with a steadiness that belied the rage flickering in her eyes.

Death's stony expression never wavered, but I noticed the slightest twitch of his shoulders.

"I only ever protected you and your mother," he snarled.

"Bullshit! You've done what you've always done; played your games and sat back moping when the shit hits the fan. We wouldn't need protection if you hadn't screwed that psychotic bitch. Chavas would still be beside you today." Evanee pointed at him before her hand cut through the air. Her body language louder than her words. "You've learned nothing from any of this."

Death's murderous expression drove shards of ice through my heart, my body quaking with fear at that thunderous expression.

"I will not warn you again, child."

"Is that all you can do—warn me? Are you that blind to your flaws you're incapable of acknowledging or even attempting to work on them?"

An intense sadness tightened my chest with every syllable Evanee uttered. "Why are you here? What do you want?"

"How do you know he wants something?" I frowned.

"Because he has repeatedly said that he cannot interfere or solve my problems for me, yet here he is once again attempting to fix something."

Death's answer stalled as two figures stormed into the room wordlessly. Erick and Tristan approached us, their eyes keeping track of Death and his position in the room.

A mercurial garnet swirl broke Erick's green eyes; their glow heightened by his rage.

It was the first time I'd seen his eyes like this. The golden flame at his hand crept further up his arm the closer he got to us. He searched Evanee with an unblinking stare. He took in the floor beside the dining table, where an imprint of Evanee's body decorated the floor, his gaze returning to hers. I'd only ever seen the gentle and fun side of Erick, but the increasing rage that filled his stare was warning enough that Erick had a completely different side to him. One I had no intention of ever crossing.

Beside him, Tristan's power rolled from his tall, flowing body. He moved with a grace only the most talented of dancers could hope to achieve. No flames clung to him or any other outward signs of power, yet the human and banshee within me sensed the threat of what he was or could do.

'Mo ghrá, are you okay?' Tristan's soothing voice caressed my mind.

'Honestly, I'm not sure. I never thought I'd have to go up against Death himself. My scream did nothing but annoy him. I had to tackle him to get him off Evanee.'

'You did well. Stalling him and defending your best friend. You should be proud.'

'Yeah, I'm not feeling proud right now. I'm feeling the distinct need to pee my pants,' I confessed.

Tristan's stony expression never wavered as he came up beside me. He positioned his body slightly in front of mine, protecting me.

Evanee caught at Erick's hand and clung to it. "I'll ask again, Grandfather. What do you want from me?"

Death's wings flared behind him, and a long-handled scythe appeared in his outstretched hand. I stopped breathing, wondering if this was it; was he about to reap the lot of us?

Tristan moved then, his hands clapping together. Evanee and I jump at the thunderous sound they emitted made. I watched fascinated as Byzantium sparks shot from between his fingers, a piece of wood lengthening between his parting hands. Milliseconds later, one end of a gnarled wooden staff thudded onto the floorboards. The dark wooded staff stopped just short of his shoulder.

'Where the hell did you get the staff from, and why haven't you shown me that trick before?' I groused mentally.

'I'll explain later, I promise.' His chuckle reverberated through my mind.

"You would challenge your All-Father, Tristan?" Death frowned.

"I would protect my king, queen and mate, Dagda. As is my sworn duty." Tristan stood tall, his resolve absolute.

"You swore an oath to me, Tristan. Don't forget that," Death barked.

"I've not forgotten my oath to serve you. I swore to serve you and protect those you hold dear. I don't believe I'm betraying that oath by reminding you that Evanee is your great-granddaughter, the very one you worked so hard to protect."

When Death stayed silent, Tristan's shoulders slumped with weariness.

"So many secrets, All-Father. Tell her what you told me. She deserves to know."

Death remained silent for a moment, then seemed to crumble before my eyes. A man with the weight of the world on his shoulders replaced the battle-ready god. The wings behind him vanished as quickly as they'd arrived, as did his scythe.

"As always, Tristan, you're right." Death scrubbed at the loose strands of his hair, teasing his cheeks. "I've been in a state of flux for so long I've forgotten what it's like to share my thoughts, hopes and plans with someone I care about. I'm sorry, sweet child. I'm not in my right mind. It is no excuse for my behaviour, but I am truly sorry."

To my left, Evanee nodded stiffly. It hit me then. Death was broken and grieved for his wife. Would Tristan transform into a replica of this broken man? Would he roam the earth lonely, his heart eternally shattered? I turned my head to the side, hiding the tears sliding down my cheeks.

A large icy hand gripped mine and placed my hand to where his silent heart sat. When Tristan did things like this, I was sure we could take on anything and win, even a bat-shit-crazy goddess like Fate.

Evanee's posture remained stiff, and it didn't take a genius to figure out she was waiting for the other shoe to drop. "What do you need from me, Grandfather?"

"Chavas, sweet child. I need your help to bring Chavas back to me. I'll need the help of everyone one of you in this room, including Jordan."

My breath stalled in my lungs at Death's plea.

"Hang on. You want us to bring my great-grandmother back from the dead?" Evanee's hands exploded into the air, taking on a life of their own, as they so often did when she talked about something she was passionate or vexed about.

"How the hell are we meant to bring Chavas back from the dead when you can't do it?" I blurted.

Erick's hands strayed to his mate's shoulders, the tiny tug of his lips and the gleam in his eyes giving his amusement away. "I think we need to stop and let Death explain things."

Erick tugged at Evanee, so she stepped backward and into his chest. Placing a gentle kiss on her neck, Erick's hands dropped to circle her waist. Arms crossing, Evanee tapped her foot impatiently, and I smirked.

Oh, he's good.

"Thank you, Erick." Death stared at each of us. "I don't need you to bring Chavas back from the dead because she's not dead."

"Come again?" The words were out of my mouth before I could censor my thoughts.

"I don't need Evanee to resurrect Chavas. I need her to break the curse Fate put on Chavas," Death implored a shocked Evanee. "She'll need the help of all of you."

Bewildered, my foot in mouth syndrome took over. "Does anyone even know where Chavas is?"

"She's in Acrasin City," Evanee whispered, her eyes widening with horror. "The Acrasin Metro Police Station, to be exact. Isn't she, Grandfather?"

Death nodded while Erick and Tristan stared in shock. I, on the other hand, had no clue what she was talking about.

"You're an arsehole. This whole time Chavas was right there, and she has no damn idea who she is," Evanee seethed.

"Uh, could someone fill this mortal in on what you're talking about?" I interjected.

"Bernard. Detective Bernard is Chavas," Evanee said through clenched teeth.

Sacred Plants

Vervain (*Verbena Officinalis*)

324

Also referred to as Verbena.

Commonly used for stimulation of lactation

and the treatment of jaundice, kidney stones, gout,

and dysmenorrhea.

May also be used to soothe headaches,

depression, anxiety, and bouts of insomnia.

Tincture may be used, but sparingly, and not

for long-term use.

– Tristan Cathbad.

Chapter Thirteen

Tristan

The rough bark of the Red Cedar beneath my smooth palm did little to soothe the constant barrage of thoughts in my mind. I was grateful for the house's silence. The floorboards in the dining room would need to be replaced unless I intended on seeing an Evanee shaped indent for the rest of my undead life.

"Today is not a day I want to repeat."

I turned toward Ellie's petite frame. She was standing in the centre of the room.

With a sad smile, I murmured, "I couldn't agree more. Death has always been one for the dramatics, but today's revelation was bigger than anything I've ever witnessed. I think Evanee may be right. There really is some invisible shoe waiting to drop."

"I feel for the man. He's been without his mate for how many millennia? I feel like he's entitled to a few blunders along the way," Ellie said, sympathising.

I remained silent, turning to face the noble tree once more. Would I become like Death if Aibell drew Ellie back to Ireland? Would I wage a war with an entire species for the sake of one?

'Yes,' my beast hissed, violence radiating from his naked body. 'No one will keep us from her. No one.'

"Hey, Mr Grumpy Pants, how about we have some fun?"

Ellie stepped up behind me, her tiny hands circling my waist to clasp at the front. The heat from her head seeped beneath my shirt and down my spine, sending shivers across my body.

My hand drifted down to rest on her clasped ones, and I smiled at their smallness. "What did you have in mind?"

"Lab setup," she whispered with mischief.

"Say that again?" I frowned, sure I'd misheard her.

"You could help me set up the lab at Erick's place. I can't lift all the equipment by myself, and I'm pretty sure Brad's in Acrasin City getting supplies. We could make it fun and have you lift everything shirtless."

I could hear the smile in her voice.

I restrained my grin, playing along. "Shirtless, you say? Just how are you intending on paying for my services as your lab assistant?"

"Oh, I'm sure I'll figure out some form of payment that's suitable for you, gorgeous," she murmured against my back. "Plus, I'd love to get my hands on a sample of your blood."

"Fine, let's go then." My long-suffering tone was met with a swift smack to my arse. I spun, and I clasped her hand. "We'll need to take the ute, the suns too high for me to be truly comfortable walking beneath it."

Ellie hesitated. "So how did you get here with Erick?"

"I sprinted beneath the canopy of the trees." When her frown deepened, I clarified, "The sun drains me more than it hurts. I'm old enough to not succumb to its effects. Erick, having been born a vampire, has a certain immunity to it that would take most at least a thousand years to build up. Evanee, well, who knows what's going on there." I shrugged.

Ellie giggled, and I grinned at her.

"Fine, let's take the ute. I want to drive, though. It'll give me a chance to show off the four-wheel driving skills I learned on the homestead in Orchard Hill." She wiggled her eyebrows at me before she snagged the keys beside the door to the garage.

My grin widened when I caught sight of Ellie's bare feet.

"Aren't you going to put on shoes?"

"Don't have any. All my stuff is still at the house. I already messaged Brad and asked him to bring spare clothes and shoes. He'll bring them by the lab when he gets back from Acrasin City."

We climbed in, and Ellie adjusted the seat and mirrors. She hit the button on the remote clipped to the visor, igniting the engine. Ellie backed out of the garage and had the ute turned around and meandering down the steep dirt driveway in no time. I sat back, silently watching her handle the ute with confidence. Pride welled up within me.

This was my mate. The one picked for me and me alone. Her confidence, tenaciousness and love for life were infectious. She threw herself into life and love like no one else I knew, and I loved her even more for it.

Twice she was forced to hit the button to shift into four-wheel drive. We emerged from the tree line at the bottom of the driveway, and I pointed to the stables to the left of the house.

"I thought we'd be going to the main house?" Ellie asked, confused.

"Erick thought it best to have the bunker beneath the stables converted to a lab for you and Brad. With our interstate and international visitors due to visit, he felt it'd be safer and quieter for you and Brad to have access without having to confront a nest of plotting vampires," I pointed out wryly.

"Yeah, that was probably a wise choice. Was it meant to be a panic room or something?" Ellie pulled to a stop in front of the stables and hopped out. "Oh man, that wind is cold. I hope Brad brings me a jumper." Ellie shivered.

We met at the front of the car, and I pulled her against my body, cursing myself for not having thought about how the cold would affect her. "Yes, it was a panic room of sorts. We designed it to be away from the house in case anyone invaded. There's a tunnel leading to it from the house. We're revamping it. Evanee and Brad both pointed out that a lab needed to be a sterile environment. Erick changed the stable entrance after they made upgrades inside the bunker, so it should be safe enough for people to enter via this entry for now. Once we receive visitors, though, we'll get you and Brad to enter through the library to be safe."

"The entrance to the lab is in the library?" Ellie laughed, her bottle-green eyes sparkling with her laughter. "If I knew any better, I'd have said Evanee designed the house and that entrance."

With a chuckle, I steered her toward the tin partition hiding the door at the side of the bard. The rustic addition would appear as though they'd added it to protect the door from the weather.

"It would seem that Evanee and I have a lot more in common than we care to think about."

The old wooden door squawked in protest, its hinges in need of oiling. I frowned at the door and made a mental note to get someone on to it.

I trod lightly, making my way toward the back of the storeroom, where a keypad lay hidden behind some old riding equipment.

"Do you think the two of you will ever get along?" Ellie's quiet question gave me pause, and I turned around as the panel in the ground slid back with a hiss of hydraulics.

"Admittedly, we got off on the wrong foot. But I think it had more to do with my concern for Erick than it did with Evanee. As I said, we have a lot in common. Her love of books and knowledge is not that dissimilar from mine. And her desire to help those who have no voice is in line with how I lived my life and still live my life. Her temper is what gets my back up. But she's young, and I'll work with her to control and channel that anger, so it has purpose and direction. I did the same with Erick."

It had taken decades to work with Erick; I prayed Evanee would be a better student.

Please All-Farther. Please let Evanee be a better student.

Ellie shook her head with a sigh and stepped around me to descend the stairs to the basement below. "I keep forgetting what an old man you are."

"Who you calling old? I could probably outlast you all despite my years before me." I feigned outrage.

"Sure you can, gorgeous. I'm not questioning your stamina." Ellie snorted.

I swatted her round arse playfully.

"Don't start what you can't finish, old man," Ellie warned cheekily over her shoulder.

My arm shot out to circle her waist, and I had her back against the wall before we could blink. My nose touched the tip of hers, and I stared into her wide eyes.

"Are you daring me?" Pressing my hips to hers, I nipped at her top lip.

"Was I? I'm sure I wouldn't do that." She feigned innocence, but the sassy smile tugging at her plump, pale pink lips said otherwise.

My cock twitched at those lips and the delicious things they'd done and could do.

I continued to nip my way along her delicate jaw toward her ear. "Ah-huh. You're lucky there's a camera in the corner above the stairs, or I'd have you facing this wall spread legged while I spanked that rather delicious arse of yours."

My seductive purr had the desired effect. The scent of her arousal drifted up to tease and taunt me.

"Chicken." She groaned against the shivers running through her taut body.

I hissed at her challenge, manoeuvring my body to block hers from the camera's lens. My left hand slid across her hip and beneath the T-shirt, she'd borrowed from me. My fingers caressed her ripped stomach, tracing the subtle edges of her four-pack.

The hitch of her breath sent a fresh wave of blood straight to my groin, and I bit back the groan on the edge of my tongue. We were on the edge of the camera's vision up the stairs and only just clear of the vision of the second camera at the entrance to the lab doors. The camera at the top of the stairs would get a clear shot of my back, but Ellie would remain hidden if I kept still enough.

"Always so brave, mo ghrá. Let's see how long you make it before you beg me to bury myself in you." I challenged in return, my hand slipping to the edge of her yoga pants.

The door above slid shut on a soft hiss, but I ignored it. My hand trailed the line of Ellie's waistband, forward then backward. Parting the material from her silky flesh, I kept my arm movements to a minimum. My hand slid further down, groaning in satisfaction when I realised she'd foregone underwear.

My tingling lips sought hers. With every brush of our lips, my hand travelled down. My fingers encountered the trimmed hairs over her pubic bone, and I bit back a groan. Ellie's kiss grew deeper, her hips bucking ever so slightly with impatience. My cupped hand glided down, then back up. I drank Ellie's groan in, my own caught in my throat.

I pulled back from our kiss to whisper, "Move your foot up one step, baby."

Ellie's foot slid up a step without hesitation, and I nipped at her jawline.

My fingers dipped just a little, encountering her silken folds. I gave into my groan when they met the warm juices coating them. "Fuck Ellie, you're going to kill me."

"Tristan, don't stop. Please," she begged, and my cock twitched, the material of my pants an unwanted barrier.

I slid my hand further down, my fingers burying themselves deep within her. From above us, the soft hiss of hydraulics caught my attention, and I hissed with frustration.

For fuck sakes, can't a man catch a break?

"Oh, for goodness's sake, you two, find a bloody room, will you? No one needs to see you two making out in the bloody stairwell."

Brad's exasperated voice snapped Ellie out of her sensual daze, and a blush crept over her cheeks and down her neck.

'Oh shit. I hope he didn't see anything.'

Ellie's mortified whisper crept through my mind.

My fingers withdrew from within her, and I eased my hand out with slow and subtle movements so as not to alert Brad. My fangs retracted, and I smirked at Ellie before placing a quick kiss on her swollen lips.

"Oi, you two. Don't make me get a hose, because I will. If you two have time to make out, you have time to help me haul supplies into the lab," Brad grumbled.

"We heard you, Brad." My calm exterior at odds with a sudden urge to throw him back up the stairs.

'*Be nice.*' Ellie smirked, then puckered up her lips and blew me a kiss as she stepped around me.

"Coming, weirdo. Did you bring my spare change of clothes?" Ellie sang out, the blush in her cheeks subsiding.

I turned to follow Ellie, my groin throbbing painfully.

"Yes, it's in the front seat of the ute."

Ellie ran up the stairs lightly, and I made to follow her when Brad muttered, "And don't think I don't know what you two were doing. I'm going to have nightmares for a week, dude. No guy needs to walk in on his sister from another mother being fingered."

I stopped, stunned into silence for a second.

With a smirk, I shrugged. "I'd say sorry, but I'm not. You'll have your turn one day."

"That's highly unlikely," Brad mumbled, and I frowned at his retreating back.

Chapter Fourteen

Ellie

An empty sack does not stand.

With my lower back resting on the icy counter of a nearby workbench, I observed the laboratory. Boxes filled with test tubes, Petri dishes and inoculation loops sat awaiting allocation to their shelves and drawers. I took in the shining surfaces and Tristan and Brad manoeuvring benches and equipment to their new spots, contentment filling me to the brim.

Tears blurred my vision, wetting my lower lashes, and I fought the urge to cry at the transformation taking place before me. The light grey floors, white walls and stainless-steel benches sparkled with their newness.

"Ellie, are you just going to stand there, or are you going to help get this bloody mess cleaned up?" Brad huffed as he shoved another bench toward the centre of the room.

With a quick swipe across my eyes, I dashed my tears away. I stepped forward and nose-first into Tristan's chest. Tristan's hand shot out to grasp my upper arms.

"Ouch. Tristan, these human eyes cannot keep up with your speed."

"Sorry, mo ghrá," he murmured, the palms of his hands rubbing at my upper arms.

I swallowed hard, Erick and Evanee's warning whispering through my mind, mocking me. I scrunched my eyes tight, praying the tears wouldn't fall.

Tristan drew me to him, whispering against my forehead.

"Do you want to talk about it?"

My breath squeezed from tight lungs, and with a pathetic sniffle, I caved in. "There's something I need to tell you, and I don't know how to say it."

"I find the best way to say anything is to open your mouth and let the words come out," Tristan mumbled against my forehead.

"You'd think so." I hiccupped.

"Ell? Everything okay?"

Brad's concern pierced my already weeping heart.

"What's got you upset? Did I order the wrong equipment? I tried to order what I thought you'd need too."

My arms shot out to wrap around Tristan. I hugged him hard, not worrying I'd hurt him. Tristan's hand dropped to my waist, holding me close to him. The sweet, clean scent of Brad's deodorant encompassed me before his warm hand rubbed circles across my upper back.

Forehead resting against Tristan's chest, I blinked down at the floor. "There's something I need to tell you two."

"Well, okay. Tell us then. Rip that Band-Aid off and let's get this show on the road," Brad encouraged.

I smiled through my tears.

"Right. Well, here it goes." I stalled, trying to find the right words and deciding there was no right way to tell someone you would die.

"My family's closing in on me, and when they do, I'll be out of time." I blurted.

The room plummeted into silence, and I kept my head down, not wanting to see the looks on Tristan's or Brad's face at my news.

"What the hell do you mean you'll be out of time?" Brad croaked.

Tristan remained still beneath where my temple rested on his chest, and I wiped at my eyes before I stepped out of both men's reach.

My tear-blurred gaze met Tristan's. His face remained emotionless, as it so often did when dealing with business. His only tell were his eyes; they spoke the words he seemed incapable of saying. The glimmer of sadness in their lavender depths and slight crinkling at their edges hinted at how my statement was affecting him.

"Perhaps you could explain why you think your time is up and what it has to do with your family?" Tristan raised his eyebrows in question.

Grief tightened my chest, and I nodded. "That's fair enough."

My gaze drifted over the two men who meant the world to me. Brad, who'd gone from my study buddy to best friend and brother since I'd first met him at university. And Tristan, the man who'd wormed his way into my barricaded heart after I'd tried so hard to keep him out.

"I've known for years I'd die young." Brad's breathing hitched, but I ploughed on, not trusting myself to do anything else. "It's why I tried so hard to keep people at bay. It's why I told you we could never be anything more, Tristan." I shrugged.

When neither man said anything, I drew a deep breath in and released it shakily. "In my family, females rarely, if ever, make it past the age of twenty-five. You both know I'm part banshee, but what you don't know is on or just before her twenty-fifth birthday, a banshee is murdered by one of her male relatives. If a relative doesn't complete the ritual, the curse supposedly activates on it's own."

My shaking hands speared into my hair, and I tugged them through roughly.

"I've always known I wasn't like the women in my family. I didn't spend my teenage years romanticising becoming some immortal broodmare as the women in my family have done before me. I've never thirsted after the chaos and fear the way my mother, sister and cousins have. I've wanted to heal, to help those less fortunate than myself, much like you two. I've spent the past four years looking over my shoulder and avoiding going home, knowing at any moment, one of my male relatives would come after me as ordered by my mother."

I lifted my tear rimmed eyes to the ceiling and sniffed indelicately, trying my best to hold my tears at bay. I was losing the battle.

"Mostly, the men in my family are a bunch of kiss-arses, who blindly follow what the women tell them. My twin brother, Ronan, and my father are the exception. From what I understand, my father flat-out refused to kill me. He's threatened to disembowel any man that took my life. He and my brother, Ronan, have brought me precious time no other woman has had, but my time's up. I still can't figure out why the curse hasn't activated yet. It should have by now, according to our lore. Unless my mother's been lying all these centuries."

"Has Ronan contacted you?" Brad gritted out, his face growing redder by the second.

"No, my family's remained silent since the last attack the other night." I held up my hand to silence a spluttering Brad, soothing his indignation before he could verbalise it. "Relax, Brad. Tristan, Evanee and Erick came to my rescue; I'm all good. Your mother's birthday didn't feel like the right time to tell you about the attack. As for how I know my time's nearing an end, that's simple. Evanee and Death confirmed it." I shrugged, wringing my hands.

Tristan frowned. "When was this?"

"Evanee confirmed it the night you stormed from the library," I muttered.

Tristan hissed, his face thunderous. "You've known that long that you were approaching your death and didn't tell me? Why? Did Erick know about this?"

"Tristan, if you want to be angry, be angry at me. Erick and Evanee warned me to tell you both, but I didn't know how to broach this subject until Death visited me. I only wanted to protect you both from any pain my death would cause."

Brad stood stricken, his eyes glazing over.

"You've both lost so much in your life. I didn't want to cause either of you anymore heartache."

"You had no right to keep this from me, Ellie," Brad choked out.

Tristan's fists clenched at his side, and he ground out, "I wish you'd have told me."

I bit my tongue, my heart aching at the hurt and betrayal clouding their eyes.

Brad was the first to shake it off.

"Okay, okay. Let's think." Brad exhaled shakily. "So, we know one of your relatives will try to attack you again," Brad said, his brain already trying to formulate a plan.

"Yes," I whispered.

"So, all we have to do is keep you hidden and alive. Between Tristan and I, surely we could keep you safe." Hope glistened in the depths of Brad's eyes.

I met Tristan's unflinching gaze. His clenched jaw a sign he knew as well as I did there would be no saving me. If Evanee and Death had both warned me about my impending death, then it was a sure thing.

"There's no protecting her from this, Brad," Tristan muttered.

"What?" Brad took a step back, shocked by Tristan's words.

Tristan spun, his fierce eyes fixing on Brad. "There's no saving Ellie from this. If Evanee foretold it, and Death has paid a visit to Ellie, then she'll…." Tristan faltered, unable to get the rest out.

Brad stilled for a second before succumbing to his grief. "No. No, we can save her. We have to save her. There has to be a way?" His voice rose with each word he uttered.

His wide, panicked gaze darted from Tristan to me.

My heart shattered, tears spilling down my cheeks.

"No, you can't. I can't lose you too. I can't." Brad begged between hiccups.

"Brad, I'm so…" I spluttered but stopped short when Brad spun, his arms lashing out at the boxes closest to him.

"No! No!" he roared through falling tears.

His fist collided with the metal table in front of him. Over and over, he punched the table, a dint forming around his bloodied knuckles. I moved to stop him, but Tristan's arm shot out, stopping me in my tracks.

Brad spun then, his arms colliding with more boxes, which met the same fate as the previous ones. His fists drove down on the metal table beneath, and I flinched at the loud clang.

His fists drove down onto the metal surface, all the while sobbing brokenly, "Not again."

His movements grew slower, fatigue setting in. Tristan stepped forward, his hand reaching for Brad's shoulder.

Brad flinched but stayed still beneath Tristan's light grip. "You're not alone in this, Brad. I'll tell you what Death told me. Death is but a state, not the end. While she might not be human, she'll still be with us, as a banshee," Tristan soothed.

Head bowed in defeat; Brad nodded before turning to make his way out of the lab without glancing my way.

The air felt heavy, and I pressed my fingertips to my mouth to silence my grief. I'd done the exact thing I'd tried to avoid all along. I'd hurt two people I cared so deeply for.

Tristan's shoulders sagged, and I waited for him to walk out too.

"Thank you for trusting me enough to tell me, Ellie," Tristan uttered, his back still to me.

I blinked, a frown drawing my eyebrows together. Swallowing my sob, my hands dropped uselessly to my sides, and I waited for Tristan to speak again. His nimble fingers combed through his shoulder-length hair, and he turned, his lavender eyes glowing.

"I won't lie to you, Ellie. You keeping this from me hurts. Erick knowing this whole time and not telling me has hurt more than I care to admit, but I understand why he remained silent. I'd have done the same thing if it were him; hell, I've done the same thing." Tristan's gaze dropped to the floor, his jaw tightening.

"I'm sorry," I whispered, ashamed. Tristan's last words hit home, and I frowned. "What do you mean you've done the same thing to him?"

"I mean that the prophecy announcing the coming of Regina Populi Mortis didn't write itself, Ellie," Tristan ground out, refusing to meet my eyes.

"Tristan, tell me you aren't saying what I think you're saying."

Dread settled in my stomach, and I swallowed heavily to keep the bile from rising.

"I was a young man when the dream first came to me. It wasn't my first vision, and it wasn't my last during my human years. I can't be sure who bestowed it on me; but, since Fate has laid claim to concocting some grand scheme to get back at the Dagda, sorry Death, I can only assume it was her. The dream was so vivid. I remember waking happy and excited that there would be a queen as fierce as the woman in my dreams. It was one of a hundred I put onto hide. Someone, I can only assume was the man that would become my sire, must have sneaked into my tent and copied the prophecy onto paper. In their haste, they screwed up the last two sentences completely."

Tristan scoffed at what had been pure idiocy on the creature's part when copying the prophecy.

"Instead of saying 'For she will rule, her king beside her. All Hail Regina Populi Moris', the fool wrote, 'For she will sit upon the throne, beside her king.' They left the all hail out completely. I didn't even realise it'd been copied until I stumbled across it in one of the many libraries the Tenebris family own in Romania. The hide I'd written the prophecy on disappeared the next night, and I assumed Dagda or Morrigan retrieved it."

A small smile tugged at Tristan's carnation-pink lips.

"I can still see the queen sitting on an enormous black throne made of flesh and bones with a crown of clasping misted hands and ruby droplets scattered around it. I remember the feel of those delicate drops of mist that crept from beneath her throne. I swear, Ellie, the mist had hands reaching from within it. They shackled me in place during the vision."

I held my breath, shocked by the words spilling from his mouth.

"Erick sat beside her, and gods was he magnificent. He sat on a throne so red; it appeared to be carved from blood, which is impossible I know." Tristan frowned as though trying to recall a detail from his dream. "A crown of blue and gold flames circled his head with sapphires scattered through it. There was a woman's body lying on its side at his feet. Ribbons of blood ran over her body, and it would shift from skeletal remains to a fully formed human body, then be stripped to the bone again."

Tristan frowned at the last part, and I waited for him to continue.

When he remained silent for some time, my curiosity got the better of my previous heartbreak and shock.

I cleared my throat, approaching him, only to stop a couple of feet from him. "What else, Tristan."

Tristan's lavender gaze met mine, and my heart clenched at the guilt I saw in their depths.

"You have to understand, Ellie. A sheer veil shrouded the queen's face. There was no way for me to see her. My visions never reveal all of what will come to pass. The gods, they don't work on the same thought pattern as we do. The only giveaway was the white hair. It's the same shade as Evanee's. Her hair triggered my memory. I'd never have wished what Evanee and Erick have been through on anyone, let alone the man I love like a son or younger brother."

My breath exploded from my lungs, and I hadn't realised I'd been holding it as he spoke.

A full-body shiver worked its way down my spine to my toes. I shrugged it off; instead, I took a tentative step toward Tristan, and when he didn't move, I approached him. My arms reached up to lock around his neck, and I combed my fingers through the feather-soft tendrils of his hair. Tristan's arms hugged my waist, his face burying in my neck. We stood there, holding each other. There was no prophecy and no banshee curse out to seek its next victim for a moment in time. It was just him and I at our rawest.

Tristan's lips moved against my pulse as he murmured, "Since we're being honest, I should probably tell you Death paid me a visit too."

My hands stilled in his hair, and I pulled my head back to stare at him.

"When?"

"Last night."

"I see. Let me guess; Death told you about my family's curse and what it entails," I grumbled.

Tristan's arms tightened around my waist as though he was afraid I might bolt.

"Yes. He also suggested there may be a way to save you but wouldn't say how."

I lowered my head to his chest. "He said the same thing to Evanee and me."

"Ellie, your mother will not be taking you back to Ireland as long as I'm still on this earth."

Tristan's chest rumbled against my head.

Fear gripped my heart, and my throat tightened.

"You promise?"

Tristan's large hands gripped my waist, pushing me back until I lifted my head to stare into his glowing eyes.

"Ellie, I swear to you that no matter where you go, I'll follow. I'll be there when you breathe your last breath. You mean more to me than life itself, and there's nothing I wouldn't do to keep you beside me. I love you, mo ghrá," he declared, passion and love radiating from every fibre of his body.

A grin tugged at my lips, and I rose on my tippy toes, my body brushing against his.

"You sound like a stalker; you know that?" I teased.

"Ellie…" Tristan groaned, but I interrupted him, my finger pressing against his lips.

"Shh. I wasn't finished. You sound like a stalker." I grinned saucily at him. "But you're my kind of stalker. I could think of nothing better than being glued to you for all eternity. Hell, maybe I could find some super glue up at Erick's place, and we really could be glued together."

Tristan laughed, and my heart lightened.

"I love you, Tristan Cathbad, son of the druid Cathbad, who sat at the side of the cursed King Conor MacNess of Ulster. Claíomh to his Royal Highness Erick Tenebris and chosen soothsayer by the Dagda himself. Did I get that right?" I smirked at a gapping Tristan.

"Where did you hear my full title?"

I shrugged. "Your beastie whispered it to me the last time I was in your mind. He likes me, you know?"

Tristan stared at me, a slow smile spreading across his face. The world spun as Tristan held me to him, and I squealed at the suddenness. His deep, melodic laughter echoed through the room, and my body responded to it, my stomach tightening.

The world stopped spinning, and my body slid down the hard planes of Tristan's stomach, my feet hovering just above the ground. A heaviness settled in my breasts, and I clamped my thighs together. When at last, my feet found solid ground again, I kept my grip on Tristan, not trusting my balance. The solid chest beneath my palms expanded. My eyes met Tristan's heated ones, and my heart skipped a beat at the smouldering heat that lay within them.

I rose to the balls of my feet, bouncing once before I lifted my legs to wrap around Tristan's waist. His hands caught at my arse, and he drew me closer.

"Did you know that when a couple declares their love as epically as we just did, they celebrate it with a few rounds of frenzied and passionate lovemaking?" I nipped at his lips once before pulling back.

"Is that so?" Tristan purred, his lips twitching at the corners as he fought to hide his smile.

"Oh yes. What are your thoughts on the table behind you?" I suggested before I waggled my eyebrows at him.

Tristan dipped his head, pressing his lips to my ear, his whisper sending shivers down my spine so that goosebumps tightened my skin. "While that table is perfectly acceptable, I don't like the idea of your naked body on display for all to see. This room has cameras that connect to a feed in Erick's office."

I groaned at my stupidity and dropped my head to his shoulder to hide the hot flush creeping across my cheeks. Tristan's hand slipped from my arse, and I raised my head.

"What are you doing?" I frowned, attempting to look over my shoulder to his raised arm.

Tristan replaced his hand on my arse with a smirk. "Flipping Erick off. He can be an annoying bugger when he wants to."

I giggled, peeking over my shoulder to the camera in the corner. I waved cheerfully at it. "Tell him to stop being a pervert and direct his eyes elsewhere."

Tristan's laughter drifted away when he suddenly spun, the room blurring until we halted at sliding doors. Pressing his palm to the panel, I held onto him and waited for the precious seconds it took for the doors to open.

"Where are we going?" I squealed, my arms tightening around his neck.

"Somewhere there's no prying eyes and teasing princes," Tristan ground out.

I suppressed my giggle, knowing Erick would tease him mercilessly.

We sped up the stairs. Tristan's fingers flew over the keypad beside the door to the storage room above us, his hand returning to my arse, where he squeezed it lovingly.

"Poor baby, what did the mean prince say to you? Do you want me to yell at him?" I offered, my gaze darting up to watch the panel above our head slide open with a hiss.

"It wouldn't help. Besides, you yelling at Erick would require us to be close to others, and I'm not sure I'd survive that right now," Tristan responded dryly, with a pained expression.

"Aww, my poor, brave druid, we can't have that, now can we?" I fought my grin, holding him tight when the world once again blurred around me.

We stopped inches from the ute, and my eyes snapped shut against the brightness of the afternoon sun. Tristan swung the passenger door open, and I found myself seated and buckled in before I could ask what he was doing. The door slammed shut, and Tristan sped around the front of the ute, sliding into the driver's seat and igniting the engine.

"What about Brad?" I frowned, trying to locate his ute but not seeing it.

"Brad will be fine. There's nothing you can do for him until he returns," Tristan reassured me.

I nodded, knowing Brad would need time to adjust to what I'd revealed.

The ute in gear, Tristan reversed. He hit the brakes hard before he slammed the gears into drive and accelerated, loose gravel spitting up behind us in his hurry to get us somewhere more private.

My thoughts of Brad, impending death and any plans for the future stayed with the cloud of dust now drifting to settle back on the ground.

"So, gorgeous, where are we going?" I purred.

I faced Tristan, sliding my hand over his thigh. It came to a stop precariously close to the bulge straining against his black slacks.

"Home," Tristan ground out through clenched teeth, his knuckles tightening on the steering wheel.

"Oh, good. I could do with a nice long, hot shower." I sighed, removing my hand from his thigh to skim it over my stomach and up over my breasts.

The ute sped up, and I bit my lip in anticipation.

Chapter Fifteen

Ellie

Tá mo chroí istigh ionat. – *My heart is in you.*

Clouds of steam billowed around my naked body and slid across the glass door and over the slick, moist rock wall at my back. Perched on a small rock jutting out of the wall, I clung to Tristan's tensed shoulders, the muscles beneath my fingertips rippling when he shifted. Legs wrapped around his waist, I clenched my thighs, drawing him closer to me, the ache within my core growing with each second, demanding he enter me. Tristan's lips stilled at my collarbone, his throaty chuckle shivering down my spine.

"Patience, mo ghrá," Tristan murmured with a knowing chuckle, feathering kisses over my collarbone and toward my nipple.

My tingling fingers speared into Tristan's wet, loose hair, and a long blissful sigh escaped my parted lips. Each caress of his lips over my sensitised skin ached; my nipples puckered, begging for his attention. As though he sensed their silent plea, Tristan's canines scrapped over my taut nipple, drawing a deep, shuddering breath from within me. His seeking mouth skimmed down, and I shuddered at the feel of his tongue darting out to tease my exquisitely sensitive classic pink flesh.

The large, smooth hand gripping my thigh drifted upward and across with slow, deliberate caresses, driving me to the edge. My core wept and tightened with need.

"Tristan." I pleaded, my body straddling that delicious edge of pain and pleasure of overly sensitive skin.

Tristan's head rose, and I fought the urge to weep with frustration. Feathering kisses along my jaw, Tristan nipped at my lip, forcing my heavy eyelids to flutter open and stare into his lavender orbs.

"Are you open to trying something new?" he whispered, his hand moving closer yet to the junction between my thighs.

I gripped his head harder, my gaze never leaving his as I nipped at his bottom lip. "Of course I am. What did you have in mind?"

His fingers slide enticingly closer to my clenched pussy. "I'd like to bite you," he murmured against my lips.

I frowned, confused. "You've bitten me before, Tristan. Why are you asking for permission to bite me now?"

Tristan smirked, and I fought to keep my eyes open when his finger brushed the tight plump nub of my clitoris.

"It's not your neck I want to bite, Ellie," Tristan murmured, his lips feathering across my jaw toward my ear, where he breathed, "I'd like to bite your breast."

His fingers stroked gentle circles over my clitoris, and I panted, my brain fogging with pleasure.

Jaw tightening, I growled. "Tristan, if you don't do something soon, I'm going into the bedroom to grab my vibrator to finish myself off. I'm wound so tight it hurts. So, for the love of my sanity, do something about it."

"Are you sure? It'll be an entirely new sensation than you're used to," Tristan warned, his finger hovering enticingly over the opening to my dripping pussy.

My fingers shackled around his hair, and I dragged his face to mine. Our lips locked, my tongue thrusting into his mouth. He met my punishing kiss with an intense one of his own.

We parted on a pant, and I ground my pussy against his exploring finger as I hissed, "I don't care, Tristan. I want you—all of you, man and beast. Now, either fuck me or get the fuck out of the shower, Tristan."

A feral light flickered in the depths of his lavender eyes. The skin beneath my tense fingers rippling as the beast that was his magic rose to the surface.

I grinned then, leaning forward to whisper into his ear, "Come and play, gorgeous."

I pressed an enticing kiss to his ear, then leaned back to stare at him through hooded eyes.

A wicked grin tugged at Tristan's usually plump lips; they'd thinned slightly, his beast now a mirage, shimmering just below the surface. Sharp fangs peaked over the top of his bottom lip, and I shivered at the sight. I released his head, sliding my hands down and across to trace the now taut skin over his cheekbones. Lips still tingling from our last kiss, I placed a light kiss to one fang and then the other. A deep purr radiated from within his chest, beckoning to my banshee. Curiosity getting the better of her, the banshee rose to the surface. A keen worked its way up my throat to slip from my swollen lips. Our magic pulsed, colliding together before merging.

We'd enjoyed sex before, but this was new; this was raw. There were no barriers, no secrets.

"More," I wept, the banshee driving my voice up an octave.

Tristan moved then. His fangs sunk deep above my aureole as his finger sunk deep within my folds. My banshee screeched her pleasure, and I gave myself over to the exquisite heat rushing through my body.

I thrust my chest forward at the first pull of his mouth, the intensity of the dragging sensation running from my breast to my wet core. Hands rising to Tristan's shoulders, I dug them into him to ground myself. Beneath my firm fingers, his muscles rippled, and I tightened, knowing how close to danger I was. His power slid beneath his skin, pressing against the skin underneath my grip.

A deep growl vibrated against my breast, and he sucked again. I groaned long and hard when he added a second finger to my tight folds, the friction obliterating the sliver of control I had over my banshee. She slammed to the surface, and I embraced her, the need riding us both. Tristan's head lifted, his fingers withdrawing from my folds to catch my hips when my legs dropped from around his waist. My feet found purchase against the course rocks behind me, and I pushed off the wall, my claws digging into his flesh, ribbons of blood seeping from beneath them. Tristan's back met the thick glass of the shower door with a bone-jarring thud. His hands gripped my arse, so my feet landed lightly on the wet floor. Fingers gripping Tristan's wet locks, I dragged his head down to mine, slamming my lips against his as I grabbed his cock in a tight fist.

Pumping him once, twice, Tristan's lips left mine, his fingers digging into the flesh of my arse cheeks as he groaned, "Fuck, Ellie."

My hands dropped to his healed shoulders, and I pushed at them. "Down. On your back," I ordered.

When a growl vibrated from deep within him, I reached for his cock once more, shackling it.

"I. Said. Down." I purred dangerously, pumping him once more so his eyes glazed over and his growl morphed into a long groan.

My hand dislodged when he obeyed, dropping to knees and onto his back. I smiled, pleased with the sight of him stretched before me, steam cocooning his body as the hot spray cascaded against my back.

I dropped to the warm stones at his feet, my black claws a stark contrast to the pale skin on his shins. I dragged them up his legs, drawing a hiss of pleasure from him. The length of his straining cock greeted me, and I leaned down to run my tongue along the length of it until I reached the tip. The silky texture of his cock slid over my moist lips and into my mouth.

My lips tightened, gripping his cock as my mouth slid down his solid cock. His hoarse cry sent a shiver of pleasure down my spine, and I reached down to cup my weeping core. I ached to have him in me.

With a pop, his cock slid from my mouth, and I slid upward, one of my breasts feathering along the length of him as I did. My right hand slithered up his taut stomach, his eight-pack straining beneath my black claws. Tristan's hands found my arse once more, his claws biting into my flesh, the sensation straddling the delicious edge that was pleasure and pain. Beneath my hands, his muscles bunched and rippled. I hissed and pushed his rising upper body back onto the stone floor and back into submission.

"Stay," I reprimanded him, and he growled at me, the garnet flecks within his lavender eyes multiplying with the intensity of his emotions.

I held his wild gaze, drawing my hips forward and allowing my weeping pussy to slid up along his twitching cock, teasing him with what awaited him.

When he made to move once more, I pressed down on his chest so his back returned to the ground as I slid the head of his cock into my opening. Tristan stilled beneath me, his eyes snapping shut, and I grinned devilishly, knowing I had him.

When I stayed still, his eyes snapped open, his heated gaze finding mine. His grip on my arse tightened in a warning, and my tight folds wept over the top of him. When I couldn't hold out anymore, I slammed down over him. Our yells of delight echoing through the bathroom.

I straddled him, my hips grinding against his pelvis. My silky folds tightened around him, gripping him with each grind of my hips. I lost myself to the rhythm.

Tristan's hands drifted from my arse cheeks and up to my breasts. The feather-light touch of his fingers trailed along their sides, his thumbs caressing my taut nipples. My hands snapped to his forearms, and I gripped them when his thumbs circled my nipples clockwise. My pussy clenched around his throbbing cock, and I arched back, grinding harder against him.

"Fuck, Ellie! Don't stop," Tristan groaned, and I grinned at his plea.

I dropped forward, my hands landing either side of his head to brace my body. The swollen folds of my core slid up and down his length, and I shuddered when the swollen head of his cock brushed over my g-spot. I slammed down with another shudder. Tristan's hands abandoned my breasts to grip my hips, his fingers digging into my flesh, encouraging me.

I lowered my upper body, so our noses touched, and I nipped at his bottom lip as my hips moved over him. Pressing my lips to his, I captured his growl of pleasure. My fingers bit into the stones beneath Tristan's head as that delicious heaviness built within my core.

Body tightening, I gripped Tristan's drenched hair. His glowing eyes met mine, drinking me in hungrily, his fangs on full display.

I leaned forward to whisper into his ear, "Come with me, gorgeous. Come with me now!"

My hips lost their rhythm with my excitement, but Tristan was there, slamming himself home, never once breaking the rhythm I'd set. A cry of ecstasy burst free from deep within me, my wet core clamping around Tristan's solid length.

Tristan's hoarse yell joined mine, his hips faltering before dropping back to the stone floor.

I slumped onto his chest, sated. Tristan's hands traced lazy circles on my back, and a small smile tugged at my lips.

"Ellie, that was incredible."

I braced myself, rising to stare down at him. "Thanks, gorgeous. You weren't so bad yourself."

He rewarded my cheeky grin with a swift smack to my arse.

With a quick peck to my swollen lips, Tristan reached up to scoop an errant strand of hair behind my ear, murmuring, "I think we should take this to the bedroom before the hot water runs out."

"Sounds like a plan to me," I smiled, my brain still fogged with pleasure.

~

Hunched over my microscope, my eyes strained and blurred. With a heavy sigh, I leaned back and scrunched my eyelids shut. Opening them once more, I rolled my shoulders back to loosen the tension that had crept into my neck and shoulders.

"You ready for a break, Brad?" I called out.

When he didn't answer, I turned to find Brad hunched over his table, his head on his arms, sound asleep. The high-pitched squeak of my chair sounded loud in the silence of the lab. I stood stretching for a moment, studying the man who'd gone from a friend to a brother in the years I'd known him. We'd spent the past five days avoiding any conversation that would inevitably lead to the elephant in the room that was my untimely demise. The tension and awkwardness between us thickened the air until I feared I would suffocate on it, but I didn't blame him for his avoidance of what would ultimately cause him heartache. He was working through this emotional trauma the best way he knew how. He'd done the same when Evanee was bed-bound. Withdrawing into himself or finding solutions to the problem was how he dealt with emotionally confronting situations. I only wished I knew how to help, but how could I when I'd been running from my death.

I slid the specimen dish I'd been studying back into the refrigeration unit before padding across the silent room. I snapped my gloves from my hands and deposited them in the closest bin. The slight tremor in my hands warned my blood sugar levels were low, and fatigue had set in. I laid my shaking hand on Brad's upper back, rubbing it in a circular motion.

"Hey, weirdo. I think it's time to take a break. We've been at it for hours now," I crooned.

With a weary grumble, Brad sat upright, shoving his hands through his auburn curls. I cringed, glad he'd had the foresight to remove his gloves before falling asleep.

"What day is it?" Brad yawned.

Hand dipping into my coat pocket, I retrieved my phone.

"It's 2 am Friday. Shit, I can't believe we've been at it that long," I groaned, wondering why Tristan hadn't come to haul my arse home by now.

"Close to forty-eight hours, nice. Time flies when your eyes are glued to the microscope. You wanna raid Erick's house for food? He has a fully stocked fridge for the humans that service the house." Brad yawned, not bothering to cover his mouth.

"Yeah, I could go with something hot. I'm surprised Tristan hasn't been badgering me, to be honest," I confessed.

"He has been quiet, hasn't he? You guys going okay?"

Brad stretched his arms overhead, then side to side, his gaze searching my face for any signs of unhappiness.

"Yeah, we're fine. Things have never been better, to be honest. The treehouse is a dream, and so is my man." I winked.

Brad's face scrunched up in revulsion. "Ew. No details, Ellie, I mean it. I don't need mental images of my sister from another mother playing doctor with her vampire boyfriend running through my head, thank you."

"Hey, you asked." I snorted. "And we don't do role play — yet." Waggling my eyebrows at him, I chuckled at his groan of despair. "You ready to present your findings to Erick and Evanee yet?" I murmured tiredly, my fingers flying over my screen as I tapped out a message to Evanee.

"Yeah. We may as well address the elephant in the room while we're at it." Brad stared pointedly at me, his voice gruff with emotion.

"I know, I know. I promise we'll talk about it," I agreed, my hand moving up to silence his retort. "I think it's something we should probably talk about as a group with everyone present."

A shimmering portal doubled in size at the centre of the laboratory, silencing Brad's response.

"They live." Evanee's dramatic announcement preceded her body.

In blue scrubs and a white lab coat, Evanee stepped through the portal, her white hair glittering beneath the fluorescent lights overhead. In the room behind her, I caught sight of a familiar figure.

"Hey, Steve." I waved cheerfully, and he rewarded me with an exuberant wave of my own.

"Hey, Ellie. Good to see you again, love. You're looking beautiful as ever. Hiya, Brad," the round security officer greeted.

"Evening, Steve," Brad greeted with a yawn and a small wave.

Evanee turned to face Steve. "You'll message me if someone needs me?"

"Go on, princess. I'll hold the fort," he nodded.

"Thanks, Steve, you're the best."

Evanee turned to face us once more, the outer edges of the portal beginning to shrink. I frowned at Steve's figure or at least the wavering outline of his body.

What the hell?

My gaze focused on the room, and I stepped forward, my face coming close to the portal. With a deep inhale, my banshee swirled lazily within me, enticed by the delicious scent drifting through the portal.

"Ellie, what are you doing?" Evanee laughed, the portal sealing shut.

"I thought I saw… Never mind." I sighed, rubbing at my temples. "I must be more tired than I thought."

Evanee's assessing gaze roved over my body. She remained silent for a second, then shrugged.

"Well, I better get Erick. He's chucking a hissy fit at my sudden departure from the lab," Evanee grumped, rolling her eyes skyward at her mate's theatrics.

A portal materialised near the door, and I chuckled, knowing full well what she meant. Tristan's curses would likely still be ringing in my ears if I'd pulled the same stunt.

Erick's broad shoulders and long deep blue denim-clad legs materialised through the portal, his deep melodic voice filling the lab. "I don't throw hissy fits, Evanee. That would be your department."

Brad and I chuckled at Erick's wry expression, and I turned my head in time to see Evanee stick her tongue out at him. I shook my head at the two of them. My gaze darted to the figure behind Erick, and I grinned. At six foot two, my man was all grace and power hidden behind his fine-looking, lean figure. Memories of our time spent in bed this past Sunday tumbled through my mind, and my body grew heavy.

My gaze found him, and his smirk told me he knew exactly what I'd been thinking and what my body wanted.

"Evening, mo ghrá. You've finally surfaced," his voice wrapped around me, caressing my body better than the finest silk.

Tristan's arms opened, and I stepped into his embrace, breathing him in.

"I missed you," I whispered seductively into his ear.

"Liar. You were too focused to know what day it was."

He chuckled, pressing a kiss into the side of my head.

"But for the record, I missed you too."

My stomach growled, and I leaned back. "Tell me you brought food, please?"

"He didn't, but I did," Jordan's deep voice boomed cheerfully throughout the lab. I stepped out of Tristan's embrace and around him to seek the giant of a man that was Evanee's guard, friend, and mentor.

"I could kiss you right now." I beamed, bouncing on the balls of my feet at the two plates of steaming food in his hand.

"But she won't, or I'll have to rip your head off," Tristan growled.

"Calm down, old man," Brad chuckled, patting Tristan's shoulder as he passed by. "She still loves you. You just don't rank at the top of her needs list right now. You could have a group of girls walk in naked right now, and I'd still walk past them for that plate of food. Jordan, buddy, best mate in the entire world, you shouldn't have," Brad teased, inhaling the delicious aroma wafting from where Jordan stood.

"Hey, I thought I was your best mate." Evanee feigned outrage.

"Hey, no food, no best mate title for you," Brad retorted, his eyes glued to the plate of food in Jordan's enormous hands. "Come to Daddy."

"Who do you think told him to bring the food," Evanee muttered beneath her breath.

I rose onto the balls of my feet, and Jordan bent his legs to accommodate my short stature. With a quick peck to Jordan's cheek, I ignored Tristan's hiss of warning; instead, I plucked the plate from Jordan's large, russet hand. The delicious savoury aroma of Shepard's pie and steamed vegetables piled high on the plate filled the room, and I grinned at the giant, earning a wink in return.

I puckered my lips at Tristan as I bypassed him and headed for the table at the centre of the room. It was the only surface we hadn't used and would be the easiest to sanitize when we finished. Hooking my foot around the stool tucked underneath, I slid it out and sat heavily, my plate barely on the table before I shovelled my first mouthful into my open mouth. Brad stepped up to the other side of the table, his mouth already full before he sat. Eyelids drifting shut, I savoured the herbs and spices dancing across my palate.

Swallowing heavily, I muttered, "Oh, this is good. Have you started cooking again, Evie?"

"I have. How d'you know?"

"The mince, it's the same as the one you used to do for your lasagne." I grinned, then shovelled the next fork-load of food into my mouth.

"You three are as obsessed with food as each other." Erick chuckled, making his way toward where Brad and I sat, followed by Evanee.

"Only Evanee's cooking. Mine doesn't touch sides with her palate, and Ellie's banned from the kitchen," Brad spoke around a mouthful of food.

My fork stalled at my lips, an objection at the tip of my tongue when Brad pointed his fork at me. "Don't even try denying it, Ell. You and the kitchen don't go hand in hand unless you're making margaritas or mojitos."

I shrugged, then focused on my next mouthful.

Tristan leaned down, placing a soft kiss on the crown of my head. "In that case, I'd like to place an order for a corpse reviver when you're next in the kitchen."

I frowned and craned my neck to frown up at him. "What the hell is a corpse reviver? Please tell me I don't have to mix blood with vodka or something because that's gross."

Tristan laughed. "No, it's a cocktail from the nineteenth and twentieth century. I've not seen it around since before prohibition ended, but I hear it's making a comeback. It comprises cognac, calvados or brandy as you know it, and sweet vermouth. I'd add a couple of drops of blood for extra flavouring."

"Bloody hell, I haven't heard of those since my last trip to America. Come to think of it, that was around the time prohibition ended." Jordan rubbed his chin, deep in thought.

"Man, you guys are a bunch of old farts," Evanee groaned, then squeaked in protest when Erick delivered a sharp slap to her arse. "Hey! It's true. Don't shoot the messenger."

Evanee rubbed at the spot where Erick slapped her.

Erick smirked at her before taking pity and sliding his hand beneath hers to rub at the spot.

"I'll show you how old I am later. For now, we have something a little more pressing to focus on. Ellie, you're the one who called for this meeting, so let's begin."

Alchemy

Transmutation: Characterisation of alchemy.

<u>Understood as:</u>

Chemical changes

Physiological changes when passing from

sickness to health

The transformation from old age to youth or

earthly to supernatural.

– Tristan Cathbad.

Chapter Sixteen

Tristan

Ellie's eyes widened, her mouth full to brimming. Brad interjected smoothly, giving me the impression he'd done this before.

"We have an update on the samples. We managed to isolate the different DNA strands from the samples you took from the original victims autopsied before your attack, Evanee. We compared the samples with your blood while you were in your coma."

Brad's fork bobbed in Evanee's direction before he dropped it back to his plate to scoop up more shepherd's pie.

"You were right, Evanee. The original strain from the male and first female victim only contained vampiric DNA; there were no signs of reaper DNA. The second female you autopsied had signs of the reaper and vampiric DNA in her bloodstream, but only a minute amount, not enough to cause a change."

Ellie took a swig of water. Her smooth, elegant throat working to get the water down.

Mouth no longer full, Ellie followed on from Brad's assessment. "The rest of the DNA comprised human and animal strains, with one other strain attached to the human. But we can't identify it. The animal strains were mostly pig and Aurelia Aurita—aka the…."

"The moon jellyfish," I murmured, surprised by the analysis.

"That's right, gorgeous. You get brownie points for that one. It's not surprising that they used the Aurelia Aurita as part of the base for the creature. The genome studies on the creatures are yielding some interesting results. Their ability to evolve from stationary polyp to a full-fledged swimming medusa are of particular interest. As for the other strain, well, I've isolated and replicated it. The strain is weak, but it's there. We're hoping one of you old farts might recognise it," Ellie teased, and I growled at her playfully.

'*I couldn't help myself. You brought it on yourself, honestly. Talking about prohibition and old cocktails. What did you think was going to happen?*'

Ellie's chuckle shimmered through my mind.

'*I guess Erick won't be the only one proving his youth when he gets home. I believe you may need some education,*' I purred, purposely stirring the banshee within her — seducing her.

My lips twitched at the subtle shiver of lust working its way over her body. Across the bench, Jordan grumbled something about feeling old these days. I ignored him and tracked Ellie across the room, where she retrieved a sample from the fridge. Not bothering with a microscope, she handed the sample to Erick.

"I won't bother showing you my slide. I'll give you the original sample from the male Evanee autopsied. It's the best sample to start with." When Erick frowned at her, Ellie gave a one-shouldered shrug. "It doesn't contain any reaper DNA. You guys have enhanced eyesight, so there's no need to put it beneath the microscope." Ellie slipped into her seat, her attention swapping to the half-finished meal before her.

Twisting off the cap, Erick sniffed at the contents, frowning hard after a second. He extended the small vial toward me, and I took it. I lifted it toward the light and concentrated on the cells within. Despite being refrigerated, the cells vibrated. It most definitely wasn't human. Sniffing at the vial, as Erick had, my instincts flared to life.

My arm shot out to Jordan, who promptly lifted the vial to his nose. His head reared away from the vial, his amber eyes glowing.

"I recognise the scent, but I can't put my finger on it," Erick frowned. "It's too weak."

"As do I. It's faint, but it's there. Whatever it is, it's no friend to vampires," I pondered.

"Jordan, can I have that for a second, please?" Evanee stepped forward, extending her hand to him.

Without hesitating, Jordan extended the vial toward her. She plucked the vial from his enormous hands, and raised it toward the light and frowned.

"Why are the cells vibrating like that?" Evanee looked toward me and then to Erick.

When neither of us could explain, she lifted the vial to her nose and sniffed delicately. Evanee's nose scrunched at whatever she smelled. A tiny electric blue spark zapped between the fingers holding the vial and into the blood. She lifted the vial toward the light again, and her eyebrows rose. I stepped forward to inspect it.

The cells within were vibrating at triple the rate they'd been previously.

Astonished, I studied Evanee. "What did you do?"

"I don't know," she murmured, bringing the vial back to her nose. "Oh, yuck! That smells like a wet dog that's just rolled in cow crap. I thought I smelled it before, but now I can definitely smell it." She gagged.

I plucked the vial from her fingers, ignoring her protest as I sniffed at the vial again.

"She's right; it does reek of wet dog. Bloody hell, it's lycanthropy," I stared at Erick, my eyebrows doing their best to join my hairline. "How did Jared get his hands on lycanthropy infected blood? The Were community is as careful as we are with our blood, not to mention their ability to blend in with the humans." I handed the vial back to Erick, who plucked it from my fingers gingerly.

"That must have been what Brian meant about Sebastian having a basement full of supernatural creatures. We assumed it was vampires and potentially reapers, but what if it extends to the other side? What if he's mixing DNA from living supernatural beings with the dead?"

Brad slid his empty plate forward with a soft snort. "No offence, Erick, but it's not a matter of 'what if'. Sebastian has combined the DNA. These samples prove it."

Ellie's plate joined Brad's, and she rose, swiping the petri dish from the benchtop and replacing it in the refrigeration unit. Ellie found her seat again, her piercing green gaze drifting between each of us. Intelligence shone in their sparkling depths, and my groin tightened at the glow emanating from within her. She was in her element. Here in this laboratory in the wee hours of the morning was where she belonged, where she excelled, and I loved her more for it.

You think I'm hot now; you should see me when I'm nearing a breakthrough for whatever virus I'm working on.

Ellie caressed my mind, her brush sensual and loving.

Her gaze found mine, and she winked before leaning forward onto her forearms.

"The virus has been developed in multiple layers. Genetic strands added and removed masterfully. Brad couldn't have done a better job himself." Ellie yawned.

"I'm not sure if that's a compliment or an insult." Brad sniffed.

Ellie stared at Brad pointedly, her eyebrows raised. "What I mean is there are few people in Australia with the ability to create a virus this complex. Aside from the human, supernatural and animal DNA, I isolated crystal structures commonly associated with the Murray Valley Encephalitis Virus."

"Is it possible that one of the patients could have been infected before Jared's virus?" Leaning my hip against the steel bench, I watched my mate rub at her brows.

Brad sighed tiredly, and he massaged the bridge of his nose. "No. The creature's DNA held traces of encephalitis, and so did the victims. It's as if they used it as part of the creature's programming."

"Encephalitis attacks the nervous system. By combining the base structure of the Murray Valley Virus with the necrotic and aggressive nature of vampiric genetics, it gave the creature its target — the brain and spinal cord," Ellie explained.

"And the creature's ability to hide from view and devour the subject's soul would have been courtesy of reaper DNA. So, where does the Lycanthropy come into it?" Evanee mused.

My gaze flicked toward the refrigerator and the sample sitting within. My brain conjured and discarded ideas until it settled on an alarming theory.

My throat constricted with revulsion. "Life and creation." I shuddered.

My gaze snapped to Erick's, my jaw clenching and unclenching. "They needed the supernatural DNA that would give the creature the ability to infect and create. Lycanthropy is the light to our dark. We are the moon, and they the sun. Our ability to procreate has been strenuous at best. Your mother and father were amongst

the few born vampires able to procreate. A vampires'
ability to create life without devouring it first has
diminished over the centuries."

"So have the reapers. Our numbers have dropped
since Chavas' disappearance," Evanee added.

"But not the wolf clans. My sources say their
numbers have remained the same," Jordan added. When
Evanee, Brad and Ellie stared at him, he shrugged.
"What? Don't tell me you think I got my general status
because of my big muscles and good looks?"

Evanee snorted, and I spoke over the top of what
was no doubt a smart-ass comment. "So Sebastian gets
his hands on a wolf, hoping it'll be enough to give his
creature life. The question is, was it incubated and
birthed from a female wolf, or did they combine the
DNA and grow it in a test tube?"

The room plunged into silence. Ellie and Evanee paled, horror tightening the corners of their eyes.

"The pain and violation that poor woman would have experienced…." Brad swallowed heavily, his fists tightening at whatever image his imagination had erected.

My gut tightened at the thought. Distress radiated from Ellie's hunched shoulders. Her top teeth bit down on downturned lips, her anxiety ratcheting up the longer she thought about my question.

"Jordan, I need you to reach out to your sources in Davide's clan. See if there have been any disappearances or deaths we haven't heard about," Erick ordered, his shoulders rigid beneath his tension.

"I'll try. Things are still strained from Belle, but I may have one or two who might swap information. You good for me to divulge our numbers to them?" Jordan clarified.

Erick's gave a brisk nod. "Yes. It may pave the way for a meeting between Davide and me."

"Who is Davide and Belle, and why are things so tense between you?" Evanee gazed up at Erick, her curiosity getting the better of her.

Ellie's eyes held the same question.

Erick's lips thinned, and I spoke up, understanding the guilt of Belle's death still lingered despite the time that had passed. "Davide is the alpha for both the Acrasin City clan and Murder Point Bay's clan. It's a rarity to be alpha of two clans, but he makes it work. Bella was his youngest sister. She was murdered five years ago."

Jordan's thunderous growl vibrated through the room. "Murder! Fuck, that little prick butchered her. She was a sweet, naïve sixteen-year-old girl."

Memories of that night stirred within me, and my beast's menacing growl at the starkness and brutality of that night shivered across my body. I slammed my mental shields in place, not wanting Ellie to glimpse the haunting images. Across from me, Erick's cold, arrogant mask slid into place, his green eyes losing the smile they'd contained upon entering the lab.

Evanee's body tensed before it hurtled past Ellie's slumped figure, stopping at the metal sink across the room. The sounds of dry heaving filled the lab as Evanee wretched repeatedly, distant memories of her not-so-long-ago trauma resurfacing.

Erick cursed, his hand scrubbing over his face.

Ellie's and Brad's astonished gazes jumped from Evanee's slumped over body to my face, then to Erick, and finally to Jordan before returning to me expectantly.

I refused to meet Ellie's seeking gaze; instead, I focused on a point beyond her shoulder, guilt a living monster slicing at me.

"Five years ago, we hosted one of the royal families from Europe at the Acrasin manor. Erick was to negotiate the terms of their return to Australia after their exile during World War II. Long story short, they deemed it necessary to bring their son with them," I gritted out.

"The little prick, as we refer to him, makes what Desmond did look like child's play," Jordan spat.

I nodded in agreement. "When we enter another master's territory, their laws are adopted by the visiting party. To break them is considered an offence and carries severe penalties depending on the law you break."

Erick approached the sink cautiously, where he laid an open palm on Evanee's back. Her body jerked as though she'd been slapped but didn't move from beneath Erick's touch.

Erick fumed, his jaw clenching beneath the onslaught of memories flooding his mind.

"It wasn't until our meeting the second night that we realised the little prick wasn't in residence. He'd dodged the guards we'd assigned to him during his stay. The three of us went on the hunt, but it was too late. Unbeknown to anyone, Belle had snuck out to meet with friends at a local restaurant. She was on her way home when he attacked her."

Evanee stood motionless over the steel sink. Her shoulders hunched, and her back bent.

"By the time Erick found her, the damage done to her body was beyond healing, even for a werewolf. I tried the best I could, but there was too much blood loss, and she couldn't shift."

I shuddered at the gore and blood that'd pooled around Belle's fragile and broken body. The silver knives he'd used to dissect her discarded beside her, as he'd fed from us. The feeling of the warmth of her blood coating my arms, hands, and chest still covered my skin in my mind's eye.

"We raced her home, but she died in Tristan's arms one block from her house. Davide was distraught, and rightly so. I delivered that little prick to Davide's front door the second I got my hands on him."

Erick's harsh bark of laughter slashed at my eardrums, and I cringed at it.

"He thought he'd get away with her murder because she was a werewolf. His parents thought the same thing until I dragged him out by his hair kicking and screaming and threw him through the open front door of Davide's house."

"It's been over twelve years, Erick. We need to heal this rift, or we'll be facing a battle on two fronts," I warned.

"You think I don't know that, Tristan. I've tried on more than one occasion. But how can I ask him to forgive me when it took me decades to come to terms with Sophia's death," Erick snapped, his teeth bared in a warning.

"Sophia's death was different, Erick. It took you at least two decades to hunt the man who killed her. You delivered the young prince to Davide's doorstep. You gave him the choice of the justice he felt was best for the death of his sister. You need to forgive yourself if Davide is to forgive you."

"Enough!" Erick slashed at the air with a stiff hand, his power rippling from him to heat the room. Ellie and Brad shifted in their seats, sweat beading across their foreheads. "I'm done talking about this tonight."

"We need to break Chava's curse, and sooner rather than later. She's the key to all of this." Evanee sniffed, her voice thick with unshed tears.

Her pale hands gripped the sink beneath them, the metal groaning beneath her strength.

Evanee's head lifted and tilted to the left so that her electric blue eyes found mine.

"She's the light to Death's darkness. They ruled as one for millennia. If my great-grandfather oversaw the people of death, then it'd be logical to assume Chavas ruled over the people of life. We need balance. We save Chavas; we unite all the species once again."

My mouth opened to agree with her reasoning when Ellie's tired voice overrode my response.

"I'm too tired to deal with this political cluster fuck. I need to sleep for my brain to process what you're all saying. Not to mention Brad's about to have kittens if we don't discuss my impending doom at some point."

The occupants of the room cringed at her blunt words, but Ellie ignored us.

"Brad, you're in no state to drive. You have two choices, you can camp out in one of our spare rooms at the treehouse, or you can crash at Evanee's place if they're okay with it." Ellie pointed toward a tired Evanee and an amused Erick.

My heart tightened with joy at her bossy attitude. She'd not bothered to ask if I was okay with Brad staying over, and it sent a thrill down my spine knowing she felt comfortable enough to invite guests to our house.

"Of course, Brad's welcome. The suite you used during your last stay is ready for you to use any time you need it," Erick offered.

"Thanks, guys. I'll camp out at Evanee and Erick's tonight. My ute's parked there." Brad sighed heavily. "It'll be easier to get home when I wake up."

"Great. Home time it is then."

Ellie hopped off her stool, and I stepped up to her, a smile tugging at my lips.

There was a tiny shift in power within the lab before a portal expanded from a speck. In the background, the grey-brown bark of a familiar Red Cedar came into focus. My gaze found Evanee's, and she gave a small, sad smile.

"I thought it might be quicker and easier for you two this way. It won't take her long to pass out," Evanee murmured.

With a brief nod, I scooped Ellie into my arms. Her weary head rested on my chest, and I tightened my grip on her. I stepped through the portal, and the power vibrating within the room vanished along with the portal.

"Let's get you into the shower, mo ghrá, and then bed," I crooned.

Ellie yawned loudly, not bothering to hide it behind her hand. "Sounds good, gorgeous."

My grip tightened a smidgen more, and I moved toward the ensuite bathroom.

Chapter Seventeen

Forearms flat to the mat, my triceps bore most of my weight, while my legs remained motionless above me. With interlaced fingers and my thumb-pads pressed together, I maintained my headstand. Eyes closed against the chaos that was the world; I allowed my mind to still, banishing thoughts of Ellie's impending death and the information she'd imparted in the early hours of Friday morning. I'd wanted nothing more than to curl up beside her as she slept all day yesterday and today, but my beast snarled and snapped at me, impatient and eager for sacrifice. The All-Father, or Death as we all now knew him, ignited something within me the night he'd visited, and I was struggling to keep my magic contained. I was struggling to contain my beast.

"You hold that handstand any longer, Elf Boy, and your head might pop off."

A cheeky feminine chuckle reached my ears, and I fought the urge to snort at it.

"You'd do well to practice yoga and meditation, Evanee. Who knows, it might help with those temper tantrums you're so prone to," I murmured, keeping my eyes shut.

Evanee's indelicate snort was the only response she gave. Abdominals straining, I slowly lowered my legs back to the ground before dropping my knees to the mat. Fingers spreading, I pushed myself into an upside-down V-shape. I stepped one foot forward and then the next until they met my grounded hands. Finally, I rose and allowed my eyes to open before I turned to face Evanee.

"What can I do for you, Evanee?" I stretched my arms forward and above my head, studying my future queen.

She'd finger-combed her snow-white hair into a loose ponytail and looked a far cry from her usual professional self.

"Truth?" Evanee whispered, staring down at her feet.

"Speak the truth, Evanee. I'll only sense your lies."

Evanee approached the mat wearily, and I held myself still when she finally met my gaze.

"I'm worried about Ellie. I'm scared I don't have the experience or power to save her. I'm worried I won't be able to save Ellie or Chavas. Death believes you have the knowledge and power to guide me, but what if it's not enough? Half the time, I'm not even sure whether you even like me or are merely tolerating me because of Erick and Ellie. How the hell do you work with someone who merely tolerates you?" she exclaimed.

"You'll find, Evanee, there are things in life we'd rather not do but are forced to do out of necessity. There will be times where you'll be forced to play the devil's advocate to achieve overall peace. It's what's in your heart that matters. And for the record, I don't tolerate you or dislike you; quite the opposite in fact."

I smirked at Evanee's slacked jaw expression at my confession.

"Seriously? Are you screwing around with me, or are you serious?"

She narrowed her eyes at me dubiously.

"I respect you, Evanee. I know you have the potential to become one of the greatest queens of my time. Life has dealt you cards most could never bear, and yet here you stand, asking for help from someone you felt merely tolerated you. You're empathetic and brave. If only you would control that temper of yours," I finished pointedly.

Evanee's throaty laugh echoed the empty gym.

"You have me there. I'm trying. You've gotta give me brownie points for that." She shrugged.

"True. To think, I thought my days of dealing with ill-tempered children had passed with Erick." I rolled my eyes.

"Hey, I'm not a child. In human years I'm nearly thirty," Evanee objected.

"Evanee, that's a baby in my eyes, compared to my two millennia." I stepped closer to her, guilt squeezing my gut. "I have a truth of my own if you'll hear me out? There's only one other soul I've told, and that's Ellie. But considering how events are playing out, I feel it might be time I shared it with you."

"Should I get my pillow and nail polish? We could swap truths, braid hair and get all chummy while we're at it. You know, all chick like," Evanee teased with a bright smile.

I snorted and shook my head. "Trust you to make a joke out of me baring my soul to you."

"Hey, I wasn't joking; I was relieving the tension. Get it right, Elf Boy." Her hand on her heart in mock outrage, she grinned before dropping onto the mat. "Please continue to pour your heart out to me."

I shook my head at the nickname she'd stuck me with. "You realise if anyone other than you ever calls me Elf Boy, I'll be forced to rip their hearts out. I can't have the guards calling me that or the fledglings."

"Hey, that's my nickname for you. Anyone else calls you that, I'll stand right beside you with a magnifying glass while you rip their heart out. I mean, someone needs to show you where the heart's located, you being an old fella and all." Evanee snorted, amused at whatever image was floating in her mind.

Exasperated, my steely gaze fixed on her. "Remind me to give you another training session. I'll show you just how quickly this *old fella* moves. As for this truth, it's been weighing heavily on my consciouses since your death. Before I can divulge this truth, I need to explain something."

My gaze darted from her wide, innocent eyes to a point over her shoulder. I braced myself and stared at her once more, my confession heavy on my lips.

"I've known Death since I was a young boy, I'd say maybe five or six, only I never realised it was Death until that night at Brad's and Ellie's house."

Evanee frowned in thought, and her frown lightened to surprise. "You called him Dagda."

"I am. And, they thought it'd I nodded. "That's right. I knew him as The All-Father or Dagda. Your Great Grandmother was known as Morrigan."

"Wait, how's that even possible? You're referring to the old gods—the Celtic Gods. It makes no sense. My great-grandfather's not life. That was, or should I say is, Chavas."

"I am. And, they thought it'd be funny to trick the humans and have a bit of fun, I believe. But that's a story for another time, one I'm sure Death would indulge you with." My hand cut through the air with impatience. "Do you know what my full title is, Evanee?"

Evanee shook her head.

"I'm known by some as Tristan Cathbad, son of the druid Cathbad, who sat at the side of cursed King Conor MacNess of Ulster. I am claíomh to his Royal Highness, Erick Tenebris, and chosen soothsayer by the Dagada himself." I paused for a moment, allowing my title to sink in. "I'm Death's soothsayer, and to some extent, I was Chava's soothsayer too, until she disappeared. As a young druid boy, I was gifted with prophetic dreams tied to the supernatural world. My first dream was of your great-grandfather walking the fields of a kingdom my mother and I were visiting. I won't bore you with the details of that dream. There have been many more since that day, most have come to pass, and some I shudder to think about being fulfilled."

Silence descended over the gym, my thoughts drifting to rivers of blood and gore. A shiver of dread ran up my spine. There were some prophetic dreams I prayed would be averted, or at the very least that I would no longer be upon this earth if they came to pass.

"Tristan, you need to finish your story because where my mind's drifting, it isn't a good place." Dread laced Evanee's quiet voice.

"I wrote the original prophecy Reagan and Erick found," I confessed at last.

Horror flooded Evanee's eyes, and I cringed when her mouth opened, then closed. I barrelled on, hoping to explain myself.

"I had no knowledge of who the woman in my dream was, only that she would be Erick's greatest love. I wrote one prophesy, but it was copied by someone and given to Erick's ancestors. Someone twisted the words to finish the prophecy when they no doubt tried to copy it and were interrupted. I swear to you, Evanee, I didn't know it was you until your mortal death. But I'll tell you what I told Ellie. The dream was vivid, as though this prophecy needed to be fulfilled. I remember waking happy and excited there would be a queen as fierce as the woman in my dreams. She sat on an enormous black throne made of flesh and bones with a crown of clasping misted hands and ruby droplets scattered around it."

Evanee swallowed hard at my description. "I know the throne you just described."

"You do?"

Evenee nodded, her glazed eyes staring off into the distance trapped within her memory.

I pressed on, knowing she needed to hear the rest. "Mist crept from beneath the throne. There were obscured hands reaching from within it, much like it did in the forest that night you and Erick fought."

I focused my pleading eyes on Evanee, praying she'd forgive me for having kept this secret for so long. When she remained silent, I continued my description of my dream, unable to stop myself.

"Erick sat beside you, and Evanee, he was magnificent. He sat on a blood-red throne; it appeared to be made of blood. A crown of blue and gold flames circled his head with sapphires scattered through it. A female body lay on her side at his feet. There were ribbons of blood running over her. She'd shift from skeletal remains to a fully formed human body, only to be stripped to the bone again by Erick's flames."

My throat tightened when Evanee bowed her head.

"Evanee, the love and happiness on Erick's face when he gazed at you was breathtaking. And while I couldn't see your face, I felt your love and joy in that moment. You two were happy; you were complete. It's how I know you can do what Death's asked. It's how I know you can save Ellie."

The words stopped coming, and I waited with a weariness that increased with each passing second of silence. I studied the crown of Evanee's snow-white head, waiting patiently for what I'd revealed to sink in.

A delicate sniff sounded, and my eyebrows rose at it.

Is she crying? Please don't let her be crying.

"Evanee, are you okay? Do I need to fetch Erick?" I glanced at the door and then back to Evanee, concern and horror tightening my shoulders and neck.

"No, Tristan. Don't bother Erick; he's busy with a conference call. Thank you." Her voice was thick with emotion and tears. "I've spent the past few months wondering how the hell I would know if Erick truly loved me or whether it was because of some damned prophecy a random person wrote."

Evanee's head lifted, and her wet eyes met mine. She rubbed at her tears with her palm, and I gave in and approached the mat to sit beside her.

"You're one of the few people I know who wouldn't speak a load of rubbish to placate me or anyone else. Weirdly, knowing you were the one to receive and write the prophecy is oddly comforting. Did we really seem happy?"

Evanee electric blue gaze swept over my face, and I smiled fondly. A relief so profound seized my heart, and I cleared my throat, fighting the tears of gratitude at her forgiveness.

"You were happy and in love, Evanee. I felt nothing but love emanating from you both. You're not angry with me?” I checked, incredulous she’d remained calm this entire time.

Evanee smiled through her tears. “No, Elf Boy, I’m not angry. Of course, I can’t speak for Erick when he finds out you’ve kept this from him this entire time. But don’t worry, I’ll put in a good word for you.”

I barked a laugh at her and slung my arm around her shoulder to give her a quick squeeze.

“I’m relieved, Tristan. More than you’ll ever know.” A stray tear escaped down the wet path of her cheeks, and I squeezed her shoulder once more.

“I’m glad.” I smiled warmly at her, glad she was Erick’s mate and Ellie’s best friend.

Without her, I might have missed my chance to meet Ellie and see Erick find his happiness.

A soft, menacing growl shivered through the air followed by a pulse of heat, and I looked up to see Erick standing tall in the doorway.

"Anyone mind explaining why my mate is crying and refusing to respond to me telepathically? And while you're at it, you can explain why you have your arm slung around her shoulder?"

"You can keep your savage dogs at bay, sexy. Elf Boy and I were having some bonding time. I told him to bring pillows and nail polish, but you know how forgetful he can be." Evanee shrugged her truth and lie, drawing a frown from Erick.

"I know you lied just then, but for the life of me, I can't seem to tell which part of that sentence was a lie."

Our laughter trickled out at Erick's confusion.

"That would be the last part of that sentence," I chuckled. "Evanee and I were discussing—" Evanee spoke over me.

"We were discussing whether I'd be able to save Ellie."

Evanee wiped at her wet cheeks, standing, so my arm dropped from her shoulder. She turned to cast a pointed look at me.

"Okay, but I can sense there's something else you're not telling me, mic luptător. What is it and why?"

Erick's arms opened, and Evanee stepped into them, rising to the balls of her bare feet to press a soft kiss to his lips.

"Leave it, Erick. It's for another night. Tristan can share what we talked about when I'm working, and there's not so much drama surrounding us."

"Coward," I hissed at Evanee, standing with one fluid motion.

"I'm not a coward, Tristan. It's self-preservation. There's only so much crying a girl can do in one night without feeling like death warmed up. Not to mention, I think Erick deserves the opportunity to digest it in private," Evanee snapped, and I rolled my eyes at her.

And there's that temper. Heaven help me.

My hand rose in surrender, and I shrugged at Erick. "It would seem I have my orders. I will defer to my future queen's decision."

Erick smirked at me, hugging Evanee closer. "Who's the coward now?"

"Think what you will." My eyebrows rose in a challenge, but inwardly I was more than a little grateful to Evanee for her distraction. "Now, Evanee, let's see if we can devise a plan to present to my mate. We're running out of time. Did Death say anything that you think might be of use?"

Evanee turned her back to Erick but remained within the circle of his arms. The subtle change in her body language drew my attention. The slight tension present before my confession was melting before my eyes. I wasn't the only one to notice the change. Erick gazed down at the crown of Evanee's head, his eyes widening subtly and the cords in his forearms moving as he tightened his hold on Evanee. Pride and hope warred within me at the sight.

"To cut a long story short, Death reminded me I'm his descendent, and along with devouring and reaping souls, there are perks. He mentioned my connection to Ellie and how he found mental connections fascinating."

Evanee studied me, her electric blue eyes boring into whatever soul I had left after all these millennia.

"Did he now?" Erick murmured, pressing a kiss to the top of Evanee's head.

Evanee's lips quirked, but her focus remained on me. "He thought you'd be able to help, Tristan."

"Did he say anything else you feel might be important?" I quizzed her.

Evanee's head stopped mid-shake. "Come to think of it. He did mention I would be responsible for reaping Ellie's soul or part of it."

My mind plucked random thoughts and bits of past knowledge I'd not thought about in centuries, discarding them as quickly as they'd appeared.

The beast within purred impatiently, and I shut my eyes, rolling my neck in an attempt to keep the elemental side of me in check. My power seeped through my shields, and my ears pricked at the sound of a shocked inhalation.

An image of an odd room with multiple doors flashed before my eyes. I frowned, noting its round shape and the glass ceiling above. Eyes still shut; my head twitched to the right, trying to decipher what I was witnessing.

It would seem the universe is not done with me yet.

An image of a blonde, sullen teenager staring wide-eyed at me slid into my mind. Recognition flared through me, and my eyes snapped open, colliding with Evanee's shocked ones.

"Do you have a sullen teenage daughter stomping around a round room?"

"She's not sullen. She's moody." Evanee replied, shocked. "And she's not my daughter; she's a version of me. How the hell did you enter my mind without my permission?"

I ignored her question, my mind spinning from what could only be a gift. "Where do all those doors lead?" I demanded.

Eyes narrowing with anger, Evanee hesitated for a second, her jaw clenching and unclenching.

"Each door contains a memory or a link to someone. If I share a blood bond with someone, a window appears in the glass ceiling of my mind. The window gives me the option of dismissing it or creating a door to link us permanently. Now, how the hell did you break through my wards?"

Again, I ignored her question, choosing to focus on the similarities of how our minds worked. For each memory, a leaf grew on the branches of my mind. Each branch belonged to an individual I shared a connection with. My beast roamed those branches, protecting each of them.

"We'll use that to our advantage," I muttered distractedly.

"Use what to our advantage, Tristan?"

Erick's exasperation drew my attention back into the gym.

"We'll use Evanee's mind as the halfway point— a meeting place. You'll reap Ellie's soul, but instead of sending her to Death, you'll bring her to me. We'll use your mind as a connecting point." I explained, praying to the All-Father and the Great Queen that it'd work.

Evanee's body stilled as only the living dead could. "That's easier said than done, Elf Boy. I'd need to share a connection with you."

"That's fine." I dismissed with a wave of my hand. "We had a breakthrough of sorts moments before. Exchanging blood should be easy enough." I shrugged, unperturbed.

A deep, dark wave of magic pulsed from Evanee's taut body, washing over and through me. It tugged at the magic deep within me. A shudder ran the length of my body, and I struggled to contain my beast. I'd not experienced this sensation since my fledgling years. The skin across my shoulder blades stretched and settled, and I rotated my neck from side to side to ease the stiffness.

"You never answered my question, Tristan. And we both know if it were that simple, it would be performed all the time."

Evanee enunciated each word.

"Like calls to like, Evanee. Power as ancient as ours cares little for barriers." I shrugged.

With a quick pat against Erick's arms, Evanee stepped from them. Erick's arms lingered beside her hips.

"I'd be allowing you into a place sacred to me, Tristan. I'd need to trust you implicitly." Anger simmered in every word. "And judging by what just happened, I'm wondering if I can." Evanee's voice bounced off the gym walls, despite the quietness of her words.

"If Erick can trust me, I don't see why you can't." I stiffened, my gaze fixing on hers intently.

She prowled around me, an elongated talon trailing the back of my neck where the skin lay stretched tight against my beast within. I shivered at the power seeping into my flesh in its wake. Erick's mouth opened to object, his fists clenching at the sight of his mate touching another male.

Evanee placed a taloned finger to her lips. "Shhh, Erick. This is between Tristan and me."

The same dark, primal magic I'd felt emanating off Death seeped from Evanee's body, washing over me in waves. My beast longed for freedom, and I ground my teeth against the internal assault, my head aching from the pressure of my clenched jaw. My insides cramped and seized against the onslaught of my magic.

"Stop now, Evanee. You're tempting something you have no comprehension of," I warned with a deep-bellied hiss so low it turned into a growl.

"Oh, I can see what's sitting beneath your skin, Elf Boy. I may not have always seen him, but I can see him as clear as day now. He's fascinating," she purred in that otherworldly voice that often accompanied that bottomless magic she housed within her.

Evanee's head angled to the side, and she studied me as a hawk might study its prey.

Obsidian lightning flashed across her pupils, electric blue and gold veins rising to break the opal surface, only to disappear again. Magic coated her skin, a mercurial mist, and I wondered how much sway her ancient magic held over her at this moment.

"Evanee, don't do this. I don't want to have to choose between the two of you," Erick pleaded.

Evanee's head turned to the side. "Erick, no one's asking you to choose between anyone. If he wants in my head, he needs to earn his spot there. You and Jordan proved your love and loyalty. I trust you both, as I trust Ellie and Brad. Tristan and I have had a difficult relationship. I need to know who I'm letting in my head, and he needs to understand what being in my mind can be like. There can be no surprises for us."

She turned to face me once more, leaning forward, so her power surrounded me.

"Come out and play beastie. Show me those pretty fangs and claws," Evanee purred, her talons snapping out to clutch my throat.

My right hand shot out to grip her wrist, the soft violet glow of my talons bright against her pale, slender wrist.

"You want to play, little girl. Let's play." My voice dropped an octave as I gave into my magic.

Chapter Eighteen

Tristan

My left arm snapped up of its own accord, my beast slithering into place. Behind Evanee, Erick cursed, and my mind flexed, catching his mental call to Jordan. I bared my teeth in a broad grin, and my beast flexed beneath the thin layer of my flesh. The pop and snap of my spine and ribs ricocheted through the room.

Sharp fangs slid past my lower lip, and I flexed my neck beneath Evanee's grip.

"There he is."

Evanee's magic expanded and retracted as though it were taking a breath. Her taunting grin would have given me pause if my beast hadn't been riding me so hard.

Growling through bared fangs, I stepped into Evanee, forcing her elbow to bend or snap. The tips of our noses touched, Evanee's roiling eyes never blinking as she stared up into my glowing lavender ones.

So many had fled or perished beneath my gaze over the centuries. It was an odd sensation to see this tiny creature embrace that stare and stand up to it.

Savage delight at the challenge exploded within my mind, and I closed the distance between us to bury my nose in the crease of her neck. I inhaled, taking in her sweet rose and cinnamon scent, an image of a blooming black pearl rose drifting through my mind. Tongue darting out, I drew it up the length of her neck, trying to taste that ancient magic coursing through her veins. A furious growl exploded from behind Evanee, and my gaze flicked up to where Erick stood, his fists clenched and his giant obsidian and sapphire veined wings spread wide behind him. He was holding on by a thread, his body vibrating with his rage. Jordan's amber eyes glowed brightly to his left, the pitch black of a long-forgotten cave creeping from his hulking body. I hadn't heard him enter, so lost was I to the power that now consumed me.

"Remove your tongue from me this instant."

Evanee's silky order shivered through me.

My lips trailed toward her ear, and my deep bellied growl slid into her ear.

"You wanted me to come and play; well, here I am, little queen. Your magic demands my obedience, yet your body and mind are too naïve to understand what it would take to hold my loyalty and trust."

"You swore an oath to me, old one. That's enough." Erick snarled, the ground vibrating with the step he took toward us.

Gold and blue flames licked at the tips of his fingers, creeping up each phalange with every step.

My claws dug a little further into the pale flesh of Evanee's neck, and Erick stopped short. "It's enough to garner my support, love and trust, where you're concerned, young king. I've sworn no oath to the little queen; nor shall I, until she proves she's worthy. I don't bow to anyone unless I deem them fit. You paid your price, so too shall the little queen."

Erick stiffened. Anger, sadness, and curiosity flickered behind his hooded eyes. At last, his broad shoulders sagged, and he issued his command. "Stand down, Jordan."

"Like fuck, Erick. No offence, but I'm her shield. I wouldn't be much of a shield if I didn't protect her from this pompous idiot," Jordan's voice rumbled.

The image of boulders shifting against each other during a landslide slid through my mind.

"I'm ordering you, as your sire, to stand down. Tristan's correct," Erick ordered, resignation in his voice.

"Erick…" Jordan started.

Only to be interrupted when Erick bellowed, "I said enough, Jordan!"

Erick's anger and frustration seeped through that calm mask he'd learned to hide behind as a young man. "Mic luptător, what do you want me to do?"

Erick stepped up behind Evanee, his hand at her back and mine at her throat.

When she remained silent, I lifted my head from her ear to gaze into her furious eyes. Her mind flexed, and I smirked, knowing she was communicating with Erick mentally. Erick gave a sharp nod, and he stepped back, his wings folding tight behind his back. Jordan looked between the three of us, his brow furrowing. His magic dropped as quickly as it'd appeared.

"Let. Go. Of. Me. Tristan." Evanee's calm command was at odds with the magic lashing at me.

"Make me, little queen," I dared her.

We stared into each other's eyes, neither of us willing to give any ground. A flicker of obsidian lightning flashed across Evanee's irises, and my beast sniffed at the air, scenting it.

Evanee's magic retreated inward, and my head cocked to the side, my nostrils flaring as I continued to scent the air for any changes. Evanee's head dropped forward, and I watched her feathery white lashes sweep over her pale cheekbones.

My grip remained firm against her neck, waiting and watching to see what she did next. Behind her, Erick clenched his hands, his need to protect his mate proving more challenging than he'd anticipated.

Evanee's head shot up a split second before a burst of power slammed into me, flinging me across the room and into the wall behind me. Behind her, Erick and Jordan fared no better, their bodies sailing through the air and out the double doors behind them.

My back slammed into the wood-panelled wall. The ground raced up to meet me, and I landed in a crouch. A sharp shake of my head sent dust and slivers of wood trapped within the fine strands of my hair cascading to the floor. My ears pricked at the slightest hiss of material, and I rolled to the side a second before a tiny barefoot slammed down where I'd crouched. Evanee shifted, an imprint of her foot remaining in the rubber mat.

With preternatural grace, I rose to take in Evanee's defiant posture. She stood silent, her shoulders set, fists loose and ready. With the slightest shift, her feet found purchase on the mat beneath, yet she remained light on her feet, prepared to move.

My beast purred, paralytic venom dripping from my claws and elongated fangs to the padded floor beneath my bare feet.

My gaze fixed on her teal lycra-clad thigh, and with a flick of my index finger, a long line appeared across her thigh. Her pained hiss slithered through the room, and a thin line of blood seeped from the wound. My beast purred with satisfaction, and with another flick of my finger, a second deeper wound appeared at her exposed shoulder.

Evanee cried out, her slim hand shooting to just above her collarbone.

My finger twitched once more, but Evanee saw it, her body blurring with speed. I cursed beneath my breath, my gaze darting around the room, seeking her out. The minx knew enough not to approach me in a straight line. Instead, she darted from one side of the room to the other, using every bit of speed her vampiric and reaper genes afforded her. On her second pass, her hand shot out, a talon catching me across my pectoral.

"Son-of-a-bitch, that stings." I spat.

A red haze slid across my vision, and I sought her slim figure once more, my gaze tracking her movement. My hand shot out at the last second, shackling her arm when she made another pass at me. My arm strained against the impact as I used Evanee's speed to my advantage. Her body jerked harshly, and her feet lifted from the ground, so her back slammed onto the rubber-lined floor. I tightened my grip on her wrist, the bones beneath my clawed hand creaking from the pressure. Evanee shrieked, pale pink tears leaking from the corners of her eyes. The slightest shudder in the air warned me she was drawing her magic to her, and I snapped my teeth at her. My foot aimed for her neck only to drop into the portal she'd summoned beneath her. Together we fell into the hole in the floor, only to drop from another portal in the ceiling. I released her wrist and somersaulted at the last second, landing in a crouch. Evanee twisted mid-air, landing in a low crouch opposite me before darting off across the room toward where the swords lay sheathed. I raced after her, my hand catching hold of the collar of her shirt and jerking it back. Evanee's body lifted backward before dropping to the ground with a heavy thud.

I towered above her horizontal body, staring down at her.

"No weapons, little girl. You'll only end up hurting yourself," I admonished her.

"Fuck you," she snarled, summoning yet another portal, only this time I was ready.

I released my grip on her shirt and stepped aside, studying the room for that shimmer of power that would signal her re-entering the gym.

"Come on, Evanee, get back in there! You've got this!" Jordan bellowed from the sidelines as Erick murmured, "Come on, baby, you can do this."

A shimmer of power in the far-right corner caught my attention, and a smirk tugged at my thin lips. My beast purred with happiness, recognising Death's presence. When Death didn't materialise as I'd expected, my gaze darted to where Evanee's magic was shimmering to life in the opposite corner of the room.

When I understood Death wasn't sure where he stood with his great-granddaughter, I chuckled to myself.

Delightful.

Another second passed, and the shimmer of Evanee's portal flickered in the corner of my eye. Evanee stepped from its depths, and I sprinted forward. The slightest widening of Evanee's eyes was the only outward sign of her fear. My body slammed into hers, and I lifted her off her feet, giving her no option but to lock her legs around my waist. Her back slammed into the far wall, and my hand shot up to shackle Evanee's jaw. I gripped her hard, twisting her head to where I knew Death hid in the shadows.

My lips pressed to her ear, and I whispered, "Open your eyes, child. Look who's come to see you fail. He hides in the shadows, yet he's still here, no doubt to rescue his precious baby great-granddaughter or watch her fail against his protege.”

Evanee’s body stiffened with rage, and I drew back, watching fury and hurt crease her delicate face. Her eyes threw daggers at the spot where Death stood.

“I’m not a child that needs rescuing,” she spat at Death. “You want a queen? Fine. I’ll give you a fucking queen. The Queen of Hearts. Off with your head, even if I have to gnaw the damned thing off with my fangs.”

Evanee’s head strained against my grip, the muscles in her neck bulging with the effort it took to face her head forward. Eyes narrowing, Evanee forced her head forward as though she were a snake striking its prey. Her teeth found their target, burying deep in my carotid artery. My beast and I roared, the pleasure of her bite searing and intense beyond anything we’d experienced. Eyes drifting shut, I savoured the delicious warmth creeping through my body. My mind struggled to latch onto a single thought, but when it did, my eyes snapped open. Evanee's words registered, and my eyes widened when her jaw worked at my neck, my flesh ripping where her fangs gnawed. It wasn't blood she was after—it was my head.

Warmth slithered down my bare torso, and Death's dark chuckle echoed within my mind. Behind me, Jordan gagged, and Erick cursed, uncertain whether to intervene or let things play out.

Spots danced at the corner of my eyes, my body growing weak, warning me my blood supply was running dangerously low. My shaking hand latched onto Evanee's loose ponytail. My teeth ground at the wet ripping sound of my flesh tearing at my neck and the fiery pain that followed it. I tugged hard at the silky tendrils in my grip in a warning. When Evanee showed no sign of stopping or releasing my neck, I flexed my hand behind her, burying my poison-laced claws deep within her spine. Evanee tensed against my body, Erick's and Jordan's roars of protest shaking the ground beneath my feet. I paid them no heed, my sight now set on the arch of Evanee's slender neck.

I lunged forward, my elongated fangs burying deep. A spurt of velvet liquid coated my mouth, the spicey notes of Evanee's blood forcing my eyes to roll back in their sockets. Dark power popped and sizzled across my palate. The sounds of chaos within the room dissolving with every draw. I swallowed greedily, needing more.

A cool breeze skimmed my body, and my eyes flashed open at the odd sensation. I stood motionless, surprise fluttering through me when I scrutinised the carpet beneath my feet and then back up to the round room surrounding me. Doors of varying shades of wood and sizes circled me. Each one different from the next.

"So, you've found your way to my round room of doors."

Evanee's soft feminine voice purred from behind me, and I whirled to face her.

She stood before a door so black; I was sure it couldn't be wood. She appeared different from when I'd last seen her. Gone were the leggings and baggy pink top, and in its place sat a floor-length inky-black silk dress. It hugged her short frame until just past her hips, where it flared out to pool at her feet. At its helm, I thought I caught the faintest glimmer of golden etching. I blinked once, then focused on it again, only to find the golden glimmer gone.

I must be delusional from blood loss.

I shook my head before meeting Evanee's electric blue eyes. "This is the round room of doors I saw in my mind." The softest carpet I'd ever felt cushioned my feet. "I have to ask, though, why the carpet?"

"Why not carpet?" Evanee shrugged before she lifted her dress. "Also, I never wear shoes in here. Nobody does. Now, shall we invite your beastie in and have a civilised conversation about who's boss? I should warn you this will be the only time your power roams my mind as a separate entity to you," she warned.

A plain door to my left popped into being, and I stared at it wearily. Not waiting for my answer, she flung the door open with a wave of her hand and the round silver doorknob embedded in the wall beside it. Behind it stood my seething beast. He stalked forward, his shimmering skin shivering and morphing to take on his surroundings, only to resume its shimmer once more. He was a replica of me, yet he looked nothing like me. Where my lips were full, his were blue, thin, and slightly drawn back to accommodate his elongated fangs. His silver hair cascaded down his back, coming to a stop just above his nude buttocks. It appeared to be alive beneath the room's soft lighting, moving even when he stopped to inspect something. The beast spun, and Evanee whistled long and low.

"Wow, I don't want even to know if his dick is a replica of yours. Ellie may kill me for even seeing this. Does he always walk around naked?"

Evanee's amusement drew the beast's attention, and he stalked toward her.

Evanee's hand shot out, and the beast stopped dead in his tracks.

"Uh-uh, beastie. You're in my territory now, and I don't take shit from anyone in here."

With a flick of her wrist, the black door behind her creaked open, and I couldn't help but wonder what terrifying monster was about to climb out from behind the door.

Instead of some hulking beast, a thick fog rolled and tumbled from the tiny crack in the door. The fog barrelled toward my beast, shackling his ankles in place.

"That's better. Now, let's have a chat, shall we?" Evanee smiled sweetly, and I inclined my head politely.

"What would you like to discuss?"

"That little display out there. Was it you or him? Or was it both of you?" Her bright blue eyes stared daggers at us.

"It was me," my beast hissed, venom dripping from his fangs and claws.

"Right, so is this like an animalistic thing where you need to establish who's more dominant?" She frowned.

I answered before the beast could open his mouth. "That's correct. This creature is my original form or my magic's true form. He operates on a more primal level."

"Okay, so I'd need to best you both to garner your joint respect?" Evanee queried, fatigue and resignation sitting heavily on her shoulders.

"In a manner of speaking. As I mentioned previously, I already respect you, Evanee. My beast is magical. Some might call it fey, but it's magic at its rawest. It's lived within me since before my conversion. My death merely gave it the ability to manifest physically." I studied my beast, pride welling within me at the creature. "There are only two things that would garner his respect or loyalty, dominance by another and his mate.”

“So, he and Ellie have bonded then?”

At the mention of Ellie’s name, the beast relaxed, a small smile tugging at his thin, blue lips.

Evanee snorted at his reaction. “I guess that answers that question.”

Evanee studied the beast before she addressed me. “And you were sincere when you said I already have your respect?”

“I don’t say things unless I mean them, Evanee.” Fatigue crept over me, and I wondered just how much blood Evanee had drained from me and how much I continued to lose.

“Not to put a time limit on this, Evanee, but I think we should get back to reality,” I cautioned.

"There's no rush, Tristan. It would appear my great-grandfather couldn't help but intervene."

With a nod toward a brick wall on the far side of the room, an image flickered to life. The room had come to a grinding halt, myself included. While my fangs were still buried deep within Evanee's neck, my mouth was no longer moving. Beside us, with his back against the wall and his arms crossed, stood Death, his pearl orbs focused on the two of us. He was at ease in a pair of black denim pants, black boots and a tight black t-shirt.

"He's frozen time. I can feel him poking and prodding, trying to gain access to my mind, but I'm not ready to deal with him," Evanee said dismissively. Her hand rose only to slash downward, so the vision of Death obliterated.

"Now, back to the problem at hand. How to garner your beastie's respect and loyalty without having an all-out war?"

Evanee's gaze found mine, and my heart clenched at the sadness I found there.

"I'm tired, Tristan. I'm tired of having to prove my worth. I'm tired of the violence that's entangled itself in my life. I'm just plain tired."

I felt for her and the burden placed upon her shoulders against her will.

"It won't all be about violence, Evanee. Yes, sometimes violence will be required, but you can garner someone's loyalty and respect through strength, determination and sheer will. Three things I know you have in abundance. You already have my respect and loyalty, so what are you going to do to gain his?" I nodded toward the other part of me.

Evanee's shoulders slumped forward. Tiredness and defeat radiated in that moment of silence.

Her head flicked to the black door behind us and then back to my beast. Evanee's shoulders pulled back, her spine straightening with it as though pulled by invisible strings. Determination flashed across her bright eyes before her gaze landed on mine, and I swallowed hard.

"I need you to merge with your beast."

Her order was not what I'd expected. "Pardon?"

"Trust me, Tristan. Merge with your beast. If what I'm about to do next doesn't gain his respect, then we'll go back to trying to rip each other's throats out," Evanee replied.

Her sureness did nothing to appease my nerves at whatever her plan might be.

I studied her and realised this was my moment to prove I wasn't full of crap, that what I'd said was true. With a quick nod, I stepped up to my beast, staring into his hazy lavender eyes. I moved to his side, and we reached out to grip each other's forearms. The pop and crackle of bone shifting echoed throughout the room, accompanied by the loud sizzling of our skin melding together. The pain was excruciating but lasted mere seconds.

When at last we were one, I rolled my neck, easing the tension in my shoulders. My eyes snapped open, and my beast roared with pleasure when he found himself no longer restrained. Muscles tensing, my body readied itself to attack Evanee once more. With a mighty roar, I pounced for Evanee.

Evanee shifted at the last second, so she stood side-on. Her hand reached toward the black door behind her. Alarm speared through my beast, but it was too late to backtrack. The door swung wide, and my mind went blank at the wall of swirling fog before me. The mist from earlier had been but a trickle of what sat hidden behind the door.

The fog raced forward, and my beast and I roared with fear and anger when my body collided with the wall of fog. Flashes of obsidian lightning forked sporadically within the fog, and I flinched at the sting wherever it sizzled across my flesh.

Evanee's soothing voice reached me over the howls of my beast.

"Don't fight it, Tristan. Whatever you do, relax, or this next part is going to hurt more than it needs to."

Next part? What the hell's she got planned that could hurt more than this.

My question was answered when a large bolt of obsidian lightning struck my abdomen. Mouth opening wide, my beast howled our pain. That's when the fog hit, racing toward my open mouth, pouring itself down my throat, forcing my beast and me to choose between drowning or swallowing.

My mind filled with a million voices, each one louder than the other. Cries of the damned scratched at my mind, and my beast whimpered at the intrusion of magic greater than him. Knees colliding with the carpeted floor, I reached up, tearing at my hair. Over and over, the deaths of thousands scraped at my insides, both human and supernatural alike. The hands I'd seen roiling within the fog gathered at Evanee's feet during more than one fight tore at me, begging to be heard, to be saved from the purgatory they'd been resigned to. When I thought I could take no more, the weight of the fog shifted, then bled out through my mouth, nose, ears and eyes.

When the last drop of power had seeped from my body, I dropped to the ground, shuddering. I lay on the carpet, a panting mess, my beast mewling and shaking within me.

The hiss of material at my shoulders heralded Evanee. Kneeling beside me, her small hand grazed my shoulder, and I flinched at that soft icy touch.

"I'm sorry, Tristan. It was the only thing I could think of," Evanee whispered her apology, her hand moving to my head where she stroked at the strands.

I rolled to my back and stared into Evanee's concerned face.

"What… what the hell did you… do?" I stuttered past my chattering teeth.

"I gave you a glimpse into what it's like to be me. I showed you the power that courses through my veins," she whispered.

"Great Dagda, you feel all of that all the time?" Nausea rose at the thought of that power coursing through my body every second of the day.

"Yes." Evanee nodded before frowning down at me. "Did it work? Does your beastie still want to rip my throat out?"

I snorted then, fatigue clawing at me. "I think you well and truly showed my beast where he stands. I can feel him cowering within me."

"I'm sorry again, Tristan."

Evanee leant forward then, one arm sliding beneath my legs while the other pulled my arm upward, so it dropped uselessly around her shoulders.

"Is it safe to say that I have his respect then?" With a soft grunt, Evanee scooped me up as though I were a sick child.

"Oh, I'd say he's more than learned his lesson. You have earned our respect, Evanee."

We approached the plain wooden door my beast had stepped through moments before, and it swung open slowly. My weary gaze fixed on the branches and leaves beyond.

"Hang on. That's my mind." I blurted; my thoughts were sluggish.

"Yup. You have your own door now, Elf Boy. Now, are you okay to find your way back into your body, or do I need to guide you?"

Evanee gazed down at me, her eyes sparkling with humour.

"I'm sure I can find my way back on my own. I'm not that incapacitated," I huffed.

"Tristan, I'm cradling you like a baby."

"Indeed you are, and I'd appreciate it if you didn't tell Jordan or Erick." I winced.

Evanee's laughter shivered through her mind, and I grinned back at her.

"I can't make that promise, I'm afraid. Well, here's your stop, Elf Boy. I'll see you on the other side." She grinned evilly, stepping to the edge of the open door. "I hope you know how to land on your feet," was all she said before she dropped me unceremoniously back into my mind.

Chapter Nineteen

Ellie

It's the lonely washing that has no man's shirt in it.

"Ellie, wake up!" A woman's urgent voice broke through the dark haze of sleep cocooning me.

"No, I don't want to go to work. Just five more minutes of sleep, please," I croaked, trying my best to pull my blankets over my head.

"Ellie, you need to wake up! We need you at the mansion. He's attacking Evanee."

The woman's words sunk through the haze, and I bolted upright, blinking with confusion.

The timber floors and heavily draped floor to ceiling windows came into focus, and my mind finally recognised the master suite I shared with Tristan.

I rubbed my eyes with a yawn. "What's going on?"

"I said, you need to come with me to the mansion. Something's happened with Evanee and Tristan. They're at each other's throats the last I heard from Jordan. I can't reach him, and I don't want to distract him."

Reagan, Evanee's mother, rose from where she'd been sitting beside me.

"What do you mean they're at each other's throats?" I scrambled out of bed, reaching for the pyjama pants I'd discarded before climbing into bed.

"I don't know. Jordan sent me a mental image of Evanee lunging at Tristan's throat. Then it all went blank," Reagan barked, a portal opening near the entrance to the bathroom.

I jogged after her, combing my wayward locks from my eyes. Reagan stopped at the portal, inspecting the swirling mist.

"Right, take my hand and don't let go. Do you understand me? My portals aren't like Evanee's. The gap between here and there is wider than what hers would be."

I nodded my understanding.

I clasped Reagan's pale, smooth hand, and my banshee moaned within me, recognising one of Death's descendants. We stepped into the portal, and my gut churned at the dizzying sensation before the gym at the mansion materialised.

I stumbled out of the portal, blinking against the tears pouring from my eyes. My tears of nausea stopped abruptly when I finally took in the chaos before me.

We'd emerged near the left corner of the gym. My gaze darted to the gym's wide open double doors and the two men frozen in motion. Jordan and Erick's bodies were bent slightly as though they'd been about to take off in a race, their eyes and mouths wide with horror. My head swung to the left, and my eyes refused to make sense of what I was seeing.

At the other side of the gym, the silvery-blonde shoulder-length hair I knew so well caught my attention. Tristan's back was to me, and I gasped at the sight of his pale skin that now held a shimmer to it, as though caught in a stage of becoming translucent. Evanee's teal covered thighs clamped tight below Tristan's ribs, one foot hooking beneath the other at his back.

My vision bled red, and my banshee shrieked in outrage at the sight of another woman straddling our mate. My foot shot forward, my thoughts centred on

Evanee's taloned fingers digging into Tristan's shoulders as though she were trying to hold him closer.

A pale, slender arm shot out, and Reagan chuckled. "Stop, young one. Not everything is as it seems. Look closer, Ellie. Study them with more than the eyes of a lover."

I frowned, shaking my head to clear the haze of jealousy. Eyes narrowing, I stepped around Reagan's arm to study my best friend and mate. Her pained expression and the vacant sheen descended over her swirling orbs were at odds with the legs wrapped around Tristan.

I was so focused on the scene before me; I failed to notice the tall figure leaning against the wall until his smooth, deep voice washed over my body. "I wouldn't get too close, banshee. It won't be long now until they return to their bodies, and when they do, I can't guarantee they'll be in their right minds."

I startled when the god himself stepped forward, his eyes darting to Reagan, a smile of affection caressing his sensual lips.

I took in his all-black attire and bit my inner lip.

Does the man ever not look hot?

"Ah, Granddaughter, it's good to see your beautiful face again."

Arms open wide, Death embraced Reagan before he pulled back to place a gentle kiss on her forehead.

"Grand-père, it's good to see you again." Reagan motioned toward Evanee and Tristan, her brows furrowed with concern. "Can you tell me why one of Erick's people is attacking my daughter?"

"I believe this was a fight for dominance," Death responded calmly, then added, "loyalty must be won from a beast such as him."

"That beast you're talking about is my mate, and he has a name," I snapped.

Death's amused face turned to me, and he nodded. "That he does, little one. But it wasn't the man I was talking about."

"Oh." I swallowed heavily, knowing full well who Death was referring to. "Sorry."

"Now step back beside us; they're near the surface," Death warned, and I scampered back to Reagan's side, heeding Death's advice.

My eyes blinked, and the room erupted into chaos. Erick's and Jordan's roars shook the ground, while Evanee's pained scream dissipated to nothing. Death's arm flew out, and Erick and Jordan slammed into an invisible wall, their bodies tumbling to the ground. Dazed, they shook their heads, taking in the three of us. Confusion creased Erick and Jordan's brows before they turned their attention back to Evanee and Tristan.

Tristan's head lifted from Evanee's blood-stained neck, and I caught his words.

"That wasn't very nice, little queen."

Evanee's feet unlocked from around Tristan's waist, and his hands lowered to her waist to steady her when she wobbled.

"Don't make me recount how I flung you back into your mind, Elf Boy." She snorted, then grimaced. "Shit, Tristan, how much damned blood did you take?"

The occupants of the room frowned at their exchange.

Are they joking? What the hell kind of twilight zone did I walk into?

Tristan's spun, his eye finding mine automatically. "Ellie, what are you doing here?"

"Don't give me that bullshit, Tristan. What the fuck is going on here? Why were Evanee's legs wrapped around your waist? And why the hell were your fangs buried in her neck?" I exploded, striding forward to stand toe to toe with my perplexed mate.

"It's not what it looked like," he stammered, his light lavender eyes drinking me in.

"Yeah, cause every woman who's ever heard those words has believed her man," Erick snorted, striding past us to where Evanee stood.

"Fuck off, Erick. Go see to your mate," Tristan growled.

"Don't you talk to him like that," I screeched. "He's not the one who got caught with his mate's best friend straddling him."

My gaze darted to his neck, and I gasped at the gaping wound that was slowly knitting itself back together. I leaned to the side, my furious gaze centring on Evanee.

"What did you do to my boyfriend? Why's there a gaping hole in his neck?" I demanded, pointing to Tristan's wound.

"He didn't give me a bloody choice. But he's fine, Ellie, see it's already healed, unlike the damned claw marks in my back. Shit, Tristan, that venom hurts." Evanee winced at Erick's inspection of the wound.

Behind me, Death's full-bellied laugh burst into the air. I stood bewildered for a second, the looks of amusement the last straw for my overtired brain.

"Enough!" I hollered.

The laughter stopped. I stood shaking with fatigue and rage.

There's not enough coffee and Cocopops in the world to deal with this crap.

"Somebody tell me what the hell's going on before I lose my shit completely? I'm tired, my brain hurts from being on a two-day bender, and I'm pretty sure my stomach is eating itself." Voice quivering with anger, I fought back the tears trying to escape as the adrenaline flooding my body faded.

"Sweetheart, I'm okay. Evanee needed to be sure she could trust me enough to share a link to her mind. She demanded trust and loyalty, which I would have willingly given. Except my…" his voice trailed off as I spoke over the top of him.

"Except your beast is too primitive to allow you to give your loyalty to her. He needed her to show strength and dominance, didn't he?" I sighed.

"Yes, he did. And Evanee more than showed her strength." Tristan smiled, then regarded Death. "I don't know how she survived the transformation, and I could never understand how she continues to hold all that power. She's a worthy successor, All-Father, and with Erick by her side, they'll do things beyond what any of us thought possible."

Death's eyes crinkled at the sides, an affectionate smile tugging at his lips when his eyes found Evanee. "I know, lad. She is perfect like her Mother and Great-Grandmother. She's the best parts of all of us. Fate may have bitten off more than she can chew."

Evanee's eyes held Death's, her mouth set in a grim line.

Death's eyes darted away first, and he murmured, "It would seem you have Chavas' way with words, sweet child."

Evanee smirked, an obsidian bolt of lightning flashing across her electric blue eyes. Their conversation was entirely telepathic.

"Enough. Evanee, there's planning to be done," Erick chided softly. He turned to Tristan with exasperation, scrubbing at the back of his neck. "Is this what it was like for you when it was my father and me at loggerheads?"

Tristan smiled benevolently. "No. Your father's an idiot with little love in his heart. This was what it was like for me between you and your brother. The man wanted nothing but to protect you, and you wanted nothing but his attention and acceptance. You were forever throwing yourself off the castle's highest tower just to see if he was fast enough to catch you. Sophia would hear your cheeky laughter and chuckle, knowing exactly what you were up to. None of us was ever far away, but we all knew it was Alexandru you were taunting."

Erick chuckled, a sadness flickering in the depths of his eyes. "Thank you. Remind me to ring Alexandru and apologise to him."

My mind brushed against Tristan's, and I smiled at the love and respect I found.

"Tell me, after all that drama and commotion, you came up with a plan to save Ellie," Jordan grumbled, and I grinned at the big fella. "Because if I have to watch you two tear chunks out of each other again, I might just knock you both out and be done with it. I taught you to fight dirty, Evanee, but that was just plain nasty."

The room erupted into laughter. Jordan's lips tugged at the corners, but he remained straight-faced.

"We were discussing Grandfather's helpful hints before the need to establish who had the bigger balls took precedence." Evanee grinned cheekily at Tristan, and I rolled my eyes when she purred, "I can't decide who's measured bigger, mine or yours?"

Tristan's head dropped back, his laughter echoing the room.

"Evanee," Erick groaned.

Reagan's hand slid over her eyes. "The words that come out of your mouth, Evanee."

I glanced at Death. With his mouth drawn back in a shit-eating grin, and mischief dancing merrily in his eyes, the family resemblance between him and Evanee was never more apparent.

"Don't you know, it's not the size of the balls that matter, Evanee," Jordan smirked, his eyes focusing on Reagan. "It's the size of the shaft that counts."

"Ew, Jordan. You can't say stuff like that to me while you're ogling my mother like that," Evanee groaned.

Reagan's calm demeanour slipped for a second, and her piercing blue eyes sparkled naughtily at Jordan. The big guy winked before he puckered his lips in her direction. Ever the elegant lady, Reagan rolled her eyes, but her lips tugged a little wider at the sides.

"Shafts and balls aside, did you come up with a plan?" My gaze searched Tristan's grinning face.

Tristan tipped his head forward, his lips brushing mine. "I may have a plan. One we'll talk at length about over the next couple of days. But for tonight, you and I are heading home to rest."

With a wide yawn, my stomach grumbled. "Rest sounds good, but after this drama, I'm going to need a large bowl of Coco pops first."

"Of course, mo ghrá." Tristan grinned, then turned to Evanee. "Would it be too much to ask for a portal?"

"I'd be happy to oblige, Elf Boy." Evanee grinned wickedly, a portal appearing beside her and Erick.

My hand found Tristan's as we approached the shimmering portal.

"Would you like a walking stick or mobility scooter to go with that portal, Elf Boy?" Evanee taunted.

Tristan shook his head, a rueful grin tugging at the corners of his rose lips. From behind me, Jordan called out, "Don't forget, Ellie. It's the size of the shaft that matters, not the balls."

Laughter erupted from the room as we stepped through, and my arm stretched behind me, my raised middle finger my only response to his advice.

~

Dry leaves crunched beneath my joggers, my breath coming out in white puffs of smoke. My lungs burned, and the stitch at my side was fast becoming unbearable, but I pushed on. It'd been over a week since I'd last jogged, eleven days since my family's last attack. Who knew how many days it'd be until my mortal body would succumb to the curse that plagued the females of my family? Beside me, Tristan kept pace, and I fought the urge to laugh at how ridiculous we must appear to the other vampires at the compound, witnessing Tristan Cathbad, the Prince's right hand, keeping pace beside his short mate. My foot hit a stone, and I cursed my distraction when I stumbled. Tristan's arms shot out to steady me.

Jolting to a stop, I hunched over. My hands dropped to my knees as I fought the urge to throw up, my humour from before vanishing. Questions of when

I'd die and who'd be the one to deliver the final blow circled my head over and over. Bile rose into my throat, and I bolted to the nearest tree, my coffee and what was left of my lunch evacuating my stomach. Tristan's large hand rubbed circles in a clockwise motion around my back, around and around his hand went.

Over and over, my stomach emptied itself until bile burned the back of my throat.

"Ellie, you need to stop. Empty your mind. Listen to my voice, listen to the birds and trees surrounding you. Take the peace nature's offering you."

Tristan's deep voice slid over me and through my mind, calming me enough that my stomach stopped protesting.

My hearing picked up the mournful notes of a family of curlews wandering between in the wild grevillea's dotted around the bush. Winter's chilly wind fluttered through eucalyptus leaves and whistled through the branches of the dotted pine trees littering the landscape. The full moon our only source of light.

"That's it, baby, you're doing fine," Tristan encouraged.

I desperately wanted to talk, but the only thing coming out of me were tears of mind-numbing fear. I lifted my face to the sky, straightening as I inhaled deeply, not caring that Tristan could smell my fear.

What if the plan to save me doesn't work, and these are the last days I'll see him?

"Breathe, Ellie. We've spoken and planned. Evanee's taken time off work, and Erick's cleared his schedule for the next two weeks. Jordan and Reagan are on standby in case something goes wrong. We're as prepared as we can be," he soothed.

His arms circled my body to pull me back into his chest.

All I could do was nod, my fear rendering me speechless.

"I think that's enough running for this evening; let's head back to the house, and I'll make you something light to snack on. We could even put on one of those girly movies you like, as long as it's not that ridiculously slow romance we watched." Tristan shuddered beneath me, and I hiccupped my giggle.

"It came highly recommended, but no, I won't subject either of us to it again." I sniffed.

"Thank the All-Father. I'd rather sit through one of Reagan and Jordan's arguments."

Tristan scooped me up, and I rested my head against his chest.

"You and me both. I think a comedy might be called for, though," I sighed, exhaustion settling over me.

"Now that sounds like a plan I could get behind. Well, that and you."

His cheeky reply barely reached my ears as he sprinted back to the house, the landscape blurring around us.

"That could always be arranged." I smiled, sadness constricting my heart.

"Don't go there, mo ghrá. What comedy do you want to watch?" Tristan came to an abrupt stop, his foot already on the first step leading up to the front door of our house—our home.

"Black Books. It's a British Comedy about an Irishman who owns a bookstore in London and spends most of his days drunk."

He stepped over the threshold before he lowered my legs to the ground, his arms never leaving my waist.

"Never heard of it. If you like it, I'm sure I will, though. Why don't you hop in the shower, and I'll make you popcorn?"

Tristan smiled encouragingly before he pressed a tender kiss to my brow.

With a numb nod, I shuffled toward our bedroom, my gaze drifting around the room that now had signs of life in it — signs of our life together. Tissues sat on my side of the bed, along with my watch and mobile phone. A leather-bound diary and pen were the only items that graced Tristan's nightstand. Shucking my joggers off near the closet, I padded toward the bathroom. Turning on the shower, I stripped and stepped beneath the warm spray, allowing my thoughts to drift to the hours Tristan,

Evanee, Erick and I had spent discussing and meditating over the weekend.

There was no stopping my death, but it would be up to Evanee to reap my soul or at the very least, part of it. It'd been Reagan's idea to try to save the entire soul instead of just a sliver. After that, Tristan and Erick had argued and debated ideas until the plan had slid into place one puzzle piece at a time.

"Ellie, your snack's ready," Tristan called from the doorway.

"Thank you. I'll be out in a second," I yelled, reaching for the taps.

I slid into one of Tristan's t-shirts, then shuffled out to the lounge room, smiling at the sight of a shirtless Tristan lounging on the couch with pillows and blankets. My bowl of popcorn sat on the coffee table, ready for my attention.

Tristan's eyes light up at the sight of me in nothing but his shirt.

"I like you in my clothes. Let's burn your clothes, and you can wear mine for all eternity."

The huskiness in his voice shivered up my spine, the heat in his eyes leaving fiery trails across my erect nipples.

My mouth opened, a sassy response at the tip of my tongue only to dissolve into a sob. It burst from my trembling lips, and my body shook. Unable to look at the man I loved with all I had, I buried my face in trembling hands. My knees buckled only for large arms to scoop me up. I buried my face against Tristan's chest, the scent of holly wrapping around me with each heaving sob.

A breeze ruffled my hair before Tristan dropped gracefully onto the couch, draping a blanket over my huddled form.

"Ellie, you need to stop crying. You're breaking my heart," he said.

"What if it doesn't work, Tristan? What if I die, or worse—transition to a full-fledged banshee?" I wept. "I can't live like that. I won't turn into my mother or sisters."

My heart raced at the thought of becoming a cold, distant creature with little to no love for anything other than fear.

My head shot up, and I stared into Tristan's concerned eyes.

"Swear to me you'll kill me if the plan doesn't work. Swear to me you'll rip my heart from my chest and incinerate it."

Pain flashed across Tristan's handsome face; his voice strangled when he answered, "Ellie, don't ask me to promise that because I can't. I'd rather have some of you than none of you."

My mouth opened to argue, but his long, pale finger slid over my trembling lips. "Baby, you need to have faith this will work. You need to have faith in us. I know this will work, and if it doesn't, I'll be holding your hand as we walk into Death's open arms."

Fresh tears spilled at the passion and love in his words. No matter what, we'd be together, here or in the next life. Burrowing into his chest, we sat in silence for a moment, absorbing the enormity of what he'd just said.

Tristan pressed a kiss to the top of my head.

"When will you grab the last of your things from Brad's house?"

"Tomorrow. I'd like to spend the day with him. I owe it to our friendship and him. He's been struggling with what's coming. His mother died from cancer, and I think my impending death has triggered some memories he's kept buried," I whispered thickly.

"I understand, mo ghrá. Erick and I have contracts that need completing. But I'll collect you from the house after dinner," he reassured me.

"Sounds like a plan, gorgeous." My smile was small, but it was there.

"Now, no more crying. Show me this drunk Irishman you were talking about," Tristan encouraged, scooping up the remote beside him.

Chapter Twenty

Ellie

Many a ship is lost within sight o' the harbour.

The afternoon's last rays of sunshine filtered through the green-stained glass of what was soon to be my old bedroom. I took in each corner, and the stripped bed at the heart of the room. There was still some cleaning to do, but I knew I'd have it done within a day or two. If I didn't, Tristan would find some excuse to visit, at which point he'd probably use that delightful supernatural speed of his to get the cleaning done.

While the idea held a great deal of appeal, it felt like somewhat of a betrayal to palm off something as significant as this to someone else. These would be my last days in this house; the last days I'd spend with Brad in the first investment home we'd purchased together.

I never thought I'd have to choose between the man I loved like a brother and the man I loved with all my heart. A headache blossomed at the back of my head, and I clenched my jaw, adding to my already strained neck muscles.

"Ellie, where the hell did you put the tape?"

Brad cursed on his way into my old room.

My eyes closed, and I smiled serenely. I'd heard that frustrated tone a thousand times, and I hoped I'd still be around to hear it a thousand more. Dread churned my gut at the thought of the plan not working.

Will it hurt? Who'll be the one to plunge the blade into my chest? Please don't let it be my brother or father. They swore they wouldn't betray me that way.

Brad placed a hand on my shoulder, and my body jolted. Turning me, so I faced him, Brad's warm, chartreuse eyes studied me, taking in my downturned mouth and wide eyes.

"Hey, Ell? You okay?"

Brushing at an errant tear making its bid for freedom, I grimaced. "I have so much to lose," I whispered. Brad's shoulders stiffened, and words tumbled from me before he could say anything. "I need you to keep your word, Brad. You can't be around me when they come for me. And remember, you swore you wouldn't seek revenge for my death."

Brad speared his hands through his tousled locks, his sigh of frustration hissing through his clenched teeth. "You're asking for a hell of a lot, Ell. But you have my word I won't stand guard out the front of Tristan's place. And yes, I don't plan on hunting down your rellies, no matter how much I want to kick their arses up and down the main street.”

He’d do it too, if I asked nicely enough. I wouldn’t, though.

We stood in silence for a moment, watching the dust motes flit in and out of the last rays of sunshine.

“The years I’ve spent with you have been some of the best years of my life,” I murmured. “You’re more than a friend. You’re my brother, and I want you to know that no matter what happens, I love you. Thank you for everything you’ve done for me and for putting out all those fires my cooking started,” I choked out.

A soft sniffle sounded from beside me, and Brad reached out to clasp my hand as we continued to watch the dust motes in silence.

“I’ll always love you, Ell. In this life and the next.”

The sun's rays faded from my old room, leaving a chill in its wake. Beside me, Brad stirred, releasing my hand to pull his mobile from his short's pocket.

Brad checked the time, then cleared his throat, gruffly asking, "You wanna grab some takeaway? My shout."

"Sure. What did you have in mind?"

"Curry?"

My eyes drifted shut, and I could almost taste the creamy lamb korma. "Oh, that sounds heavenly. No vindaloo this time, Brad. I mean it. That stuff burned a hole through my stomach and tongue the last time I ate it." When he laughed at me, I frowned. "I mean it. My arse was glued to the toilet the whole of the next day. I had to buy pseudo cream to stop the damn burn."

At the mention of pseudo cream, Brad braced himself against the wall, his arm supporting his weight as he leaned over, laughing long and hard.

I snorted with laughter, trying my hardest to give him my best grumpy glare. "Wanker."

~

The warm scent of garam masala, coriander, cumin, and turmeric filled the house. I inhaled deeply, salivating. The soft glow of the dimmed downlights in the lounge room came into view, and I rubbed my hands together regarding the feast laid out on the coffee table.

"Wow, Brad! You've outdone yourself. Is that garlic naan bread I see there?" I wiped at the corner of my mouth before I made a fool of myself and drooled on the floor.

"It is. Figured I better go all out tonight." Brad chuckled.

"Damn straight. Now let's eat before it gets cold. It's nippy tonight?" I frowned.

"It is a bit on the cold side. I need to restock the woodpile; we're running low. Erick said I could take what I needed from his property. The joys and perks of knowing a mega-rich vampire. I chop, and they can haul my load back to the ute."

We grinned at each other. The loud knock at the front door stopped us short.

Brad rose to his feet, dumping the napkin he'd just picked up on top. "You expecting visitors?"

"Nope. Tristan promised me the night with you, and Evanee wouldn't knock."

Brad approached the door, his hand at the handle, when a thought occurred to me.

"Brad, wait." He swung the door open and stopped short.

I was on my feet and rushing toward him only to stop short when his hands rose into the air, and he took a step back. The cold glint of the barrel of a pistol came into view, and my heart dropped.

Shit. They're here.

'Who's there, Ellie?' Tristan's bark filled my head.

'My family's here, Tristan. It's time.'

A cold sweat broke out over my body, and I held my breath waiting for the person at the door to come into view.

The sight of short dark blond spikes seized my heart, and I stared at the stubbled chin and sharp cheekbones I'd recognise anywhere.

'Ronan. It's Ronan.' My cry of betrayal shattered the psychic walls of my mind, my pain splintering, so they pierced Evanee and Tristan's minds.

Their flinch and disorientation went unnoticed; my grief was all-consuming.

"Ronan," I sobbed, tears searing my cheeks.

"I am sorry, Ellie. It was father or me, and his heart wouldn't survive this." Ronan's bruised green eyes stared back at me, betraying the sleep he'd already lost over what he was about to do.

"You… you have me. Let Brad go. He has nothing to do with…with this." My garbled speech and attempt to negotiate for Brad's safety ignored by the man I called my brother.

"Not a chance in hell, Ell. Like fuck I'm letting this traitorous bastard murder you without someone who at least loves you being by your side as you take your last breath," Brad spat venomously.

Ronan flinched, the barrette in his hand wavering before he twitched the barrel to the left, indicating for

Brad to move into the lounge room. "You told him? You betrayed our family's secrets to your housemate? Why? You know the penalty?"

My hand reached for Brad's, and he clasped it, his large, calloused hand engulfing mine. Brad tried his best to shield my body, but we both knew it was pointless.

"He's not my housemate," I spat. "He's my brother, and as my brother, he deserved to know what was coming. Brad is teaghlach é." I purposely used the Irish phrase to drive home that Brad was family. I aimed to hurt.

"He's not family. We are. Blood runs thicker than water." Ronan's anger darkened the green of his eyes, his thick Irish accent so different to Tristan's softer one.

White-hot rage at the hopelessness of the situation rose on swift swings within me, and the loose tendrils of my hair lifted from my shoulders. I didn't need a mirror to know my eyes had bled black; I felt the banshee hovering beneath my skin, where it sat trapped by my human body.

"That's rich coming from the bastard about to betray the promise he made to his twin sister," I snarled.

"You left Máthair no choice. How many of us did you put in the hospital? You killed one of us." His voice got higher and higher the longer he yelled.

"Oh, boohoo. My heart's bleeding for them. Those arseholes got what they deserved and more. And I killed no one; my mate, on the other hand, does not take kindly to attacks against me. Neither does my queen."

"If they care so deeply for you, iníon, then where are they now." Mother's cold, cruel taunt skittered down my spine, and I shoved past Brad to step in front of him, my body shielding his.

"Máthair. Have you come to drive the knife into my heart yourself?" I stood tall, defiant against the woman who claimed to be my mother.

"That's not our way, and well you know it." Aibell sniffed at the air delicately, her bright green eyes bleeding to pure white. "My, my, but your friend smells delicious. All that fear and impending death would make for a wonderful evening snack."

A slithering sensation across my ribs below my left breast distracted me for a split second, and I didn't need to guess what was happening. The scales Evanee had seared into my flesh were moving, no doubt tipping from neutral to death. I'd seen it more than once on Jordan's bicep. The thought of Evanee's power flowing through my veins, offering me support when she wasn't here in person, gave me the boost I needed. Knees locking, I stood tall, a hiss of warning echoing through the room. The link I shared with Evanee flared to life, and I drew from the deep black well that was her power.

"He's been marked by my queen. To touch him is to declare war on Evanee and Death himself. Now lock it up." My command slapped Ronan's and my mother's faces, firm and uncompromising.

I lifted my foot and stomped down, channelling that dark power into it, so the entire house shook.

Ronan's arm dropped to his side, and he stumbled backward on wobbling legs. Startled, my mother's white eyes widened.

A biting cold poured through my veins as Evanee's magic filled every inch of me.

"Ell, your lips have turned blue," Brad muttered beneath his breath.

"Not now."

"You'd challenge your máthair, your chief, over some pathetic human," Aibell snapped, regaining her composure.

"Careful, Máthair, your human son stands not three feet from you."

"Enough of this nonsense. Ronan, fulfil your part of the deal, or suffer the consequences," Aibell commanded, her patience at an end.

Evanee's power ebbed, held at bay by my weariness.

"What deal? Ronan, what did she offer you in exchange for your betrayal?"

My gaze switched to Ronan, and I studied him, knowing he'd never been good at hiding his emotions.

Anguish washed over his face, and it suddenly clicked. There was only one thing my mother would have exploited to get her way. Love.

"What's her name?" I whispered.

"Ellie, I'm so sorry. I had no choice," he implored.

"I asked what her name was, Ronan?"

"Marie. Her name is Marie. Máthair has kept me locked in the compound since you left. If I don't do this, Marie's as good as dead. Liam and Cian are positioned on her farm, ready to strike if I don't follow through."

Ronan's guttural confession landed where it was intended—right through the centre of my already fractured heart.

"If I do this, Marie lives, and I'm free to leave the clan and be with her. A new life for a fated one." He delivered his confession on a broken sob.

"And you dared to preach to me about blood being thicker than water. You're a fool, Ronan. There's no leaving the clan; no one ever has. What do you think will happen if you and Marie produce females? Do you honestly think, Máthair will allow them a normal life?”

“That won’t be an issue.” Ronan sighed heavily. “Marie can’t have children.”

Mistaking my astonishment for disbelief, he stumbled on.

“She has endometriosis. She’s had one of her tubes removed already, and she may face a hysterectomy soon. They think she has adenomyosis.”

I cringed. The pain and heartbreak Marie experienced and would continue to experience was not something I would wish on my enemy.

“I’m sorry.” Was all I could say. There were no words that could convey my sympathy and grief for what his girlfriend was going through.

‘*Ellie, we’re here.*’ Tristan’s voice breathed through my mind.

Relief soared through me, and I sighed, '*Thank you. Will you make sure Brad isn't hurt?*'

'*Of course. Evanee's communicating with Brad as we speak.*' Tristan reassured me.

Pain gripped my heart, and fresh tears leaked from the corner of my eyes. '*Where are you exactly?*'

'*In the corner to your left. You forgot to dust behind the bookshelf.*'

'*Seriously, I'm about to bite the dust, and you're inspecting the corners to make sure I didn't miss any dust bunnies?*' I hiccupped mentally.

'*No, but it worked to distract you, didn't it?*' He chuckled half-heartedly, despite the underlying tension seeping through our connection.

I fought the urge to not poke my tongue at him and instead focused on the issue at hand.

"Right, well, the night's not getting any younger, so let's get this over with." I shrugged before moving my neck from side to side. A loud crack released, and I almost sighed in relief when a fraction of the tension eased.

A spark of hope flickered in Ronan's eyes. "So, you'll come willingly with us and complete the ceremony on the farm?"

I snorted in disbelief at my brother's naivety. "Hell no. The only way you're dragging me back to that shit hole is in a coffin. My heart belongs right here in Australia with the man and family I love. My loyalty is to my queen and king."

Not waiting for him or my mother to respond, I twirled, shoving Brad to one side. Twisting back, I charged forward, my gaze set on Ronan. Right shoulder connecting with his mid-riff, I drove him backwards until he hit the wall behind him. His pained 'oomph' fell on deaf ears, my upper body twisting and lifting in one fluid motion. My left elbow arched across the distance, smashing up into his nose just below his nostrils with a thud. Bright crimson blood exploded through the air, but I was already moving. I'd taken the element of surprise, but it wouldn't last long.

'*Keep going, baby,*' Tristan encouraged, his pride lighting up my mind.

'*Hell yeah, Ell. Look at you go. He'll need a hospital trip to fix that break.*'

Evanee's cheer joined Tristan's voice within my mind, and a warmth that had nothing to do with the strain of my muscles radiated through my body.

I stepped to the side, ready to strike once more, only to stop short at the painful grip on my shoulder. My right knee slammed into the floor, pain shooting from my shoulder to my brain. Sweat dripped from my forehead and my vision darkened at the sides. My panicked eyes darted to where Tristan and Evanee stood cloaked by her power.

Just as suddenly as the hand had clasped my shoulder, it lifted, and I dropped to the ground, rolling to avoid an attack that never came. My gaze darted to where my mother stood, with a livid Brad towering over her. His arm rose to stop my mother's punch, exposing his ribs. Aibell took full advantage. Balancing on one leg, she delivered a solid kick to his rib cage. The dull crack of his ribs fracturing preceded his pained bellow, and I watched horror gripping my heart as he dropped to the ground.

"Brad!" I screamed.

My hand slapped over the butter knife on the coffee table, and I scooped it up, the forgotten curry containers sliding from the table. Putting every ounce of power I had into my arm, I hurled the knife. It buried hilt deep in my mother's shoulder. When she didn't flinch, I dove across the distance, tackling her, so we both crashed into the corner of the couch.

Strong hands gripped my ankles, and my face hit the wooden floorboards. I winced, tears pouring from my eyes as I twisted, coming face to face with Ronan. He was seething, but my care factor was bottoming out at zero.

"You're a selfish brat; you know that? Always have to make things so damned hard. Why couldn't you come home like you were supposed to? You put me in this fucking position; you put Marie in danger with your bull-headed stubbornness. Do you have any idea what tonight will do to Dad and me? We'll never be the same.

You and I will never be the same," he roared, his rage and fear radiating from his trembling body.

"Cry me a fucking river, Ronan. You're an oath breaker. You had a choice to make, and you made it. Don't think I won't remember this night long after I've risen." I panted.

"Who said anything about you rising, Ellie? You pissed Máthair and the clan off one too many times. I'm not here to help you transition; I'm here to put you in the fucking ground. I'd hoped you would come to your damned senses when you saw me, but no, you had to be your usual stubborn self."

Ronan panted with the effort it took to keep me from twisting out of his grip. I stilled momentarily at his words, and my eyes widened with panic.

He's here to kill me for good?

My eyes locked with Ronan's familiar green eyes, and I watched blind panic flicker through them.

Shit, he is going to kill me! He's not here to complete the ritual.

I could feel Tristan's alarm from across the room, and I knew if I wanted my brother to walk out of this room alive, I needed to decide for him. I loved the idiot. His betrayal was no different from mine. I'd betrayed my family's biggest secret for a chance at more time with Tristan.

In a split-second decision, I dropped flat on my back and arched back to locate the other butter knife I knew sat in the middle of the coffee table. Screaming with frustration when my fingers nudged the edge of the shattered wooden table, I flattened myself once more before twisting my body with a sharp jerking movement. Ronan cursed, readjusting his grip. I bucked and kicked my legs hard. Ronan's sweating hands slipped from my bare ankles, and I rolled over to scamper across the floor for the knife.

'*Ellie, behind you!*' Tristan's fury and helplessness at being forced to watch consumed my mind. I shoved the helplessness to the back and latched on to that fury swirling within me.

My hand shot forward, my fingers snatching at the knife. My head jerked back violently, and pained tears sprang to my eyes when the roots of my hair strained against the hand holding my ponytail. Twirling, I kicked out blindly and almost grinned when my foot connected with Ronan's knee. He collapsed in a heap with a holler of pain, and I scuttled over him. I drove him to the floor, straddling him, my butter knife pointed at his bobbing Adam's apple.

We panted, staring daggers at each other.

"You always were better at close quarter combat." He moaned.

I studied his face, taking in the blood still seeping from his nose and the paleness of his cheeks.

"How long before you broke?" I demanded.

"You know how long," he ground out.

I knew because he was here. He'd only caved out of fear for his girlfriend.

With a sharp nod, I sneered at my mother standing over a pained Brad. "You will step away from him, Aibell, or I'll drive this knife through your son's neck," I spoke slowly, enunciating each word.

Aibell's cold eyes found mine, and we watched each other. "I'm your máthair, and chief, you will address me as such," she spat.

"I already told you I don't want anything to do with the clan. We're no longer teaghlach. You're just the bitch that gave birth to me."

Aibell stepped over Brad's body, her lips rigid with fury. "You've grown reckless and spoilt during your time away from the clan. You've forgotten our ways."

"No, I haven't. I've grown stronger. I found a family who loves me no matter what or who I am. I've chosen to follow the true ways of the banshee and command of my queen and king. It's you who's forgotten your true purpose, and Death knows it."

At the mention of his name, Aibell froze.

"That's right. He knows how far you've strayed from the path, and your day of reckoning is coming. I pray you and the rest of your family can stand before him and justify your actions. If not, the veil of mist and despair awaits you all."

With a subtle flick of her wrist, I flew into the same wall I'd tackled Ronan into. My back hit hard, air leaving my lungs with a whoosh, so I was left gasping for breath. It took precious seconds to draw air back into my mouth. By then, Aibell stood before me, black sparks flickering at the corners of her white eyes. Her dark red hair whipped and twisted around her head, reminding me of Medusa.

"Death is a pathetic excuse for a god. Do you honestly expect me to believe you've met the god of death? No one's seen or heard from that pathetic excuse of a god in millennia. The man lost his head all because his beloved Chavas was taken from him," Aibell mocked. "He wasn't and isn't fit to rule over us, and his wretched offspring are no better. But that's all about to change. There's a new leader on the rise, and he has his sights set on that precious queen of yours. With Death's descendant under his command, he'll be the one to remake this pitiful excuse for a world. The humans will be nothing but fodder under our feet. They'll be nothing but food for us all. Why do you think I allowed you to stay away from home for so long? You were one of three girls placed to track Reagan, but you, Ellie, surpassed even his greatest expectations when you befriended Reagan's daughter."

Bile pushed its way up my throat at the evil grin spreading across Aibell's slim face. Ronan, who now stood behind her, grew paler with the realisation I'd been right. He and Marie would be no safer out of the family than if they'd just stayed in it.

Pity welled up within me when his face turned puce. His eyes flicked from mine to the back of our mother's head, hatred and rage growing in his dark green eyes the longer he stared at it. The slightest movement of his shoulders warned me he was going for a weapon, but I knew it wasn't me he was coming for.

I stood stock-still, not wanting to give his actions away.

I might make it out of this intact after all.

Needing to distract my mother, I smirked at her. "Yeah, well, Sebastien Moissonneuse can kiss my arse. He can come all he wants. I'll be waiting right here along with every other person who cares for Evanee." Aibell's mouth opened and closed, giving me the distinct impression of a fish on dry land. "What? Do you think we didn't know? Of course, we know all about that egotistical twit."

The slightest waver in the air at the back of the room drew my eyes over Ronan's shoulder.

"I hope you said goodbye to the family because you won't be seeing them again. Now, Ronan," I commanded.

Ronan didn't need telling twice. He stepped forward, thrusting whatever weapon he held toward my mother. But Aibell was ready for it, her body shifting to one side at the last second.

One second my brother was standing behind our mother, the next, we were nose to nose.

It took a moment for either of us to realise what happened. When it finally registered, Ronan's eyes widened in panic, and he blinked down to where the black hilt of his hunting knife now stuck out of my chest. Tristan's pained yell echoed through my mind while my mother's sadistic laugh breached the roar of blood in my ears. Ronan and I stood staring at each other. None of us was willing to move. Finally, my head turned to the right, and I reached out to where Tristan and Evanee materialised. Tristan never hesitated, appearing beside me. He gripped Ronan's shoulder.

Aibell's shriek, "What's the meaning of this?" went unheard by all.

"Step back from her, but don't remove the knife," Tristan ordered, his voice thick with the unshed tears glistening in his eyes.

"Ellie, I'm sorry. It was supposed to be Máthair. I swear I wasn't going to go through with it," Ronan sobbed brokenly.

"It's okay, Ro. This had to happen." My legs gave out, and Tristan caught me in one smooth motion.

He cradled me close to him, stepping toward the couch. "I've got you mo ghrá. I'm right here."

Pale pink tears coursed down his cheeks. The knife grated at my ribs, and I winced at the feeling, my emotions numb with shock. A slow burn increased to an all-out blaze in my chest.

"Brad. I need… to see… Brad," I panted, my teeth clenching against the pain.

Tristan moved to where Brad lay unmoving. He dropped gracefully to his knees and laid me out beside Brad. Tears of pain and grief trailed down the side of Brad's face. His hand found mine and gripped it.

"I'm here, Ell. I got you," Brad groaned, trying to roll to his side and failing. He panted heavily through the pain of his broken ribs. "You're going to be okay. You're going to make it through this. We'll spend Christmas together like we always do, only this time we get to add a dysfunctional lot of vampires and reapers to the mix. We could get Evanee to make Jordan dress as Santa."

I smiled at the image of Jordan in a white beard and a Santa hat.

Beside me, Tristan snorted at the image in my head. "If Evanee can't make him dress as Santa, I will."

A fuzziness descended on my mind, and I fought it, fearful that this was the last moment I would have with the people I loved.

"Don't you worry, Ell. I'll make him dress as Santa. I'll call the big guns in if I have to. My mother knows how to get her way."

Evanee smiled down at me over Tristan's shoulder, her lips quivering at the edges and her pearl irises clouded with grief.

With a small smile and a tiny nod, I focused my wavering eyesight on Tristan.

"Remember… this was… wasn't Ro's fa… fault." My words faltered, a chill leeching into my limbs.

"Of course, baby." Tristan nodded. "I love you, Ellie." Tristan sobbed.

I love you too, gorgeous. I whispered with the last bit of strength I had.

The darkness that'd been lingering around the edge of my vision finally took hold, and I sunk into oblivion.

Tree of Life

We are born of it.

It embraces us, nourishes us, and bestows

wisdom if we but accept it.

The Tree of Life demands sacrifice, not to hurt

us but to teach us the value of life, of love

You, my love, will be my greatest sacrifice.

I will lay and wait until your soul finds its

way back.

There will never be another such as you, just as

there will never be another as grand as the Tree of

Life. – Tristan Cathbad.

Chapter Twenty-One

Tristan

Ellie's eyes fluttered shut, her blonde eyelashes standing out against her pasty cheekbones. I bent close, my ears struggling to hear the stuttering beat of her heart. It strained against the knife still lodged in her sternum. The bloody stain on her pastel pink T-shirt widened with each sluggish pump of her heart.

"Forgive me, mo ghrá?" My guttural sob was of little comfort to the woman dying in front of me. Grasping the hilt of the knife, I gingerly removed it. The rush of blood was louder than any wave I'd witnessed in all my years on this earth.

My fingers grew limp, and the blade clattered to the ground, forgotten. I lay beside Ellie, uncaring of the chaos about to erupt around us. Resting my head gently against her chest, I listened to her heart stutter and struggle. When it beat one last time, my lips found her lips, and I took her last breath into me. What took seconds felt like a lifetime.

At last, my lips left hers, and my shaking fingers caressed her face. The beast in me howled his pain and despair, and I moaned, my pain too much to bear.

I knew this needed to happen. My brain knew Ellie needed to die for her to be by my side for eternity, but my heart ignored my brain.

Evanee's strained voice reached me, and my dazed stare found hers. She'd taken her place at Ellie's head.

"Tristan, we need to act fast before her soul fractures and finds its final resting place. Are you ready?"

I moved onto my knee, nodding when I was in place. A large hand on my shoulder forced my head up, and I blinked into the swirling depths of Death's grieved eyes.

"I'll be here, lad. I'll guard you all."

"As will we," Erick spoke from beside Aibell.

Erick, Reagan and Jordan surrounded her, leaving her no room to move.

I hadn't felt or seen their presence during the chaos. My attention centred on the woman before me.

A nod was all I could muster. Evanee's damp cheeks drew my attention, and I reached out, so our hands met and clasped. My eyes drifted shut, and when they reopened, I stood at the base of the tree that was my mind. I hauled my body up into the thick branches of my mind. To my right, the warped and beastly version of myself kept pace beside me. Ellie was ours, and we'd get her back.

We reached the top, and my hand reached for the shoulder of my beast. We merged seamlessly; the pain sharp but brief. I gazed out across the last branch of my mind and found the door to Evanee's mind. Sprinting across the length of the branch, my hand reached for the handle, and I twisted it, pushing the door inward.

Evanee stood at the centre of her round room of doors. She was pure grace and elegance in the same long ink-black silk dress I'd seen her in the first time I'd entered her mind, only this time veins of gold interspersed throughout the bottom of the dress. Atop her head sat a crown of misted hands clasping and ruby droplets; the same crown she'd worn in my vision.

I bowed my head, knowing what I was seeing would come to pass in reality. Her crown would be added when she released the hold she had on her magic.

"You ready for this, Tristan?"

With a sharp nod of my head, I strode toward her.

"Let's go get our girl."

Evanee breezed past me, heading toward where I'd just emerged. My gaze caught on a door that appeared to be made of driftwood.

"Is this Ellie's door?" I whispered in awe.

"Yeah, it is. She's always loved the sounds and smell of the ocean. It's only natural her door would be driftwood, don't you think?" she mused.

"It's perfect." I sighed.

Evanee reached for the handle, flinging the door wide. My eyes collided with Ellie's bright green ones, and I moved past Evanee, reaching for Ellie. I pulled her into my arms, holding her so tight I thought I might never let her go.

"Hey, gorgeous," her sweet voice whispered.

"Hello, my love. Are you ready for this next part?" I released her slightly so I could inspect her smiling face.

"Definitely."

Behind her, the gaping white figure of her banshee floated toward us, her silent screams contained within Ellie's mind. The banshee's features resembled Ellie's in almost every way, except for the deep red of her hair and the white sightless orbs that were her eyes. Jet black sparks flickered at the corners of her deepset eyes.

"You need to merge with her fully. It's about your two halves coming together as one. You'll both need to accept each other as you are for this to work." I stared at the banshee, and her weeping face smiled back at me through her black tears.

I grinned at her, the purr of my beast vibrating through my body. There wasn't one part of Ellie I didn't love. She was who she was, and I'd never want to change that.

Ellie eyed me wearily before she nodded. "All right, let's give this a go."

Her shoulders drew back, and she turned toward the banshee. The creature stopped smiling. They stared at each other for a second before Ellie slowly lifted her hand. The banshee bared her razor-sharp teeth, issuing a menacing hiss. Ellie jumped, her hand snapping to her chest where she cradled it as though the banshee had bitten her.

"I can't do this. She doesn't want to merge with me. Tristan, I've spent so long keeping her hidden; she doesn't trust me." Ellie winced. "To be honest, I don't trust her either. What if she overtakes me and I'm no longer me? What if I become like my mother?"

My hand brushed her back, offering what little comfort I could. "Ellie, to earn the trust, you must put yourself in a position of disadvantage. Put your hand out again. Show her she has your trust, and in return, she may reward you with her trust. Speak to her."

Ellie mulled over what I'd said for a few seconds, then released her death grip on her wrist. Her hand trembling, she stepped closer to the doorway. At the threshold, she lifted her hand, her palm facing forward.

"I'm sorry. I kept you bound and hidden. If I'm honest, it had nothing to do with you and everything to do with my fear of becoming reliant on you. I've been so scared I'd lose myself to you when the fact is you're a part of me. We're two sides of the same coin."

The banshee remained still, staring at Ellie, her white eyes leaking black tears. Ellie remained motionless, watching and waiting.

"We need to hurry this along," Evanee warned from beside me.

"Shh. It takes time for beast and companion to merge. These things can't be rushed." I responded.

As though she understood Evanee's warning, the banshee floated forward wearily. Her hand mimicked Ellie's, her palm rising to hover just above Ellie's. Their fingers inched closer until their fingertips touched. Hand to hand, their fingers interlaced, clasping tight at last. Bubbles hissed and popped, the skin of their clasped hands melting so you couldn't tell where one began, and the other ended.

The two women dropped to their knees, their moans and cries painful to hear. I knew it would pass; mine had.

"Be ready, Tristan. I can feel the darkness rushing toward them. It'll be close." Evanee danced from foot to foot, her hand hovering over the door handle.

"I've never been more ready in all my life," I reassured her.

My power and beast flexed, ready to catch her the moment the merge was complete. I prayed the banshee wouldn't fight, but her smile had offered some hope.

At last, the merge was complete and not a moment too soon. There, barrelling toward us was a large and ominous wall of black smoke. I lunged; my clawed hands shackled Ellie's waist and pulled her away from the doorway. Her body went taut beneath my grip, and I readied myself. The driftwood door slammed shut in front of us, and Evanee stood tall, the crown at her head weeping droplets of blood from the rubies scattered around it. Her wings flared, and I shuddered at the opaque liquid dripping from her talons. Sharp fangs erupted from beneath her upper lip, her hiss long and low.

"Hear me, banshee," Evanee commanded. "You will submit to me, or I'll stick you back in that darkness with my great-grandfather where your soul will be lost to him forever. You and Ellie are now one. To tear yourself apart now would be to commit suicide. What's your decision?" Obsidian lightening flashed across her pearl white orbs, her voice regal and commanding, and I couldn't have been prouder if I'd been her father or Death. She would make a magnificent queen.

Ellie stilled in my grip, her chin dropping to touch her chest as a sign of submission.

"Life, my Queen," she moaned mournfully.

"Good." Evanee nodded.

Her piercing gaze met mine.

"She's yours to keep safe. Don't disappoint me, Tristan."

I bowed my head as best I could, then spun Ellie to face me.

Black tears bled from her eyes, stark against the paleness of her cheeks. Her hair, now a deep coppery red, lay in straight layers. Her waves long gone.

"Will you fight me, banshee, or will you come with me where you'll be loved and cared for?" I purred, and my beast stretched beneath my skin as though trying to get closer to his mate.

The white of the banshee's eyes receded, and the bright green of Ellie's eyes returned. "I love you too much to fight with you, Tristan. Unless it's over who gets what side of the bed." She grinned.

My lips found hers, my kiss deepening with the first brush of our tongues.

Evanee cleared her throat. "Um, do you guys mind? I'd appreciate it if you'd take your X-rated behaviour and conduct it in your mind, Tristan."

My head lifted from Ellie's, and I grinned at Evanee. "I didn't pick you for the shy type," I teased.

"Oh, I appreciate a good love scene as much as the next. My boyfriend, however, does not take kindly to me witnessing another man naked in my mind, let alone his second in command."

At the mention of Erick, his deep velvety voice drifted through the room. "No, he does not. Get back to your mind, Tristan or I'll come in there and give you a not so helping hand out."

Ellie snorted at his threat, and I quirked my eyebrow at her. "Shall we go?"

"I think that may be best." She chuckled.

I caught her beneath her knees, an arm closing around her rib cage to sweep her into my arms. My smile refused to dim. I had her, and I'd keep her safe until she could re-enter her body. I stopped beside Evanee, who'd opened the intricately carved oak door to my mind.

"Thank you. Thank you from the bottom of my dead heart. You've given me back my Ellie, and I don't know how I'll ever repay you."

Evanee shifted subtly, her gaze darting from mine to stare at Ellie.

"Keep my mate safe like you've been doing all these centuries, and you can consider your debt repaid." My throat tightened at her words. She wanted nothing from me I hadn't already been doing all these centuries. With a tight nod, I passed her.

The door was drifting shut behind us when I caught Evanee's devilish chuckle.

"But don't think I won't be calling you Elf Boy. Your door may as well have been carved in J. R. R. Tolkien's Rivendell. Look at all those pretty swirls and edges."

Erick's deep bellied laughter drifted through the gap of the closing door, and I joined him.

~

Midway down the trunk of my mind, my beast pried himself from my body. He kept pace beside me, his eyes never straying far from Ellie. We approached one of the larger branches within my mind, and I crouched low, laying Ellie down. My beast slid past me to curl around her.

"Take care of her until I return," I ordered sternly.

With a nod, the beast nestled closer, its deep purrs eliciting a tender smile from Ellie as her eyes drifted shut. Satisfied she was safe in his arms, I returned to my body.

My eyes sprang open, and I blinked up to see Evanee sitting tiredly across from me. To my right, Brad cried unashamedly, his grief at losing someone he loved all-consuming. I reached across Ellie's cooling body, releasing his grip from Ellie's hand to clasp his forearm.

"Rest easy, brother. She's safe now." I smiled warmly at him, and he blinked back at me.

"It worked?" He hiccupped.

"It did. We got to her before Death's curse could. She's resting as we speak."

"Okay. Thank whatever god is listening," Brad sobbed. "I think I might pass out now. Fractured ribs hurt like a bitch." And with that, his head lolled to the side, his breathing shallow and pained.

My gaze found Evanee's, and I murmured, "We should probably heal him."

"Yeah. Give me a second. My body's feeling a bit on the jelly side."

"It's okay. I'll heal him." Erick stepped past Aibell, the hard glint of anger in his glowing eyes the only hint of the rage that simmered just below that calm exterior.

A loud clapping echoed through the lounge. Death, who'd found a seat in one of Brad's lounge chairs, placed his hands on his lap and grinned at everyone and no one in particular.

"Now, that right there was beautiful. The complexity of what the two of you have achieved this night is breathtaking."

"Yeah, whatever. Next time you can pull the rabbit out of the bloody hat," Evanee groaned, her bruised eyelids heavy with fatigue.

I rose to my feet, scooping Evanee into my arms.

'What are you doing?' she eyed me wearily as her words filtered through my mind.

'Putting you beside your great-grandfather. Aibell's words have confirmed an uprising is on the way. You need to show a united front with Death. I'll be here to guide you and Erick, as I always have,' I reassured her.

'Oh, joy. The politics, I mean, not your help.' If she'd been human, I'd have seen a red tinge blossoming across her cheekbones.

'I knew what you meant.' I chuckled.

"Ronan, collect your sister's body. We need to return it to home soil. I doubt she'll rise, but at the very least, she'll be buried beside her ancestors. Not that she deserves it." Aibell's heartless command to Ronan was ignored by all, including a weeping Ronan.

I placed Evanee on Death's right side, my head dipping in acknowledgment of the All-Father before I stepped to one side.

"Always so diligent, Tristan. Thank you. Your loyalty won't be forgotten."

Death's smile was friendly enough, but there was something about it that had me itching to summon my staff. There was a coldness to that smile.

"You, Aibell Arnam, on the other hand, have forgotten who you pledged your loyalty to." That pleasant yet wintry smile never wavered as he transferred his focus to Ellie's mother.

Reagan stepped from Aibell's side, her hand skimming Jordan's bicep as she passed behind him. Without hesitation, Jordan followed her, coming to a stop behind Evanee. They stood silent; their loyalty clear for all to see.

"I was loyal to you for millennia, and yet you proved no better than all the other men I've known. Utterly useless and downright pathetic. You lose your soul mate, and suddenly you're a blithering mess, hell-bent on undertaking some sabbatical," Aibell spat, disgust dripping from every word she uttered. "Ronan, are you deaf or useless? I said, pick up your sister. We're going." Aibell's impatient snap at her grieving son set my teeth on edge.

This is the woman Ellie grew up calling her mother? How the hell did she turn out as beautiful as she is? I remained silent, knowing now was not the time to voice my opinion.

"Your daughter won't be returning to Ireland with you, Aibell. She'll remain here with her mate in Australia." Death clicked his fingers, and Ellie's body disappeared from the room.

Alarm flooded my mind, and I made to move, only to stop at the whisper of Death's voice through my mind.

'Relax, lad, your mate is safe. Her body rests at the foot of the Red Cedar, at the heart of your home.'

'Thank you, All-Father,' I acknowledged.

"You've lost all sense. She'll not rise here. She needs the soil of the motherland to regenerate." Aibell grinned cockily. "Not to mention she needs her heart carved from her chest before the last beat, or did you forget that little detail?"

That bit of knowledge sunk in faster than a boulder dropping to the murky depths of the river.

'Have faith, Tristan. I've altered the soil so that her body will transform. She lacks nothing.' Death reassured my frayed nerves.

I fought to hide my relief; instead, I assessed Aibell's confident posture. She assumed she knew better than Death. Oh, how wrong she was.

Death rose smoothly, and the room darkened at the edges, his anger a living shadow.

Erick adjusted his body, so it blocked Brad from Death's sight as though he worried Death might reap anyone and anything he saw.

"You dare to tell me what I can and cannot do? You've forgotten who created your species and why you were allowed to live," Death thundered. "I am Death, father and creator to all those who walk in the realm of the dead. I've left you to your own devices for too long, but no longer."

Aibell cowered, fear widening her eyes so that the whites were evident to all in the room.

She shook her head to clear the fog her fear had created within her mind. The air pulsed around her with power. Aibell's boot-clad feet lifted a few centimetres from the floor, her challenge clear.

Stupid woman.

"I don't think so," Death drawled, and with a flick of his wrist, Aibell crumbled to the floor.

Behind her, a portal to the farm I'd seen through Evanee's portal days earlier appeared. Ronan shuffled across the floor, coming to a stop at my feet. I frowned down at him, unsure whether I should comfort him or pick him up by the collar of his shirt.

'He's scared, Tristan. He would have saved me if he could.' Ellie's sleepy whisper came from within me.

'Always so forgiving.'

I reached down and grabbed Ronan beneath his arms. The man jumped beneath my hands, and he swung around in bewilderment and fear.

I nodded grimly at him and hauled him to his feet. Guiding him behind me, I shielded him from the room and All-Father's rage.

"Marie, she's at the farm. Please!" Ronan begged, his eyes flooding with fresh tears of dread and worry.

'All-father, the human's mate, is on the farm. She's being held captive. Her name is Marie. He's begging for leniency.'

My thought left my mind, and I prayed to the Great Queen the Dagda wasn't too far gone not to hear my request.

'You would have me spare the mate of the man that murdered your mate?'

Death's dark hiss slithered through my head.

I stood taller, fighting the urge not to bow to that power flooding my mind.

'It's what my mate would want. I would never be able to face her knowing I'd doomed her brother to a life of misery in addition to the weight that already sits on his heart.'

'I will spare his mate.' Was his only reply before his power receded from my mind.

I caught myself before my body could sag with relief.

To my right, Erick scooped up Brad's now slumbering figure. He stepped around the couch and behind me, where he hid Brad from view. With Brad hidden from Death's impending wrath, Erick found his seat beside Evanee.

From beyond the portal, armed figures stepped forward, their guns drawn at the sight of another portal.

Women with red hair floated forward, their white dresses shimmering as though the moon shone from beneath them.

"Hear me daughters and sisters of Aibell." Death's power and voice drifted through the portal, halting those beyond. "You've forgotten who it is you serve, what your true purpose is. No more. You will kneel before me and mine, or I'll do to you what I should have done centuries ago—bring you to heel."

He turned to the banshee cowering on the floor and snagged a handful of her red hair. Aibell rose, her body shaking with fear only Death could illicit in his victims.

"Your true death will pave the way for a new Ua Briain in Ireland, and she'll either come to heel, or she'll suffer the same fate as you. I thought Ellie would be a suitable choice as ruling Ua Briain, but I see now that her role here at Evanee's side is far more important,"

Death growled. He leaned forward, and I strained to hear his harsh whisper, "And we both know removing a banshee's heart has nothing to do with the curse. Your sadism and vanity festered within your heart long before the curse took hold. It's why you had your daughters and other females murdered at twenty-five. You enjoyed seeing the light fade from their eyes before their time. You got off on seeing them in pain, and I allowed you your secret fetish. But no more."

Within me, Ellie roused from her slumber, outrage and horror shaking her fragile soul at the knowledge her mother was a monster. My gut clenched at Death's words and the knowledge this woman was responsible for murdering her kin to satisfy her twisted needs.

Death dragged Aibell before him, giving those who'd assembled beyond the portal an unobstructed view of her quivering body. A subtle movement in my peripheral vision drew my attention to Erick's firm grip around Evanee's abdomen. To everyone in and beyond the room, it appeared as though he were embracing his mate, yet the power radiating from his palm suggested he was using more than just physical strength to restrain Evanee.

I don't envy Erick right at this moment.

The fleeting caress of Ellie's soul against mine was all the energy she had. She fell asleep once more, regaining her strength for when she would enter her body. My body strained against my willpower, needing to move or to leave and seek Ellie's body. I fought to return my focus to Death and his exhibition.

He now gripped his scythe. A shudder clawed up my spine at the glint of the arched blade. In one fluid motion, the thin blade thickened and extended to that of a sword's blade. Death's supple fingers gripped the handle with tight fingers; the glinting tip pointed at Aibell's back. She was out of time, and Death was out of words. The blade plunged to the hilt, piercing Aibell's heart, so the blade erupted out of her chest cavity. Death tugged at the crimson hair he held in his grasp, forcing Aibell's head to tilt back. His lips lowered to hover over Aibell's parted ones, and I flinched when from those parted lips a sliver of shimmering soul drifted up and into Death's mouth.

In and in, he sucked, his eyelids drifting shut, euphoria lighting his face. Upon rising, Death stood tall once more, and the room bowed with his power. The sword slid from Aibell's lifeless body, the metallic scent of blood permeating the air. My vision narrowed in on the long finger Death ran over the length of the sword. His thumb slipped between his parted lips, and he hummed with satisfaction. To my astonishment, the rest of the blood slowly disappeared, and I realised the blade itself was consuming it.

"Make your choice now, young ones. Will you suffer your leader's fate, or will you once more serve your true purpose?"

A dozen red and blond-headed females had by now gathered near the portal, their men behind them, guns raised, mouths gaping at their fallen leader's crumpled body.

My gaze darted to the half a dozen women who dropped to their knees, and I marked their faces. When their men failed to follow, they hissed as a clowder of cats would warning off a stray dog. The men eyed Death one last time before dropping their weapons to their sides and kneeling as their women were.

"Traitors," shrieked one of the taller copper-haired women.

Death grinned, and his shirt misted from his chest to reveal what appeared to be large wings tattooed between his shoulder blades, sweeping down the length of his back to end above his tailbone. They rippled and shimmered as they would have if they'd been on full display. They were alive yet infused into the upper layer of his skin.

"And so it begins," Death relished, and a dread that had everything to do with an ingrained fear that had cautioned beings since the dawn of man clawed at my mind.

The collar of Aibell's shirt in his clenched fist, Death dragged her lifeless body through the portal until he stood before the banshee who'd hissed at her sisters. Aibell's body flopped to the ground at the banshee's feet. The world erupted into chaos as the portal shrunk in on itself, the screams of terror and battle cries travelling through to assault our ears. The portal shut,

and the room plunged into silence. No one moved.

Chapter Twenty-Two

Minutes passed, and no one moved or spoke. A shuddering breath and whimper of pain rose from the floor. Brad rolled to his knees behind the couch with a loud, long groan, his ribs now healed but still tender thanks to Erick's blood.

"Marie! My Marie, how the hell is she going to escape Death himself?" Ronan worried, his body almost convulsing with hysteria.

"Relax. Death has agreed to spare her," I said through gritted teeth.

The thud of Ronan's body hitting the floor was his only response, and I turned to find him passed out cold.

Evanee sprang from the couch, her brows furrowed with anger and her eyes glassy from unshed tears.

"I could have stopped him, Erick," she raged.

"Mic luptător, there was nothing you could have done to stop what he was about to do. He loves you, yes, but these were his people, and this is his way of pulling them into line," Erick reasoned. The slight pinching at the corners of his eyes belied how badly Death's actions had affected him. Like Evanee and I, he was not immune to the cries of terror and horror that awaited those that would defy Death.

"He's right, Evanee," I confirmed. "Until your coronation, Death's free to do as he pleases with his subjects or creations. He's not himself right at this moment, and we all know why that is."

Reagan nodded sadly from behind the couch.

"Chavas," Evanee grimaced.

"Exactly. Until Death's reunited with her, there'll be no reasoning with him. His balance is off." I hoped my explanation would help ease her guilt.

"Chavas was the other half of him; to lose that and have true immortality…" Reagan swallowed, grief shadowing her pale blue eyes.

Jordan's arm snaked around her waist to tug her closer to his side and placed a tender kiss on the side of her head.

I shivered at the thought of losing Ellie permanently.

"Would be to endure a fate worse than true death. Death has lasted far longer than I would have." Erick finished, then gazed at Evanee, his shoulders slumping. "If I lost you, mic luptător, I would seek my true death.

The earth and its creatures would not be safe with me in that state," he confessed quietly.

"As would I," I echoed.

Brad coughed. "Well, this isn't half morbid."

"I don't know if you've noticed, but today is a day full of morbidness. We still have to replace Ellie's soul in her body." Evanee tipped her head back and stared unseeing at the ceiling, her hands rising to spear into the loose hair. "At least we won't have to carve her heart from her chest. I can't say that golden nugget didn't shock the hell out of me."

"Agreed. Death has adjusted the soil beneath the Red Cedar at our home. Her body will heal beneath the soil," I reassured Evanee.

"Good, good. Once we replace her soul, I'm assuming she'll need time to adjust?"

With a quick nod, I cleared my throat. "I'm estimating a week. Ellie won't crave blood as we do, but she'll need to feed on fear, and I dare say she'll need your help for that, Evanee."

"Yup, because that's what my family does best. Create fear," she complained dejectedly.

"Evanee…" Reagan and I stuttered simultaneously but stopped when Erick shook his head and stood from the couch.

"Let's drop Ronan to his partner, then go home. Tristan, I'd appreciate it if you drove Brad to the house. I don't think he's in any state to drive, and you need to conserve your power and energy. I'll organise for the house to be fixed before you resume living here, Brad."

"Thanks, mate. I appreciate it. Funds are tight with Ellie leaving." Brad sighed.

I cringed inwardly at that last part. I'd need to find a way of helping him through this. If not for Ellie, then as thanks for all he'd done and his eternal loyalty to us all.

Erick circled Evanee to scoop Ronan from the floor. Striding to where Evanee now stood in the hallway, they disappeared.

Reagan and Jordan nodded to Brad and me before they disappeared through one of Reagan's portals

Brad cleared his throat, staring down at the floorboards beneath his knees. "And then there were two."

I took pity on the guy and approached him before extending my hand to him. "Let's get Ellie's things packed in your ute, and I'll get you to the mansion. I think you need food and a good night's rest."

We grasped forearms, and I hauled him upright.

"Somehow, I don't think a night's rest is going to cut it. I may need at least a week and copious amounts of alcohol before I get over this shit," Brad huffed in frustration.

"What, no therapy?"

"Like any shrinks going to believe this shit happened. I'd be a permanent fixture at Acrasin General's mental health facility," Brad scoffed before making his way to the hallway and Ellie's old bedroom.

~

Leaves rustled above, allowing me glimpses of the starry night sky above. My back firmly pressed to the wooden floor, I crossed my hands over my abdomen, biding my time. Evanee would soon arrive, and the process to bring Ellie back to me would begin. Within my mind, Ellie still slumbered, and my beast held her close, his body shielding hers. He growled a warning, and I studied Ellie a little closer. The light of her soul had dulled, but only infinitesimally. A cold sweat broke out over my body, and I instantly reached for Evanee relaying the image of Ellie's soul.

"Relax, Tristan. I'm here," Evanee said, her voice soothing.

My eyes snapped open, and I fought down the rising panic. "I didn't expect this. I should have, though," I chastised myself.

"No one expected this to happen, Tristan. This is unfamiliar territory for us all," she calmed me. "Now get off your arse, Elf Boy, and help me bring my best friend and your mate back to the land of the living."

I rolled my eyes and rose to my feet.

"Nice feet. I don't think I've ever seen you this casual. It makes you seem more human."

Evanee tilted her head to the side slightly, and I snorted at her assessment.

"I don't like it. You need to keep dressing all professional-like, or Elf Boy will never stick."

I shook my head, chuckling.

She was incorrigible.

"Evanee." Erick's warning shook the windows as he strolled through the portal behind her.

"What? I was paying the guy a compliment."

Evanee groused, and I smirked at her.

"Keep smirking, Tristan; I'm not dropping the nickname. And now that you're mated to my bestie, you'll be stuck with me until I bite the dust."

My smirk vanished, and Evanee beamed.

Erick rubbed at his forehead as though he were a father attempting to hold on to his patience amid his children arguing. "You two will be the death of me. I believe we have a banshee to raise if you two are done?"

Evanee rolled her eyes before winking conspiratorially at me. We knelt beside the raised earth under which Ellie was resting. Evanee placed her hand atop the mound and shut her eyes.

'I have to keep him on his toes somehow, or he'd get bored with me and all the drama I've bought to his doorstep,' Evanee said, her tone suggesting she was teasing.

She stepped through the door that connected our minds, her presence sinking through the branches of my mind.

My eyes drifted shut, and I opened them, finding myself standing beside my beast and slumbering mate. *'As his second in command, I don't believe he needs any more stress on his plate. But as his friend, give him hell. The man needs to lighten up again.'* I grinned.

Evanee grinned back at me.

My beast padded forward and came to a stop in front of Evanee. He sniffed once before his arms circled Evanee's waist. He stepped in close, sniffing once more before drawing her even closer.

'Um, Tristan, this is getting a little on the personal side here.'

Wariness drew her upper body away, her hips locked against my beast.

I held Ellie closer. *'He's paying tribute to his queen.'* I smirked.

'Well, unless he wants his arse set on fire, I'd suggest you teach him a less personal way of communicating his loyalties. I don't think Erick would

find it amusing having a naked male rubbing up against

me, do you?' She warned.

'Ah, yes, you may have a point there.'

'That's enough. We have work to do,' I

commanded.

My beast regarded Ellie and me over his shoulder.
He turned back to Evanee to place a tender kiss on her
forehead, then retreated.

Evanee nodded stiffly. *'Right, well, let's head on
up. Erick's waiting to guide you through what you need
to do.'*

Together we climbed the branches of my mind. At
the top, my beast and I merged.

Evanee winced. *'That looks so damned
uncomfortable.'*

'*We've been a part of each other for so long I don't notice the pain anymore.*' I shrugged and stood back for Evanee to pass through first.

My bare feet met soft powder-blue carpet, and I frowned. '*What is it with you and bare feet? And did the carpet change colour?*'

'*Hey, my mind, my rules. I don't need you tracking muddy mind-matter through my squeaky-clean mind. And thanks for noticing.*' She beamed.

'*Your mind is not what I'd call squeaky-clean, Evanee.*'

'*The man has a point.*' Erick chuckled, reclining against a dove-grey round banquette lobby sofa.

'*You two better stop ganging up on my girl. She'll kick both your arses with her eyes closed,*' Ellie whispered.

'*Yeah, that's right. You tell 'em, Ell.*' Evanee stepped forward and placed a gentle kiss on Ellie's temple. '*It's good to hear your voice again. What do you say we get you back in your body, and you and I have a spa day with no men invited?*' Evanee's voice cracked despite her attempts to joke with Ellie.

'*Um, there'll be no spa day until I've spent at least a week with my mate at my house—alone,*' I protested.

Ellie chuckled weakly, and I frowned at the dimness.

'*Right, well, that's my cue to show you the way. A heads up, you're going to want to hold on to her tight,*' Erick warned, approaching Ellie's door.

Evanee floated up beside him. They stood before Ellie's door, and she nodded for Erick to depress the handle. '*You have to shield her as best you can. My psyche still hurts some nights after guiding Evanee back, but the pain is lessening.'*

With a nod, my mind turned to the task at hand.

Erick flung the door open, and Evanee threw her arms wide. The pitch-black nothingness beyond the door surged forward, stopping short at Evanee's outstretched arms.

Evanee's back stiffened, and her shoulder muscles flexed against the weight of that blackness.

'*Erick.*' Evanee's whimper was swallowed by that nothingness. It pressed forward, determined to breach her restraint. '*It's the same.*'

'*I see mic luptător. You can do this. You came through it once; you'll do it again. You have to,*' he urged.

'*What's the same, Erick?*' I demanded.

Erick's lips tightened into a thin line, and he studied me with a graveness that chilled me to my core.

'This is going to hurt both of you. That black wall Evanee's holding back is the same power Evanee sat cocooned in during the initial phase of her infection. I experienced the pain for only a few seconds, and it sent me into a rage, so be prepared, Tristan. Ellie isn't strong enough to do this on her own, but with your help, I believe she'll make it through to the light.'

I clenched my jaw, and the beast within growled long and low. We were up for the challenge.

'Change of plans, Erick.' Evanee grunted beneath the strain. *'You're coming with us. Tristan, we'll guide you in as best we can.'*

'Mic luptător, are you sure? Can you support me and the other two?' Erick frowned.

'Erick, you're supposed to be the future king to my bloody queen. Sometimes logic, a calm touch and gentle encouragement are needed, and then there are times where stubbornness, brute force and strength come in handy. Right now, I need you, your stubborn-arsed nature and your strength.'

I wanted to laugh at her tone, but nothing about what I was staring at seemed to warrant laughter.

'Fair point. Tell me what you need from me. And I'll have you know I prefer to think of it as sheer determination,' Erick said grousing.

Evanee and I snorted at Erick. 'I don't know what to do. I can feel the power pulling at me, and my power is responding, but I'm too scared to let go.'

Understanding dawned on me, and my beast purred. 'Let your power take over, Evanee.'

'What?' she screeched.

'I know we've been trying to teach you control of your power, but life is chaos, not order. It's a beautiful cacophony of love and hope. To live is to hurt. Without pain, we can't know happiness—ying to yang. There's a reason Death hasn't created any new beings. He didn't have life, love, and hope. He didn't have Chavas. You're her descendant and his. Embrace what's been seeking you out.'

Erick's eyes widened with understanding.

'Right, so we're working on the assumption I should embrace all this nothingness that's going to hurt like hell. I don't like either of you,' Evanee whined.

Erick winced but floated toward Evanee to press a tender kiss to the forehead. *'We can do it, baby. For Ellie.'*

'For Ellie,' she sighed with a resolute nod.

My throat tightened with pride and respect for the people I considered my family. These two beings who'd been thrown together by a vengeful goddess.

Erick clasped Evanee's hand, giving a quick squeeze. A light purple shield snapped around Ellie and me, my magic pulsing with menace and excitement at the prospect of a new challenge. Evanee's arms dropped to her side, and with them Erick's arm. The wall of darkness she'd kept at bay barrelled into the room, plunging it into darkness so pure it felt solid. I held Ellie tighter, praying to the All-Father and the Great Queen we'd make it out the other end as the pain ate at my shield and down to my flesh. In my arms, Ellie wreathed and whimpered.

My will wavered at my mate's cries of pain. Had I'd made a mistake and doomed us all?

An explosion of blue and gold flames flashed to life in front of me. I twisted my head to the side to avoid direct contact with the eye-burning brightness. Inch by inch, I reopened my eyes, allowing them to adjust but still wincing. When at last my eyes adjusted, the sight before me and around me filled my heart with hope and pride so great a tear escaped. My very essence wept at the magnificence of this moment. The blinding electric blue and golden flames from before now surrounded Ellie and me, shielding us from the endless darkness swarming at the edges.

Evanee and Erick stood tall, their hands clasped tight.

I could only marvel at Erick and Evanee's determination, devotion and love for their people and loved ones. It was a force, not even the eternal darkness could breach. They would rule as one, and I'd be there to help and guide them when they stumbled.

I peered down at Ellie and grinned. We would be here for them.

'Tristan, be ready. We've gone as far as we can. Stay true and don't waiver, no matter what pain you experience. It's going to hurt you both,' Evanee said, her teeth gritted against the agony I imagined she was experiencing.

Erick hissed, his fury and sheer willpower funnelling into the surrounding shield. *'She's yours to love and protect. This next part will go against everything you believe in. You'll want to protect her, but you can't. See her soul to its resting place and leave.'*

I frowned. *'How will I know her soul's where it should be?'*

'Ellie will be the one to tell you. It's time. Come as close to the front as you can.' Evanee released a grunt, and Erick growled long and low, red flashing across his eyes.

I stepped through the middle of them and came to a stop when I caught sight of Erick's eyes.

'What are you staring at?' Erick gritted out.

'Your eyes. They're like Evanee's; only they're green instead of white. You two are nearing the end of your transformation. Soon what we're witnessing here will come to pass in reality.' I directed a warm smile at Evanee. *'You two are truly breathtaking, and I look forward to seeing you reign.'*

'He's not wrong, Evanee. I'm looking forward to what the future holds with you two ruling,' Ellie added, her voice soft with her fatigue and weakness.

Evanee leaned forward to place a tender kiss against Ellie's forehead. Tears glittered like diamonds against her cheeks, some coming to rest on Ellie, where they were soaked in immediately. *'I will see you on the other end, bestie. Don't give up, no matter how much it hurts. You are too precious to me to lose you now.'*

My grip tightened at her words, and I pressed forward resolutely.

'Hang on tight, mo ghrá. I'll get us to where you need to be.'

'I've never doubted you before; I don't see any reason to start now,' Ellie murmured.

I grinned.

'Good luck, my friend. Ellie, we'll see you on the other end.' Erick's words reached my ears, forgotten when the shield surrounding us dropped.

Agony like nothing I'd ever felt seared every nerve ending, my scream of pain swallowed whole by the darkness compressing my body. My beast shrieked and thrashed, and I fought to hold him to me, knowing we'd be doomed without him.

On and on it went for what I was sure was an eternity. Evanee had endured this for months. How the hell had she come out as sane as she did? How the hell was Ellie going to come out of this intact?

My body stopped thrashing at the thought of Ellie. She needed to be somewhere, and I was supposed to take her there.

I reached for the rage simmering beneath the surface, pushing the pain to one side. It was that blind rage that accompanied pain. That rage that kept you up at night wondering if you could have done things differently. That same pain that kept you going just so you could stick your middle finger in the air at life.

I snarled and hissed, jutting forward. Inch by inch, I moved until I picked up the pace. My beast surged to the front, bringing with it a blast of magic. A dark magenta aura surrounded mine and Ellie's body. Her cries and whimpers of pain pushed me forward, and we trudged on and on, my determination to get her to where she needed to be never wavering.

At last, after what felt like hours, Ellie croaked, *'Tristan, stop. We're here.'*

I came to a halt, more exhausted than I'd been in my undead life.

'Let me go,' she whimpered.

'I let you go, and the darkness I've only just kept at bay will surround you,' I gritted out.

'*Let me go. I have to do this next part on my own. You know I do.*'

I knew she was right. Erick had warned.

Jaw clenched, I lowered her feet to the ground. My arms remained around her waist, unable to let her go completely.

Unbidden thoughts crowded my mind, installing a fear that had no right to be there at this moment.

What if this was the last time I'd hold her? What if I let her go, and the darkness swallowed her soul whole?

'*I can't do it. I can't let you go.*' I moaned, the questions spinning through my mind.

Ellie snuggled against my chest, her hands reaching up to my chest. '*I love you,*' she whimpered before she pushed hard with her hands and power.

Shocked, I had no time to prepare. My body flew backward, Ellie's screeches of pain fading as I catapulted from her mind and back into Evanee's. The door slammed shut, and I dropped to the ground. I rolled to my knees, lunging forward to smash my fists against her door before I could form a solid thought. My hoarse cries of protest garbled.

'*Come on, old friend, it's time to return,*' Erick whispered, his voice weak.

His bunched forearms pushed beneath my arms and hauled me upright.

'*I can feel her gaining strength. It won't be long now.*' The dark rings of fatigue beneath Evanee's eyes were a warning she'd reached her limit for the night.

Resigned, I allowed Erick to guide me toward my door. I hesitated for a second, then grasped my handle and stepped over the threshold, eager to return to reality.

I blinked down at the mound of earth covering Ellie and then to the brightening sky through the leaves of the red cedar.

A movement past Evanee's shoulder drew my attention, and I watched as Erick stumbled toward Evanee, catching her as she slumped backward.

"I've got you, baby." Erick kissed the side of Evanee's head, lips lingering.

"When all this is over, you and I are going to have a long conversation. It will involve my undying gratitude and your explanation of how the hell you stayed sane after being trapped in that world of pain for as long as you were," I said solemnly.

Evanee nodded before she shuddered. I stiffened when that electrifying power I'd felt in Ellie's mind crawled over my skin.

"You need to let go, hot stuff. Don't you know there's no rest for the wicked?" Evanee groaned and tried to lean forward.

When her body refused to do what she needed it to do, Erick manoeuvred them around so he could lie Evanee beside the mound.

"This is going to hurt like a mothertrucker," she groaned.

"What do you mean? What are you doing, Evanee?" Erick gripped Evanee's shoulder, his fingers tightening.

"I don't know. My fingers are tingling. It's as though there's all this pent-up electricity, and I need to release it. I have to reach Ellie." She flopped onto her side, then dug her hands into the earth. "Come on, Bestie, it's time for you to rise and shine."

A pulse of electric blue and gold sparks shot down Evanee's arm and into the soil. Evanee moaned loudly, and her body grew stiffer the longer she pushed power into the ground.

Evanee rolled to her back, tears pouring down the side of her face as she wept with the pain and fatigue now weighing her body down.

"I can't do any more. I can't."

Evanee wept, and I withdrew my hand from the soil to place it on her dirt-covered forearm.

"Rest, Evanee. Your work is done here." Tears clogged my throat, making it difficult to get the words out.

I resumed my vigilance over the mound of earth. A shudder vibrated beneath my body, and I gaped when the earth parted to reveal Ellie's body.

The changes were slow at first, a lightening of Ellie's skin to match my pale skin. Then came the darkening of her blonde strands. They grew redder with each passing second.

Ellie's eyelids fluttered once, then snapped open to reveal white sightless orbs. "Ellie?"

Did it work? Is her soul back within her body, or are those the cold eyes of the banshee?

Dread curled deep within me the longer I stared at those white sightless orbs. When Ellie didn't blink, I steeled myself for the worst.

Chapter Twenty-Three

Ellie

However long the day, the evening will come.

The faint light of dawn played peekaboo between the fluttering dark green leaves dancing high above my head. Pain slashed at my body with each passing second I stared up through the branches. Every nerve hurt right down to my small toe, and I dared not move, fearing I'd cause myself more pain. My fingers flinched, digging into the loose soil beneath me.

How long have I been gone?

"Ellie?"

The uncertainty in Tristan's voice cut at my heart, and I blinked my gaze finding his.

Lavender and garnet irises glowed back at me. "Ellie. Baby, are you okay?"

"You must give her a moment, lad. Banshees are not the happiest of risers, and judging by your mate's eyes, she's yet to settle into her new body. The pain will still be present, not to mention the hunger."

My head lifted at Death's smooth, husky voice coming from in front of me. I stared unblinking into his white and obsidian eyes.

He wasn't lying about the pain. Molten lava that was blood flowed thickly through my veins. Hunger gripped my stomach, the spasms coming in waves.

Death glided forward, his footsteps silent against the wooden floor. "Erick, I believe you and my great-grandchild require rest and nourishment."

His words registered, and my head twisted to the right. Erick knelt, exhausted yet still alert enough to protect his mate. Evanee lay spent beside me. Her heavy hooded eyes parted, and she smiled at me.

"Told you I'd protect you," she murmured, her voice husky with fatigue.

"You did. Thank you," I whispered back.

Her eyes drifted shut again, a pained frown marring her beautiful heart-shaped face.

"Always, bestie."

My head turned left, and I pursed my lips at Tristan. "Did you miss me, gorgeous?"

Death and Rebirth

To be born into this world, you must die in the otherworld.

I will celebrate your birth, despite your death. – Tristan Cathbad.

Chapter Twenty-Four

Tristan

Those five words were my undoing. I grinned like a madman, laughter bubbling up from deep within my gut, the vibrations rolling through my body and into Ellie's. The longer I laughed, the more it took on a note of hysteria.

Realising what was happening before I did, Ellie rolled to her knees, wincing at whatever pain she was experiencing. She shuffled closer to me, reaching up to circle her arms around my neck.

"I'm here. You did it," Ellie whispered. "All of me is here."

Despite all that had happened to her, Ellie reassured me her soul was still intact and not just the customary sliver.

My laughter slowly died, and I buried my head in the crease of her delicate neck to inhale her intoxicating scent, trying to memorise it.

The barrier I'd kept in place containing my fear fractured, and my shoulders shook softly at first. The emotions I'd held leaked through the cracks before I could contain them. Relief, anxiety, and exhaustion collided until my vision blurred. Tears dropped from my unseeing eyes to land on Ellie's dirt-caked shirt.

Her arms tightened around me, her own body now shaking.

"Today, you've made an old man's heart beat once more. The four of you have filled me with the hope that I'll one day reunite with Chavas."

Death coughed to clear the emotion from his hoarse voice before he finally managed, "Thank you."

Ellie was the first to pull back. She cupped my cheeks, peering deep into my eyes. Black tears marred her pale flesh.

"I love you, Tristan Cathbad, with all my soul and heart," she declared through her tears.

"I love you too," I whispered back, my gaze never leaving hers.

Ellie pressed her lips to mine, hard. This was no tender kiss, only a deep well of eternal love.

The moment broke when Erick leaned close to Evanee and whispered, "Now why haven't we had a simple 'I love you' moment like that?" He joked, but the edge in his voice said otherwise.

"Simple, my arse. I just walked through hell and back for those two," Evanee said through clenched teeth, avoiding his question at first. "Besides, like I told Elf Boy, I've got to keep you on your toes. Why else would you keep me around otherwise?"

Evanee groaned, and Erick shook his head, concern drawing his brow into a frown.

The growl of Ellie's stomach broke the tension simmering in the air.

"Tristan, your mate needs to feed, as do you all. I'll summon a portal for the four of you. Tonight, you'll feast like kings," Death announced, an icy, gleeful glint flickering across his face.

A portal shimmered to life, and we staggered to our feet, exhausted and starving.

The four of us staggered and stumbled through the portal and into a starlight sky. I inhaled deeply. The scent of death drifted along with the dry, smoke-filled wind. Screams of pain and terror rang out into the winter night. Beside me, a shiver erupted across Ellie's petite body. Dark tears slid down her pastel cheeks, her moan of pleasure altering to a high-pitched keening. I stood back, watching Ellie's feet lift from the ground. A pale white dress shimmered to life, replacing her bloodied clothes. Her ethereal body floated just above the red dirt, lost in the panic and fear permeating the air.

Desire and pride flooded my body, and my hand latched onto her deathly pale one. Her eyes snapped open, and she glanced at where my hand clasped hers before she lifted her head to stare at me. With a quick squeeze, I grinned at her, pouring the desire and pride I felt for her into it.

"Where are we?" Erick hissed, his eyes taking in the silhouettes of armed humans darting between thatched huts, slashing at fleeing people with glinting machetes.

Beside me now, Death shrugged. "Does it matter, Tenebris? You're here to feed, and I'm here to escort souls to their resting place."

I spoke up, understanding Erick's reluctance. "What if we're seen? The council's looking for any excuse to bring us in."

"Erick has Evanee and her ability to keep them hidden from human eyes. Ellie will only be seen by those close to death, and you, lad, are free to give in to that pure elemental magic running through your veins," Death encouraged.

I replied stiffly, "That would require me to undress, All-Father."

"Don't worry, Tristan, it's nothing I haven't seen before," Evanee taunted, eliciting deep hisses of rage from Erick and Ellie.

'When did she see you naked, Tristan?' Ellie snapped, her jealousy lashing out at me through our link.

Before I could respond, Evanee shrugged, her eyes sparkling with mischief as she answered. "Hey, it's not my fault his beastie wandered into my head naked. I haven't seen Tristan fully naked, just his beastie."

"When were you going to tell me this?" Erick asked, his voice rising with exasperation.

Evanee lifted a shoulder. "When the time was right, I guess. Surprise!"

Erick and Ellie groaned, and I shook my head at her mischievousness. Taking advantage of their distraction, I tugged at my blood-stained shirt and unzipped my slacks, dragging them down my hips. I'd barely risen to my full height when my body shuddered and rippled. My shirt dropped to the dry dirt beneath my bare feet, and I grinned, embracing the temporary pain of my skin stretching and settling. The loud cracks of my body giving way to my beast drew the group's attention.

Jealousy forgotten, Ellie's adoring gaze drank in my shimmering body as it adjusted to blend into my surroundings, much like a chameleon's skin.

Beast purring with happiness, I grinned playfully at Ellie before purring, "Catch me if you can, mo ghrá."

I laughed with a freedom I'd not felt in centuries. My feet barely touching the ground, I raced toward the chaos. Behind me, Ellie's laughter turned to screams that breached the warm night air to mingle with those of the dying. I reached my first victim, and with a flick of my wrist, a deep crimson slash appeared over his heel, severing his Achilles tendon, incapacitating him. My claws buried deep in his abdomen, shackling him to me as I bit down hard on his neck. I spun him to face my mate and feasted on the prettified insurgent, gulping his life force down, my gaze never leaving her gleaming one. She drifted forward, her cupid lips parting to swallow the man's screams.

To my left, Evanee and Erick glided silently amongst armed insurgents, feasting on the blood and souls of those marked for death by the god himself.

The dead insurgent dropped to the ground, and I trailed after Ellie. My beast humming with happiness and contentment. It had taken nearly three millennia for us to find our mate, and we would spend the next three millennia and every day after that making the most of every moment we had together. Ellie and I would stand beside Evanee and Erick as they ushered in a new era.

Epilogue

Ellie

I tracked the forest surrounding the house from the treehouse's balcony with my newly enhanced vision. It'd been over a week since I'd completed the transformation to a full banshee. As promised, Tristan refused entry to anyone who showed up at our front door. He'd demanded all of my attention in between taking me out to feed.

Tonight would be my first time out amongst humans and friends. My stomach tightened at the thought of being amongst humans and losing control of my banshee, but I shrugged it off.

I can do this.

"Of course you can. You were raised amongst banshees, and you fed well today. I can sense the banshee within you. She's sleeping and content."

Tristan's voice broke the silence of the night.

Strong, brawny arms circled my waist before pressed a kiss to my cheek.

I clasped his arms tightly, remaining silent.

"You look beautiful, as per normal. We might have to stay home, I think."

Chuckling at his suggestive tone, I patted his arms to release me. I turned to face him, my arms circling his neck.

"Despite how good that sounds, we're going out." When he groaned playfully, I pouted and murmured huskily. "How else will everyone see the new bracelet you gave me?"

The black maxi dress I'd chosen to wear was a stark contrast against my fair skin. The emerald and gold leaf bracelet in question lay lovingly against my wrist, contrasting beautifully with my bright green eyes. I'd admired its beauty in the mirror as I'd applied my makeup.

"Fine." Tristan rolled his eyes dramatically before grinning at me. "Are you ready to leave?"

With a quick peck to his smiling lips, I whispered against their softness, "Whenever you are, gorgeous."

~

Tristan and I stepped into the shadows of a shop front, the ute now cooling from the drive. We regarded the brightly lit club across the road. The salty scent of the ocean drifted along with the tepid breeze. Spring was on its way, and with it, the heat and humidity Acrasin City was well known for.

I could feel Tristan's heated gaze on me as I stood quietly observing the glaring lights of the club's sign.

"You ready to go in, mo ghrá?"

He tugged me closer, his arm dropping to the top of my hip as he placed a tender kiss on my shoulder.

A warm heat grew from within, and I smiled up at him before I leaned in and captured his mouth with mine. I nipped at his lower lip, my tongue darting out to soothe the spot. Tristan's solid arm looped below my shoulder blades, shackling me to his body. His moan of pleasure speared through my body and down to my core, and I kissed him harder, our tongues dancing a dance known only to us.

I pulled back with reluctance, grinning at his dazed expression. "Now I'm ready."

"I'm not quite sure I am. Maybe we should just go to Erick's residence. It's not far from here."

I grinned at the pained yet hopeful look in his eyes, then stepped out of his arms. A soft, mournful melody danced along with the breeze.

My head cocked to the side ever so slightly as I sought the direction of the melody. "Do you hear that?"

Tristan went on alert instantly, seeking out whatever threat I'd detected. "No, what are you hearing, Ellie?"

The tune flowed over and through my body, beckoning to my banshee. She rose to the surface, and my hair lifted on a breeze that had nothing to do with the wind dancing around us.

"My Queen's calling to me. Death comes on swift wings to those she chooses." My ruby red lips drew back into a feral smile, and I reached out to clasp Tristan's hand in mine. "Where my best friend dances, so shall I."

"Lead the way. Where you go, I'll follow."

Tristan's large, smooth hand encased mine, and we stepped out of the shadows.

"My own stalker. What more could a girl ask for?" I teased.

Tristan chuckled before giving my hand a light squeeze. We stepped onto the warm bitumen and made our way across the road before disappearing into the crowds gathered out the front of the club.

Acknowledgement

Thank you to you, my readers, for your support and reading yet another one of my novels. I hope you enjoyed The Kingmaker's Banshee as much as I loved writing it. Before I wrote this novel, Tristan was one of my least favourite characters in Evanee's world. Whenever he popped into my head, I got the distinct impression he thought he was better than everyone else. Oh, how wrong I was. Tristan fast became one of my favourite characters, and I've loved getting to know him. I hope you fell in love with him, just as I did.

There are a few key people I need to thank. Without them, The Kingmaker's Banshee would not be the book it is today. To my critique partner, Helen, you are amazing and patient while I bounce ideas off you. Your support and encouragement mean the world to me, and I will endeavour to do the same for you. To my superb editor, Dannielle, your expertise and kind words have helped refine my dreams into the book it is today. Finally, Amanda from Smoking Hot Covers, thank you for the gorgeous cover. You never fail to bring the images in my head to life for all to see.

Chapter 1

Salty popcorn and freshly baked chocolate chip cookies scented the air, drifting lazily through the cosy, open plan cottage. A lone lamp in the dining area cast a gentle glow around the snug interior, the only other light coming from the flickering television.

Outside in the evening's gloom, mist snuck its way through winding streets, creeping across lawns to lap gently at closed windows—the perfect evening for a date with my TV boyfriends.

When you lived in a smallish town like Murder Point Bay, whose only source of evening entertainment included a night out at one of the two local pubs; the 24hr drive-thru fast-food chain, where local teenagers hung out; and any harebrained schemes the locals thought of, evening fun was in short supply. If you were single and had workaholics for friends as I did, well, evening fun was even more limited. Not that I minded too much. I usually worked on weekends, and on the rare occasions that I had a night off, I tried to catch up with my workaholic friends for a night of drinks and laughter.

Tonight, however, I wanted some peace. I needed some time with two of my main men—Dean and Sam. Oh, I had others, but tonight was their time to shine.

I had all thirteen seasons of Supernatural lined up and ready to go, with the first disk of season two already playing. I turned the sound up; the scene unfolding with Dean being all tough man after losing his father, while Sam was attempting to deal with his loss in a more therapeutic way, which pissed Dean off to no end.

Bliss. Pure bliss.

~

I was jerked from my reverie when someone knocked sharply on the front door. I was loathed to get up from the horizontal position I was occupying on my super comfortable couch. No one could resist *the couch* once they sat in it, no one.

Assessing my energy levels, I debated whether I wanted to rise when another series of knocks sounded.

"Come on, Evanee, I know you're in there. I can hear the TV. Don't make me stand out here in the cold." Cassandra's whine crept through the spaces in the door frame, shattering my relaxed mood.

Damn it. I thought she was out partying with Jared tonight, not bloody harassing me.

I took my time hauling my backside off the couch. I didn't bother to hit pause as I placed my bowl of popcorn onto the coffee table. I'd already watched all the seasons of Supernatural enough times to quote most of the lines.

Feet dragging along the fluffy caramel carpet, I took my sweet time, hoping she would give up and leave.

Tiptoeing across the cool, dark wooden floors, I stood at the front door, hesitant to open it. There were only a few steps between my lounge room and the front door.

A third series of impatient knocks echoed in the little hallway.

"I'm coming, I'm coming. Keep your panties on."

Impatient woman.

"I don't have any on, another reason my butt is freezing out here." Her high-pitched whine scraped at me as nails would on a chalkboard, grating every one of my nerves.

I wasn't in the mood for any company tonight. I'd had a long week and just wanted some veg-out time.

"Well, whose bloody fault is that, Cass?" I didn't bother hiding my annoyance, hoping she might take the hint and go?

Although this was Cassandra—she never listened. Not anymore, anyway.

Unlocking and pulling the door open, crisp fresh air raised goosebumps along my exposed arms. There, in all her glory, stood Cassandra. Her ebony hair was down and tousled to perfection. She had a figure enough to make even the most seasoned model jealous.

Looking her over, I noticed she was dressed to party. A gold metallic dress clung to what little curves she had, somehow enhancing them; whilst her legs were on full display, amplified by a pair of black stilettoes any stripper would cry over.

"I can't wear underwear with this dress," she complained. "Besides, Jared likes it when I keep him guessing what's underneath."

I just bet he does.

"Yeah, yeah. Are you coming in, or you going to stand out there and give Steve across the street a heart attack?" I could see him nosing through the curtain as I spoke.

Steven Mors worked in Security at the same hospital as me, Acrasin General Hospital. We'd known each other since my first day of work placement at the hospital morgue, during high school. He'd taken me under his wing my first day, showing me where all the best vending machines were and which café to get my lunch from.

Cass stepped through the door and I waved to Steve before gently closing the door.

"What can I do for you, Cassandra? I'm in the middle of something."

Picking my way back to the couch, I flopped back into it and grabbed my bowl of popcorn.

"Oh, I can see that. Is this how you're planning on spending your Friday night?"

Nodding in response, I stuffed more popcorn into my mouth.

"Haven't you seen this like a thousand times already?" Said with exasperation.

She glided towards the two-seater against the wall. Dropping gracefully, she arranged herself as a Queen might on her throne. Me, I was going for the sloth look.

"Yes I have, but a thousand and one times never hurt a girl," I spoke through a mouthful of popcorn.

Poor Sam was getting his ass kicked by a demonic clown. He never could catch a break.

"Oh, come on, Eve, it's not even that good of a show. Never mind the lack of talent." Cassandra bitched.

"You're treading on thin ice, Cassandra James. I'll put up with you showing up at my front door with no text or phone call. I'll even put up with you walking into my clean house in your dirty stilettoes. What I won't put up with is you throwing shade at Supernatural. Some things should never be messed with and my favourite show is one of them." Arching my neck, I looked back at her. My cranky expression must have been enough, as she raised her hands in surrender.

"Okay, okay, sorry. Psycho much?" she sniffed.

She pursed lips and raised eyebrows, hinting at how she couldn't care less about the fact that she'd just insulted me.

"Why are you here, Cassandra? I thought you and Jared had a party to go to?" I mumbled distractedly as I hit the skip button, bypassing the credits for the episode.

Cassandra picked at non-existent fibres on her pristine dress, her boredom coming through loud and clear, as she pouted, "Yeah, we're still going. I was intending to go after I came here and checked if you wanted to tag along? I knew you wouldn't answer your phone or a text, so I thought I'd show up in person. Besides, I thought it might do you good to get out and socialise."

"Hey, I socialise, thank you very much. Almost every night, in fact." I objected weakly.

I wasn't interested in going to any party. I knew who would be there. Thinking about it left a nasty taste in my mouth.

"Socialising with other staff members at the hospital does not count and you know it, Evanee. Now get your butt off the couch and into something pretty so we can go celebrate," Cassandra ordered.

"Celebrate what? There's not a lot going on our lives that needs celebrating at this point. Is there?" I looked over at her, waiting for her answer.

"There may or may not be something to celebrate, but I'll only tell you if you get off that couch and into something other than that atrocious nightie."

The little minx, she knew my weakness all too well. Curiosity. It had been my ultimate flaw since childhood.

"Can't you just tell me here? You don't need me to go to a party just to tell me good news, do you?" I whined.

I don't want to leave my couch, and I like this atrocious nightie!

"Nope. You want to know the secret, you need to come with me to the party. Look, don't consider it as just a party, consider it a celebration. Come on, Eve, you also know you want to know my secret," she taunted.

Damn it, she has me backed into a corner. Damn you, curiosity.

"Humph, fine, I'll come." I relented, to Cass' obvious glee. "But I'm only staying for an hour or two. You also have to tell me your big secret while I'm getting dressed."

Sitting up, I stood to turn the TV off, already mourning the loss of my peaceful evening. Clapping with delight, Cassandra followed me into my bedroom.

I flicked the light switch, and I shuffled in, smiling to myself at the sight that greeted me. I loved how everything had come together. It was a haven and my sanctuary after a busy night at work.

"Now what's this big secret you have to tell me?" I called back as I retreated into my walk-in closet.

The closet was a thing of perfection. Colour co-ordination at its best. Flicking through my dresses, I was looking for something specific—a dress my mother had sent. It'd arrived on Monday.

I wasn't particularly interested in fashion per se, but this dress had caught my eye. It was edgier than I normally went for, but the cut was beautiful, as was the midnight fabric. No one knew my figure better than my mother.

Placing the dress on the back of the door, I went to grab the black stiletto knee-high boots that had accompanied it. They were divine. The heel of the boots were silver-coated, with the rest of the boot made up of supple, genuine leather.

Sliding the boots just under the dress, I stood back to admire the effect.

Stunning.

I returned to an impatient Cass.

"Don't keep me waiting," I chided as I made my way to the ensuite bathroom. "A deal's a deal. What's the big news?"

Starring at my bedraggled reflection in the mirror, I pondered what makeup and hairstyle to do.

My eyes drifted from where I stood to a hovering Cassandra, who, if I wasn't mistaken, looked rather shy.

What on earth would make Cassandra shy?

She hadn't done shy since before year 12. *Intriguing.*

Clicking my finger, I pointed at her. "Out with it, woman, don't make me beg."

I watched and waited as she twisted her hands. Whatever it was, it was big. It surprised me she'd kept it in this long.

"The thing is… Um… You see, Jared kind of asked me to move in with him when he moves back to Acrasin." She spoke hesitantly.

Well colour me blind, I did not see that coming. Quick, say something reassuring before she sees!

I knew it was only a matter of time before my disgust for her newest boyfriend peeked through.

I'd met Jared Miller at the hospital two years ago when he'd taken up a position as one of the many researchers at the newly established Aeternum Ltd. Scientific Research Department at Acrasin General Hospital. Coincidentally,

Cassandra had met him the same night I had. She'd paid a surprise visit to my office one Friday evening asking if she could bum a ride with me back home after my shift.

My dislike, well, that had grown over time. There was something off about him, and I couldn't quite put my finger on it, but every inch of my skin crawled whenever he was in my presence.

"That's wonderful news. It is, isn't it?" I checked to be sure she was happy with this recent development in their relationship. After all, she'd flittered between men more times than a butterfly between flowers.

"Yes, of course, its wonderful news. I'm thrilled about it. I'll be getting out of Murder Point Bay, what more could I ask for?" Her hands went into the air in exasperation, as if I'd asked a stupid question.

"What about love? You could ask for love."

"That's the thing. I… I think I might love him. I'm not sure. I mean, it's not like I've ever been in love before! He makes me feel special, like I'm the only woman in the world for him. That's love, isn't it?" Her uncertainty had returned, and now I understood why. She was nervous, almost scared of taking such a monumental step, even though it was something she'd been aiming for since graduation.

I stepped up to her, knowing right now she needed reassurance that she was making the right decision.

I placed both hands on her tiny shoulders and smiled the most reassuring smile I had in my arsenal. "It sounds like love to me. I'm thrilled for you. I know you'll love living in Acrasin. Now help me with my hair, woman, and I'll do my makeup, while you tell me all about your plans."

I prayed she hadn't seen through my smile.

~

For the next half hour, we chatted about her plans to play house. Cassandra wasn't sure when they were intending to move, but it was likely to be sooner rather than later. Nothing was tying Jared or her to Murder Point Bay. She'd already begun looking for a job in the city, hopefully, close enough to the area Jared had said they should start looking for an apartment.

Happiness radiated from her with the intensity of the sun.

With my hair straightened and secured in a high ponytail and my makeup applied to perfection, I made my way back to my walk-in wardrobe.

"I'll wait for you in the lounge room, Eve. I'm just going to call Jared and let him know we'll be leaving soon," Cassandra called out as she left the room, not waiting for my response.

Cassandra was impatient.

Sliding my dress from the coat hanger, I slipped the exquisite material over my head. Stepping into my boots, I turned carefully towards the full-length mirror in the corner of the room.

I'll be damned. Mum, it looks like I owe you a serious thank you for this one.

The dress not only made me look slimmer, but it also made me look taller, with the help of the heels. The simple cut and plunging neckline did wonders for all my assets; including giving me a semblance of cleavage—an unusual thing. The long sleeves were perfect for a cool evening like this one. Opting for understated jewellery, the necklace my mother had gifted me on my eighteenth birthday nestled snuggly against my chest.

It had shocked me the day my mother, Reagan, had presented me with the scale pendant. It'd been the first time she'd mentioned her family and the significance of the pendant as a crest worn only by those born into the family. I'd loved it with all its intricately woven strands of white and yellow gold.

Until my eighteenth birthday, my mother had never once spoken about her family. I'd mistakenly asked about her side, after being tasked with an ancestry assignment in primary school. Reagan had gone pale before walking out of the room.

Distraught at the fact that I'd done something wrong, my father had sat beside me soothing me, whilst calmly explaining that her family had disowned my mother for choosing to marry him. I'd found it difficult to understand how anyone could disown someone they loved over who they married.

The grief and guilt that had hung over the family that day had been bad enough for me to never question my heritage again; although the curiosity had lingered well into my adulthood, I'd respected my mother and father's decision to not broach the topic. That and the fact that Reagan's temper was just as bad as mine, if not worse.

Clutch in hand, my heels click-clacked quietly on the wooden floors as I made my way to the lounge room. Cassandra's slack-jawed expression was confirmation enough that I was in fine form tonight.

"Wow, Evanee, you look fantastic! Is that a new dress, and if so, where d'you get it? I need to be shopping in the same shop." She made a circling motion, and I complied, turning around so she could get the full effect. "Add to that the place where you got those heels. You look like sex on legs, girl."

Rolling my eyes at the absurdity that I could ever look like sex on legs, I made my way towards the front door, snagging my keys from the bowl on the cabinet by the door.

"The shoes and dress arrived on Monday, courtesy of my mother. I can only imagine she purchased it from one of her designer friends' latest collections. Are you ready to head off?" I called out.

Cool night air rushed in when I opened the door. Cassandra was already striding past before I could snatch my jacket from the coat stand, and a cloud of the latest Chanel perfume trailed behind her.

"Yeah, I'm ready. Jared took the day off to help Desmond, and the boys set up."

Oh goody, Desmond will be there. He must have swapped his shift. It's not enough I have to see the arse at work, now I have to see him on my night off too. Awesome.

Deflating just a little, I tried hard to keep my voice perky. "Sounds good. Look, I'm going to take my car just in case I get bored and decide to come home early." Holding up my hand before she could object, I continued, "I promised I would go for a couple of hours and you know I don't go back on my promises. Now let's go, before we freeze to death on my doorstep."

"You know the way to Jared and Desmond's place, right?"

"Yep. I think everyone knows where their place is. I won't be far behind you." I scoffed as I locked up and made my way towards my little Audi hatchback.

Sliding in, I looked up in my rear-view mirror in time to notice Cassandra's Lexus pull off. I hated driving with her. She scared the hell out of me with her inability to focus on what was going on around her.

Reversing out, I braced myself for the night ahead, and the inevitable interaction I'd be forced to endure with Desmond.

Desmond Reilly had transferred to Acrasin General Hospital Mortuary Facility roughly six months after I'd started. We never worked directly with each other, and I was grateful for it. I usually came in to do my night shift as he was finishing his shift. I'd taken an instant disliking to him the first shift I'd worked with him.

As part of his induction during his first week of work, I'd been required to acquaint him with the facility and AGH's procedures. One of the forensic assistants had fallen, twisting her ankle. He'd politely offered to examine her ankle, while I rushed to grab a seat for her to sit in, but upon returning I'd walked in on the young woman crying, begging him to stop touching her. The unfriendly smile he'd worn had chilled me to the bone; it was almost as if he'd enjoyed the assistant's pain.

After that day I'd been weary and grateful to never be on the same shift as him. The problem was it hadn't taken long after he'd arrived before he decided a working relationship wasn't enough. I'd put up with his obnoxious flirting for two months, politely declining his invitations before I'd lost my limited amount of patience and told him in no uncertain terms I was not interested.

That proved to be more of a challenge than a deterrent to him. I'd eventually had to call the regional boss, Bob Johnston, last week after I'd noticed Desmond sitting in the car park, watching me from his car. To say I was a little weirded out would be an understatement. Bob assured me he would personally deal with the situation.

His anger and frustration at Desmond's actions had come across loud and clear during our conversation on the phone the other evening.

I'd loved working for Bob from the moment I'd stepped foot in the morgue during my work placement in high school. That he was a family friend helped. He'd been the one to suggest I complete my placement at the morgue after picking up on my love of forensics and the many forms of decomposition during a family barbeque before my Dad had died.

I'd been curled up on the couch watching a medical documentary when he and Aunty Marg had arrived. He'd also persuaded me to qualify as a Forensic Pathologist and had been delighted when I'd put in for a transfer to my old haunt.

Not long after settling in, he'd taken a position as regional manager of Far North Queensland, confident I could handle the job on my own. He lived in Brisbane and still consulted on the particularly troublesome cases; although they didn't pop up all too often in the outer towns and smaller cities.

How Desmond secured a spot at Acrisin General was beyond me. I wasn't even sure Bob knew how he arranged a transfer. His work was sloppy and rushed; his disrespect for his charges well known amongst his colleagues.

I sighed heavily and drove away from the house, already missing my date night, popcorn and freshly baked cookies.

AN EVANEE SHEPERD NOVEL
EXITUS
DEATH IS BUT A STATE, NOT AN END
T.S. PETERSEN

Prologue

Hand in hand, Erick and I stepped through my portal, leaving behind the carnage that was once Aeternum's Science Laboratories at Acrasin General Hospital. The scents unique to Murder Point Bay drifted enticingly through one of the open French doors lining the top floor. The shadowed wrap-around veranda beyond the doors beckoned, whispering of rest and relaxation as the sounds and scents of sunrise cast their spell over me. With a tired sigh, I ignored the call and focused on the door that led to Erick's room.

A sudden shift in the pressure turned Erick's, Jordan's, and my head towards the veranda. Jordan stopped short and inhaled the new scent drifting into the hallway on the cool air. The air surrounding him responded, growing denser as the shadows in the hallway crept along the floor and roof. His hands clenched into fists, the dried blood that caked them cracking. He was frightening in this moment, and I was glad the focus of his attention wasn't on me. Erick dropped my hand, placing his body between me and whatever, or whoever was responsible for the shift.

Focusing on the power emanating from outside, I sensed my mother's presence seconds before she emerged from the shadows, her hands raised to show she meant no harm.

"Relax Jordan, I'm not here to reap."

Jordan visibly relaxed as Mum stepped further into the hallway.

"Apologies Reagan, we didn't realise it was you."

Dropping her hands, Mum spoke with a quiet urgency. "No need to apologise, it's me who has dropped by unannounced. There's something I feel needs our attention—sooner rather than later. Jordan, where's that prophecy you were referring to at the hospital?"

"I asked him to put it in my study for safe keeping," Erick responded.

"Good. The fewer people who know about this, the better. Erick, if you would lead the way, I don't have much time." Nodding at my mother's request, Erick moved towards his bedroom doors.

I stalled momentarily, not sure I wanted to know what the prophecy said.

I don't know how much more drama I can take.

Jordan's raised eyebrows had me sighing with weariness, and my shoulders slumped in defeat. The action forced the dried blood covering my body to crack, pinching at the tiny hairs on my body. I grimaced at the unpleasant sensation.

Entering Erick's room behind my mother, my gaze zeroed in on the turquoise love seat near the fireplace, reminding me of the vision Fate bestowed upon me before my death. My eyes darted away, and I made my way towards Erick's desk in the corner.

"Hello sweetheart, sorry for the haste."

Mum's rose-lipped smile was laden with hope, and I cringed inwardly.

"Hi Mum," I mumbled. Things were far from being resolved between the two of us, but that didn't mean I didn't love her. She was my mother.

Looking for Erick, who'd disappeared into his walk-in closet as soon as we'd entered his room to retrieve the vampire's prophecy from his safe, I prayed he'd hurry. I wasn't even close to being ready to talk to my mother about her years of betrayal and lies. If she forced me to address it now, I knew we'd both walk away feeling worse than we did now.

Mum looked me up and down as though she finally noticed my bloodied appearance.

"I hear you kicked arse at the hospital. Jordan said you were magnificent."

Wow, she didn't even bat an eyelid at the blood. At least now I know who Jordan was texting before we left Acrasin General.

"Apparently. Let's not forget I also started an interspecies dilemma, and all in my first month of being a vamper. Personally, I call that talent. Erick will probably refer to it as a pain in his royal arse."

'Play nice, Evanee.'

Erick's hiss slithered through my mind as he emerged carrying a small leather-bound scroll.

"Vamper. That's cute. Vampire and reaper combined, am I right?" Mum asked.

Nodding silently, I stood back from the desk making room for Erick.

Together the four of us crowded around the desk as Erick gingerly unwound the brittle paper. We took a few minutes to absorb the words scrawled across the middle of the page.

"Well, that settles that." Mum recovered first. "The good news is we found the correlating prophecies. The bad news is that the one I have in my possession is one of our forbidden prophecies, which was why my memory was vague. What the Mors family prophecy refers to is something my parents have worked hard to ensure didn't come to pass."

Mum looked to Erick and Jordan.

"Mors… wait that's what… umm," I stalled, realising I hadn't informed my mother about everything that had happened before my death and during my conversion. "Someone called me that name just before I died. Your maiden name was Mors?" The pieces were sliding together, everyone seemed to have guessed who I was except me.

"Yes, it was."

Mum stared at me for a heartbeat before she moved on.

"One reason my family cut me off was because they worried my marrying a human meant I was the woman in the prophecy."

"What does the Mors prophecy say, Mum?"

Pulling a torn, rolled piece of tanned paper from her pocket, Mum placed it on the table in front of Erick and stepped to one side. I leaned forward and gazed at the looped writing on the piece of what I prayed was paper. It was far too thick and rubbery to be paper, and a shudder of foreboding clawed at my skin.

Order out of chaos, chaos out of order. Death she comes, uniting the divided. Sword and shield at her side; she is their salvation, or their doom. For she will rule, her King beside her. All Hail Regina Populi Mortis.

"Interesting. The prophecies are the same, with one exception the last sentence." Erick tapped on the ancient scroll just in front of him. "Ours indicates she will sit upon the throne, beside her king. It also leaves out the 'All Hail the Queen of the People of Death.' I take it your family doesn't have a ruling monarch like ours does?"

"No, we don't. If there is a ruler of any kind, it would be my grand-père—Death," Mum clarified. "As you three are aware, my grand-père has not been seen since the day of my naming ceremony as an infant. My father, sensing the chaos approaching, tasked himself with overseeing the family and reapers; however, his abilities have waned substantially since I last saw him, as has the rest of Death's remaining direct living descendants. Except… umm… myself and… umm you, Evanee."

Curious. I wonder if any of Great Grandfather's reapers have noticed any changes?

Mum cleared her throat, distracting me from my thoughts.

"Now, it's been some time since anyone's seen Death. My father has grown accustomed to his rule, and fears being overthrown from his position. From what I've been able to gather since my return, there has been no attempt to locate my grand-père. I'm not exactly in any rush to remind my father about the prophecy or my suspicion that it refers to Evanee."

I could just imagine how that would go over with my mother's family. *'Hey Papa, I'm back. Oh, and by the way, your long-lost granddaughter is your new queen.'*

"I can see how they might not accept that with open arms."

I rolled my eyes at Erick's dry tone, as he echoed the words he'd surely heard me think.

"I don't see your family or that vampire council you're all so afraid of taking the news any better." Sarcasm dripped thicker than honey as I spoke.

"Evanee." Mum's note of warning did nothing to deter the fear churning my gut.

"What? You're all standing around insinuating that some cockamamie prophecy that that bitch, Fate, concocted, is supposed to be about me. How would you like me to react to this?" Looking between my mother and Erick, I resented the hell out of the fact I was once again being thrown in the deep end with no floaties.

"I mean, if this prophecy is really about me, then that would make you and I." My hands jerked angrily towards Erick. "Nothing more than Fate's pawns in some morbid game of supernatural chess."

Erick stood immobile, as he took in my words.

That would mean what we feel for each other is all a farce, something programmed into our brains by Fate.

"What did you say? Evanee, tell me. What did you mean by Fate concocting the prophecy?"

Mum's worry fell on deaf ears. I was done being a pawn in everyone else's game.

"You heard me, Mum. I know Fate drummed up this useless prophecy. She admitted as much the night she appeared to Erick and me while we were in the cocoon." Shocked into silence by my confession, it took a second before the wheels in my mother's mind began to churn.

Stepping around the desk, I bade my farewell. "Now, if you'll all excuse me I think I've had enough bullshit and drama over the past few weeks to last the rest of my undead life."

I made my escape, leaving Erick's room as Mum rounded on Erick firing questions at his startled face. I couldn't care less what they had to say. A hot shower and peace were what I sought.

Chapter 1

Curlews crooned softly in the cool night air, their eerie cries drifting around me. For some their cries were haunting. To me they were lovers beckoning to their mate, gently reminding them they would always find each other no matter how great the distance between them.

Chaotic thoughts swirled through my mind, but I pushed them aside instead focusing on placing one foot in front of the other as I forced myself to walk at human speed. My powers showed no signs of abating since my death three months ago. While this wasn't a bad thing, the downside meant it was harder for me to function as a human.

I gazed up at the twinkling stars and cheerful moon smiling down at me, mocking me and my sombre mood. Being dead had not been as fun and carefree as the books and movies made it out to be. I still stared down that black tunnel some days, hoping the light would eventually emerge. The hunger, which Erick and Jordan had assured me would go away, only seemed to get worse. Not that I was in any hurry to reveal this to Erick or my mother for fear of their reaction. The last thing I needed was my freedom curtailed any more than it already was.

Breathing deeply, the familiar scents of tea tree and eucalyptus saturated bushland drifted along the breeze to surround me. My one attempt at showing Erick I could be strong, that I deserved the title I would inherit, had ended with a beheaded vampire. Not to mention Erick fearing some all-powerful vampire council would come swooping down from the sky to bring justice upon me. You could cut the air in the mansion with a butter knife, it was that tense.

A gentle pulse of my birth mark at my lower back elicited a shiver of anticipation from me. Whispering, my words drifted along the breeze. "It didn't take you long to find me."

With a weary sigh, Erick stepped from behind a magnificent Paperbark tree. "I didn't want to disturb you, but I thought you should know I just got off the phone with Bob. I'm sorry, *mic luptător*, they lost the last infected human last night."

I cringed at his endearment, *mic luptător*, little fighter. I didn't feel like a fighter tonight, I hadn't for a while now.

"Thank you." I said between gritted teeth, trying my best to hold on to my temper. I had no desire to lose control over my power and accidentally kill anything around me.

"I know what you're thinking, I can see it in your shoulders. They carry the weight of the world, when they don't need to."

When I remained silent, he continued.

"You couldn't have known this would happen. The humans appeared to be stable, and there was nothing any of us could say to tip the doctors off about what happened without causing more drama and getting the government involved."

"You think I don't know that, Erick? Why the hell do you think I kept my mouth shut all these months? It sure as hell wasn't for my benefit." *I should have just let Jordan kill everyone that night in the laboratory and saved them and their families the months of agony.*

"You weren't to know that the decomposition of Jared's creatures would be lethal. How were any of us to know that?"

I knew he was trying to make me feel better, but the more he spoke the more I wanted to punch something or someone.

"No Erick, you're wrong. I should have known." A resounding thud of my fist hitting my chest did little to comfort me. "I mean, come on, the initial virus and her eggs lived in an acid, not to mention the creatures were made up of an acidic compound. I should have known they'd need to be removed surgically; but no, I was too bloody distracted with all the bullshit and melodrama of becoming the first ever vampire-reaper." My body shook with fury, and I refused to turn and face him just yet.

"So, do me a damn favour…" Breath hitching, I paused. "Please, just stop talking, okay. I was a self-centred bitch, and as a result innocent people lost their lives." The slow unfurling of something ancient and powerful rose from deep within me, responding to the overwhelming anger and pain squeezing my dead heart. My clenched fingers loosened their tight grip, flexing so onyx and electric blue sparks drifted down to land atop of the brittle foliage beneath my booted feet. The leaves that had once held life in them, turned to ash as the embers touched down.

"Evanee, you need to calm down. I know what you're feeling, because I feel it too, but now is not the time to fight about it. Aeternum compensated the families of the victims. I've had my people monitor transactions to the victims' families to combat possible lawsuits. I wanted to keep you up to date, so that it wouldn't be something else you could put between us."

"You want to choose your next words carefully, Erick." Hurt pierced my heart, but I pushed it aside, choosing to embrace the anger simmering beneath the surface instead.

"I understand you're angry with being sequestered to the mansion. But you can't deny that when it comes to your mother and I, your temper ignites quicker than drought-stricken bush during an electric storm these days."

He wasn't wrong. Staring into the distance, my mind drifted back to the night I'd finally set eyes on Fate's prophecy. The realisation what I felt for Erick, and what he felt for me in return, might be nothing more than a result of Fate's interference had really hit home. To think under normal circumstances I wouldn't have been someone Erick would've chosen of his own free will, hurt. I'd withdrawn into myself, choosing to spend my days reading, walking in the state forest, or training with Jordan and Aunt Paige whenever she was at the mansion.

Breathing in deeply, I struggled to pull my power back within, when what I wanted was to lash out at anything and everything. Reigning that ancient power in, the hunger lurking in the dark corners of my mind, assaulted me once more. Despair followed close behind it. *Why am I so hungry? Surely it should simmer down by now?*

"Evanee, you need to give yourself credit. You've made so much progress in such a short amount of time. The hunger will gradually become easier to control."

"Reading my mind again?" My lips quirked to one side.

Cheeky bugger.

"I only caught that last thought, but I try not to. Although, I'll take advantage of whatever opportunity presents itself, if it means I'll be one step closer to healing this rift between us."

His confession hurt. A part of me wanted to build on the friendship we'd initially built, but a larger part of me was too afraid of being hurt or worse—hurting him.

"Give me some credit, Erick. At least I'm trying. Being cooped up at the mansion all day, every day, isn't helping. Neither is the fact that I'm cut off from everything I once knew. I haven't seen or spoken to Ellie or Brad for over two months," I said, the venom clear in my tone.

"Enough Evanee. You need to accept there'll be things you'll never be able to do again without betraying the supernatural community. Seeing Ellie and Brad would still be out of the question if they were in Murder Point Bay, because you're still having problems controlling your hunger and speed."

Holding up a hand to silence me, Erick stepped closer as he spoke.

"Don't bother denying it. It's only been a little over three months since your conversion, and we still don't know what powers you've inherited."

"And what about you? I can't have been the only one who inherited new powers. As I recall, you were trapped in the cocoon right along with me."

Huffing in frustration, his pale hand combed at dark spiky locks, only for them to spring back into place.

"You're being purposefully obtuse, Evanee. I have over 500 years of experience with controlling the powers I already have. I don't think my new powers will be any harder to control."

Gesturing at me, Erick's exasperation came across loud and clear.

"You barely knew your abilities before the conversion."

So, he has received new powers. He could have at least given me a heads up.

'That would've been hard considering you've been avoiding him since the prophecy. Give the poor man a break.'

My inner bimbo snapped in frustration at my bull headedness, all the while applying a fresh layer of red lipstick.

Erick was speaking again, dragging my attention back to him.

"Without testing, we have no idea what your weaknesses are. You've built an immunity to the sunlight at an accelerated rate. We're yet to determine if a stake to your heart will kill you. We have no idea what vulnerabilities reapers have, as you keep avoiding your mother like the plague. Aside from Death, his creations, and your extended family, is there something or someone else who might pose a risk to your life? Then there're your damn temper tantrums, and the fallout from them."

Silence settled around us as he registered what he'd just blurted out.

The power I'd been struggling to contain barrelled upwards, a cold rage settling over my mind. My anger lashed at the surrounding air and I snarled, "You want a temper tantrum, Erick, I'll give you a tantrum like you've never seen before."

Erick's calmness further fuelled my temper as my voice rose. "Who exactly gets to determine whether I have a handle on my newfound abilities, Erick? Who determines when I will regain my independence? You?"

The surrounding air thickened, compressing my empty lungs a little more, and I was grateful I no longer needed to breathe as Erick stared unblinking at me.

Finally, his power receded, and he addressed me with a composure I'd have imagined him using to address members of the council or during his many staff meetings, but not during an argument.

"Stop this now, Evanee. I will not be held accountable for my response if you continue to behave like a child."

Passion and conviction drove me onward as I yelled at the steadfast male before me. "If I'm behaving like a child, it's in response to your shitty parenting skills. I want to see Uncle Bob, Aunty Marg, Steve, Brad, and Ellie. I miss my work and the help I gave to those needing justice. Instead, I'm stuck here listening to Tristan and Jordan bitch at each other day in and day out."

A sudden intense urge to scratch at an itch at the top of my spine, between my shoulder blades, distracted me. As it continued, my eyes shifted around the area, subtly looking for the nearest stick. Argh, m*an that's itchy.* Erick's retort drew my attention back to the now seething vampire before me.

"Your ungratefulness astounds me, you know that? I've been putting out the damn fires you started with your little stunt outside the lab. I have my father pressuring to meet you, and the council isn't far behind him. Between the transformation and my absence during it, your poorly timed killing at the lab, and that damn prophecy, I've had my hands full. So, you'll have to put up and shut up until things quiet down. I don't have the time to deal with your insecurities and melodramas right now."

Power glowed from the depths of his eyes, as he lost what little patience he'd been holding on to. If he'd been human, he'd have been breathing heavy from sheer anger and frustration.

Needing a distraction from the itch that had re-emerged at my shoulder blades, I stepped forward so Erick and I came face to face. We stared unblinking at each other, neither willing to budge first.

When the itching grew too much, I blinked, whispering, "I'm drowning here and all you can see is that I'm a pain in the arse."

Erick stood unmoving and non-pulsed, the glint in his hooded gaze betraying his resolve. Tugging me closer, he bent his head to whisper in my ear.

"You will not leave this property, Evanee. I have my reasons for limiting your access to the outside world, and they're my own. You leave without my consent and I will lock you in the basement right beside your best mate, Jared. I'm your sire, Evanee, and I won't tolerate your insubordination. Don't screw with me on this."

Releasing my hands hard so I stumbled backwards, he turned and disappeared into the darkness from which he'd emerged.

Clenching my jaw against the sob of anguish lodged deep within my throat, I dashed at a single tear making its escape down my cheek, the itch in my spine forgotten. "I'm done. I'll give you bloody insecurities and temper tantrums."

Summoning my reaper's portal, I stared into a darkened bedroom beyond. Sounds of beeping machines drifted through from beyond, at odds with the crickets and rustling leaves of the eucalyptus trees swaying in the light breeze around me.

I'm done being everyone's little puppet, and we all knew this was a long time coming.

Without hesitation I stepped through the portal and into another kind of hell.

www.ingramcontent.com/pod-product-compliance
Lightning Source LLC
Chambersburg PA
CBHW022358110726
47903CB00004B/1041